Harvest Moon

NATIONAL BESTSELLING AUTHOR
ROCHELLE ALERS

Harvest Moon

A Hideaway Novel

ARABESQUE®

Recycling programs
for this product may
not exist in your area.

HARVEST MOON

ISBN-13: 978-0-373-53444-9

Copyright © 2011 by Rochelle Alers

www.kimanipress.com

Printed in U.S.A.

Dear Reader,

It wasn't until the release of *Heaven Sent* that I realized how much readers had connected with the characters in the Hideaway series. Thus began the next generation of the Cole family, whose stories continue in *Harvest Moon*.

This is the first title in the daughters and sisters trilogy that features Regina Cole, who also appears in the first novel in the series—*Hideaway*. In *Harvest Moon,* Regina takes a sensual journey from Mexico City to West Palm Beach and finally to the breathtaking, natural beauty of Brazil. She is forced to face a childhood trauma and learn to trust, or risk losing a love that promises forever.

Don't forget to read, love and live romance.

Rochelle Alers

HIDEAWAY SERIES

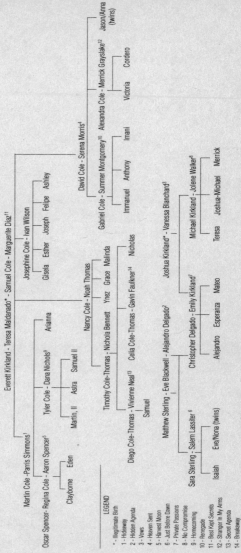

Everett Kirkland - Teresa Maldanado* - Samuel Cole - Marguerite Diaz[11]

Martin Cole - Parris Simmons[1]

Oscar Spencer - Regina Cole - Aaron Spencer[5]

Claybourne

Eden

Tyler Cole - Dana Nichols[6]

Ariama

Martin, II   Astra   Samuel II

Josephine Cole - Ivan Wilson

Gisela   Esther   Joseph   Felipe   Ashley

David Cole - Serena Morris[4]

Gabriel Cole - Summer Montgomery[10]

Immanuel   Anthony   Imani

Alexandra Cole - Merrick Grayslake[12]

Victoria   Cordero

Jason/Anna (twins)

Nancy Cole - Noah Thomas

Timothy Cole-Thomas - Nichola Bennett

Ynez   Grace   Malinda

Diego Cole-Thomas - Vivienne Neal[13]

Samuel

Celia Cole-Thomas - Gavin Faulkner[14]

Nicholas

Matthew Sterling - Eve Blackwell

Christopher Delgado - Emily Kirkland[7]

Alejandro   Esperanza   Mateo

Alejandro Delgado[2]

Joshua Kirkland* - Vanessa Blanchard[3]

Michael Kirkland - Jolene Walker[8]

Teresa   Joshua-Michael   Merrick

Sara Sterling - Salem Lassiter[6]

Isaiah   Eve/Nona (twins)

LEGEND
* - Illegitimate Birth
1 - Hideaway
2 - Hidden Agenda
3 - Vows
4 - Heaven Sent
5 - Harvest Moon
6 - Just Before Dawn
7 - Private Passions
8 - No Compromise
9 - Homecoming
10 - Renegade
11 - Best Kept Secrets
12 - Stranger In My Arms
13 - Secret Agenda
14 - Breakaway

Chapter 1

Mexico City, Mexico—August seventeenth...
Oscar Clayborne Spencer died today at the age of seventy-seven after a decade-long bout with lung cancer.

The multiple award-winning film director, who won an Academy Award for his last film, *Silent Witness,* also earned more than a dozen awards from the Cannes, Venice, and Sundance Film Festivals during his illustrious thirty-five-year movie career.

Spencer is survived by his wife, Regina Spencer, and son, Dr. Aaron Spencer, of Bahia, Brazil.

Funeral arrangements will be private.

Regina Cole-Spencer's left hand trembled noticeably as she reached for the telephone on her bedside table. She loathed having to make the call. It would have been easier if she had called Aaron when his father was first diagnosed with the illness that had laid claim to his life second by second, minute by minute, and day by day for a decade.

Her fingers curved around the receiver. She knew the telephone number without glancing at the yellowing, frayed business card lying atop the highly waxed surface of the table; she had picked up the receiver and dialed the South American country's international code more than a dozen times over the past week, only to replace it in its cradle before the impending connection. But this time the call would be completed.

Oscar had issued an explicit order for her not to contact Aaron until after his death. Now was that time.

Her husband died quietly in his sleep, slipping away from their life together and into the next with the aid of the potent narcotic the doctor prescribed to make Oscar's pain more tolerable toward the end.

Pressing the buttons, she punched in the numbers and then closed her eyes and listened to the sound of the steady, measured ringing.

"Olà. São Tomé Instituto de Médico Pesquisa."

Regina heard the feminine voice speaking Portuguese, and was instantly reminded that Brazil was the only South American country whose official language was not Spanish.

"Hola," she responded in Spanish, a language she had learned from her Cuban-born grandmother and had perfected since living in Mexico for nearly a decade. "I would like to speak to Dr. Aaron Spencer."

"Lo siento," the receptionist replied in the same language, "Dr. Spencer is not scheduled to work at the institute today."

There was a long silence. It was obvious the receptionist wasn't going to be forthcoming with any information regarding Oscar's son's whereabouts.

"It is imperative that I reach him. This is a family emergency," Regina added.

"I can page him and have him return your call."

She let out an audible sigh. "Thank you." She gave the woman her name and the telephone number to her house in a remote town nearly a hundred miles south of Mexico City, and hung up.

Rising from a tapestry-covered armchair, she walked over to the French doors and stared out at the lush property surrounding *El Cielo*. An expression of profound sadness settled into her delicate features as she opened the doors. The cloudless summer sky made the Sierra Madre Del Sur mountain range seem close enough for her to reach out and touch. She had lost count of how often she had awakened to stare at the jagged peaks blending with the sky. The first time she stood on the veranda staring down at the valley she had felt as if she had come to heaven. The mountain peaks had appeared to pierce the verdant, rolling hills of the valley to rise heavenward like spires on a Gothic cathedral, prompting her to call the property *El Cielo*. It had become heaven and a safe haven for her, as it was to become a final resting place for Oscar Spencer.

For eight years she did not have to concern herself about whether someone recognized her as Regina Cole, the actress who at seventeen had been nominated as Best Actress in her first film. No one had ever stared at her or whispered behind their fingers whenever she and Oscar dined out or shopped in town. They were allowed their privacy as private citizens, to share their lives uncensored as a married couple.

The telephone chimed softly, and she returned to the bedroom to answer the call. *"Hola."*

"This is Dr. Spencer," came a deep, powerful voice speaking fluent Spanish.

Regina inhaled, then let out her breath slowly. "Dr. Spencer," she continued, switching to English, "I'm Regina Spencer. I called you because I want to inform you that your father passed away earlier today." Her eyes filled with tears. "He did not suffer."

There was an interminable silence before Aaron Spencer spoke again. "What was the cause of death?"

"Lung cancer." Tears she had kept at bay now overflowed and stained her cheeks.

"When was he diagnosed with cancer?"

"His doctor discovered it ten years ago."

"Ten years! You waited ten years, and for my father to die, to call me, Miss—"

"I was just following his wishes, Dr. Spencer," she countered, interrupting him. "He forbade me to call you until after he'd died." She felt a rush of heat suffuse her face. He had no right to yell at her, and he had no right to accuse her of something he knew nothing about.

"What do you mean, he forbade you? Just who the hell are you, anyway?"

Her fingers tightened on the receiver. "I *was* your father's wife."

A soft curse came through the wire as Aaron Spencer mumbled angrily under his breath. "And now you're his widow." He had not bothered to hide his sarcasm. "Have you made funeral arrangements?"

Sitting down on the armchair, Regina pressed her back against the cushion, closing her eyes. She hadn't realized how tired she was, or how great a strain she had been under for more years than she could count.

"No, I haven't. I waited because I wanted to call you. If you intend to come to Mexico, then I'll hold off until you arrive. If not, then I'll proceed with my original plans."

"Don't do anything until I get there."

Nodding, she opened her eyes. "When shall I expect you?"

"I'll try to be there sometime tomorrow. Give me the address where you're staying."

She blotted her cheeks with the back of her right hand as she gave her late husband's son the directions to the sprawling property she had occupied with Oscar since they fled Southern California.

He repeated the information she had given him, and without offering the ubiquitous "goodbye" or "have a safe flight" she hung up.

All she had shared with Oscar swept over her as she left the chair and lay down on the large bed where she had slept alone since becoming Regina Spencer. She thought she had prepared herself for this moment. She had thought she would welcome the time when Oscar would slip away from her to a place where he would never feel pain, or see the sadness she valiantly tried to conceal from him.

She'd thought she had a lot of time to get used to the day when she would eventually become a widow, but she was wrong. She was wrong, because when she married a man fifty years her senior she never thought she would come to love him as much as she did.

Aaron Spencer sat in the dark long after he'd called a carrier which would take him from Salvador to Mexico, numbed by the news that his father was dead. It had been twelve years since he last saw or had spoken to Oscar, and despite their estrangement he had never envisioned him not being alive.

There had been one time when he picked up the telephone to call Oscar and set things right between them, but it had been too late. His father's telephone had been disconnected, and the recorded message indicated no forwarding number.

The anger he had carried for years diminished with time, but the pain hadn't. And now, with Oscar's death, there would never be peace between them. He could have forgiven Oscar for anything, but not for marrying the only woman he had ever loved.

A heavy sadness descended upon him like a leaden blanket, and he was swallowed up in a morass of despondency. He sat motionless in the sanctuary of his study, staring into nothingness, until a light knock on the door pulled him from his self-pitying reverie.

"Yes."

"Senhor Spencer, Miss Elena is here to see you."

Aaron scowled, squeezing his eyes tightly. He should've told his housekeeper that he wouldn't be receiving guests.

"Tell her I can't see her now."

There was a whisper of soft feminine voices, then a rapid tapping on the solid mahogany door. "Aaron. Please open the door."

He groaned audibly. At any other time he would've opened the door for Elena Carvalho, but not now. He wanted to be alone, alone to reexamine his life over the past twelve years.

"I'll call you, Elena."

"When, Aaron?" came the soft, pleading voice on the other side of the door.

"Tomorrow."

There was a pregnant silence before Elena spoke again. "*Boa noite,* Aaron."

"*Boa noite.*"

He counted off the seconds until he heard movement in the alcove outside his study, indicating Elena Carvalho had left, then he let out his breath. He lost track of time before he left the chair to lie down on a chaise, sleeping fitfully until he rose to prepare himself to leave Salvador for his flight to Mexico City.

Chapter 2

"*Señora Spencer. El abogado està aquí.*"

Regina Cole-Spencer registered her housekeeper's softly modulated voice. She did not know how long she had stood at the window, staring at the undulating landscape.

"Thank you, Rosa. Please send him in."

The solid oaken door closed quietly, only to open again within minutes. Ernesto Morales stepped into the large, richly appointed room, waiting until his vision adjusted to the dimly lit space. All of the drapes had been drawn across the expanse of one wall except for six inches, and it was at these six inches that Regina Spencer stood at the wall-to-wall window, peering through sand-beige silk at the verdant property she had owned with her late husband.

His admiring gaze swept over the tall, slender figure of the young widow clad in a pair of black linen slacks with a matching, short-sleeved blouse. Her trademark waist-length, curly, black hair was secured in a chignon on the nape of her long neck. A slight smile touched Ernesto's mouth. Even in mourning she was beautiful and very elegant.

When word had reached him that Oscar Spencer had finally succumbed to the disease laying waste to his frail body, he had experienced an uncharacteristic emotion of forgiveness. Now, with Oscar Spencer's death, he no longer had to experience guilt about coveting the man's young wife.

"*¡Buenas tardes!* Señora Spencer."

Turning slowly, Regina stared across the room at her late husband's attorney. She smiled at him—a sad smile.

"*¡Buenas tardes!* Thank you for coming so quickly."

Ernesto crossed the room, his footsteps silent on the priceless handwoven rug. "I came as soon as I could. I was scheduled to appear in court this morning, and unfortunately I couldn't postpone it."

He stood inches from her, his dark gaze measuring the undisguised pain in her large eyes, the tension ringing her full, generous mouth, and the resignation in her stance that indicated she had done all she could for Oscar Spencer, that she had honored her marriage vow to love him in sickness and in health. And now her husband was dead, but she was alive—alive and breathtakingly beautiful at twenty-seven.

His hands went to her shoulders, tightening, as he lowered his head and placed a kiss on both cheeks. "*Lo siento mucho,* Regina."

"*Gracias,* Ernesto," she returned, lapsing easily into Spanish. She wondered how many more times she would have to hear the *I'm sorry* phrase before she left Mexico to return to the States. As soon as the doctor confirmed Oscar's passing, the household staff had come to her, one by one, offering their condolences. And now it would be Oscar's business associates.

"Please sit down. Can I have Rosa bring you something to drink?"

Ernesto waved a hand. "No, thank you." He waited for Regina

to sit before he took a comfortable armchair near hers, staring intently at her as she closed her eyes and pressed her head against the cushioned back.

"I've placed a call to Aaron Spencer to let him know about his father." She opened her eyes and met Ernesto's steady gaze.

"What did he say?"

"He said he'll arrive here today." She smiled again, this time indicating a weighted fatigue. "Oscar gave me my instructions, and I've followed them. What did he tell you?"

Ernesto nodded slowly. It was apparent Regina had known her late husband very well. Even on his deathbed Oscar Spencer continued to direct. He had given him specific instructions as to how he wanted his estate divided.

"You'll have to wait for Dr. Spencer's arrival before I make the conditions of the will known. I can assure you that you will be adequately provided for."

Sitting up straighter, Regina glared at the attorney. "You think I married Oscar for his money?"

"No! Oh, no," he apologized. "I happen to know that you've never needed your husband's money."

Visibly relaxing, she nodded, her frown disappearing as quickly as it had appeared. Ernesto was right. She did not need Oscar's money, or for that matter any man's. She was a Cole, and the name symbolized wealth and prestige, not only in the United States but throughout the Caribbean and in many Latin American countries.

Ernesto also relaxed. He had made a grievous *faux pas*. If he hoped to court the young widow, he was not beginning well. Like many others who met Regina Spencer for the first time, he had found it hard to believe she had married a man whose age eclipsed hers by fifty years, but during the years he had observed them together he realized she truly did love him. There also were times when he thought her youth, beauty and repressed passion had been wasted on the elderly man.

How many times had he fantasized running his fingers through her long, curly hair? Feasting on her perfectly formed, full, lush mouth? Caressing her slim curves and full breasts? Too many for him to count.

"I'd like to ask you a question," he began slowly, softly. "And if you choose not to answer it, I will respect your decision." She inclined her head. "I've been your husband's attorney since he moved from California to Mexico, and we've discussed many things. Many, many personal things. But not once did he ever disclose why you married him."

A slight frown marred Regina's high, smooth forehead. Ernesto was asking what so many had asked over the years. Her answer was always the same.

"My reason for marrying Oscar will remain my secret."

What she did not tell him or the others was that she and Oscar had promised each other that only their families would know the real reason behind their union.

It was Ernesto's turn to incline his head. His gaze shifted, lingering on the length of Regina's long, graceful neck. It was only the second time he had seen her with her hair pinned up off her neck. A secret smile touched his spare lips. He would wait for what he thought would be an appropriate time for her to mourn. Then he would make his intentions known to the very young and very beautiful widow. He was confident that she would not reject his subtle advances. After all, he was Ernesto Morales de Villarosa, and he could trace his family's ancestry to the period of the Spanish grandees who had settled Mexico in the early sixteenth century.

A swollen silence filled the room as the brilliant summer sun began its slow descent behind the nearby mountains. Regina leaned over and turned on a lamp on the table between the armchairs, flooding the space with soft golden light.

Ernesto stood up and reached across the distance separating him from Regina. He grasped her hand, pulling her gently to her feet. "I must be going. I've promised my mother I would share dinner with her."

Tilting her chin, she smiled at him. "Are you certain I can't have Rosa bring you something to drink?"

Squeezing her fingers, he returned her smile. "Maybe another time. Perhaps, after everything is settled, I hope you will allow me to…" He stopped, struggling to rephrase his statement.

Her smile faded as she tried meeting his furtive gaze. "To what?"

He registered the coldness in the two words. Had he moved too quickly? "I hope you'll allow me to handle your legal affairs," he continued, lying smoothly.

"Of course, Ernesto. I see no reason to change legal counsel at this time."

He offered a mock bow. "*Gracias. ¡Buenas noches!* Regina."

"*¡Buenas noches!* I'll see you to the door."

She led the way down a carpeted hallway to the entry, feeling the warmth of Ernesto's steady gaze on her back. She knew the attorney was interested in her, and had been for a long time.

Oscar had retained him to settle his estate, and she would concede to her late husband's wishes, but what Ernesto Morales did not know was that—if Oscar had willed her the house and its contents—she planned to dispose of everything as quickly as possible before she returned to Florida. She had been away from her family and the country of her birth for too long, and she found it hard to believe that it had been eight years since she had called the United States home.

She and Ernesto stood at a set of massive, ornately carved mahogany doors, staring at each other. She offered her right hand and he took it gently and placed a kiss on a knuckle.

"I'll call you to let you know the time for the service," she reminded him.

He nodded, released her hand, opened the door and walked out of the large house and through the courtyard of the magnificent structure built on a hill overlooking a picturesque valley. He glanced over his shoulder just before he turned in the direction of the garages and saw that Regina hadn't moved. She stood in the doorway, a slim, shadowy figure against the rapidly waning daylight.

Regina was in the same position when she heard the sound of Ernesto's car drive away and the arrival of another. Straightening from her leaning position, she recognized the car as a taxi. She saw the driver stop, exit the vehicle and come around to open the rear door for his passenger. Not realizing she had been holding her breath, she let it out slowly when she saw the figure of a tall man emerge from the backseat.

Even in the encroaching darkness there was something about the man that reminded her of Oscar, and without seeing his face she knew the passenger was Dr. Aaron Spencer.

Reaching into the pocket of his suit trousers, Aaron withdrew a money clip, peeled off several bills and handed them to the driver. He then waited for his luggage to be unloaded from the trunk. It was only after he had hoisted a garment bag over his shoulder at the same time the driver picked up two carry-on bags and set them down in the entryway of the house that he noticed the door stood open and a woman stood at the entrance awaiting his arrival.

He counted the steps which brought him face-to-face with a young woman dressed entirely in black. His large, dark, slanting eyes widened in shock. *She couldn't be!* He shook his head. This woman couldn't be Regina Spencer. There was no way she could be his stepmother!

Regina took several steps backward and opened the door wider to permit Aaron Spencer to enter. "Please come in, Dr. Spencer."

The instant she opened her mouth she confirmed what Aaron did not want to accept. The deep husky sound of her sensual voice had resounded in his head hours after he'd hung up from her call. He had sat in his study, staring into darkness, and recalling her statement: *Dr. Spencer, I'm Regina Spencer. I called you because I want to inform you that your father passed away earlier today. He did not suffer.*

After hearing her statement he had wanted to cry, but did not—because he could not. He could not because he had spent twelve years hating the man who had given him life.

He walked into the opulently decorated entryway, then turned and looked down at the woman who had been his father's wife. He visually examined her, complete surprise freezing his expression. Not only was she very young, she was also stunningly beautiful. He did not notice the slight puffiness under her large, dark eyes which indicated she had not gotten enough sleep. All he saw was the delicacy of her features, the lushness of her perfectly formed mouth, the flawlessness of her brown skin and the soft curves of her womanly body.

She extended her hand. "I'm Regina."

Lowering the garment bag to the floor beside the matching leather carry-ons, he took the proffered hand. He inclined his head, his gaze fixed on her mouth. "I'm sorry we have to meet under these circumstances."

Regina felt a tingle of awareness when her hand was swallowed up by Aaron's much larger one. "Yes. It is unfortunate." She withdrew her fingers, still feeling the warmth of his flesh lingering on her palm.

Aaron Spencer had inherited his father's height and lean face, but that was where the similarities ended. His features were nothing like Oscar's. Her gaze caught and held his as she silently admired the exotic slant of his eyes. His nose was bold, almost aquiline, and his mouth was strongly masculine with firm upper and lower lips.

She watched him watching her, a knowing smile flashing the dimples in her cheeks. He was intrigued. It was obvious he hadn't expected his stepmother to be younger than he was. He gave her a lazy smile, and his lips parted to reveal a set of perfect white teeth.

Regina felt her pulse quicken and she glanced around his shoulder at her housekeeper, who had approached silently. "I'll have someone show you to your room. Rosa, please see Dr. Spencer to the guest room in the east wing."

Rosa nodded, smiling. "*Sí, Señora* Spencer."

She watched Aaron pick up his luggage and follow Rosa through the entryway to a flight of curving stairs leading to the upper level. Even after he'd disappeared from sight she was able to recall the width of his broad shoulders under his expertly tailored suit jacket. And in one glance she had taken in his close-cropped, gray-flecked black hair, the richness of his sun-browned dark skin and the masculine sensuality he wore as proudly as a badge of honor.

She realized Aaron Spencer wasn't as handsome as he was sensually attractive. Even his voice was erotic—deep, powerful and seductive.

What she did not want to acknowledge was that she was attracted to the son of her late husband.

A man who was her stepson!

Aaron stood in the middle of the bedroom where he would reside during his stay in Mexico, staring at the queen-size bed's wrought-iron headboard. Twin emotions of rage and sorrow assaulted him as his hands curled into tight fists. He had flown thousands of miles and across several time zones to attend the funeral of a man whom he had symbolically buried years before— a man he hadn't seen or spoken to in twelve years. Just this once he wanted Oscar alive, so he could damn him for destroying the love and trust between them, and for not permitting him to trust a woman.

Closing his eyes, he relived the scene which had haunted him for years—the one where Sharon had come to him, her eyes awash with tears, when she told him she couldn't marry him because she was going to marry his father.

She had waited exactly one week following his graduation from medical school to disclose her intentions. She returned the engagement ring he had given her for her birthday, then stood up and walked out of his life and into his father's. He did not attend their wedding, telling himself that he did not have a father.

But he did have a father—a man whom he despised. But Oscar Spencer had spent the last ten years of his life dying from a disease that had ravaged his body; a disease that left him racked with pain and suffering; a man whose last days on earth he could have helped make comfortable because of his medical training.

Slipping out of his jacket, Aaron placed it over the back of a plush armchair. He hadn't spoken to Oscar, and his father had forbade anyone linked to him to contact his last surviving relative. A wry smile tugged at a corner of his mouth. Whatever Oscar's reason for not contacting him no longer mattered.

"And that suits me just fine," he whispered between clenched teeth. *Now, we're even,* he added silently.

It took an hour for him to put away his clothes, shave, shower and change into a pair of black slacks, an oatmeal-hued, short-sleeved silk shirt and a pair of black, Italian-made loafers. He dimmed a lamp on one of the bedside tables, closed the door to the bedroom and made his way down the hallway to the staircase leading to the main level.

It was apparent his father hadn't spared any expense when he purchased and furnished the sprawling house for his young wife. Priceless, colorful handwoven rugs covered wood floors, and the tapestries covering the seat and back cushions of various chairs, chaises, and settees were exquisite. Walking into the living room, he ran his fingers over a side table boasting a marble inlaid surface. The dark-green, gold-veined marble was the perfect complement for the surrounding gleaming oak.

His footsteps were silent on a sand and ocher blend print rug as he moved over to a hand-carved, Mexican stone fireplace. He stared at a pair of massive, gilded candlesticks flanking an ornate ormolu clock resting atop the mantel. The candlesticks and clock were a bit too fancy for his more Spartan taste.

His gaze shifted upward and he stared into the mirror hanging above the mantel, seeing the reflection of his stepmother standing under the arched entrance to the living room. He went completely still, wondering how long had she been there.

His pulse quickened as he noted the ethereal slimness of her body in a black, floor-length slip dress and the cloud of ebony curls falling over her bare shoulders and down her back.

Turning slowly, he watched her walk into the room, seemingly floating toward him and closing the distance between them within seconds. An unfamiliar tightening in his groin caused him to gasp, and his eyes seemed to darken with an emotion he knew was lust. His body's violent reaction had betrayed him. It had been a long time—in fact years—since the mere sight of a woman had aroused him physically. He prided himself on his iron-willed control. Women who set out to seduce him always failed in their attempts to get him to commit to a future with them.

Regina was different, because she was seducing him unknowingly. She stood two feet away, golden light from an overhead chandelier shimmering on her exposed, velvety flesh. Transfixed, he inhaled the hauntingly clean smell of her body. The scent was reminiscent of the lingering fragrance of a refreshing rain shower. His penetrating gaze searched her face, lingering on her lips. She had not applied any makeup except to outline her lush mouth in a vermilion-red.

Perfect, he mused. *Incredibly perfect.* It was no wonder his father had been drawn to her. Regina Spencer was a temptress—a modern-day Delilah. What man could resist her once she set out to lure him into her beguiling web?

Arching a sculpted eyebrow, he wondered if she was aware of her seductive powers. If she was, he pitied the hapless man who would become her next victim. There was one thing for certain—he would not be the one.

She managed a forced smile, offering him an enchanting display of matching dimples in her silken cheeks. "I don't know whether you're hungry, but I had the cook prepare a simple repast. We'll dine on the patio," she said, not giving him time to accept or decline her invitation.

Turning gracefully, she walked out of the living room, leaving him to follow. He followed numbly, staring at the wealth of curling black hair falling to her narrow waist.

Regina led him outdoors to a patio overlooking the lighted courtyard. A small, round table had been set for two. A dozen blackened antique iron lanterns, suspended from stanchions, bathed the space in a warm yellow glow. She extended her left hand, and the light caught the circle of diamonds on her third finger.

"Please be seated."

He did not sit, but walked around the table and pulled out a chair for her. "Thank you," she murmured softly, permitting him to seat her.

Aaron lingered over her head, feasting on the soft swell of her breasts rising above the dress's décolletage and the sensual fragrance of her body before he reluctantly rounded the table and sat down opposite her.

She removed the cover of a soup bowl, watching Aaron follow suit. It was only a week ago that she had shared her last supper with Oscar. There were days when he hadn't been able to tolerate eating solid food, but he awoke one morning complaining that he was hungry. They'd shared breakfast in his bedroom, and an early supper on the patio. Oscar was more animated than he had been in weeks. They'd laughed and danced together, humming to their own music before he returned to bed, complaining of fatigue. That night was the last time his feet would ever touch a solid surface.

Aaron spooned the rich, flavorful fish soup into his mouth, watching his stepmother closely. She ate as if in a trance, and he knew she went through the motions because it was necessary to sustain her life. Laying aside his spoon, he reached over and picked up a bottle of chilled white wine.

"Regina?" Her head came up quickly. "May I serve you some wine?"

"No, thank you." Her husky voice had dropped an octave, and he was enthralled with its cloaking pitch. "I don't drink." She picked up a goblet with mineral water and took a sip.

Tilting his head at an angle, he narrowed his gaze. "Are you recovering?"

She laughed softly, the sound floating up in the warm, summer night air. "No. I just have no tolerance for anything alcoholic."

"How does it affect you?"

"Migraine."

He nodded. "That's enough reason not to drink."

They ate in silence, both content to listen to the strumming of a flamenco guitar. After twenty minutes a woman joined the guitarist, her clear, lilting voice lifting in song and sending chills throughout Aaron's body. He had forgotten why he'd flown from Brazil to Mexico. He wanted the reason to be different from the fact that he would bury his father without having cleared his conscience, to let Oscar Spencer know how deeply he had hurt him. And if he had to sit across from Regina, he didn't want it to be because she was his stepmother. He didn't want to be reminded that she had and still belonged to his father—a man he had not forgiven for his deceit, not even in death.

He finished the fish entrée, dabbing his lips with a cloth napkin while watching his stepmother. There was a weariness about her that should not have been apparent with someone her age. And he wondered about that. She said his father had been ill for ten years, which meant she probably had been in her early twenties when she and Oscar had become involved with each other.

How could she? he mused. How could she sleep with a man old enough to be her father, possibly her grandfather? What was there about Oscar Spencer that young women could not resist? Had Oscar seduced her, or had Regina seduced him? There were a lot of questions he needed answers to with regard to Oscar and Regina's marriage, but he decided they could wait.

"Where did my father die?"

She went completely still. It was the first time Aaron had mentioned Oscar, and she had to remind herself the reason she was meeting with Aaron Spencer was because Oscar had died.

"He was at home. He did not want to die in a hospital."

"You said he did not suffer."

She shook her head. "No. His doctor made certain he wasn't in any pain toward the end." Aaron sat motionless, staring at her, his expression impassive. Her gaze narrowed. "Do you think I would've permitted my husband to suffer more than was necessary, Dr. Spencer?"

"Aaron," he chided in a deep, quiet tone. "I'd prefer that you call me by my name."

"Then Aaron it is."

Placing his elbows on the table, he rested his chin on a clenched fist. "Did my father give you any specific instructions on how he wanted to be buried?"

"You didn't answer my question, Aaron."

"And you didn't answer mine, *Regina.*"

The strain of caring for a sick husband for the past eight years suddenly overwhelmed her, and she wanted to scream at Aaron Spencer that he had no right to question her role as wife and caretaker. Closing her eyes, she filled her lungs with deep drafts of nighttime mountain air. All she wanted was for it to be over; she wanted to bury Oscar and leave Mexico—forever.

Opening her eyes, she glared at him. "He'd talked about being cremated. Then said he'd allow me to make that decision."

Vertical lines appeared between Aaron's eyes. "Have you considered cremating him?"

"No."

He nodded, seemingly letting out his breath in relief. "Where do you intend to bury him?"

"I thought I'd leave that up to you."

"I won't make that decision. You're his wife."

"And you're his son," she retorted. "You and Oscar share bloodlines. Don't you have a family plot somewhere?"

Raising his chin, he averted his gaze. "No. My mother was buried in Chicago, her parents in South Carolina and her only sibling in Bahia."

"How about Oscar's family?"

"He was an only child. He has a few distant cousins, but he lost contact with them years ago."

Running a hand through her hair, Regina pushed a wealth of curls off her forehead. "Then we'll bury him here at *El Cielo*. He will be closer—to…heaven."

Her voice quivered as she struggled to regain control of her fragile emotions. She would not permit anyone to see her cry. She would do what she had been doing for years—she would grieve in private.

Rising to her feet, she placed her napkin beside a plate of untouched salad. Aaron also stood up. "I'm sorry, Aaron, but I must retire. Please stay and finish your meal."

She took a step, but he reached out, his fingers snaking around her wrist and halting her departure. "There's one thing I *need* to know," he said in a dangerously soft voice.

For the second time since she had come face-to-face with Aaron Spencer, Regina registered the fiery brand of his touch. "What is that?"

"Did you love my father when you married him?"

She flinched, then squared her shoulders. He was just like all the rest. Everyone thought she had married Oscar for his fame, or for his money. Her head came around slowly as she tilted her chin to stare up at the man standing inches from her.

"I did not love him when I married him," she answered as honestly as she could. "But I did fall in love with him before he died. And I made certain to tell him I loved him—every day. Is there anything else you *need* to know?"

Aaron released her wrist, his gaze boring into hers. "That's enough, for *now*."

"Goodnight, Dr. Spencer," she said softly, her eyes narrowing.

He opened his mouth to reprimand her about using his professional title, but swallowed back the words. At that moment he felt vulnerable because Regina Spencer disturbed him, disturbed him in ways that aroused old fears and uncertainties. He watched her until she disappeared into the house.

He would stay and bury his father, then leave Mexico and not look back. His life and his future were in Brazil, and that future did not include interacting with Oscar Spencer's widow.

Chapter 3

Regina returned to her bedroom and changed out of the dress and into a pair of cotton eyelet pajamas. She much preferred sleeping nude, but had acquired the habit of wearing pajamas to bed because she had never known when she would be summoned to Oscar's bedroom and she hadn't wanted to waste time getting dressed.

Walking over to the French doors, she opened them and stepped out onto the second-story veranda. The calming silence of the Mexican night swallowed her whole, filling her with a peace she had not felt in years. The past ten years had changed her into someone who had become a stranger—even to herself.

She had missed a lot of milestones a woman her age should have experienced: dating, traveling with her girlfriends and attending parties. She had missed seeing her brother and sister grow into adolescence, and she felt detached from her parents, grandparents, aunts, uncles and her many cousins.

She met Oscar Spencer at seventeen, married him at nineteen

and he left her widowed at twenty-seven. She had given him a total of ten years of her young life, and she wondered about the next ten. For the first time in her life she was alone—alone to make decisions that would not include anyone but herself.

A soft chiming shattered her musings. Leaving the veranda, she returned to the bedroom to answer the telephone. *"Hola,"* she said softly.

"Cupcake."

A bright smile softened her delicate features. "Daddy!"

Minutes after her husband died, she had called her parents and left a message with their housekeeper. The woman informed her that her family had gone up to West Palm Beach for a few days.

"We just got back and heard the news. How are you, Baby?"

"I'm fine, Daddy."

"Hold on a minute, Cupcake. I can't talk to you and your mother at the same time."

Regina sank down to the bed and pulled her knees to her chest. Hearing her father's voice reminded her of what was waiting for her once she tied up all of the loose ends of her life in Mexico; she never realized how much she missed her family until she heard their voices or they left after a visit. They had always come to see her in Mexico, because most times Oscar was too weak to travel more than a few miles from home.

Martin Cole's soft, Southern drawl came through the wire again. "Your mother says you should expect us within two days."

"No, Daddy, don't. I don't want you to come."

"Why not? I'm not going to let you go through this by yourself. Hasn't Oscar Spencer taken enough from you?"

Biting down hard on her lower lip, she chose her words carefully. Her father still hadn't forgiven her for marrying Oscar, and whenever he came to visit her and Oscar, it had been obvious he afforded the older man a modicum of respect because of his age, not because he was her husband. Oscar had been twenty years her father's senior.

"I'm not alone, Daddy. Oscar's son is here. And after we bury him and settle the estate, then I'm coming home."

There was a noticeable silence before Martin responded. "Are you coming home to visit?"

Her smile returned. "No. I'm coming back to stay."

"I like the sound of that. Are you certain you don't want your mother or me to come? She can come without me."

"I want to handle this myself. I'll keep in touch, and let you know when to expect me."

"Okay, Baby. Let me put your mother on before she has a fit."

Regina spent the next quarter of an hour talking to her mother. She laughed, the low, seductive sound of her voice filling the room when Parris Cole confided that seventeen-year-old Tyler Cole had shown a marked interest in a girl at his school.

"I can't believe it," she chuckled. "My little brother in love."

"I wouldn't call it love," Parris countered. "But I must say that he's quite infatuated with her."

"Is she at least a nice girl, Mommy?"

"She's lovely, but as quiet and shy as he is."

Wincing, Regina shook her head. "Do they talk?"

"He spends hours on his phone with her."

"I guess that means that they talk. How's Ari?"

She missed her brother, but missed her sister more. They were thirteen years apart, and she did not know why but she felt more like Arianna's mother than her older sister. Arianna called her every week to talk, and she usually wound up giving Ari advice about everything from interacting with her parents to dealing with the erratic behavior of her peers.

Parris offered an update on Arianna's latest escapades. She

ended the call with a promise that she would contact all of the Coles for a family reunion once she confirmed a date for her return.

"As I told Daddy, I'm not certain how long it will be before Oscar's estate is settled, but I'm hoping to be back within a month."

"Today is August eighteenth. Which means we can expect you the middle of September," Parris stated firmly.

"Let's say October first."

"I can't wait, Angel. I don't think you realize how much I've missed you."

"I know, Mommy, because I've missed you more than I want to admit. But you know I had to fulfill my marriage vows."

"And you did. Now it's time for you to live."

What she wanted to tell her mother was that she had been living, that marrying Oscar had been her choice and that she had loved him as much as Parris loved Martin. She had given Oscar Spencer eight years, eight years she did not regret.

She rang off, replaced the receiver in its cradle, then lay across the bed. Closing her eyes, smiling, she remembered the night the Academy of Motion Picture Arts and Sciences honored Oscar with his namesake for his directorial effort for *Silent Witness*.

She had crawled into bed with him and held him while he shed shameless tears of joy. She had not shared his joy, because she blamed the Academy for waiting until the brilliant director was sixty-seven, ill, and at the end of his career, to honor him. It was at that moment that she swore she would never make another film, but Oscar had persuaded her to accept one more—one more before she left the business for good. And his prediction had come true when he said he doubted whether she would complete more than three films.

Now, opening her eyes, she leaned over and turned a switch on the bedside lamp, leaving one bulb lit in the crystal base. There was enough light for her to see the familiar objects in the room. Pulling a sheet up over her body, she closed her eyes and slept a dreamless sleep.

Regina overslept for the first time in years. The sun was up, the household stirring, while Aaron waited for her on the patio. He'd declined Rosa's offer of breakfast, preferring to wait for her. He wanted to conclude the arrangements for his father's funeral, then confirm his return trip to Brazil.

He had slept fitfully, his mind filled with painful and agonizing memories—memories of pain, rage and guilt. His father had wanted to explain his decision to marry Sharon, but he wouldn't listen. He had turned his back on his father, knowing no amount of rationalizing could counter his deception.

His dark gaze was fixed on a small green lizard that had attached itself to the sand-colored wall. The tiny reptile was joined by another, and the two lizards regarded each other for a full minute before one scampered away.

He detected Regina's approach seconds before he saw her. The familiar fragrance of her perfume wafted in the warm morning air, filling his sensitive nostrils. Rising to his feet, he stood, turned and stared numbly as she crossed the patio. His respiration quickened. She was awesome, more shockingly beautiful than he remembered.

She was elegantly attired in a black business suit with a slim skirt ending several inches above her knees. A fitted, hip-length jacket claimed a single button, calling attention to her tiny waist. A pair of black, patent leather pumps and a single strand of large, magnificent cultured pearls with matching earrings completed her attractive presentation.

Extending her right hand, Regina gave Aaron a bright smile. "I'm sorry to have kept you waiting."

The wait was worth it, he mused. "It's all right. My body's circadian rhythms still have not adjusted to your time zone."

Ignoring her proffered hand, he leaned over and kissed her cheek. "Good morning."

Her eyes widened, and she pulled back. "Good morning," she mumbled softly.

Aaron moved over to the table under the shade of a brightly colored umbrella, and pulled out a chair. She thanked him while allowing him to seat her. He circled the table and sat opposite her. What he had not been able to observe the night before was ardently displayed in the full sunlight.

She had brushed her hair off her face and secured it in a simple twist at the back of her head. Sleep had erased the slight puffiness under her eyes, and they gleamed like polished onyx. His mesmerized gaze catalogued the sweep of her naturally arching eyebrows, the delicate symmetry of her features, and the stubborn set of her rounded chin. Her face was slender, with cheekbones set high enough for her to be thought of as exotic.

Her gaze locked with his as each engaged in a silent examination of the other. She studied his face, feature by feature, wondering if he, too, had disapproved of his father marrying someone as young as she was.

"How old were you when you married Oscar?" he questioned softly, verbalizing her musings.

She arched an eyebrow. "Nineteen."

He recoiled as if she had struck him. "And how long were you married?"

"Eight years."

He frowned. "He was fifty years older than you." He made it sound like an accusation instead of a fact.

Tilting her head, she stared down her nose at him. "Fifty years older than me, and twenty years older than my father."

He couldn't believe it. *She's only twenty-seven.* He knew she was young, but he had hoped that she was at least in her thirties. He was thirty-seven—ten years older. That meant she was practically still a child when she married Oscar. At least Sharon had been twenty-four, and a woman—a very experienced woman.

"Did your father object to you marrying a man so much older than you?"

"He couldn't object. He didn't know I was married until a week after Oscar and I had exchanged vows."

"He disapproved?"

She shrugged a shoulder. "I'm not one to seek approval from anyone—especially my parents."

Sitting up straighter, Aaron draped an arm over the back of his chair. He was intrigued with Regina Spencer, intrigued enough to want to know more about the woman who had seduced Oscar and had gotten him to marry her. And he did not want to deceive himself because he knew his father, regardless of his age, was a suitable catch for any woman. Not only had Oscar been considerate, gentle and brilliantly creative, but he also had been a very wealthy man.

There was no doubt Regina had married Oscar for his money. Why else would a nineteen-year-old girl marry an old, terminally ill man?

Whatever his suspicions, he knew they would be revealed at the reading of Oscar's will. Only time would tell why she had married his father. She had admitted that she did not love Oscar when she married him, so it had to be for money.

Regina glanced at the watch on her wrist. "We're scheduled to meet with the funeral director at eleven-thirty."

Aaron looked at his own watch. It was after eight-thirty. "How long should it take us to get there?"

"We *should* make it within two hours, but one can never tell with the city traffic." That meant they had to eat breakfast, then leave within half an hour. And as if on cue, Rosa appeared, pushing a serving cart filled with juice, fresh fruit, freshly baked bread and a steaming pot of strong, fragrant Mexican coffee.

Rosa placed the dishes on the table, then poured coffee into translucent china cups painted with delicate blue flowers. "Will there be anything else, Señora?"

"Tell Jaime to have the car ready for nine-fifteen. Dr. Spencer and I will be going to the city."

"*Sí*, Señora."

Aaron waited until the housekeeper walked away, then turned his attention to Regina, studying her with a curious intensity. Everything about her indicated she had been spoiled and pampered. She issued orders to others as if she had been doing it for years. The night before she hadn't waited for him to acknowledge whether he had wanted to eat when she said, *We'll dine on the patio.* She had turned her back and walked away, expecting him to follow her. What surprised him was that he had—he'd followed her like someone in a trance.

And he had also spent a restless night dreaming—dreaming of the rare occasions when he shared more than two months in a given year with Oscar Spencer, and dreaming about the woman who had offered his father companionship during the last eight years of his life. And it was now—in the full sunlight—that he knew he wanted to know everything about Regina.

Buttering a slice of bread still warm from the oven, he said, "Where are you from?"

Regina, caught off guard by the questions, nearly spilled the cream she poured into her coffee cup. "Florida."

He arched a questioning eyebrow. "You don't sound as if you're from the South."

She took a sip of the rich, strong brew. It was perfect. She had grown to love coffee and everything about it: taste, smell, and its soothing properties.

Placing her cup on its saucer, she met Aaron's questioning gaze. "I was born in New York, and spent the first nine and a half years of my life there. Then I moved to Florida. How about yourself?"

"My father didn't tell you about me?"

She shook her head. "Your father did not discuss his past with me. I knew he'd been married twice before he married me, and that he had a son from his first marriage."

A muscle flicked noticeably in Aaron's left cheek, and at the same time his mouth tightened into a thinning line. It was apparent Oscar hadn't told her the reason for their estrangement.

"I find that odd," he remarked in a quiet tone.

"Odd? Why?"

"Because a husband and wife should not have secrets between them."

Sitting up straighter, Regina leaned forward. "Is there something Oscar should've told me about why he did not want me to contact you until after his death?"

"What you're asking me is something you should've questioned your late husband about."

"I did." The two words exploded from her mouth.

His eyes widened when he registered her rising temper. A rush of color suffused her clear, gold-brown skin, and her breasts rose and fell heavily under the lightweight fabric of her suit jacket.

Spreading his hand out, palms upward, he drawled, "And?"

"And he wouldn't tell me."

Placing his hands on the table, Aaron leaned forward, a feral grin curving his strong, attractive mouth. "And neither will I."

Regina recoiled as if he had slapped her and slumped back against the cushioned softness of her chair. Whatever it was that kept father and son alienated would remain untold. Oscar had carried the secret to his grave, and no doubt Aaron would do the same.

It no longer mattered to her. She planned to begin her life anew, and her future would not include either of the Spencer men. She would always love Oscar and carry his memory within her heart, but that was what he would be become—a memory— while Dr. Aaron Spencer would return to Brazil and his research projects, which had become his lifelong obsession.

She would return to Fort Lauderdale, Florida, reconnect with her family, then put into motion what she wanted to do with the rest of her life.

Picking up her cup, she flashed Aaron a dazzling dimpled smile. Surprisingly, he returned it with a bright one of his own.

He took a sip of coffee, rolling it around on his tongue before letting it slide down the back of his throat. It was excellent. In fact, the quality was far superior to the beans grown on his coffee plantation.

"Did you learn Spanish after you moved here?" he queried, still wanting to know more about his enticing dining partner.

"No. My grandmother taught me."

"Cuban?"

"How did you know?"

"Lucky guess." What he didn't say was that the largest concentration of Spanish-speaking people in Florida were of Cuban ancestry.

"How about you, Aaron? Why do you prefer to call Brazil home?"

He hesitated, savoring the soft, husky sound of his name rolling off her tongue. It was the first time she had said his name without his prompting her. Whenever she addressed him as Dr. Spencer he felt her sarcasm.

"My research."

"Is that the only reason? Couldn't you do your research in the States?"

"I could, but there's no way I could manage my coffee plantation from thousands of miles away."

What he did not say was that living in Brazil was far enough away from the States so that he wouldn't have to hear or read about Oscar Spencer, though the news of his winning the coveted Academy Award for his last film had reached him when he sat down to view the evening news ten years ago. The moment he'd heard his father's name mentioned, he turned off the television. The pain of Oscar and Sharon's deception still had not faded, after two years.

"Why don't you hire an overseer to manage your plantation?"

"I have one."

A slight frown wrinkled her smooth forehead. "I don't see the correlation." Her family's business conglomerate, ColeDiz International Ltd., owned coffee plantations in Belize, Puerto Rico, and Jamaica, yet her father or uncles were never directly responsible for planting or harvesting the crop.

Aaron smiled a full smile, the gesture transforming his face and causing Regina to catch her breath. His eyes tilted higher in an upward slant, and his full upper lip flattened against the ridge of his teeth, offering her a glimpse of their perfection. Her gaze moved slowly from his mouth to his eyes as they appeared to wink at her. She found his smile so infectious that she returned it with a dimpled one of her own.

"At the risk of sounding like an elitist, do you actually think I went to medical school to labor in the fields?"

Her smiled faded. He was laughing at her. Did he think she was totally ignorant? She struggled to control her quick temper.

"Save your sarcasm, Dr. Spencer, because I'm not in the mood for it right now."

He sobered quickly. "I wasn't laughing at you, nor did I mean to insult your intelligence."

"Tell me, Aaron, what exactly do you mean?"

He now understood why Oscar had been drawn to the young woman sitting opposite him. Beneath her overt beauty it was apparent that Regina Spencer's mien was that of entitlement. She was spoiled, as well as demanding. She'd met Oscar, wanted him for whatever her personal reasons, then claimed him as her husband.

And he knew he had to be careful—very, very careful—not to fall into the same trap. He'd been in Mexico less than twenty-four hours, and in that time all of his thoughts were filled with the image of the woman with whom he was sharing breakfast. He usually did not explain his work or himself to any woman, yet he found himself wanting to with Regina.

"Hospitals in South America were recruiting American-trained doctors, and I signed up to do my pediatric internship and residency in Brazil."

Regina paused, a spoon filled with fruit poised in midair. "Why Brazil, and not one of the other countries?"

"I had lived half my life in Brazil. After my mother died in childbirth, my father agreed to share responsibility for my up-bringing with her twin sister. My very proper schoolteacher aunt had declared openly that she would never marry. She quickly changed her mind after going to Brazil on vacation, where she fell in love with a man who was a coffee grower. She married him after a whirlwind courtship, then worked out an arrangement with Oscar in which I would spend the school year in Brazil and the remaining time in the States.

"Her husband died during my second year in medical school, leaving my aunt heir to a small but very profitable plantation in Bahia. She was a woman who never wanted to learn anything about coffee except how to brew it, but when she found herself totally ignorant about the product which afforded her her income she quickly changed her mind. Within a year she became an authority on every phase, from growing the plant to harvesting it. So when I was offered the chance to return to Brazil to be close to her, I accepted it."

Regina was fascinated by his story. "Does she still run the plantation?"

Aaron wagged his head slowly. "No. She died three years ago."

"I'm sorry, Aaron." The three words came out of their own

volition, those words she had heard people offer her so often since she had become a widow.

He pulled his lower lip between his teeth, staring directly at her. "I miss her, Regina. I miss her more than I can verbalize. She may have been my aunt, but she became more than that. She was my mother."

Reaching across the table, Regina covered his larger hand with her slender fingers. For the first time she noticed the difference in their coloring. Both were brown—hers a gold, his a rich, warm sienna. His fingers were long, his hand well-formed—the hands of a healer whose touch made her aware of her dormant sexuality for the first time in her life. And what she did not want to admit was that his touch was also that of a seducer.

His free hand closed over hers. "I decided to live in Bahia after I completed my residency. I became interested in microbiology, and joined a research institute that relies solely on the government and private donors for funding. I now head that institute. I'm also its largest benefactor. Every penny of profit I squeeze from the plantation I put into the institute."

His fingers tightened on hers. "I will not leave my research, nor will I ever leave my plantation. Not for anyone or for anything."

But you have left it, Aaron, she wanted to remind him. He'd left it so he could pay his last respects to his father.

"Now I understand," she replied quietly.

He released her fingers, then picked up his coffee cup. He took a sip, savoring its rich taste on his tongue. His gaze met his stepmother's over the rim, and he registered a curiosity that hadn't been there before. It was apparent she was as intrigued about him as he was about her, but he knew whatever he felt or was beginning to feel for his father's widow would never manifest itself. As soon as Oscar was buried, he would take his leave. Oscar was his past, and Regina Spencer was certain to become his past, too.

They finished their breakfast in silence. Half an hour later both were seated on the rear seat of a late model BMW sedan as the driver maneuvered expertly down the winding narrow roads toward the bustling, smog-filled, overcrowded streets of Mexico City.

Chapter 4

Aaron stared out the side window rather than glance down at the length of Regina's long, shapely legs in the sheer black hose. He realized she was tall, and the black patent leather pumps added another three inches to her already impressive height, putting her over the six-foot mark. It was apparent she was secure with herself—quite secure, very beautiful, and now no doubt an extremely wealthy young widow.

"The funeral service will be private," Regina stated, her low, husky voice breaking the comfortable silence. Not turning his head, he nodded. "Oscar wanted it that way," she continued. "He made all of the arrangements a month ago. He wrote his obituary, eulogy, and updated his will."

Shaking his head, Aaron mumbled a colorful expletive under his breath. "I thought he would've changed, but it's obvious he was controlling up until the end."

Regina bristled at his sarcasm. "It was his life, and he had every right to control it."

This time he turned and glared at her. "And everyone else's around him."

"He wasn't that way with me," she said in defense of her dead husband, but the instant the words were out of her mouth she knew it was only a half-truth. Oscar's decision to marry her had come with a stipulation: that she attend college after she completed her second and final film. She agreed, and when they relocated to Mexico she enrolled in the *Universidad* with a major in landscape architecture.

His grim expressions fading, Aaron gave her a tentative smile. "Then he was *very* different with you."

There was no mistaking the softer quality of his voice. Oscar had agreed to share custody of his son with his sister-in-law, but had issued his demands once she decided to move to Brazil: Aaron would live in Brazil during the school year, but return to the States for every school recess; he would attend an American college and—when he considered a career in medicine—an American medical school.

It wasn't until he returned to the United States to attend college and medical school that he came to know the man he called Dad. He wasn't a man to whom he felt close enough to confide his secrets. He was Oscar Spencer, the brilliant movie director; the man whose word was the final one on a movie set; the man whose acting techniques were followed and executed by actors earning millions of dollars a film; the man whose methods were taught in many drama schools all over the world.

Shifting his expressive eyebrows, he offered Regina a warm, open smile for the first time since their meeting. It was apparent she had not known her husband *that* well.

"How did you meet Oscar?"

It was her turn to gaze out the window. "I met him on a movie set."

His body stiffened in shock. "You worked in film?"

She nodded. "Yes. I was an actress. Oscar directed me in my

first film. His genius secured me an Academy Award nomination, and of course his own award."

Slumping back against the leather seat, Aaron felt as if someone had put their fingers around his throat, closing, squeezing, and not permitting him to draw a normal breath. *She was also an actress!* Like the first two women Oscar Spencer had married, Regina had also been an actress. What was it about these women that his father had not been able to resist?

He also had to ask himself why he, too, was drawn to actresses. His own mother had been one. Then he had fallen in love with Sharon, who had been a drama major. And now there was Regina Spencer—his father's widow, and now his stepmother.

What he was forced to admit to himself was that he *was* attracted to Regina. It just wasn't her beauty. Only a blind man would not see her most obvious appealing characteristic—her face—but it was the total package: her voice, body, and most of all the controlled sensuality she probably wasn't aware she possessed. It was apparent her youth and her sensuality had prompted Oscar to offer marriage, while it was evident that greed and cunning made Regina accept his proposal.

Like father, like son? No, he prayed silently. He had wanted a lot of things in his life, but he never wanted to be Oscar Clayborne Spencer.

Aaron sat on a straight-back chair beside Regina, listening to the funeral director. His father had delineated every phase of his funeral, including specific instructions for a graveside, closed-casket service only. There was not to be a wake.

He waited for the conclusion of the arrangements, then asked, "May I see my father's body?"

The solemn-looking director glanced at Regina. She lowered her lashes, signaling her approval. "*Sí,* Dr. Spencer," he replied, rising to his feet. "Excuse me, Señora."

She nodded, acknowledging their departure. She did not know

why, but Aaron's request to see his father's body surprised her. Not once since his arrival had he exhibited any emotion which had indicated sorrow or grief. She thought perhaps because he was a doctor—who was familiar with death and dying—that he had become an expert in concealing his feelings. It was either that, or his and Oscar's alienation had vanquished any or all love between father and son.

She could not imagine not having her father in her life, even though she had spent the first nine years not knowing who he was. Closing her eyes tightly, she mentally dismissed the repugnant family secrets that had forced her twenty-two-year-old pregnant mother to flee Florida and hide from Martin Cole for a decade. If Martin hadn't gotten his half brother to find her mother, her existence would have mirrored Aaron's—not knowing where her father resided or whether he was dead or alive.

She shook her head, not opening her eyes. That was not what she wanted for herself, and, if she ever remarried, for her children.

"Are you all right, Señora Spencer? Perhaps you would like me to get you something to drink?"

Regina opened her eyes, realizing the funeral director had returned. His expression mirrored his concern. Offering him a gentle smile, she said, "No, *gracias,* Señor Padilla. I'm fine."

And she was. She and Aaron had finalized the arrangements for the graveside service, and within another three days the earth would claim Oscar's body as it had every existing organism since the beginning of creation.

Aaron walked into the small, air-cooled antechamber and stared at his father's cadaver. The sight of the emaciated form numbed him as he stood motionless, holding his breath. The man lying on a table bore no resemblance to the one he remembered. The Oscar Spencer he knew was tall, proud, elegant, not withered with age and disease. The angular face—which had been a collage of African and Native-American features that had afforded him a refined handsomeness both men and women had found attractive—was now a shrunken death mask.

Scathing, acerbic words he had rehearsed for years died on his tongue, and the longer his gaze lingered on his father's body the more he knew he had made the most grievous mistake of his life. He should not have permitted a woman to come between them. It should not have mattered that he loved Sharon enough to offer marriage. She should have become the recipient of his venomous fury, not Oscar.

They had been father and son—bound by blood. And there had been no doubt that his father had loved him, loved him more than he deserved to be loved.

Turning on his heel, he walked out of the room, closing the door behind him. He delayed returning to the director's office, pressed his back to a wall, and struggled for control of his fragile emotions. Covering his face with both hands, he mumbled a prayer of forgiveness.

"I'm sorry, Dad. I am so sorry, Father." His voice seemed to rumble in his chest, the very sound of it knifing his heart and leaving him to hemorrhage unchecked. Why hadn't he followed through after the telephone call? Why hadn't he hired someone to find his father? The whys attacked him relentlessly as he stood in the shadows, wanting to bellow out his pain and frustration.

His mother had given up her life giving birth to him, and his father had wasted away slowly in a foreign country without the flesh of his flesh at his side. Pushing himself away from the wall, he retraced his steps and made his way back to the director's office.

His tortured gaze impaled Regina as she rose to her feet at his return. He didn't know why, but he wanted to blame her— blame her for not contacting him sooner. What had she been trying to prove by playing the dutiful little wife and *obeying* her husband's demands? As he moved closer to her something unknown communicated that Regina was anything but a docile or submissive woman.

He stood over her, his eyes conveying the fury warring within him. "I'm finished here."

She tilted her chin and shifted an arching eyebrow. "So am I." Taking purposeful steps, she walked out of the office, her head held high and her back ramrod straight.

Aaron found himself doing what he had done the night of his arrival—following her lead. He wondered whether she had been the one doing the leading in her marriage. Had she talked Oscar into not contacting him until after his death? Had she feared that his reconciling with his father would leave her with a smaller portion of her husband's estate?

Quickening his stride, he caught up with her as she pushed open the door and walked out onto the sidewalk, his fingers tightening around her upper arm. She lost her footing, falling back against his chest. His free arm curved around her waist, pressing her hips to his middle until she regained her balance.

Turning in his embrace, she stared up at him, her breasts heaving in a measured rising and falling rhythm. The restless energy of Mexico City's populace crowding the wide avenues, the raucous sounds of honking car horns, and the incessant babble of spoken Spanish along with native Indian dialects faded as Aaron lost himself in the fragrant softness of Regina's curving body.

He noted the obsidian darkness of her large eyes for the first time, eyes so black no light would ever penetrate their midnight depths. His gaze lingered leisurely on her lush, succulent mouth—a mouth that begged to be kissed.

The conflicting emotions of anguish and defeat that had assailed him when he saw Oscar's body hadn't faded, and he wanted to ravage Regina's mouth until she pleaded with him to stop. He wanted to punish her, make her feel pain, and in doing so hopefully eradicate his own. Her eyes filled with tears, turning them into gems of polished onyx as she struggled valiantly to keep them from overflowing and embarrassing her.

Aaron held her to his heart, feeling her warmth, the fragility of her slender body, the sweetness clinging to her flesh, and registering the shudders she was helpless to control. Tightening his hold on her waist, he molded her length to his, burying his face against her silken neck.

"I just want it over, Aaron," she sobbed softly.

Inhaling deeply, he enjoyed all that made Regina Spencer who she was. Holding her and reveling in her sensual femininity made him realize that he did not think of her as the woman who had married his father, or as his stepmother.

She was a temptress who managed to lure him into her web of seduction without saying a word, and he was more like Oscar Spencer than he wanted to admit, because, like his father, he was trapped in a spell from which he did not want to escape. He had known her less than twenty-four hours, yet he wanted to know her in every way possible. She was a woman of mystery, and he wanted to peel away the layers under the overt beauty, to discover the real person who appeared secure and mature beyond her years.

"It will be over—soon," he crooned in a deep, comforting voice.

Nodding, she touched her fingertips to her eyes. "I want to go home."

He led her around the building and to the parking lot. Their driver stood beside the car, holding open the rear door. Aaron helped her in, then slid onto the seat beside her. She sat, back pressed to the seat, eyes closed. Reaching over, he took her hand in his, holding it protectively. Her fingers stiffened momentarily, then relaxed in his grip.

She opened her eyes and smiled at him through a shimmer of sparkling tears. "I'm sorry I fell apart back there."

He returned her smile with a wink. "You're entitled. I know it hasn't been easy for you."

"What I had to go through was nothing. It was Oscar who suffered—"

"You don't have to talk about it," he interrupted.

"Yes, I do. I promised Oscar I would tell you."

Vertical lines appeared between his eyes. "Tell me what?"

She pulled her hand away from his. "Everything. I met Oscar for the first time when I was seventeen...."

Chapter 5

Ten years ago

A black, stately Mercedes-Benz sedan maneuvered silently up to a set of iron gates rising upward to twelve feet. A man, standing more than half that height, appeared seemingly from nowhere and tapped on the tinted glass on the driver's side of the vehicle. The chauffeur pushed a button, lowering the window, and extended a printed invitation.

The guard's sharp gaze swept over the square of vellum, then shifted as he tried catching a glimpse of the woman sitting on the rear seat. His gaze did not falter at the same time he raised a small, palm-size cellular phone to his ear.

"Cole," he said quietly into the receiver. The gates opened and the Mercedes-Benz eased forward up an ascending, curvilinear driveway.

Regina Cole stared out the window, noting a series of gardens, a guest house, and a tennis court. The driveway ended at a *porte cochere*. Beyond were two more welcoming areas: a covered courtyard with scrolled gates, and an open courtyard with statuary and more gardens. She knew every inch of the house. Designed with the features of a Tuscany villa, it fused the grandeur and comfort afforded a man of Harold Jordan's station.

She had come to the sprawling mansion six months ago, spending a week under twenty-foot high ceilings and lazing around the Olympic-size swimming pool with the Pacific Ocean as the backdrop. Harold Jordan had summoned her and award-winning director Oscar Spencer to his home to discuss the film he decided to finance—a discussion which lasted only an hour.

Harold had invited her back more than half a dozen times during the filming of the virtually unknown artistic masterpiece, *Silent Witness,* but she had deftly sidestepped each request with a preconceived, rehearsed declination. There was something about the thrice-married producer which made it impossible for her to relax in his presence. At forty-nine, he was thirty-two years her senior. However, their age difference had not stopped him from pursuing her with the craftiness of Machiavelli.

This evening was different. Harold had summoned everyone who had had anything to do with the production of *Silent Witness* to his home to celebrate the film's eleven Academy Award nominations. She still had five months before she turned eighteen, yet she had garnered a Best Actress nomination for her first film.

The news had numbed her for hours. Then she had picked up the telephone in the sparsely furnished Los Angeles apartment she shared with another actress and called her parents in Florida. Hearing their drawling Southern cadence reminded her of how far she was from home, and despite her joy she felt more alone than she had ever been in her young life. She had wanted her parents and the other members of her family present when she shared her jubilation, not strangers; she needed people around her whom she loved, and who made her feel safe.

And there were times when she did not feel safe, despite sharing the apartment with another young woman and hiring drivers to take her everywhere. Years of therapy helped her cope with her fears, but hadn't eradicated them entirely. It was only on the set, in character, that she was no longer Regina Cole, but whoever her character was. It was then she no longer feared close, dark spaces. It was then she could breathe without a suffocating darkness crushing her body and her mind. And it was then that she could look out at the audience and smile, because she was completely free of the demons who attacked swiftly, silently, and without warning.

The car stopped at the entrance to the Jordan residence and a white-jacketed valet opened the rear door. The young man extended a tanned hand and Regina laid her slender fingers on his palm. His gaze widened appreciably as she placed one black, silk-shod, sling strap-sandaled foot on the terra-cotta path, then the other. Smooth, incredibly long legs were displayed under a body-hugging black dress in a stretch knit with a wide neckline and cap sleeves.

His mouth went suddenly dry as he pulled her gently to her feet, she meeting his gaze. He was an even six-foot in height, and Regina Cole's head was level with his. A warm wind blew in from the ocean, lifting her waist-length curly hair. Turning her face into the breeze, she smiled. His smiled matched hers. She was even more beautiful in person.

Tucking her hand in the crook of his arm, he led her toward the glass-paned mahogany doors. "This way, Miss Cole."

Regina's trademark dimpled smile faded the moment she spied Harold Jordan standing in the entry waiting for her arrival. He was as casually dressed as she was. He had selected a pair of black linen slacks and a white raw silk shirt with a Mandarin collar piped in black.

He extended both hands, his fingers encircling her tiny waist. "My queen," he crooned, pulling her to his slim, hard body.

Tilting her head, she avoided his wet kiss and it landed on her chin. "Good evening, Mr. Jordan."

The warmth of his gaze grew cold, his eyes resembling pale-blue topaz. They were a startling contrast in a face deeply tanned by the brilliant, Southern California sun.

"How many times must I remind you to call me Harold?" His reprimand, although spoken softly, was cutting.

Forcing a smile, she said, "You're old enough to be my father." He flinched as if she had struck him. "And because you are, I can't address you by your name."

"You can't, or you won't?"

Her smile faded. "I cannot."

Harold Jordan's patience had been worn thin with his continued attempts to seduce the very beautiful and very talented young woman who managed to occupy his every waking moment. If she had not been the daughter of a wealthy man she would've shared his bed as soon as she hit the streets of Hollywood.

But Regina Cole wasn't a starving actress waiting tables or auditioning on a casting director's couch to land a role. She had arrived in Los Angeles trained by the best drama coach her father's money could procure, and the training paid off. She had been nominated for Best Actress amid a field of veterans for her first film.

It wasn't just her acting talent which had drawn him to her, but the total package. She was the antithesis of the flaxen California blond. Her jet-black hair flowed to her waist in loose, shiny curls, a perfect foil for golden-brown skin further darkened by the hot sun.

The moment he stared at her black-and-white head shot he had been transfixed by the perfection of her delicate features. The large dark eyes, staring out at him from the photograph, along with her straight nose and lush, full mouth, had held him spellbound until she walked into his office. She'd smiled at him, displaying a set of deep dimples and greeted him in a low, smoky voice which belied her youth. He'd stared, temporarily paralyzed, and a slight arching of one sweeping eyebrow let him know she was aware that he was not unaffected by her startling natural beauty.

He did not remember his interview with her until after she'd left his office. All he recalled was her height, the sensually haunting fragrance of her scented body, the boyish slimness of her hips, and the firm, fullness of her thrusting breasts.

Regina Cole had successfully parried his advances, but this night he would not be denied. Having her share his bed would make the eleven nominations for *Silent Witness* pale by comparison.

Grasping her hand, he led her through an arched hallway off the opulently furnished living room and out to the patio. A state-of-the-art sound and lighting system filled the area around the pool with music and flattering lights. The glow of the setting sun bathed every light surface in a fiery orange.

Harold gave her a warm smile. "May I get you something from the bar?"

"Club soda, please."

His hand moved up her back, his fingers catching in the wealth of hair floating over her shoulders like curling black ribbon. "Can't I interest you in something stronger? I can assure you you won't be carded tonight."

"Club soda with a twist of lime."

He stared at her, a polite smile in place. "Even if you were old enough to drink what would be your preference?"

"Club soda," she insisted stubbornly. She had experimented with drinking with her friends during her sixteenth birthday celebration, and she woke with a severe migraine the following day. The episode was enough for her to never drink alcohol again. Along with her mother's voice, she had also inherited Parris Simmons-Cole's intolerance for most alcoholic beverages.

"Then it's one club soda with a twist for the pretty lady," Harold whispered close to her ear.

Regina watched him make his way to the bar before turning and searching the crowd for her mentor. She saw Oscar Spencer as he listened intently to one of the film's supporting actresses; the skimpily attired woman gestured wildly, the many bracelets on her wrists sliding noisily up and down her bare, tanned, well-toned arms.

Resting her hands on her hips, Regina smiled at the bored expression on Oscar's face. She found him to be the most patient man she'd ever had the pleasure of knowing. And if it hadn't been for his genius, she knew, her performance would never have been good enough to earn an award nomination.

"Congratulations, beautiful," whispered an assistant director as he walked past her in his quest to find some much needed liquid refreshment.

She flashed her celebrated smile. "Thank you, Neil."

Oscar turned in her direction, nodding his acknowledgment. She beckoned with her forefinger and he excused himself from the chatting, clinging actress. He wove his way through the swelling throng, reaching her at the same time Harold arrived with her drink.

The producer handed her a goblet filled with a clear, chilled, carbonated liquid with a sliver of green. "A club soda with a twist."

Regina took the glass, giving him the smile he had come to expect from her. "Thank you."

Harold nodded, dropping an arm over Oscar's shoulder. "Have your feet touched the ground yet?"

Shaking his head, Oscar offered a shy smile. "Actually, they've never left the ground."

Regina slipped the cool, refreshing drink, peering over the rim at the director. She knew he was apprehensive about celebrating his nomination prematurely. It had taken him more than thirty years to prove his genius in an industry that had employed its own efficient strategy of excluding people of color from the major studios. But Oscar had quietly made a name for himself, directing low-budget independent projects.

Then, at sixty-six, he did what he had never done before—he made the rounds of the studios to finance a script sent him by a recent graduate of an avant-garde film school. His instincts told him he had a winner, and he was right—once he finally convinced Harold Jordan to underwrite the cost of the project.

She had answered the casting call along with hundreds of others, knowing she was born to play the role of a young woman who, while on vacation in Mexico, falls in love with a priest who is living a double life. Like Oscar, she knew her instincts were correct once she received the call from her agent telling her she had gotten the part.

Her parents had flown out to the West Coast with her younger brother and sister to congratulate her on winning her first starring role, but she knew the reunion was more of a reconciliation than a celebration. Martin and Parris Cole had indulged what they had thought was her fleeting passion for acting, hoping and praying it would wane with maturity.

However, it did not wane, but intensified, and a week after she graduated from high school she packed her bags and left Fort Lauderdale, Florida, for Los Angeles, California.

She checked into a hotel, then called her parents to give them her address. Within twenty-four hours her father had set up an account in her name at a major California bank, permitting her to withdraw enough monies each month to maintain the life-style she'd had in Florida. And two weeks after her arrival she found a comfortable, two-bedroom apartment in an upscale L.A. neighborhood. She lived alone for a month before she offered her spare bedroom to another actress who had just separated from her boyfriend.

She had now been a Californian for nine months, and during

that time she had made one film and had not gone out on one date. It wasn't as if she hadn't been asked out by men of varying ages, but it was her own age which kept her away from the clubs and the private parties. She was old enough to drive, yet still not old enough to vote, smoke, or drink. And the realization was sobering, because legally she was not an adult.

Harold removed his arm from Oscar's shoulder, his pale, penetrating gaze never straying from Regina's face. "Do you think we have a chance at the triple crown—Best Picture, Director, and Actress?"

She took another sip of her drink. "I'm not so certain the Academy will want to give me a Best Actress award, given my age and inexperience."

Oscar's dark brown eyes narrowed in concentration. "Your age and the fact that *Silent Witness* is your first film should have nothing to do with it."

She shifted her expressive eyebrows. "Must I remind you of politics, my friend?"

The director shook his head. He had been involved in the film industry longer than his talented protégée had been alive, and had known firsthand how politics had played havoc with his own directorial tenure. He'd won numerous awards at the Cannes, Venice, and Sundance Film Festivals, but never his namesake—the coveted, gold-plated statuette.

He was now sixty-seven, and he knew he did not have many more years in the film industry. He had planned for *Silent Witness* to be his last project, but changed his mind after working with Regina Cole. At first he thought her garnering the lead for *Silent* was a fluke. However, he had quickly changed his mind after working with her.

He found her intelligent, extremely talented, and uncannily perceptive. She usually knew what he wanted even before he outlined what he required of her. Watching her transform herself into a character usually sent chills through his body. She always sat apart from the others on the set, meditating. Once the signal was given for her to take her place for a scene, the transformation was complete. She was no longer Regina Cole, but her character.

He wanted to direct her once more before he officially retired. He wanted and needed to know if the magic was still there, if they could become a winning combination for the second time.

Harold excused himself, walking away and leaving Regina alone with Oscar. She took another sip of her drink, then lowered the glass and smiled at the tall, spare, elegant black man. Oscar Spencer was old enough to be her grandfather. In fact he was twenty years older than her forty-seven-year-old father, but somehow she did not regard him as a father figure. She saw him as a protector. Quietly, surreptitiously, he had shielded her from the obvious and lecherous advances of some of the men on the movie set.

When she was first introduced to Oscar she had found herself staring mutely at the man whose quiet voice and gentle manner put her immediately at ease. After working with him she realized he never had to raise his voice to issue an order. A withering glance and a noticeable tightening of his moustached mouth usually indicated his displeasure, and no one appeared willing to challenge his authority on the set.

Oscar's private life had remained that—private—though the tabloids did uncover that he had been twice married, both times to actresses. His first wife died in childbirth, giving him his only child, a son. The second divorced him within the first year of their marriage, citing irreconcilable differences.

She noticed that women of all ages were drawn to him, but at sixty-seven he did not seem the least bit interested in initiating an ongoing relationship. She had shared an occasional dinner with him, but only at his home. He always sent a driver to pick her up from her apartment, and after they shared a meal and several hours of intelligent conversation, the driver drove her back home.

Taking another sip of the club soda, she noticed an unnaturally bitter taste on her tongue. A slight frown marred her smooth forehead. Perhaps the sliver of lime had given the liquid an acrid flavor.

"Is there something wrong with your drink?" Oscar questioned, seeing her frown of distaste.

She shrugged a slender shoulder, taking another swallow. "I don't know. It was fine when I first tasted it, but now it seems so bitter." Her words came out slurred, in a singsong fashion. She blinked furiously, eyelids fluttering rapidly as she tried focusing. Why was the room spinning? And why couldn't she see Oscar's face clearly?

Oscar's graying eyebrows met in a frown when he noticed her dilated pupils. Reaching out, he pried the glass from her hand and poured the contents into a large planter.

"Let's get out of here," he ordered quietly. Curving an arm around her waist, he led her across the patio and around the rear of the house to an area where several dozen cars were parked.

Supporting Regina's sagging body, he made his way over to a middle-aged man who jumped up from a chair at his approach. "Preston, please tell my driver to bring my car around."

"Yes, sir." He raced away to do the director's bidding.

Regina felt her knees buckle as her head rolled limply on her neck. "Oscar." Her voice was barely a whisper. "I think I'm going to be sick."

Pulling a handkerchief from the breast pocket of his jacket, he held it close to her mouth. "Let it come up and you'll feel better."

She did not want to throw up—not in public. Then, whatever she had eaten or drunk refused to stay down. "No," she moaned, pushing his hand away and swallowing back the rush of nausea.

Oscar solved her dilemma when he held her jaw firmly and thrust a finger down her throat. Within seconds she purged the contents of her stomach onto the octagonal-shaped flagstones. Her eyes filled with tears, which streamed down her cheeks. Her throat burned, her stomach muscles ached from the violent contractions, and she couldn't keep her knees from shaking.

"It's all right, Regina. You're going to be all right," he crooned over and over, wiping her mouth with the handkerchief.

The odor of undigested food was revolting, and Regina thought she was going to be sick all over again. What was wrong with her? What had she eaten or drunk to make her throw up?

The caretaker returned with the driver and stepped out of Oscar's car. His eyes widened when he noticed the splatter on the flagstones. Wrinkling his nose, he cursed to himself. He hated the superficial, self-centered people who attended Harold Jordan's parties. They always drank too much and wound up throwing up, and he always had to clean up after them. There were times when he let them lay in their own filth, while calling them pigs, and they were—overpaid, plastic pigs who wallowed in slop but were able to clean themselves up and then flash their perfect smiles to their adoring fans, who worshiped them as if they were royalty.

The chauffeur alighted and opened the back door. Oscar settled Regina onto the backseat of the car, then reached into a pocket of his slacks. He withdrew a large bill and handed it to Preston. "Here's a little something for having to clean it up."

The caretaker pocketed the money, smiling. "Thanks, Mr. Spencer."

Oscar managed a smile he did not quite feel and slipped onto the backseat beside Regina. He pulled her limp body close to his side, struggling to control his temper. What he wanted to do at that moment was return to the house and put his hands around Harold Jordan's throat and squeeze the life out of his body. He stared at the driver's broad shoulders instead.

Not turning around, the driver asked, "Where to, Mr. Spencer?"

"Take me home." The three words were quiet—quiet and lethal.

Chapter 6

Regina drifted in and out of sleep, succumbing to the smooth motion of the car rolling over the hills and through the canyons of Los Angeles. She remembered someone picking her up and carrying her from the car, but not much else.

She was totally unaware that Oscar Spencer's housekeeper had undressed her and covered her nude body with a freshly laundered pajama shirt belonging to her employer. She slept throughout the night as Oscar sat at her bedside watching her sleep. It wasn't until the following morning that she awoke—disoriented, wondering why she wasn't in her own bed at her own apartment.

She lay in bed, trying to remember what had happened the night before. Pushing a wealth of ebony curls off her forehead, she sighed audibly. She had gotten sick at Harold Jordan's house. Oscar had compounded her dizziness and nausea by forcing her to regurgitate.

Oscar! Sitting up quickly, she realized she was at Oscar's

house. She swung her legs over the side of the bed and managed to make it to the adjoining bathroom; she washed her face and rinsed her mouth with a cool, mint mouthwash, then searched the spacious, Spanish-style residence for its owner. Within minutes she found him in his study. He sat at his desk, his back to the door, talking on the telephone.

"You stinking son of a bitch!" he ranted through clenched teeth. "You know damn well what you did. You drugged her, Jordan! Don't lie to me. All I have to do is have a doctor pump her stomach and have a lab analyze the contents. Don't tell me what I won't do. It's over. I'll make certain you'll never get near her ever again. Don't threaten me, you perverted cretin. One call to the police and you'll be wearing a pair of bracelets that will require a key to remove." He slammed down the receiver, his shoulders heaving.

Regina's legs felt like blocks of ice. She hadn't gotten sick because she had eaten something that hadn't agreed with her. Harold Jordan had drugged her, and she did not have to guess why. He wanted her—in his bed. And because she hadn't come to him willingly he had taken the initiative of putting something in her drink.

"Oscar."

He swiveled the chair at the sound of her husky voice. Her hair spilled over her forehead and shoulders in a cloud of curling, raven spirals. The hem of his nightshirt ended above her knees, allowing for a generous view of her long, shapely legs.

Forcing a smile, he rose to his feet and closed the distance between them. He was impeccably dressed in a pair of dark linen slacks and a matching raw silk, long-sleeved shirt.

"Good morning. How are you feeling?"

Her large, dark gaze was fixed on his mouth. "Well, considering I was drugged."

He shifted a thick gray eyebrow, nodding slowly. "I suppose you overheard my conversation?"

Her expression was impassive. "I heard enough. How did you know he drugged me?"

"It's not the first time a woman has gotten *sick* at one of Harold Jordan's parties."

Closing her eyes, she wagged her head from side to side. "But why me, Oscar? I've seen Harold Jordan with enough women whom I assume are sleeping with him."

He moved closer, cradling her slender face between his hands. "Don't ask me why, Regina. All you have to do is look in the mirror. You're a stunning young woman. And there will be a lot of Harold Jordans who will want you to share their beds."

"But some of these women were very beautiful," she insisted.

Oscar held her tortured gaze. "You are young. Very, very young. And there are some older men who like young girls."

Hot, fat tears squeezed from under her eyelids and made their way down her cheeks. "When I sleep with a man I want that to be my decision. And only when I am ready."

Kissing her on both cheeks, he pulled her closer. "There is a lot of ugliness beneath Tinseltown's glitter and glamour, ugliness someone your age should not have to encounter. You should've been told that before you left home."

Opening her eyes, she stared up at him. "I heard it, Oscar. I heard it all, and still I *had* to come."

A wry smile curved his mouth under his clipped moustache. "You've heard it, yet you still had to come. The bright lights had your name on them, and they were calling you. You have it all, Regina Cole, yet you had to come. You have a perfect face, a perfect body, and an acting ability which rivals Katherine Hepburn's and Bette Davis's and you had to come to see if you could make it. Instead of you having to fend off Harold Jordan's advances, you should be in a college lecture hall taking notes."

She smiled through her tears. "You sound like my father."

"That's because I'm old enough to be your father." He returned her smile, wiping away her tears with his fingers. "In fact, I'm old enough to be your grandfather. And if I *were* your father, I'd cut you off without a penny and force you to come back home."

She took in a quick breath of astonishment. "Daddy would never do that to me."

Oscar's smile widened. "Of course he wouldn't. That's because you're his precious little princess." His expression sobered. "If you were my daughter I doubt whether I'd be able to do it, either."

Her expression matched his, giving her the appearance of being much older than seventeen. "My parents weren't thrilled that I decided to pursue an acting career instead of going to college. But there was nothing they could do about it once I graduated from high school."

"But you graduated two months shy of your seventeenth birthday. Legally you are still a minor and their responsibility."

"That's true. We had round-the-clock marathon discussions, and in the end they gave in. Both knew that I had to fulfill my dream or I would spend the rest of my life floundering while trying to find myself."

"They are truly exceptional parents, Regina. I still don't think I would've let my seventeen-year-old daughter leave home for a movie career."

"That's because you don't have a daughter, Mr. Spencer. I bet you wouldn't have raised the roof if your son left home at seventeen."

He shrugged a shoulder, the gesture both masculine and elegant. "Boys are different."

"And you're a sexist," she teased, offering him a warm smile.

"I suppose I am. I must remind you that I'm a product of my generation. We raised our sons and protected our daughters. And because I don't have a daughter, as of right now I'm unofficially adopting you. I'll make certain what Harold Jordan did to you will never happen again."

Combing her fingers through her hair, Regina pushed it off her forehead, her gaze never straying from the older man's face. "You think I need another father?"

"No. What you do need is someone to look out for you until you're able to protect yourself, or until you come to your senses and return to Florida."

She stared up at him from under her lashes, her delicate jaw tightening with a surge of determination. "I'm not leaving. A thousand Harold Jordans will not force me to walk away from my acting career until I'm ready to leave."

"And you're going to leave, Regina Cole," Oscar predicted sagely. "I doubt if you'll complete more than three films."

She felt a shiver of apprehension snake its way up her spine. "Why would you say that?"

"Wisdom and instinct, my child. And I'm going to live long enough to tell you I told you so."

Regina did not want him to be right. She did not want the heated, verbal confrontations with her parents, the thousands of hours she spent with drama coaches while sacrificing the time she should have spent with her friends and family members, to be negated.

Oscar Spencer was wrong. She would not walk away from her acting career. Not until she tired of it. And she hoped she wouldn't tire of it until she was an old, old woman.

Oscar Spencer kept his promise. He became her surrogate father and protector. Regina continued to rent and share her apartment with the other actress. However, in the coming weeks she found herself spending more and more time at the director's house. They established a habit of sharing dinner—every night. There were times when he sent her home with his driver, but many more when she slept over in the bedroom where she had spent the night following her drugging episode at Harold Jordan's house.

She hadn't heard from or seen Harold since that night, but realized that in less than a week she would be forced to come face-to-face with the man who had maliciously and methodically planned to rape her. She would attend the Academy Awards ceremony with Oscar, but regardless of the outcome she had made a decision not to attend any of the post-awards parties.

She sat at the table in the dining area at her apartment, studying the script her agent had delivered to her the day before. Vertical lines appeared between her eyes as she shook her head. It had taken only one reading for her to reach a decision. She could not consider the leading role.

The soft chiming of the telephone startled her, and she reached for the cordless phone lying inches away on the table. Pressing a button, she said softly, "Hello."

"How do you like it?"

She recognized her agent's gravelly voice immediately. "I like it, but I can't consider it."

"Why?"

"You know I won't take my clothes off."

A long, lingering sigh of frustration came through the receiver. "Regina—Baby Doll—don't do this to me. You know you're perfect for the part."

Her frown deepened. "Simon, don't fight with me. You know I don't do nude scenes."

"You're a big girl now, Baby Doll. By the time filming begins you'll be eighteen and—"

"It wouldn't matter whether I was eighteen or eighty," she interrupted. "I'm not going to do nude scenes."

Simon Garwood smothered a savage curse under his breath. "What do you want me to do?"

"Tell them to take out the nude scenes and I'll consider it."

"What if I tell them to use a body double?"

Regina heard a distinctive beep come through the wire. "Hold on, Simon. I have another call."

As soon as she depressed the button she heard the excited babble of raised male and female voices. "Hello?"

"Oh, my goodness—"

Her pulse quickened as she heard Oscar's housekeeper's trembling voice. "What's the matter, Miss Brock?"

"Mr. Spencer just took sick. The emergency medical people are here and…"

Closing her eyes, she tightened her grip on the telephone. "Is he alive?"

"I think so. But he's so still."

Even though she was sitting, Regina felt her knees shaking uncontrollably. "Where are they taking him?"

Sobbing, Miss Brock gave her the information, and a minute later she told Simon she would get back to him, then called the car service to pick her up.

She did not remember changing into a pair of faded jeans, oversize T-shirt, and a pair of running shoes. At the last moment she braided her flowing hair into a single plait and covered it with a navy-blue baseball cap. It was only when she was seated in the back of the late model Ford sedan that she pulled a pair of sunglasses from her purse and slipped them on. When she strode through the doors of the small, private Los Angeles hospital she was unrecognizable as the actress who had been nominated for her role in *Silent Witness*.

She asked the clerk at the admitting desk for Oscar Spencer's condition, lying smoothly when she introduced herself as his granddaughter. The clerk told her she had to wait until the admitting doctor completed his examination.

Regina lost track of time as she sat waiting on a nearby chair. She alternated staring at a clock and counting off the minutes with pacing. Two hours had passed before a middle-aged doctor approached her. His somber expression told her what she loathed hearing.

He extended his hand. "I'm Dr. Rutherford."

Rising to her feet, she shook the proffered hand. "Regina Simmons." She had decided to use her mother's maiden name. "How's my grandfather?"

The doctor pointed to the chair she had just vacated. "I think you'd better sit down, Miss Simmons." She complied, and he sat down beside her. "Your grandfather's condition is grave."

Her eyes widened behind the dark lenses. "How grave?"

"A CAT scan detected a large mass on his right lung. We're going to need you to sign some papers so we can remove it."

Closing her eyes, she swayed slightly as she bit down hard on her lower lip. How could she sign? She wasn't a relative. And besides, she was only seventeen. What did she know about giving permission for an operation?

Oscar had a son. A son who was a doctor. A son who hadn't seen or spoken to his father in more than two years. She studied the doctor's angular, patrician face. The green scrubs were not flattering to his sallow complexion.

"If…if he doesn't have the operation…" She couldn't continue.

"Without the operation I doubt whether he'll survive the year if the tumor spreads to the other lung."

"And with it?"

"We won't know if the mass is benign until it's biopsied. If it isn't, then the worse case scenario will be that he'll probably have to undergo radiation or chemotherapy to save the other lung, or keep the cancer from spreading. These procedures could possibly prolong his life by several years."

A wry smile curved her mouth. Oscar Spencer had promised to protect her, while the responsibility for his very existence was suddenly thrust upon her because she had elected to masquerade as his granddaughter.

She did not have a choice. That was taken out of her hands the moment he led her out of Harold Jordan's house.

"Where do I sign?" she asked in a firm voice.

The doctor patted her hand in a comforting gesture. "You've made the right decision, Miss Simmons. The clerk in the admitting office will have everything ready for you."

After signing the necessary documents for Oscar's surgery Regina lost track of time. She waited in a small, sunny room filled with large potted plants and colorful prints on the cool, beige walls. She made three trips to the hospital's coffee shop, each time purchasing large containers of the strong brew.

Becoming a Californian had changed her. She now drank coffee though she had never consumed it before, while eating less meat and more vegetables. She wasn't quite a vegetarian, but there were weeks when she did not eat fish, chicken, pork, or beef. The result was a loss of nearly ten pounds; ten pounds she could not afford to lose. Standing five-ten in her bare feet, she now tipped the scales at one hundred twelve pounds.

When her parents had come to Los Angeles to see her they hadn't been able to hide their shock at her weight loss. Her father promptly made a reservation at a restaurant and ordered every high calorie selection on the menu. Meanwhile, her mother had stared at her with tear-filled eyes before asking whether she was feeling well. She had spent more than two hours reassuring them she felt wonderful and that she was healthy. The elder Coles' fears were allayed once they saw her image on the screen. Their daughter was sensually entrancing.

She thought of her parents, brother, and sister as she sat sipping coffee, realizing how much she missed them. She missed five-year-old Arianna following her around and imitating her every motion, and seven-year-old Tyler. Her brother was quiet, reflective, appearing mature beyond his young years. He rarely smiled, and if he did it was a shy, attractive one. Everyone teased him and called him "old man." Tyler did not seem to mind. He existed in his own private world, daydreaming and keeping his fantasies to himself.

Sighing heavily, she closed her eyes, willing back tears. In a moment of melancholy she realized she was homesick. She wanted to go home—back to Florida. She was only seventeen, and Harold Jordan's drugging attempt and planned rape had compounded earlier childhood fears.

Her eyes opened and she stared at the highly waxed black and white vinyl floor tiles, a slight smile curving her mouth. As soon as Oscar recovered from his surgical procedure she would return home for an extended visit. The upcoming film her agent wanted her to accept would wait, wait until she was ready to step onto a movie set and in front of a camera again.

Chapter 7

Present day

Regina stared at Aaron, who stared back at her in obvious astonishment. "I wanted so much to go home. But…"

"Did you ever return to Florida?" he questioned after her words trailed off into a prolonged silence.

"It was another two years before I was able to go home. Meanwhile, I'd moved into your father's house, even though he had a twenty-four-hour private duty nurse. His moods vacillated from highs to lows. *Silent Witness* won seven Academy Awards, taking Best Picture and Director. Oscar had finally earned his namesake, but his depression continued."

"You did not win for best actress?" he queried.

"No, and I hadn't expected to. I made one more film before I left the business completely."

"Why?"

"Because Oscar was dying. The cancer returned, and this

time he lost the lung. I completed the second film, and we flew to Vegas and married. And when I returned to Florida it was as Oscar's wife." Her slender fingers curled into tight fists.

"My family was shocked. My father in particular was very angry, because I'd married a man who was so old. They didn't know that Oscar was terminally ill. The mass the doctors removed from his lung had been filled with malignant cells. He spent more than six months undergoing chemotherapy, which weakened him so much that he couldn't get out of bed for days at a time.

"We arrived in Florida in time to attend my uncle's wedding, spent a week at my parents' home, then returned to California to close up the house. We left the States for Mexico to avoid the photographers and reporters who had gotten word that we had married, and rented a small house near Acapulco. I thought living near the ocean would lift Oscar's spirits, but it didn't. Six months later we purchased *El Cielo*."

Her eyes filling with tears, she tried blinking them back. "He loved living at *El Cielo*. Every morning he would get up and make his way over to the window and stare out at the mountains. He'd shake his head and smile, saying he loved the higher elevation because he felt closer to heaven. It took Oscar almost ten years to die. His will to live was so strong that it confounded every doctor who treated him." She smiled through her tears. "He always protected me, even though I couldn't protect him."

"He was ill, Regina," Aaron countered. "Terminally ill. There was nothing you or anyone else could do to change the manner in which he died."

She bowed her head and bit down hard on her lower lip. "I refused to let him suffer. I made certain he was never in pain toward the end."

A suffocating silence ensued, Regina and Aaron lost in their private musings. She was relieved that she had finally unburdened herself. She had told her parents she married Oscar because he was sick, yet had never disclosed the details of her near-rape at the hands of Harold Jordan. That was a secret she had carried for ten years—until now.

Aaron swallowed several times before he could bring himself to speak. "Words cannot convey my gratitude. You truly were an extraordinary wife."

What he could not say was that it should have been him, not Regina Spencer, who should have taken Oscar to the hospital for his chemotherapy. He should have given his father the injections of morphine whenever the pain had become unbearable. And he should have been the one who sat at Oscar's bedside, holding his hand when he drew his last breath. He should have been there for his father at the beginning and at the end of his illness, but he wasn't because of his so-called wounded male pride—a pride that had kept him from a father whom he knew loved him with his last breath.

"I did nothing extraordinary," Regina stated softly. "I did what I did because I promised Oscar I would take care of him."

"And I thought you'd married him for his money." Aaron could not help verbalizing what he had rationalized the moment he laid eyes on his father's widow.

Her body stiffened in shock. She knew he had been stunned by her youth, but she did not think he would be like the others who thought she had married Oscar for his money.

"Do you actually believe that?" she whispered. She could not disguise her annoyance as the query flowed tremulously from her lips.

Shrugging a broad shoulder in a manner that reminded her of Oscar's elegant body language, Aaron ran a hand over his face, nodding. "I'm ashamed to admit I did," he confessed. "When I first saw you that's what came to mind. Why else would a woman marry a man old enough to be her grandfather, if not for material gain?"

"Maybe other women, but not Regina Cole," she stated arrogantly.

A frown furrowed his high, smooth forehead. "Cole?"

"Yes, Cole," she confirmed, smiling.

Aaron studied her intently for a moment, his eyes narrowing in concentration. "Are you related to the ColeDiz Coles?"

He might have lived most of his life in Brazil, yet he had always kept abreast of the American business market. His diligence paid off, because three U.S. pharmaceutical companies had agreed to underwrite the cost of several of his research projects for five consecutive years. He remembered ColeDiz because *Black Enterprise* and *Forbes* had listed the company as one of the wealthiest in the United States.

Regina watched Aaron with smug delight. He was no different than the others, whose expressions had given them away whenever Oscar introduced her as his wife. Some of them thought, and many had whispered, that Oscar was her *sugar daddy,* and she was only waiting for him to die so she could inherit his money. Oscar Spencer had earned less money than his comparable contemporaries, and three-fourths of his wealth had come from astute investments.

"Yes." The single word was a soft, husky whisper.

"Ouch," he gasped, grimacing. He saw the slight smile tugging at the corners of her lush mouth, and let out his breath slowly. "I'm truly sorry, Regina. Can you forgive me for being a narrow-minded fool?"

"There's nothing to forgive. And I've never apologized for marrying your father—not to anyone. I was the one who proposed to him."

Aaron placed a forefinger alongside his lean jaw. "That really must have shocked Dad."

"Believe it or not, he was speechless. He refused to give me an answer until I threatened to move out and leave him with the live-in nurse, whom he had come to despise. He fired her once, but I rehired her as she was walking out the door."

"Why?"

"Because she was the only one who would put up with his mood swings. There were days when his food ended up on the floor or on the walls."

"And you were the only other person who would put up with him."

Regina heard a measure of gentleness in his voice for the first time. "I was Oscar's wife, and the nurse was a trained professional. I paid her well to take care of her patient."

"She stayed because you paid her. But what about you, Regina? You didn't have to stay. And most of all, you didn't have to marry him."

She had asked herself the same questions over and over, but was never able to come up with a plausible answer. Was it gratitude because Oscar had saved her from becoming a rape victim? Or was it because of her own fears—fears that returned and attacked whenever she found herself alone? Living with Oscar and taking care of him had not permitted her time to think about the six days of terror which she would carry with her to her grave.

There were times when she had thought of returning to her acting career, but she dismissed the notion as soon as it came to mind. She had been away too long, and the lure of the bright lights had lost their appeal. She would follow through with her plan to return to Florida and start over.

"I stayed because I loved him."

Aaron shifted his attention to the passing landscape, Regina's statement reverberating in his head. *I stayed because I loved him.* Sharon had said almost the same thing: *I can't marry you because I'm in love with your father. Try to understand that I can't leave him.*

He had not understood—not at the time, because he had felt betrayed by the two people he loved most in the world. But Sharon and Oscar were his past, and it was time he began anew.

He was thirty-seven, in excellent health, all of the institute's research grants had been renewed for another year, and his coffee plantation was thriving. It was the first time in a long time he looked forward to reaping a bountiful harvest.

His father's death reminded him of his own mortality, and he realized it was time he existed for more than his research. Oscar had his movies, but he also had taken time to marry and beget a child to carry on his name and bloodline.

Aaron wondered how he had become so obsessed with his work that he had neglected himself, as well as ignored his own need to share his existence. When had he become so selfish that he had not permitted a woman into his heart and into his life? How had he survived the past twelve years, interacting with women only when he sought physical release?

There had been one exception. He had had a fleeting liaison with a woman two years ago, but decided to end it when she broached the subject of marriage.

Closing his eyes, he tried conjuring up Natalia Estevào's face and failed. What he did see was the hauntingly delicate face belonging to Regina Cole-Spencer. He opened his eyes and turned around to look directly at her. As he studied her with a curious intensity, his gaze seemed to undress her as she observed him through lowered lashes.

His strong, masculine mouth curved into a sensual smile, and she returned it with one of her own. He was transfixed with the dimples in her velvety cheeks as they winked back at him. Reaching over, he held her hand, squeezing her fingers gently and not letting go until the driver stopped the car in the courtyard of the house built on a hill overlooking a picturesque valley.

He and Regina were connected by a bond, and the bond was Oscar Spencer. She had taken on the role as his father's helpmate and comforter, and for that he was grateful. Eternally grateful.

Their smiles were still in place when he helped her from the car. She squinted against the blinding, brilliant rays of the blazing summer sun. Mexico was experiencing one of its hottest summers in decades. Even in the mountain region the daytime temperatures peaked in the nineties.

"I'm going to take *siesta* in my garden," she informed Aaron in the low, smoky tone he had come to listen for whenever she opened her mouth. "Feel free to take advantage of anything at the house. I'll let the household staff know that they're to take care of your requests. If there is something they can't provide for you, just let me know."

The front door opened at their approach and Rose greeted Regina in rapid Spanish, exclaiming excitedly about *el abogado* and *una carta.*

She smiled at her efficient housekeeper. The petite, forty-something woman had never cut her hair and a single, black, silky plait hung past her knees. "Dr. Spencer and I will see Señor Morales in the solarium. We will also need some liquid refreshment."

Aaron waited until Rosa left before he turned to Regina. His gaze raced quickly over her face. "Are you having a legal problem?"

A slight frown formed between her eyes. "I don't know. I suppose we'll find out once we talk to Ernesto Morales. Oscar retained him to oversee his legal matters."

She led the way down a long, narrow corridor that opened out to an expansive hallway laid out in the shape of a cross, with arched passages leading in four different directions. Turning in a northerly direction, they walked into a large, cool room filled with rattan furniture and massive potted plants. Thick, pale plaster walls kept the heat of the sun from penetrating the space, making it a cool place to sit and enjoy the beauty of the surrounding foliage, outdoor garden, and the towering peaks of the nearby mountain range. Decorative wrought-iron grillwork on arched windows brought to mind a Moorish, rather than a Spanish, influence.

Aaron walked over to an antique armoire rising more than ten feet in height above the brick floor, running his fingers along the smooth surface of the nearly black wood. He did not have long to admire the quiet magnificence of the space when a slender man entered the room, cradling a leather portfolio under one arm. The lawyer's eyes caught fire as they caressed Regina's face and body. He watched Ernesto Morales lean over and place a kiss much too close to her smiling lips. It was more than apparent that the man was attracted to his father's young widow.

"*¡Buenas tardes!* Regina," Ernesto whispered in her ear.

Her smile widened. "*¡Buenas tardes!* Ernesto. I'd like you to meet Oscar's son, Dr. Aaron Spencer."

Ernesto jumped back as if someone had seared his flesh with a white-hot branding iron. Turning slowly, he widened his gaze as Aaron moved from the shadows and into the middle of the room. He drew himself up straighter, knowing he could never match the height of the tall American looming above him. Oscar Spencer had been tall, at six-two, but Aaron Spencer eclipsed his father's height by at least another two inches.

Extending his hand, Ernesto inclined his head slightly. "Señor Spencer. Ernesto Morales. I'm sorry we have to meet under these circumstances. However, I must say that your father was truly a great man."

Aaron shook his hand. "Aaron, please. And I'd like to thank you for handling my father's estate."

Regina waited until the introductions were concluded, then extended a hand toward a cushioned sofa. "Gentlemen, please be seated."

Both men waited until she was settled on a matching loveseat before they sat down. She turned her attention to Ernesto. He was fashionably attired in a melon-green linen suit which flattered his dark hair and suntanned face. She had always found him attractive in a delicate sort of manner. He was of medium height, slender, and his features were too fragile for a man. They would have been better suited on a woman.

Her gaze shifted to Aaron, widening appreciably. She much

preferred his strongly defined masculine face and body, and his deep, powerful voice. If she had to choose between the two men, there would be no doubt that Aaron would be her choice. He hadn't just sat on the sofa, but had draped his tall body on the cushions while crossing one leg over the opposite knee. There was something about the manner in which he sat that reminded her of her own father.

"Ernesto, Rosa mentioned something about a letter."

The lawyer blinked slowly as if coming out of a trance, then unsnapped the lock on his leather case and withdrew a single sheet of paper from an envelope.

"Oscar Spencer gave me specific instructions as to how he wanted me to handle his estate. I was not to open this envelope until forty-eight hours after his death." He stared at Aaron before shifting his gaze to Regina. "I cannot reveal the terms of the will until ten days following his burial."

"Why the delay?" she queried.

"*Lo siento,* Regina," he replied. "I'm only following your husband's wishes."

She, too, was sorry. That meant her life was on hold for the next two weeks. As it was, she had to wait three days to bury Oscar, then wait another ten. It was as if she were in suspended animation. There was no going back and no forward movement.

She glanced over at Aaron, who hadn't taken his gaze off her from the moment he sat down. "How soon do you have to return to Brazil?"

He blinked once. "I have an open reservation for my return flight. I'll stay as long as it will take for *you* to conclude everything here."

What he did not say was that he would remain in Mexico as long as it took for him to shield Regina from men like Ernesto Morales, who looked at his father's widow as if she were a sacrificial lamb offering herself up for his personal agenda.

Oscar might not have been able to protect her, but as long as she remained in Mexico *he* would. He owed her that much.

Rosa entered the room, carrying a tray with a carafe and three glasses. She quickly and expertly filled the glasses with a frothy fruit drink, handing one to Regina. Within a minute the men were served, and then the silent, efficient housekeeper walked out.

Ernesto, not bothering to taste his drink, placed his glass on the tray beside the carafe. He gave Aaron a sidelong glance. "There's no need for you to stay away from your research, Dr. Spencer. As Regina's legal counsel I will make certain to safeguard her interests."

Turning his head slowly, Aaron glared at Ernesto. "I have no doubt about that, Señor Morales. But because Regina is *mi familia* it has become my responsibility to protect her."

A rush of color darkened the lawyer's face with his increasing annoyance. "Do you think Señora Spencer needs protecting?"

Aaron arched an expressive eyebrow. "Not now. But there may come a time when she will."

Regina stirred uneasily on the loveseat. The two men were discussing her as if she were not in the room. She decided to change the subject, because there was one thing she did not need at this juncture in her life, and that was protection from either of them.

"Ernesto, you should know that the service has been scheduled for Friday morning at ten o'clock. It will be held here at *El Cielo.*"

He nodded, vertical slashes appearing between his eyes. "I'll be here. If the funeral is Friday, then the reading of the will shall take place on Monday, September first, at eleven o'clock in my office." Rising to his feet, he forced a false smile. "Please excuse me, but I must get back to my office."

Aaron rose with him, extending his hand, but Ernesto busied himself with his case, pretending not to see it. "I'll have Rosa show me out," he mumbled angrily under his breath.

Waiting until Ernesto left the room, Regina stood up. "What was that all about?" she shouted at Aaron.

Slipping his hands into the pockets of his suit trousers, he closed the distance between them until they stood only inches apart. He was close enough to feel the moist heat of her breath on his throat.

"Don't tell me you didn't know what was going on?"

Running a manicured hand over her neatly coiffed hair, she closed her eyes, then opened them. "No. All I know is that you insulted him."

Leaning down from his superior height, Aaron flashed a feral grin. "The man could've called you with the same information he felt compelled to deliver in person. Can't you tell that the man has the *hots* for you?"

Regina stared at his mouth, then laughed, the sound bubbling up from her silken throat like warm honey. "You're imagining things."

She knew Ernesto was attracted to her, but it wasn't something she would admit to Aaron—not when she was no better than Ernesto. She was equally attracted to her stepson.

"And you're in denial, Mrs. Spencer. Do you ever look in the mirror? You have to know that you're a beautiful woman. I don't blame the little man for salivating. What annoys the hell out of me is that he can't wait until his client is six feet under before he—"

"You've said enough, Aaron," she warned quietly, cutting him off.

His jaw tightened in frustration. She was wrong. He hadn't said enough. What he wanted to tell her was that she was the first woman in a long time who made him physically aware that he was a male—a male who desired a female for more than a slaking of his sexual urges. He longed to tell her that she had unknowingly rekindled a fire he thought long dead—that she was a woman who made him examine himself and acknowledge his weaknesses and shortcomings, a woman he needed to repay for her selflessness. She had sacrificed ten years of her life to care for his father.

His head jerked up and he stared at the wall behind her. "Forgive me. I was out of line."

"Don't apologize to me. It was Ernesto you insulted."

Aaron's expression darkened with an unreadable emotion. "Ernesto got what he deserved. I will not apologize to him."

Regina's fingers curled into tight fists. "I will not have you insult my guests in my home."

Removing his hands from his trousers, he brought them up and cupped her face between his palms. "I'm sorry you feel that way, but I will not apologize to your *abogado*." Leaning over, he pressed his lips to her forehead. "I'm going to take *siesta* now. I'll see you later, Stepmother." He released her and strolled out of the solarium, leaving her with her mouth gaping.

"Don't you dare call me that!" she shouted at his broad-shouldered back.

The deep, rumbling sound of his laughter floated back to her, then faded with his departure. Regina folded her arms around her body in a protective gesture and floated down to the loveseat. A mysterious smile flitted across her full mouth. Aaron Spencer bore no facial resemblance to his father, but he truly was his father's son, willful and stubborn.

He had accused Ernesto of having the *hots* for her, but what Aaron did not know was each and every time he touched her she melted like a pat of butter on a heated surface.

Closing her eyes, she prayed the two weeks would pass quickly. Aaron was never to know how much he affected her—how, from the moment they met her whole being seemed to be filled with a waiting, a waiting to experience what it was to be born female.

Chapter 8

Aaron spent his *siesta* pacing the floor of his bedroom. When he tired of staring at the same objects, he opened the French doors and stepped out onto the veranda. He stared at the mountains until the heat finally drove him back inside, where he changed from the dress shirt and slacks to a pair of walking shorts, a T-shirt, and running shoes.

The inactivity was beginning to play on his nerves. His normal day usually began at sunrise, when he drove down to the coffee fields to meet with his foreman. Three days of the week were committed to seeing patients at Salvador's municipal hospital, and the other three were spent at the research institute.

He returned to the veranda and strolled leisurely down its length. He turned a corner, then stopped. Moving to the wrought-iron railing, he leaned over, his gaze narrowing when he saw Regina talking to a man. She pointed to a profusion of ivy climbing over a pergola.

Aaron smiled when he noticed she had changed from her suit

into a pair of white cotton, straight-leg slacks, a sleeveless, white shirt, and a pair of black ballet slippers. A curling ponytail was secured at the nape of her neck with a large, shiny hairclip.

She gestured, her delicate fingers caressing the leaves of the white blooms interspersed with the ivy. She took a few steps, the man following her lead and listening intently as she pointed to differing flowers and shrubs.

Reluctantly pulling his gaze away from Regina, he surveyed the exquisite beauty of the mountaintop garden. He recognized a large stone sundial, several statues, solid slabs of stone steps leading over a rise, and the reflection of the sun's rays on a shimmering pond. The lushness of the land reminded him of Bahia.

He had retained his American citizenship, yet he could not understand why he felt more at home in Bahia than he did in any place he had ever visited or lived. Maybe it was his African ancestors who called out to him in Bahia, the most African part of Brazil, that quieted his restlessness. Or perhaps he thought of it as safe haven—a place where he could hide, and divorce himself from everything that had to do with his past. But the hiding was over. He had been forced to confront his past, because he had returned to North America to bury his father.

Regina went down on one knee, extracting a clump of weeds growing too close to the rocks surrounding the man-made fish-pond. The fish darted in and out of the plants growing in the cool, clean water, some of them floating to the surface when she sprinkled a handful of dehydrated fish food mix into the pond. One large carp pushed a smaller one away from the floating particles, his gaping mouth swallowing up the food as if it were a shovel.

"That's no fair," Regina said, laughing softly under her breath. "Let the little guy get some."

"That's the way of the world. The big get better, and the small stay the same," rumbled a deep voice above her.

Startled, she fell back and stared up at Aaron standing over her. He had been so quiet that she hadn't heard his approach.

"The next time you sneak up on me, try to make some noise. You nearly gave me a heart attack."

Instead of helping her regain her footing, he sat down beside her, his large body shielding hers from the direct heat of the sun. Reaching over, he placed two fingers on the pulse in her neck, counting the beats of her rapidly pumping heart.

He removed his hand. Smiling, he said, "You'll survive."

Bracing her elbows on the damp earth, she closed her eyes. "Just barely."

He gave her a questioning look. "If you want me to perform CPR, then you'll have to lie back down."

Her lids flew up, her gaze fixed on his mouth. If he had to perform CPR on her, he would have to place his mouth over hers.

"No," she replied in a breathless whisper.

His eyes were dark, unfathomable, as they moved slowly over her face, down to her heaving breasts under the cotton fabric, then back to her mouth. "Are you sure?"

She nodded, her head bobbing up and down like a buoy on the water. "I'm sure."

She jerked her head as his right hand came up and touched her hair. "Don't move, Regina. You have a few weeds in your hair."

The moment he touched her, she froze. Aaron Spencer was too close, his body too large, and he was much too warm. She suffered his touch as he methodically picked every particle of dirt and grass from her hair. Running his fingers over the antique silver hairclip, he examined it. Then without warning, he released the clasp, freeing her hair until it spilled over her back.

He ignored her gasp of surprise, turning the exquisite piece of jewelry over on his palm. "What are these stones?"

Regina was certain he could hear her heart pumping when she sat up and folded her knees under her body. "The blue ones are sapphires and the white ones are—"

"Diamonds," he said, finishing her statement. She nodded, grasping her hair and braiding it into a fat plait. "White gold?" he questioned.

"No. It's platinum."

He examined the Art Deco piece more closely. "It looks like a family heirloom."

"It is. It was my grandfather's gift to my grandmother for their first wedding anniversary. I'm the only one of her granddaughters who still has long hair, so she gave it to me when I got married."

"Hold still and I'll put it back." Aaron lifted Regina effortlessly until she sat between his outstretched legs. Then he undid the braid and secured her hair within the hairclip.

She suffered his closeness, the press of his hard chest against her back, the sensual scent of his cologne, and his fingers combing the tangle of curls until they hung loosely down her back.

Chuckling softly, she glanced at him over her shoulder. "You missed your calling. You should've been a hairstylist."

He leaned forward, his rumbling laughter floating seductively over her. "Didn't you know that I was multitalented?"

"No." She giggled. "What other talents are you hiding?"

"I cook."

She affected an expression of surprise. "No."

He nodded, smiling down at her. "Very, very well."

"What else?"

"I'm an excellent horseman. How about you, Regina?"

She tingled when he said her name. His voice had lowered, and it sounded like a caress. His nearness was overwhelming, and she did not know how, but she felt the movement of his breathing keeping rhythm with her own.

"I act, and I dabble a little in dirt."

Aaron curved a thick, muscular arm under her breasts, pulling her closer to his body. "What do you mean by dabble?"

"I design gardens."

His arm tightened before relaxing. "Look at me, Regina." Half-turning in his embrace, she stared up at him over her shoulder. "Did you design this garden?"

Her heart was thundering uncontrollably, and she knew he had to feel it. Every muscle in his chest and abdomen was molded to her back, bringing a wave of moisture that settled between her breasts.

"Yes, I did."

His expression was one of disbelief. "But you said you were an actress."

"You asked me how I met Oscar, and I told you I met him as an actress. What I did not tell you was that I attended college and earned a degree in landscape architecture."

"When did you find time to attend classes if you were caring for my father?"

"Each semester I scheduled classes around his doctor visits and therapy sessions. It took me nearly eight years to complete a six-year degree program."

Aaron's gaze swept over the lush beauty of the garden, which had an exquisitely simple planting scheme of timeless romance and classical landscape design.

"How many gardens have you designed?"

"Just this one."

"It is truly a masterpiece."

A feeling of confidence swept over her at the same time an expression of satisfaction showed in her eyes. "Thank you."

Tightening his grip on her waist, he lifted her again until she sat beside him. He curved an arm around her waist, pulling her close. She felt the heat of his bare thigh through the cotton fabric covering hers, and for a brief moment she lost herself in his protective masculinity. She rested her cheek against his shoulder as if it were a gesture she had made before.

Even when Oscar led her out of Harold Jordan's house she hadn't felt as protected as she did now. She wasn't certain when it had occurred, but within the span of time Aaron curved an arm around her body she had unconsciously looked to him to protect her. Perhaps it was what he had said to Ernesto about her being his family, and therefore his responsibility.

She had put up a brave front for ten years, and she was tired of being a martyr. She had loved Oscar, but becoming his wife had exacted more than she expected once she gave him all of herself, leaving no reserve whenever she found herself bogged down in a tormented helplessness once his condition worsened. She'd ached with anguish and loneliness, refusing to cry because she did not want Oscar to know that she had weakened. Her mantra had become "stay strong and smile through all of the adversity." What she hadn't expected was for him to survive ten years. Each time he lived to celebrate another birthday she had weakened and aged with him.

But now she could lift her face to the sun and dance in the rain. She could laugh and cry without having to censure herself. And she could look forward to falling in love again, and to experiencing her sexuality for the first time.

Lowering his head, Aaron touched his mouth to her hair, reveling in the soft curls caressing his lips. "Are you sure you want to leave all of this?"

Sighing audibly, she nodded. "I'm sure, Aaron. More sure than I've ever been in my life."

And she was.

What she wasn't sure about was her intensifying feelings for the man holding her close to his heart.

"What about Oscar?"

"What about him?"

"You're going to leave him—"

"I'm burying him here because he loved it here," she countered, interrupting Aaron. "I didn't say I'd never come back. I just need to get away for a while."

"I'd like to offer you a deal."

"What kind of a deal?"

"I'd like to buy this property from you."

Pulling back, she stared up at him. "Why?"

He swallowed painfully, trying to form the words stuck in his throat. "I shut my father out of my life for twelve years, and I'm not very proud of that. I don't want strangers to trample over his final resting place. I know that may sound silly, but…" His words trailed off.

"It's not silly," Regina countered. "I can't promise anything until after the reading of the will. But if I'm left the property, then you won't have to buy it, because I'll give it to you as a gift."

Aaron curved a hand around her neck, then lowered his head. "Thank you," he whispered before his lips brushed against hers.

A brief shiver of awareness rippled through her body as Regina stiffened momentarily. She savored the feel of his firm lips on hers, the contact leaving her mouth burning with a lingering fire.

The kiss ended seconds after it began, and she wanted it to continue. She wanted to lose herself in the mastery of his mouth, and more. But common sense reared its head, reminding her of who she was and who Aaron Spencer was.

What was wrong with her? She was sitting in her garden, kissing a man who was the son of the man who lay on a table in a funeral home in Mexico City. Her husband wasn't even buried, and she was lusting after his son.

Pulling out of his loose embrace, she stood up and walked back to the house, her face aflame with shame when she realized what she wanted to share with him, because she had spent more years than she could remember denying her femininity.

Quickening her stride, she mumbled a fervent prayer. She wanted Aaron Spencer gone. His presence and his masculinity were constant reminders that at twenty-seven she was still a virgin.

Regina sat in her sitting room, watching intermittent drops of rain slide down the windows. In less than half an hour the graveside ceremony would begin. Earlier that morning the heavens had opened up to shed their own tears for Oscar Clayborne Spencer. It had rained heavily for an hour, then stopped, and now a watery sun broke through the heavy dark clouds to dry the earth.

The gravediggers had come the day before and dug a grave within the perimeter of the garden. Oscar's final resting place would be surrounded by a five-foot stone wall covered with a profusion of bougainvillea and Cherokee roses.

She closed her eyes. *I'm ready,* she told herself. She was ready to close a chapter on a part of her life, and hopefully she would never have to reopen it.

Opening her eyes, she glanced across the room to find Aaron standing in the doorway to her bedroom, arms folded over his chest, waiting for her. An expertly tailored black suit, startling white shirt, and a black silk tie caressed his tall, muscular body as if each item had been created expressly for him.

"Please come in." Her voice was low and cloaking in its timbre as she gestured to a chair facing her own.

Aaron walked into the bedroom, successfully curbing the urge to examine the space where Regina had sought solace since his arrival. After their encounter in the garden he'd seen very little of her, except at the evening meal. It was as if she had revealed too much of herself, and had elected to hide to fortify herself for the next phase of her life: burying her husband.

Undoing a button on his double-breasted jacket, he sat down

opposite her and draped one leg over the other. "How are you holding up?"

Regina tilted her chin and stared up at the ceiling. "Well enough, I suppose."

Leaning forward, he reached out and captured her hands between his. They were trembling, and icy cold. "I can ask your doctor to give you something to calm you down."

She gave him a direct look, her eyes widening. "I'm okay."

As he lowered his head and his voice, Aaron's gaze narrowed. "Are you certain?"

She let out her breath slowly. "Quite certain." She glanced at the watch showing beneath the French cuff of his shirt. "I think we should go down now."

Nodding, he stood up, pulling her up with him. He curved an arm around her waist and led her out of the bedroom and down the staircase to the lower level.

Regina knew she had lied to Aaron. She wasn't all right, and she needed something to stop the trembling which had begun when she awoke earlier that morning. But she was too much of a coward to request a sedative.

She paused before walking out of the house, picking up a black raffia and silk hat with a wide, turned-up brim and matching, satin, grosgrain ribbon circling the crown from a small, round table and placing it on her head. Her dress was a simple black silk sleeveless sheath, and her only accessories were pearl earrings and a matching, single strand floating from her long neck.

Nodding to Aaron, she placed her hand in the bend of his elbow and permitted him to lead her to the tent where rows of chairs were set up for the attendees.

She recognized the doctors and nurses who were responsible for Oscar's medical care, all of *El Cielo*'s household staff, Ernesto Morales, and Pablo Vasques, the artist whose works Oscar had collected since they attended a showing in Mexico City the first year they moved to *El Cielo*.

ething he would live to regret. The nostrils of his nose
s he compressed his lips tightly.

not speak of something you know nothing about," he
in a dangerously soft voice.

n why don't you enlighten me?" There was no mistaking
llenge as she folded her hands on her narrow hips.

on glanced over her head, staring at the open French doors
t tell you about it. Not now."

hen?" The single word was soft, coaxing.

gaze shifted, lingering on her seductive mouth. "Before
to Brazil I will reveal why I hadn't seen or spoken to my
in twelve years. Now, will you walk with me?"

e had to smile. "You'll say anything to get me out of this
, won't you?"

lmost anything," he admitted truthfully, "except lie to you.
there is one thing you should know about me, Regina, and
s I will *never* lie to you."

he studied his face, noticing the softening of his lean jaw.
e was a lethal calmness in his expressive eyes as he regarded
"Or I to you, Aaron."

The tension vibrating around Aaron vanished, replaced by
arm, peaceful feeling which made him want to reach out
hold her close to his heart. He hadn't lied when he told her
wanted her to walk with him, even though he would have
n content to just sit beside her. After burying Oscar she had
eated to her bedroom, locking herself away from the world.
few times he had knocked on her door she had refused him
, claiming she was tired.

fter the second day Rosa approached him, reporting that
ra Spencer was still not eating the food she prepared for her.
assured the housekeeper that Señora Spencer was grieving
at she would eat when she became hungry. And she did
lost times she picked at the food, taking small portions, but
enough to keep her alive.

The priest, who had heard Oscar's last confession before he administered the last rites, moved into position behind the dove-gray casket, which rested on a device which would finally lower it into the damp, dark earth.

Regina heard the softly spoken words of the priest as he began the funeral mass, silently mouthing the prayers and the responses. A warm breeze filtered over the assembled, bringing with it a sweet, lush, redolent fragrance of fresh flowers. Leaning heavily against Aaron's solid shoulder, she cried softly, holding the hand-kerchief he had given her over her mouth.

Aaron closed his eyes, willing his own tears not to fall. He had to be strong, strong for Regina. Curving an arm around her tiny waist, he held her until her sobbing subsided. He was amazed at the gamut of emotions her sobbing wrang from him as he vowed silently that he would take care of her. When he returned to Brazil he would take her with him.

The mass ended, and Regina and Aaron thanked the priest for what he had offered Oscar before and after his death. Then they extended an invitation to all to stay for a light repast before they returned to their homes and places of business.

Chapter 9

Regina felt a restlessness akin to an itch she could not scratch. It had been five days since the funeral, and with the advent of each new day she felt as if she had been confined to a prison without bars.

"Why, Oscar?" she whispered angrily at the brightening sky as she stood at the open French doors. Why was he testing her by making her a prisoner? What had he hoped to prove by mandating that she remain in Mexico an additional ten days? She thought about calling her father and requesting that he send the ColeDiz corporate jet to pick her up and fly her to Florida for a few days, but quickly changed her mind after she realized that if she left Mexico she would not return—not for a long time. She had to think of the people she employed at *El Cielo,* who would now have to seek other employment. She had to see to their immediate needs before her final departure.

A sharp knocking on the bedroom door shook her from her reverie. Crossing the room, she opened the door to find Aaron

standing on the other side. The sun wasn't [...] for the day. Her gaze moved slowly over h[...] body-hugging jeans, and work boots.

Folding his arms over his chest, he rega[...] disheveled beauty. Her damp hair curled [...] provocative disarray. She wore a pale blue[...] pair of faded, laundered jeans that flaunte[...] womanly body.

"Good morning," he drawled softly, winkii[...] expression on her face. "I decided to take a w[...] and wondered if you would like to accompany[...]

She knew what he was up to. "I am not depi[...]

He arched an eyebrow. "I didn't say you were. [...] you to come for a walk with me before we share[...]

"I'm also not hungry."

His arms came down as he glared at her. "Wh[...] to do, Regina? Join Oscar? You're not eating, and[...]

"How do you know I'm not eating?" she count[...]

"Because Rosa says you barely touch what she p[...] tray. You've locked yourself away in this room for t[...] days—"

"Mind your own business, Aaron Spencer!" she[...] him. She didn't need him spying on her. All she had[...] five days. Then she would be free.

He took a step, bringing him close enough f[...] the warmth of his moist breath on her face. "Oh, [...] aren't my business, Mrs. Spencer? You became m[...] moment you called me to tell me my father had [...] tinued without waiting for her reply. "And you a[...] because you married my father."

"A father you turned your back on," she said[...] temper rising quickly to match his.

A tense silence filled the room as Aaron brea[...] quick gasps, successfully curbing his runaway t[...]

"I'll wait for you in the courtyard." Turning on his heel, he walked out of her bedroom and down the hallway.

It was Regina's turn to watch him walk away, leaving her to follow, and it was another ten minutes before she made her way to the courtyard. She had brushed her damp hair and secured it with an elastic band at the back of her head.

She saw him leaning against a stone fountain with his arms crossed over his chest and his legs crossed at the ankles. The rising sun turned him into a living, breathing statue of burnished gold. The power of his upper body was clearly displayed under the jeans and T-shirt, and she tried to imagine him taking care of patients, and failed. She wasn't sure what she expected a doctor to look like, but it certainly wasn't the way Aaron Spencer looked.

"Where do you plan to walk to?"

His head came around slowly as he lowered his chin and smiled at her. "Not far," he said mysteriously, reaching for her hand. "Maybe we'll go as far as the road, then come back."

"It's over a mile to the road."

He gave her a questioning look. "Is that too far for you?"

"No."

And it wasn't. There had been days when she walked every acre of the land surrounding *El Cielo*. Those were the days when Oscar slept for hours after the doctor administered the drugs which took away his pain.

They walked in silence for over an hour, enjoying the dawning of a new day as birds called out to one another while hopping and flying nimbly from branch to branch.

"Come this way," she urged, leading Aaron up a hill. They climbed the rise, stood on its summit, and gazed down at the verdant valley below them.

Shaking his head, Aaron stared at the natural beauty of the panoramic landscape unfolding before his eyes. "It's incredible."

Regina extended her left hand, the rays of the sun glinting off the precious stones encircling her finger. "Look, Aaron. There's a golden eagle."

He squinted, staring at the large bird soaring with the wind currents. "Are eagles usually this far south?"

"Yes. They're more common in the Rocky Mountains, but we see them here because they build their nests along the Sierra Madre Occidental and Del Sur mountain ranges."

"There's another one."

She nodded. "That's the male."

"He looks smaller than the female."

"That's because he is. I don't know why, but the females are slightly larger than the males," Regina explained.

Aaron stared at the magnificent birds as they dropped several hundred feet without flapping their enormous wings. "They probably have a nest hidden away somewhere close by."

"They do. I observed them for weeks, bringing back pieces of leaves and twigs for a nest. Then they disappeared. When I saw the female again she was bringing back food in her beak, and I assumed it was for her babies. Weather permitting, I used to come up here every day and watch for them. Then one day I saw the babies leave the nest. They weren't quite as magnificent looking as their parents, but they were a sight to behold."

She and Aaron watched the eagles until they disappeared in their mountaintop retreat, then turned and retraced their steps. "I have a confession to make," she said softly as they neared *El Cielo*.

Aaron gave her a sidelong glance. "What's that?"

"I'm hungry."

Lowering his head, he hid a smile. They had walked for nearly ninety minutes, and there was no doubt she had burned calories she could not afford to lose. She was slimmer now than when he first met her.

Releasing her hand, he said, "Race you to the kitchen."

Regina was one step behind him as she sprinted toward the house. They reached the front door at the same time, Aaron stepping aside to let her enter.

He bowed from the waist. "After you, *Princesa*."

Affecting a haughty pose, she strolled into the house, glancing back over her shoulder at his smiling face. He was good for her, but she wasn't going to tell him that. It would remain her secret.

Rosa smiled when she saw the couple walk into the kitchen. "Your breakfast is ready."

Regina returned her smile, heading for the small bath off the kitchen. "I'd like to eat in the kitchen this morning instead of on the patio."

"*Sí,* Señora."

Rosa set the large table in the corner of the kitchen while Aaron waited for Regina to wash her hands before following suit. He crowded into the small space as she dried her hands, his large body pressing intimately against hers.

"Stop, Aaron," she whispered harshly at the same time she tried concealing her anxiety with a nervous smile.

He pressed closer. "You're taking too long."

"Let me out first."

Ignoring her demand, he reached around her waist, turned on the faucets, and washed his hands with her anchored between the sink and his body. She stared at the corded muscles in his wrists and forearms. The heat in her face increased until she found it difficult to draw a normal breath.

"Aaron!"

"*¿Sí, Princesa?*" he whispered, his lips grazing her ear.

Closing her eyes, Regina breathed in and out through her mouth. "What do you think you're doing?"

"I'm washing my hands before I sit down to eat." His voice was deep, even. Reaching for the towel she clutched to her chest in a deathlike grip, he pulled it gently from her stiff fingers and dried his hands.

Regina turned slowly to face Aaron. The very air in the small space was energized as an invisible thread of awareness began to form between them. Her gaze was fixed on his face when she saw his gaze slip down to her chest, where the outline of her distended nipples were clearly visible through the sheer fabric covering her bra under the cotton T-shirt.

It did not matter that they shared the same last name. It did not matter that she had married his father, or that she was his stepmother, either, when Aaron leaned down and pressed a kiss along the column of her slender, scented throat.

"Let's eat before I start something I can't finish," he whispered savagely.

Her fingers caught and tightened on the front of his T-shirt, holding him fast. "Start what?"

His eyes widened as he stared at her. "You don't want to know."

"Yes, I do, Aaron. I do want to know."

What she wanted to tell him was that he couldn't tease her and then end it when he felt his control slipping, that he had lit a fire within her, reminding her that she was a woman who had yet to experience what it was to be born female, that he was the first man who made her conscious of her repressed sexuality.

Shaking his head, he said, "No."

Regina tightened her grip on the cotton fabric. "If you can't explain yourself, then stop playing games, Aaron. Remember, I had to grow up faster than most girls, and I was not given the opportunity to perfect techniques for teasing boys."

She released his shirt, pushed past him, stalked into the kitchen, and somehow still managed to give Rosa a warm smile. *"Mil graçias, Rosa."*

"De nada, Señora Spencer."

Sitting down at the table, she had spooned small portions of

The priest, who had heard Oscar's last confession before he administered the last rites, moved into position behind the dove-gray casket, which rested on a device which would finally lower it into the damp, dark earth.

Regina heard the softly spoken words of the priest as he began the funeral mass, silently mouthing the prayers and the responses. A warm breeze filtered over the assembled, bringing with it a sweet, lush, redolent fragrance of fresh flowers. Leaning heavily against Aaron's solid shoulder, she cried softly, holding the hand-kerchief he had given her over her mouth.

Aaron closed his eyes, willing his own tears not to fall. He had to be strong, strong for Regina. Curving an arm around her tiny waist, he held her until her sobbing subsided. He was amazed at the gamut of emotions her sobbing wrang from him as he vowed silently that he would take care of her. When he returned to Brazil he would take her with him.

The mass ended, and Regina and Aaron thanked the priest for what he had offered Oscar before and after his death. Then they extended an invitation to all to stay for a light repast before they returned to their homes and places of business.

Chapter 9

Regina felt a restlessness akin to an itch she could not scratch. It had been five days since the funeral, and with the advent of each new day she felt as if she had been confined to a prison without bars.

"Why, Oscar?" she whispered angrily at the brightening sky as she stood at the open French doors. Why was he testing her by making her a prisoner? What had he hoped to prove by mandating that she remain in Mexico an additional ten days? She thought about calling her father and requesting that he send the ColeDiz corporate jet to pick her up and fly her to Florida for a few days, but quickly changed her mind after she realized that if she left Mexico she would not return—not for a long time. She had to think of the people she employed at *El Cielo*, who would now have to seek other employment. She had to see to their immediate needs before her final departure.

A sharp knocking on the bedroom door shook her from her reverie. Crossing the room, she opened the door to find Aaron standing on the other side. The sun wasn't up, yet he was dressed for the day. Her gaze moved slowly over his stark white T-shirt, body-hugging jeans, and work boots.

Folding his arms over his chest, he regarded her delightfully disheveled beauty. Her damp hair curled over her forehead in provocative disarray. She wore a pale blue camp shirt with a pair of faded, laundered jeans that flaunted the curves of her womanly body.

"Good morning," he drawled softly, winking at the surprised expression on her face. "I decided to take a walk this morning, and wondered if you would like to accompany me."

She knew what he was up to. "I am not depressed."

He arched an eyebrow. "I didn't say you were. I'm just inviting you to come for a walk with me before we share breakfast."

"I'm also not hungry."

His arms came down as he glared at her. "What do you want to do, Regina? Join Oscar? You're not eating, and—"

"How do you know I'm not eating?" she countered.

"Because Rosa says you barely touch what she puts on your tray. You've locked yourself away in this room for the past five days—"

"Mind your own business, Aaron Spencer!" she screamed at him. She didn't need him spying on her. All she had was another five days. Then she would be free.

He took a step, bringing him close enough for her to feel the warmth of his moist breath on her face. "Oh, you think you aren't my business, Mrs. Spencer? You became my business the moment you called me to tell me my father had died," he continued without waiting for her reply. "And you are my business because you married my father."

"A father you turned your back on," she said accusingly, her temper rising quickly to match his.

A tense silence filled the room as Aaron breathed in shallow, quick gasps, successfully curbing his runaway temper before he said something he would live to regret. The nostrils of his nose flared as he compressed his lips tightly.

"Do not speak of something you know nothing about," he warned in a dangerously soft voice.

"Then why don't you enlighten me?" There was no mistaking the challenge as she folded her hands on her narrow hips.

Aaron glanced over her head, staring at the open French doors. "I can't tell you about it. Not now."

"When?" The single word was soft, coaxing.

His gaze shifted, lingering on her seductive mouth. "Before I return to Brazil I will reveal why I hadn't seen or spoken to my father in twelve years. Now, will you walk with me?"

She had to smile. "You'll say anything to get me out of this room, won't you?"

"Almost anything," he admitted truthfully, "except lie to you. And there is one thing you should know about me, Regina, and that is I will *never* lie to you."

She studied his face, noticing the softening of his lean jaw. There was a lethal calmness in his expressive eyes as he regarded her. "Or I to you, Aaron."

The tension vibrating around Aaron vanished, replaced by a warm, peaceful feeling which made him want to reach out and hold her close to his heart. He hadn't lied when he told her he wanted her to walk with him, even though he would have been content to just sit beside her. After burying Oscar she had retreated to her bedroom, locking herself away from the world. The few times he had knocked on her door she had refused him entry, claiming she was tired.

After the second day Rosa approached him, reporting that Señora Spencer was still not eating the food she prepared for her. He reassured the housekeeper that Señora Spencer was grieving and that she would eat when she became hungry. And she did eat. Most times she picked at the food, taking small portions, but it was enough to keep her alive.

"I'll wait for you in the courtyard." Turning on his heel, he walked out of her bedroom and down the hallway.

It was Regina's turn to watch him walk away, leaving her to follow, and it was another ten minutes before she made her way to the courtyard. She had brushed her damp hair and secured it with an elastic band at the back of her head.

She saw him leaning against a stone fountain with his arms crossed over his chest and his legs crossed at the ankles. The rising sun turned him into a living, breathing statue of burnished gold. The power of his upper body was clearly displayed under the jeans and T-shirt, and she tried to imagine him taking care of patients, and failed. She wasn't sure what she expected a doctor to look like, but it certainly wasn't the way Aaron Spencer looked.

"Where do you plan to walk to?"

His head came around slowly as he lowered his chin and smiled at her. "Not far," he said mysteriously, reaching for her hand. "Maybe we'll go as far as the road, then come back."

"It's over a mile to the road."

He gave her a questioning look. "Is that too far for you?"

"No."

And it wasn't. There had been days when she walked every acre of the land surrounding *El Cielo*. Those were the days when Oscar slept for hours after the doctor administered the drugs which took away his pain.

They walked in silence for over an hour, enjoying the dawning of a new day as birds called out to one another while hopping and flying nimbly from branch to branch.

"Come this way," she urged, leading Aaron up a hill. They climbed the rise, stood on its summit, and gazed down at the verdant valley below them.

Shaking his head, Aaron stared at the natural beauty of the panoramic landscape unfolding before his eyes. "It's incredible."

Regina extended her left hand, the rays of the sun glinting off the precious stones encircling her finger. "Look, Aaron. There's a golden eagle."

He squinted, staring at the large bird soaring with the wind currents. "Are eagles usually this far south?"

"Yes. They're more common in the Rocky Mountains, but we see them here because they build their nests along the Sierra Madre Occidental and Del Sur mountain ranges."

"There's another one."

She nodded. "That's the male."

"He looks smaller than the female."

"That's because he is. I don't know why, but the females are slightly larger than the males," Regina explained.

Aaron stared at the magnificent birds as they dropped several hundred feet without flapping their enormous wings. "They probably have a nest hidden away somewhere close by."

"They do. I observed them for weeks, bringing back pieces of leaves and twigs for a nest. Then they disappeared. When I saw the female again she was bringing back food in her beak, and I assumed it was for her babies. Weather permitting, I used to come up here every day and watch for them. Then one day I saw the babies leave the nest. They weren't quite as magnificent looking as their parents, but they were a sight to behold."

She and Aaron watched the eagles until they disappeared in their mountaintop retreat, then turned and retraced their steps. "I have a confession to make," she said softly as they neared *El Cielo.*

Aaron gave her a sidelong glance. "What's that?"

"I'm hungry."

Lowering his head, he hid a smile. They had walked for nearly ninety minutes, and there was no doubt she had burned calories she could not afford to lose. She was slimmer now than when he first met her.

Releasing her hand, he said, "Race you to the kitchen."

Regina was one step behind him as she sprinted toward the house. They reached the front door at the same time, Aaron stepping aside to let her enter.

He bowed from the waist. "After you, *Princesa*."

Affecting a haughty pose, she strolled into the house, glancing back over her shoulder at his smiling face. He was good for her, but she wasn't going to tell him that. It would remain her secret.

Rosa smiled when she saw the couple walk into the kitchen. "Your breakfast is ready."

Regina returned her smile, heading for the small bath off the kitchen. "I'd like to eat in the kitchen this morning instead of on the patio."

"*Sí*, Señora."

Rosa set the large table in the corner of the kitchen while Aaron waited for Regina to wash her hands before following suit. He crowded into the small space as she dried her hands, his large body pressing intimately against hers.

"Stop, Aaron," she whispered harshly at the same time she tried concealing her anxiety with a nervous smile.

He pressed closer. "You're taking too long."

"Let me out first."

Ignoring her demand, he reached around her waist, turned on the faucets, and washed his hands with her anchored between the sink and his body. She stared at the corded muscles in his wrists and forearms. The heat in her face increased until she found it difficult to draw a normal breath.

"Aaron!"

"*¿Sí, Princesa?*" he whispered, his lips grazing her ear.

Closing her eyes, Regina breathed in and out through her mouth. "What do you think you're doing?"

"I'm washing my hands before I sit down to eat." His voice was deep, even. Reaching for the towel she clutched to her chest in a deathlike grip, he pulled it gently from her stiff fingers and dried his hands.

Regina turned slowly to face Aaron. The very air in the small space was energized as an invisible thread of awareness began to form between them. Her gaze was fixed on his face when she saw his gaze slip down to her chest, where the outline of her distended nipples were clearly visible through the sheer fabric covering her bra under the cotton T-shirt.

It did not matter that they shared the same last name. It did not matter that she had married his father, or that she was his stepmother, either, when Aaron leaned down and pressed a kiss along the column of her slender, scented throat.

"Let's eat before I start something I can't finish," he whispered savagely.

Her fingers caught and tightened on the front of his T-shirt, holding him fast. "Start what?"

His eyes widened as he stared at her. "You don't want to know."

"Yes, I do, Aaron. I do want to know."

What she wanted to tell him was that he couldn't tease her and then end it when he felt his control slipping, that he had lit a fire within her, reminding her that she was a woman who had yet to experience what it was to be born female, that he was the first man who made her conscious of her repressed sexuality.

Shaking his head, he said, "No."

Regina tightened her grip on the cotton fabric. "If you can't explain yourself, then stop playing games, Aaron. Remember, I had to grow up faster than most girls, and I was not given the opportunity to perfect techniques for teasing boys."

She released his shirt, pushed past him, stalked into the kitchen, and somehow still managed to give Rosa a warm smile. *"Mil graçias, Rosa."*

"De nada, Señora Spencer."

Sitting down at the table, she had spooned small portions of fluffy scrambled eggs, potatoes with peppers, and sliced *chorizo* onto her plate, and had filled her cup with steaming coffee by the time Aaron made his way to the table to join her.

Aaron's expression was a mask of stone as he glared across the table. She was a fine one to talk. Just being who she was, just looking like she did, was a tease. *She* was the tease—an unsuspecting, innocent one.

He was the one who slept restlessly, his dreams plagued with the image of her incredible face. Even in his sleep her sensual, velvet voice whispered in his head. And whenever he closed his eyes he could detect her presence as the haunting fragrance of her perfume wafted in his sensitive nostrils.

She had accused him of playing a game, but what he was beginning to feel for Regina Spencer was not a part of any game. The simple truth was that he wanted her. Not just her body, but all of her!

He poured coffee into his cup, added a teaspoon of milk, took a sip, then lowered it slowly. Placing an elbow on the table, he rested his chin on his fist, his gaze never straying from Regina's face.

"I don't play games," he said so softly she had to strain to catch the words. "What I do play is for keeps."

She arched an eyebrow, her fork poised in midair. She was aware that Aaron still smarted from her verbal spanking, and knew he wouldn't be content to let her get away with it.

"I'm impressed," she countered facetiously.

"You should be."

Regina felt a sense of foreboding sweep over her when she registered the three words. Even though Aaron's mouth had curved with a smile, his gaze held no humor. It was flat and cold, narrowing until his eyes resembled slits.

"Are you threatening me, Aaron?"

His expression did not change. "No. I just want to remind you that I stopped being a boy a long time ago, which means I don't remember how to play, as you put it, *games*."

She searched for a hidden meaning behind his words. The silence grew more tense with each passing second as they stared at each other. Her fingers curled tightly, leaving half-moon impressions on her palms.

She knew without a doubt that she was attracted to him, and now and only now did she realize Aaron was equally intrigued. She was conscious of his virile appeal and knew that many of his mannerisms reminded her of Oscar, even though he looked nothing like his father. He claimed the same quiet magnetism of Oscar, yet there was more, much more, that drew her to him. She grew more uncomfortable as his gaze was riveted on her face before moving slowly over her upper body.

Her eyes narrowed, holding his steady gaze. "What is it you want from me, other than *El Cielo?*"

He leaned forward and lowered his voice. "I'm very surprised that you have to ask me that. You should know."

Regina went completely still as she stared wordlessly at him. An oddly primitive warning shouted at her that she wasn't quite ready to offer herself to a man—especially Aaron Spencer. She had been on a roller-coaster ride for the past ten years, and even though she had finally gotten off she still hadn't fully recovered from the harrowing emotional experience.

Swallowing several times to relieve the dryness in her throat, she said softly, "Why don't you tell me *exactly* what it is you want from me?"

His gaze softened as he flashed her a sensual smile. Reaching across the table, he captured her fingers and held them firmly within his warm grasp. How could he tell her that he was no different than his father, because he, too, could not resist her, that he wanted her in his life?

"I want to protect you, Regina," he stated instead. "And to do that I need you to come back to Brazil with me. I know I'll never be able to repay you for what you've been to my father, but I hope to be able to offer you a little of what you've had to sacrifice over the years. Spending some time with me in Bahia will give you the opportunity to relax and see another part of the world. I'll rearrange my work schedule at the institute and show you a Brazil that is a primordial, tropical paradise."

A nervous laugh escaped her parted lips at the same time she slumped back against her chair in relief. Luckily, he did not want to sleep with her.

"I can't go back with you now."

"Why?"

"Because I have to go home. I've been away too long. I'll be all right once I'm with my family."

"When do you think you can come?" There was no mistaking the disappointment in his voice.

"I don't know. I need time to get used to living on American soil once again."

He released her fingers. "Whenever you decide to visit, I just want you to know the invitation will always be open to you. You don't have to call me in advance. Just come down."

"Thank you." Her soft tone matched her smile.

He shrugged his broad shoulders, the gesture so elegant that Regina had found herself watching for it. She wondered how a man as tall and muscular as Dr. Aaron Spencer could appear so masculine and graceful at the same time.

She sipped her coffee, listening intently as Aaron told her of a Brazil she had never learned about in her geography classes. He related the mad passion of Carnival to the enormity of the dark Amazon. He told her of the vast size of a country encompassing nearly half of South America, whose population was clustered around the Atlantic coast, leaving much of the country and the massive Amazon Basin scarcely populated and inaccessible.

Regina and Aaron talked for hours, unaware of the tightening bond in which they were unable to know where one began and the other ended.

Chapter 10

Regina and Aaron stared at Ernesto Morales, both astounded by the contents of Oscar Clayborne Spencer's will. It was a simply worded document, but its stipulations were shocking: she was awarded the house and all of its contents, but she was restricted from selling *El Cielo* and the surrounding property for twenty years; the fourteen paintings by Pablo Vasques, appraised at over a million dollars, were also left to her, but were not to be sold during her lifetime; the three people who made up the live-in domestic staff would continued to reside at *El Cielo,* maintaining its upkeep while earning their full annual wages for the twenty years; cash, stocks, and bonds worth more than one million, eight hundred-fifty thousand dollars would be used to set up a medical foundation in the names of Oscar and Arlene Spencer at the *São Tomé Instituto de Médico Pesquisa* in Bahia, Brazil. The funds would be disbursed over a ten-year period with Regina Cole-Spencer as the foundation's sole administrator.

It had taken Ernesto less than three minutes to confirm that

Oscar was still controlling; he had become the master puppeteer, pulling the strings and manipulating lives from his grave.

Regina rose to her feet, the two men also rising. Leaning across the table, she extended her hand to Ernesto. "Thank you for everything."

He grasped her slender fingers, coming around to stand next to her. "It's been my extreme pleasure. If you need legal advice setting up the foundation I'll be available for you."

She smiled. "Thank you for the offer, but I'll have someone at my father's company do it. ColeDiz accountants are experts in setting up tax-exempt, not-for-profit foundations."

Aaron moved closer to Regina, curving his left arm around her waist, while offering Ernesto his right hand. "I want to thank you for the trust my father placed in you."

Shaking the proffered hand, Ernesto seemed genuinely surprised by Aaron's approval. "It's been my honor to have known a man such as your father." He turned his attention to Regina. "I will need your power of attorney if you want me to manage the payment of wages for your employees."

"Thank you again, but I'll continue to pay them."

He successfully concealed his disappointment behind a polite smile. Now that he had revealed the contents of Oscar Spencer's will, there was no reason for his widow to continue their association. He did not blame Regina as much as he blamed Aaron Spencer. He did not know why, but since the man's arrival he had felt as if he had waged an undeclared war with the younger Spencer. Within a span of days Aaron had appointed himself as his stepmother's protector. Who did he expect to protect her from? Certainly not Ernest Morales de Villarosa.

Regina picked up her handbag. "I will be in touch with you before I leave Mexico."

Ernesto flinched noticeably as his face paled under his deep tan. "You are *leaving* Mexico?" There was no mistaking his surprise.

She nodded. "I'm going home to see my family."

"When—when will you return?"

"I honestly don't know."

His dark eyes showed disbelief and confusion. Regina Spencer's decision to leave Mexico had turned his world upside down. "Please keep in touch."

"I will," she whispered softly.

Turning, she walked out of the attorney's office, Aaron following closely behind her. He held her arm and escorted her to the parking lot. It wasn't until they were seated in the rear of the car and their driver had maneuvered out of the lot that they stared at each other; both had elected to conceal their emotions behind a mask of indifference. Oscar Spencer had skillfully bound them together.

Regina Cole-Spencer would become a part of Dr. Oscar Spencer's future, and he hers.

The return trip to *El Cielo* was accomplished in complete silence as she seethed inwardly, wanting to resurrect Oscar so she could scream at him for being a Machiavellian miscreant. She couldn't sell *El Cielo*, she couldn't sell the paintings—whose strange and macabre images disturbed her rather than soothed—and she would be responsible for disbursing and approving funding for a foundation named for Aaron Spencer's late parents.

She wanted to design gardens, not become a foundation administrator. *Damn you, Oscar*, she cursed silently. Damn him for forcing her to become involved with Aaron, because it had only taken two weeks for her to realize that her feelings for her stepson went beyond logic and reason. As she lay in bed before the sun rose to signal the beginning of another day, she knew she could not ignore the truth: she wanted to lie with Aaron; she wanted her first sexual encounter to be with him.

The driver pulled into the courtyard at *El Cielo*, and she did not wait for him or Aaron to help her from the car as she stepped out and made her way to the garden. Ignoring the blinding rays of the intense sun, she sat on the low stone bench facing Oscar's gravesite.

"You had to do it," she whispered angrily. *You just had to force us to be together, didn't you?* she continued in a virulent, silent tirade.

Squeezing her eyes tightly shut, she tried to fathom why Oscar would draw up a will with so many restrictions. Why had he made it so complicated, when their marriage hadn't been?

She shuddered, opening her eyes; she detected someone standing behind her. Without turning around she knew it was the man whose presence had disturbed her the moment he stepped from the taxi and onto the property of *El Cielo.*

Patting the space beside her, she said, "What do you think, Aaron?"

He sat, stretching his long legs out in front of him. His gaze was fixed on the headstone, which had been placed on the grave a week ago. "Oscar was a class act up until the very end. He didn't have to leave me anything."

Regina smiled. As annoyed as she was with Oscar, she had to agree with his son. "He left it to your research institute."

"It's the same thing. He knew how much medical research means to me. That's all I ever talked about when I was in medical school."

"If you liked research so much, why didn't you specialize in microbiology instead of pediatrics?"

He turned and smiled at her. "At the time I loved pediatrics more."

Who or what do you love more now, Aaron? she mused, watching a tiny lizard making its way over the cool, pale pink marble marking Oscar Clayborne Spencer's final resting place. His father had left him a considerable amount of money to continue his research projects, and she wondered if he would relax enough to make time for something or someone else in his life.

"We've made a breakthrough in predicting cerebral palsy in

newborns," he continued, the pride in his voice clearly evident. "A team of neurologists at the institute detected that high levels of key markers in the blood of newborns may predict who will go on to develop cerebral palsy, a motor disability that affects a half million Americans."

"What is the cause of the disease?"

"We're not certain of the cause. There have been theories that cerebral palsy is linked to maternal or fetal infections during pregnancy, but there's no proof of this."

Nodding, she smiled. "You're very lucky, Aaron. You've executed a marriage of pediatrics and medical research with wonderful results."

"We have a long way to go before we can prove our theory."

"One of these days I'll read about you accepting your Nobel Prize for Medicine, and I'll tell everyone that I know that doctor."

He concealed a smile. "It's not about prizes or awards. It's about making human life worth living."

For the first time she saw Aaron Spencer as the healer he had been trained to be. It was the first time he had broached the subject of his research.

"I'll arrange for the transfer of *El Cielo* to you as—"

"Don't bother," he interrupted. "You can't sell the property for twenty years, so let it remain as it is. As long as you own it I know I'll always be able to come back here."

"Twenty years sounds like a long time."

"It is, and then it isn't." And it wasn't. The twelve years he had been estranged from his father seemed more like three. He still could recall everything about his last volatile encounter with Oscar as if it had been two weeks ago.

Regina stared at his impassive expression. "When do you plan to leave for Brazil?"

He turned his head slowly and stared at her, his gaze cataloging and committing to memory the exquisite features of her incredibly beautiful face. "I'll wait for you."

"It may take me a month before I finalize everything."

He shrugged a broad shoulder. "It doesn't matter. I'll still wait."

"But what about your research, your plantation?"

"They will be there when I get back."

She twisted the circle of flawless diamonds around the third finger on her left hand in a nervous gesture. "But you told me that you would not leave your research or your plantation. Not for anyone or for anything."

Aaron crossed his arms over his chest, resting the forefinger of his right hand alongside his jaw, his eyes narrowing as he quickly read the letters carved into the marble headstone. "That was then, Regina." His voice was low, rumbling sensuously in his chest.

"And now?"

Her pulse was racing so uncontrollably that she doubted whether she could stand if called upon to do so. She knew what Aaron was going to say before the words left his lips.

"Now there's you."

Closing her eyes, she bit down hard on her lower lip. "What about me?" She jumped, startled, when his fingers curved around the slim column of her neck.

He leaned closer, their shoulders touching. "I have to take care of you."

"I don't need your protection. I don't need any man's protection. Not anymore."

Placing a finger under her chin, he raised her face to his. The bright sunlight illuminated the liberal sprinkling of gray in his close-cropped hair, and she wondered what he would look like if he allowed his hair to grow. Had he cut it short to conceal the fact that he was graying prematurely? It would not have mattered to her, because all of the men in her family were mixed gray before their fortieth birthdays—her father, uncles, and male cousins.

His lids lowered over his expressive slanting eyes as he flashed the sensual smile that always sent shivers racing up and down her spine. "What if I tell you that I *want* to take care of you?"

Her eyes widened. "Why?"

The sound of her husky voice floated around Aaron like a cloaking fog, drawing him under and seducing him with its hypnotic timbre. How could he tell her that what he was beginning to feel for her was so different and foreign that it frightened him? That he did not know what drew him to her as if he had been caught in a spell from which there was no escape—a spell he did not want to escape?

"I don't know," he replied truthfully.

Reaching for his hand, she laced her slender fingers between his. "Everything will fall into place in its own time," she predicted sagely.

Will it? he wanted to ask her. *Will you come to love me as much I think I love you at this time?*

The realization that he was falling in love with his father's widow was not as traumatic as it had been when he first recognized the emotions which had not permitted him to feel completely at ease in Regina Cole-Spencer's presence.

He found her more secure at twenty-seven than most older women he had been involved with. She also challenged him in a way he had never permitted a woman to challenge him.

He also realized that he was more like Oscar Spencer than he wanted to admit, because he, too, wanted Regina Cole for himself. Oscar had appointed himself her protector to keep her from the clutches of a perverted movie producer, while he wanted to protect her from anything seen or unseen which would cause her harm. And to do that he would have to marry her.

He would remain in Mexico with her, hoping it would give

him the time he needed to help her grieve, heal, and then love again.

"I want you to understand something, Aaron."

"What is it?"

"I'm going to leave *El Cielo*," she predicted quietly, "and when I do everything I will have shared with you *here* will end."

He successfully concealed a smile. She had challenged him again, and this time he would accept the challenge.

"Point taken," he replied in a dangerously soft tone.

Pulling her hand from his, she stood up and walked out of the garden and back to the house. She did not tell Aaron that she had grown to depend on him more than she had thought she would, that she hadn't wanted him to return to Brazil because then she would be alone—left to the demons who attacked relentlessly while she woke up screaming for someone to rescue her.

He had offered to remain in Mexico with her until she verified a date for her return to the United States. She would take the time given them, then walk away from Aaron Spencer and not look back.

Regina sat on a chair in the sitting room of her bedroom, staring out at the mountains as she spoke to her father. "I know he left me with a lot of responsibility, but I can handle it."

"Have your lawyer fax me all of the particulars and I'll have Philip Trent set up everything for the foundation." The soft-spoken, efficient attorney who had headed ColeDiz's legal department for the past twenty years had been responsible for filing the legal documents changing Regina's name from Simmons to Cole.

"I also need another favor, Daddy."

"What else, Cupcake?"

"I have fourteen paintings I want shipped to the States."

"What are they appraised at?"

"In excess of a million." Martin whistled softly under his

breath. "I hate them," she said. The lifeless looking subjects and dark colors depressed her.

"Why did you buy them?"

"I didn't. They were Oscar's."

"Why don't you sell them?"

"I can't. Not as long as I'm alive."

There was a swollen silence before Martin Cole's soft, drawling Southern cadence came through the wire again. "Oscar Spencer is lucky he's dead, or I would break his neck. What the hell kind of life did you have with him where—"

"I don't want to talk about it," Regina snapped angrily, interrupting her father. "He's dead, Daddy. Let him rest in peace."

"I'll send a courier to pick them up, and I'll have them stored for you. What else do you need?"

There was no mistaking her father's annoyance when his tone changed. His voice was softer, more controlled.

"I need you to set up a payroll and a household account for *El Cielo*. Oscar made provisions for the permanent live-in staff for the next twenty years."

"That was very generous of him."

"I agree." This time there was no evidence of facetiousness in her father's voice. "How long do you project all of this will take?"

"Hold on while I talk to Philip."

Regina ran a hand through the hair she had unpinned from its elaborate chignon. Twisting a black curl around her finger, she examined it; she realized her hair was too long. Unbound, it reached her waist, and the only styles she affected were a single braid, ponytail, or a chignon. The long, curly hair and her dimpled smile had become her trademarks when she was an actress, but that phase of her life had been over for years.

A few times she had thought she would return to the stage, but changed her mind. Now she loved the entire process of designing gardens, from drawing up the plans to seeing the blooming plants harmonizing with the surrounding landscape.

"Cupcake?"

The endearment wrung a smile from her. Her father had not let go of his childhood nickname for her. "Yes, Daddy."

"Philip projects it should take about three weeks, give or take a few days."

She glanced down at the open desk diary on the round rattan table. "If that's the case, then expect me back around the first of October."

"I'll tell Philip to make this a priority."

"Thanks, Daddy. I don't know what I'd do without you."

"I want you to promise me one thing."

"What's that?"

"When you come back this time you'll stay for a while. I'm getting too old to fly around the world searching for my first-born." She laughed, the low, husky sound reminding Martin of his wife's voice.

"You're not old, Daddy. You're only fifty-seven. Wait until you're eighty-five, like Grandpa. Then you can say you're old."

"Your grandfather has been asking for you."

"You tell him that I'll be home soon."

"You know your mother is planning a big party for you."

"I figured she would. I'm looking forward to seeing everyone again. Daddy, I love you."

"And I love you," Martin stated quietly.

"I'll see you."

She hung up, then closed her eyes. Everything was falling into place, and she looked forward to returning to her family with the same obsession which had made her leave Florida for Los Angeles two months before her seventeenth birthday. It had taken ten years, but she had finally come full circle.

Chapter 11

Regina met with the gardener, chauffeur, and housekeeper, informing them that they would be guaranteed a place to live while collecting salaries if they maintained a residence at *El Cielo* for the next twenty years. All were too stunned with their former employer's offer to say anything as they stared at her with gazes filled with shock and gratitude.

"I'm going to hire someone to oversee the property," she continued. "He will be responsible for repairs and the general upkeep of *El Cielo*."

"Are you going away, Señora?" Rosa questioned, taking furtive glances at the others.

"*Sí*, Rosa."

"Will you be back, Señora?" Rosa had appointed herself spokesperson for the group.

"*Sí*," Regina repeated. "I will be back, and so will Dr. Spencer. We may not come back at the same time, but I promise you both of us will return here many, many times." This seemed to satisfy the housekeeper, and her lips parted in a warm smile. "Rosa, I'd like to talk to you," she continued at the same time the gardener and driver walked out of the kitchen, patting each other on the back.

"Señora?"

Her dark gaze met the equally dark one of Rosa Galan. "You can take the rest of the day off."

"But, Señora, who will prepare dinner for you and Dr. Spencer?"

"I will."

"*Sí*, Señora."

It was not the first time she had taken over the cooking duties. Regina shared her father's love of cooking, but hadn't indulged herself with concocting new and exotic dishes. She had spent so much time looking after Oscar, and whenever she cooked for him most times his sensitive stomach would not tolerate anything but soft, bland food.

Once she returned to the States she would look for an apartment, decorate it, then plan her career as a landscape architect. Florida would be an ideal location because of its abundant sunshine and tropical conditions.

Aaron changed his clothes, made two calls to Bahia, then went in search of Regina. *Siesta* had ended, and he knew he would find her in one of two places: the garden, or her bedroom. He knocked on her door and encountered silence. He waited and knocked again. It was apparent she wasn't in her bedroom.

His footfalls were silent as he descended the staircase and went to the garden. He asked the gardener if he had seen Señora Spencer. The man informed him that he had left her in the kitchen with Rosa.

Returning to the coolness of the house, he found her alone in the kitchen. Standing in the entrance to the large, modern, functional space, he leaned against a wall, crossed his arms over his chest, and stared at her.

He thought she looked younger today than at any time since he had met her. She had pulled her hair back and braided it in a single plait, securing the curling end with a red elastic band. Wisps of black curling hair fell over her forehead and ears. She had also changed from her tailored dress into a pair of well-worn jeans, a navy-blue T-shirt, and black ballet slippers. Her overall appearance was one of unabashed feminine innocence.

She hadn't noticed him watching her as she busied herself sectioning a chicken on a cutting board. She wielded a cleaver with consummate skill, which verified that she was more than comfortable with the inside of a kitchen. .

"What's for dinner?"

Regina dropped the cleaver, it falling with a dull thud onto the cutting board. A slight frown marred her smooth forehead. "Stop creeping up on me," she gasped, wanting to scream at Aaron, but couldn't, not when her heart was pounding like a rapid-firing piston.

He closed the space between them with long, fluid strides and grasped her wrist between his fingers, monitoring her pulse. "I really did frighten you, didn't I?"

"Yes." She stared at his throat rather than meet his gaze.

His brow furrowed in a frown. "What makes you frighten so easily?"

She snatched her hand from his loose grip. "Nothing. It's just that I didn't expect to see you standing there, that's all."

"What do you want me to do?"

"Whistle. Sing. Just make some noise."

His frown deepened. She was afraid of something, and he knew he wasn't the cause. "How's your blood pressure?"

"It's normal. Why?"

"I don't want you stroking out on me."

She gave him a saucy smile. "I can reassure you that I won't have a stroke or a heart attack."

He returned her smile. "Good. And I promise I'll whistle before I come up on you again." Moving closer, his chest only inches from her back, he examined the different foodstuffs on the counter. "It's been a long time since I've had gumbo."

Regina suffered his closeness as she pretended indifference to his presence. She wanted to flee the kitchen and hide behind the door to her bedroom. It wasn't that she wanted to hide from Aaron so much as that she needed to hide from herself, and the feelings he aroused in her.

"Do you mind if I help?"

"Not at all," she said a little too quickly, realizing she would agree to anything to make him move away from her. Then she remembered his admission that he was a very good cook.

"I'll take care of the chicken while you slice the peppers and the okra," he said.

"Okay."

Aaron washed the chicken, patted it dry, then tossed the pieces in a large plastic bag filled with flour seasoned with salt and pepper. He preheated the oven, added butter and vegetable oil to a Dutch oven, and placed the chicken in the pot, then into the oven to brown.

"How spicy do you like your food?" he questioned as he picked up several CDs from a countertop next to a compact disc stereo system.

She glanced at him over her shoulder. "I don't mind if my food bites back."

"All right," he drawled, grinning broadly. "So, the girl likes it hot and spicy."

"If the truth be known, I like it *real* hot *and* spicy."

He gave her body a raking gaze, then slipped six CDs onto the carousel. "Like your music?" She gave him a lingering stare.

"I doubt very much if my father listened to the Barrio Boyz, Babyface, India, Jon Secada, Marc Antony, or DLG."

"He liked Babyface and Jon Secada."

Picking up a case for DLG—Dark Latin Groove—he read the selections aloud. "*La Quiero A Morir.* That's heavy, Regina. Dying for love. Dad was more comfortable with Frank Sinatra, Nat Cole, and Sarah Vaughan."

She sucked her teeth at the same time she continued to trim the okra. "Don't be so cynical, Aaron. One of these days love is going to jump up and bite you on your behind so hard you won't have time to holler."

"You think so?" he questioned, stalking her and reminding her of a large cat.

Holding a small paring knife in front of her, she warned softly, "Stay away from me, Aaron."

"Put that thing away." Before she could inhale, he caught her wrist and took the knife from her loose grip. "I didn't bring my medical bag, so let's try to act civil." Pulling her up close to his body, he swung her around in tempo with the pulsating Latin rhythm. "Dance with me," he urged when she went stiff in his arms. He tightened his grip on her waist, molding her to the length of him until they were fused from shoulders to knees. "It's been a long time since I've danced with a woman."

Curling her arms around his neck, Regina relaxed, closed her eyes, and inhaled the hauntingly sensual scent of his natural body fragrance mingling with his cologne.

"What's the matter, Aaron? You don't get out much?"

He laughed, the sound rumbling like thunder in his broad chest. "Apparently not enough. I'm usually invited to a lot of parties during the Christmas season, but I manage to make it to only one or two."

Pulling back, she smiled up at him staring down at her. "What about Carnival?"

He shifted his eyebrows. "I stay away from Carnival."

"Why?"

"It's become a little too boisterous for me." He swung her around, his hips moving sensuously against hers as he kept pace with the throbbing rhythm.

She nodded, concentrating on the intricate dance steps Aaron executed. He had failed to mention that he was also an excellent dancer. She followed his every move. The selection ended but he did not release her, and she did not want him to.

Dancing with Aaron reminded her of what she had missed. She had never been given the opportunity to date, dance, or flirt with a man. He was offering her that, and more. She registered the changes within her whenever he tightened his grip on her waist, making her aware of how different their bodies were. She successfully swallowed back a moan when she felt his rising hardness press against her middle, bringing with it a heaviness in her breasts she was unable to control. She was certain he was cognizant of the changes at the same time his breathing deepened.

Then, without warning, he went completely still, and she was certain she would have fallen if he hadn't been holding her and possibly injured herself.

His hands moved from her waist to cradle her face. She tried escaping him, but he tightened his hold. "Don't," he whispered, his moist breath caressing her mouth. "Please don't move."

Closing her eyes against his intense stare, she realized she couldn't move. She couldn't escape him even if she wanted to. It was too late. Aaron Spencer had become the itch she couldn't scratch. Within two weeks he had become a part of her existence, and try as she could, she could not remember when he had not been at *El Cielo*.

She looked for him when she woke up, and before she retired for bed. They had taken to sharing all of their meals and walks together, and many times *siestas* in the garden. And there were occasions when they were content to sit beside each other without initiating conversation.

She knew he was going to kiss her, and she was helpless to stop him. It wouldn't be the first time a man kissed her, but it would be the first time she would not have to take her cue from a director.

Aaron stared at Regina as if seeing her for the first time. He hadn't realized the length of the lashes brushing the tops of her high cheekbones, the smooth, velvety texture of her skin, and the narrowness of her delicate nose. His hand splayed over her cheek, his fingers entwining in the curls framing her face. His head came down slowly, inch by inch, until his mouth hovered over hers, capturing her breath as she exhaled.

Angling for a better position, he slanted his mouth over hers, increasing the pressure until her lips parted slightly. That was what he needed to stake his claim, his tongue meeting hers in a heated joining which raced through his body like the rush of molten lava.

He tasted her mouth tentatively, kissing every inch of it. Then, with a rush of uncontrollable desire, he devoured its sweetness like a child who had been deprived of candy for years.

Regina moved closer, shocked at her own eager response to the feel of his lips on hers as she returned his kiss with a reckless abandon she hadn't known she possessed.

He drew back to catch his breath and she collapsed against his chest, her fingers tangling in the fabric of his shirt. Not only had he heated her blood, but his repressed passion had scorched her soul.

"Please, let me go, Aaron." Her velvet voice came out in a breathless whisper.

Burying his face in her hair, he shook his head. "I don't want to—but I will." Releasing her, he stepped back, staring at her staring back at him. Passion had dilated her pupils, while her breasts rose and fell over her narrow rib cage.

"Aaron—"

"It's all right, *Princesa,*" he crooned, interrupting her with a knowing smile. "If you don't want me to kiss you again I won't."

Her lids fluttered in confusion. "I didn't say I didn't want you to kiss me."

Crossing his arms over his chest, his gaze narrowed. "Then what is it?"

"I want you to check on the chicken. I can't abide burnt food." He stared at her, complete surprise freezing his features. "If you're not going to help me, then get out of my kitchen," she challenged, pushing him aside to open the oven door.

He laughed, the sound exploding from his throat, as he watched her turn over pieces of chicken with a long-handled fork. His hungry gaze devoured her slim body in the revealing jeans, his laughter fading when she turned and glared at him.

"What's so funny?"

He sobered. "How can you turn your emotions on and off like a faucet? You kiss me passionately, and then in the same breath you talk about checking on the chicken."

"I can kiss you passionately because I've been trained to turn on the passion. You keep forgetting that I was an actress."

His eyes widened, anger glimmering in their dark depths. "Are you saying that what we've just shared was an *act?*"

Rising on tiptoe, she pressed her mouth to his. "That's for me to know, and for you to find out."

His arm snaked out and held her fast. "Don't play with me, Regina."

Leaning closer, she bared her straight, white teeth. "Or you'll do what, Aaron?" Their gazes fused, locking in a battle of wills where neither wanted to concede. *"¿Qué?"* she spat out.

She was asking him what he was going to do, and he couldn't come up with an answer. *"Nada,"* he replied in the same language. If she continued to tease him there was absolutely nothing he could or would do. He would take everything she threw at him until he won. And he would not stop until she was his wife.

* * *

Regina sat on the patio with Aaron, enjoying the warmth of the late summer night. It had cooled down considerably, and she lay on a chaise, staring up at the starlit sky.

Dinner had been a success, the gumbo flavorful and spicy from the piquant chili powder. She had prepared a side dish of savory white rice, with an accompanying avocado and orange salad, and baked a small loaf of Rosa's homemade bread. Her beverage was iced tea, while Aaron had opted for a frozen citrus fruit drink.

"How about a walk?" he asked lazily, his voice floating above as he stood over her.

Extending her hand, she permitted him to pull her to her feet. "I ate too much."

"You don't eat enough."

"I do eat," she protested.

"Not enough," he argued softly.

"Do I look anorexic to you?"

"No." And she didn't. Her height and narrow hips made her appear much slimmer than she actually was. He glanced down at her sandals. "Do you want to go into the house and change your shoes?"

She smiled up at him through her lashes. "Where are you taking me?"

He shrugged a shoulder. "Nowhere in particular."

"I'll keep the sandals on."

After cooking, both had retreated to their bedrooms, where they showered and changed. Aaron had exchanged his jeans and T-shirt for a pair of khakis, a matching shirt, and a pair of woven leather loafers, while she opted for a red silk shell, matching slim skirt, and leather sandals.

Aaron was transfixed by the rich color contrasting with her golden-brown flesh. Of all of the colors he had seen her wear, he preferred her in red.

Taking her hand, he led her down the patio, across the courtyard, and toward the garden. A half-moon lit up the clear sky, providing a modicum of light along with the lanterns strung around the perimeter of the courtyard and along the path leading to the garden.

The brush of flying insects on their exposed flesh, the sounds of scurrying night creatures, and the cloying fragrance of blooming flowers hung heavily in the air, and the more they ventured into the garden the closer Regina pressed against Aaron's body. He felt the slight trembling of her hand as they left the light behind and were swallowed up by a blanketing darkness.

"What is it?" he whispered at the same time she turned and clutched at his clothes in a desperate clawing that quickened his pulse.

"Take me back," she gasped frantically, hyperventilating.

"Where, *Princesa?*"

"Back to the light!"

Her trembling increased until she shook uncontrollably. Bending slightly, he swept her up effortlessly in his arms and retraced their steps, not stopping until he mounted the staircase and placed her on the large bed in his bedroom.

Turning on a bedside lamp, he sat down beside her, counting the beats of her runaway pulse. It was as fast as if she had run a grueling race. Leaving the bed, he walked into the adjoining bathroom and returned within minutes with a cool cloth, placing it over her moist forehead.

Tears leaked from under her eyelids as she cried silently, praying for the demons to flee and leave her in peace. Even after seventeen years they refused to relinquish their hold on her mind.

Running his fingertips over her moist cheeks, Aaron leaned down and pressed a healing kiss on her mouth. "It's all right, *Princesa.* I'm here for you," he crooned, hoping to calm her.

"They won't leave me in peace," she cried, burying her face

against his strong throat. "After so many years they still come back to haunt me."

"Tell me about it, Baby."

Opening her eyes, she stared up at his dark, handsome face through her tears. Would he understand? Would he laugh at her for something she should have gotten over years ago?

"I'm afraid of the dark," she whispered.

He gave her a tender smile, nodding. "Go on, Baby," he urged in a quiet tone.

"It happened a week before I turned ten."

"Go on, Baby," he repeated when she hesitated.

"I was kidnapped."

Lowering his head, Aaron pressed his lips to the side of her scented neck, cursing to himself. Didn't her family know how to protect their children? Why weren't they aware that their children were the most vulnerable when it came to kidnapping and extortion?

"Can you tell me about it?"

She nodded, savoring his warmth, strength, and protection.

Chapter 12

"My parents left me with my grandparents in West Palm Beach for a few days so I could visit my cousins, who lived in Palm Beach. My aunt Nancy asked me to sleep over at her house, but I decided to stay with my grandmother and grandfather because one of their pedigreed cocker spaniels had delivered a litter of puppies. I remembering sitting on a stool in a gardening shed watching them, but I can't remember any of what happened next."

"You don't know who abducted you?"

She shook her head. "No. The only thing I remembered was waking up in a locked closet and pounding on the door until my hands were swollen. And when I pleaded to be let out to use the bathroom, I was gagged and blindfolded. Someone watched me whenever I had to relieve myself to make certain I would not remove the blindfold."

"Was it a man or a woman?"

Her face burned in remembrance. "It was always a man. Each

time I was let out of the closet to eat or use the bathroom I was blindfolded."

"How did you manage to see to eat?"

"I didn't. They bound my hands behind my back and fed me."

Aaron's shock turned to a white-hot fury as he listened to the horror no one—especially a nine-year-old child—should have had to endure.

"How long were you held captive?"

Sighing heavily, she mumbled, "Six days."

Shifting, he eased her over his body, his arms tightening protectively around her waist. "What happened after that?" His voice was soft, coaxing.

"My uncle and his friend found me. They made it seem as if it had been a game where they had to rescue me, and somehow I managed to repress the entire incident until I returned to Florida."

"Where did you go after the abduction?"

"Ocho Rios, Jamaica. My mother and I lived with my uncle for six months before we moved back to Florida with my father."

"Why did you move back?"

"My mother was pregnant, and she was experiencing complications, so my father moved us back to the States."

Running his hand over her hair, Aaron closed his eyes. She had relaxed so that her slow, even breathing was a soft whisper under his ear. He had wanted Regina in his arms and in his bed, but he hadn't wanted his role to be that of comforter.

"Is there anything else you want to tell me?"

"I used to wake up screaming, and it would take hours before the household would settle down after each episode. I stopped visiting my cousins because I didn't want them to know that I was afraid to sleep without a light on in the room. My parents sent me to a psychiatrist, who prescribed a very mild tranquilizer to help me sleep."

"I don't advocate medicating children."

"My father shares a similar belief. He took me to a prominent child psychologist who helped me work through most of my anxiety. I joined the drama club when I entered junior high school and found a way to escape completely. On stage and in character I did not have to be Regina Cole, but could be anyone I chose to be."

"Are you saying that acting became a form of therapy for you?"

"It *was* my therapy. As Regina I was always looking over my shoulder, wondering who was following me. But on stage I was Hamlet's Ophelia or Othello's Desdemona, with nothing to fear except the audience's reaction to my performance."

Sighing, she closed her eyes, feeling safer than she ever had in her life. She'd relived the entire ordeal in her head, and she was no longer afraid to allow the images to surface. They came back, rushing through her mind like frames of film—the suffocating darkness, the blind humiliation of someone watching her relieve herself, and the macabre laugh whenever the food shoved into her mouth dribbled down her chin onto her soiled clothing. She had slept in the small, dark space with only the smell of her unwashed body to remind her that she still lived.

"You're safe now, *Princesa*."

Smiling, she nodded against his chest. "I know, Aaron."

They lay together, their breathing deepening until they fell asleep, entwined in each other's arms.

Regina woke up in complete darkness, her heart racing. She was wrong. The demons hadn't left. They had vanished when she related her abduction and captivity to Aaron, but once the lights were extinguished they'd come back like a silent, creeping fog blanketing her sanity. The humming began, low and seductive until it grew louder and louder, becoming hysterical screams which sounded like someone being tortured.

"Help her," she pleaded as tears flooded her eyes and stained her cheeks. "Oh, please help her. Don't leave her to die in there."

Aaron came awake immediately. He sat up, reaching out for Regina, who thrashed wildly on the bed. Holding her firmly against his body, he pressed his mouth to her ear.

"They're gone, Regina," he crooned. "They can't hurt you."

"They—they're still here." She sobbed uncontrollably. "They want to kill me."

Stroking her hair, he shook his head. "No, Baby. They can't get you because I won't let them. Didn't I promise to protect you?"

Regina heard the man's deep, soothing voice and the demons fled, leaving her in peace. The voice sounded familiar. At first she thought it was her father's, but it did not have the soft, drawling cadence that identified Martin Cole was from the southern region of the United States. This voice was more nasal, claiming a midwest twang. As a drama student she had studied accents and regional dialects, and there was a time when she could identify the country or region of anyone who opened their mouths to speak.

She inhaled deeply, identifying the now familiar cologne worn by Aaron Spencer. Then she remembered. She was in Aaron's bedroom, and in his bed.

"Aaron." His name came out in a long, shuddering whisper.

"I'm here," he whispered. "I'm here for you."

"Turn on the light."

He continued stroking her hair, his hand moving over the curls spiraling around his fingers. "No, Baby."

Her breathing quickened. "Please." She managed to swallow a sob.

"Nothing's going to happen to you in the dark."

"Take me back to my room." There was no mistaking her rising anxiety as her trembling voice broke.

"No. You're going to spend the night with me, and when the sun comes up you'll realize—"

"Take me back now!" she shouted, interrupting him.

Aaron tightened his hold on her waist as she tried escaping his grip. "No, Regina."

Her right hand came up, but he was too quick for her. His fingers caught her wrist, holding her with a minimal of effort. "Don't fight with me," he warned between clenched teeth. "I promised you I would take care of you, and I will," he continued, this time in a softer voice. "I won't let anyone or anything hurt you." He felt some of the rigidness leave her limbs. "My father protected you and, like him, I'll also protect you. You trusted Oscar, didn't you?"

Biting down on her lower lip, she nodded. After a pause, she said, "Yes."

"I'm his son, *Princesa*. Blood of his blood and flesh of his flesh. And I've taken an oath that I will protect you the same way he did when he was alive. If I never ask anything of you, I'm going to ask that you trust me."

Regina half-listened to Aaron as she struggled with the lingering vestiges of her fear. How could she vanquish seventeen years of fear in one night? Could she actually trust Aaron to protect her from her unseen enemies? He could not spend the rest of his life looking after her. He had promised to remain in Mexico with her until she left for the States, but had he hoped he could help eradicate the fears she had carried for more than half her life in less than a month? What did he intend to do—sleep with her every night?

She could demand that he let her return to her bedroom, but something told her Aaron Spencer would not relent. He was determined to force her to remain in his bed, and in the darkened bedroom.

Going completely pliant in his arms, she curved her body into his. "I'll try."

He let out an audible sigh. "Thank you."

They lay together, monitoring each other's heat and respiration. Aaron had removed only his shoes, but Regina felt every muscle of his body as if he were completely nude. Lying in his embrace made her aware of the solid hardness of his chest and thighs, the power in his upper arms, and the unleashed strength in his large hands.

What was she doing? She was sharing a bed with a man whom she desired from the moment she saw him. There was something so subtly virile about Aaron Spencer that the times she caught herself staring at him she found it difficult to draw a normal breath.

Whenever he caught her staring, he did not look away but returned it boldly with one of his own. She had come to look for the intensity in his dark, deep-set, slanting eyes, wondering what was he thinking. And she did wonder if he knew how much she wanted him, and that the wanting was of a physical nature.

Resting her head on his thick shoulder, she closed her eyes. The demons had finally left her, and in their place was a deep, silent longing to know what it was that made her crave the man holding her to his heart.

Her breathing deepened in a slow, measured rhythm, belaying the rush of desire racing headlong throughout her body as the realization washed over her again that she wanted Aaron to make love to her. She wanted him to introduce her to a world of passion she had never known.

She had never known or glimpsed passion—not even when her two movie roles called for on-screen lovemaking with handsome and very popular male costars.

Turning to her right, she pressed a light kiss at the side of his strong mouth, eliciting a slight intake of breath from him. "Thank you for being here for me."

Aaron smiled, lowering his head until his lips were inches

from hers. "You're very welcome," he murmured seconds before his mouth closed over hers.

What had begun as a gentle brushing of lips deepened until Aaron moved over her body, pressing her down to the mattress so that there was a sweet, deep intimacy to their kiss.

He felt the blood pool in his groin, and knew he was lost. The desire he had fought from the instant he saw Regina Cole-Spencer exploded uncontrollably until he was shaking from the passion, struggling not to erupt and embarrass himself. He did not want to pour out his passions on the bed, but inside of the woman writhing under him.

Pulling back, he buried his face in her unbound hair, which spread out on the pillow in a cascade of black, silken curls. *"Princesa,"* he groaned as if in pain.

"Aaron?" She answered his groan with her own moan.

"I don't want to take advantage of you. Tell me now if you want to take this further."

Her breath was coming faster. "And if I say I don't?"

"Then I'll stop."

A haze of passion swept over Regina, her mind reeling in confusion. Her body wanted Aaron, needed him, while she knew it was wrong to remain in his arms and in his bed. Could she sleep with him in the dark and not experience guilt in the full sunlight? Could she successfully affect indifference after sleeping with him when it came time for her to leave Mexico? What was it about Aaron Spencer that made her so wanton and so reckless? She knew the answers to all of her questions would come from offering herself to him.

Aaron did not want to stop. He wanted to take off her clothes, then his own, and feast on her body like a man dying of hunger and thirst. Making love to her would right all of the wrongs, heal all of the wounds, reconcile his past with his present.

She's your father's widow, a silent voice reminded him. She might be Oscar's widow, but Regina Spencer was the woman he had fallen in love with—the woman who had bewitched him, the woman who challenged him to his face, and still he wanted and desired her, the woman who warned him that whatever they might share in Mexico would become a part of their past and remain their past.

He cradled her face gently between his large hands. "What is it going to be?" he whispered against her parted lips. "Yes or no?"

Regina closed her eyes, knowing he couldn't see her expression in the darkness. The heat flooding her breasts increased, sweeping down and settling between her thighs while bringing a fiery heat that made it impossible for her to remain motionless. At the same time, she felt Aaron's surging hardness throbbing against her thighs. It was too late. Too late for her retreat. It was too late for both of them.

"Yes!" she gasped.

She wasn't certain of what was happening as everything fused into a slow-moving act which made her feel as if she were an observer instead of a participant.

Aaron left the bed and removed his clothes, she listening to the whisper of fabric grazing his skin as he took off his shirt, slacks, and briefs. He returned to the bed, the heat of his muscled physique enveloping her when he relieved her of the dress and the delicate scrap of silk concealing her virginal body.

She hadn't realized that she had been holding her breath until after he had pulled her into a tender embrace where her nakedness touched his, making her aware of how different their bodies were.

"Aaron?" Her voice was soft, tentative.

"Yes, *Princesa?*"

Swallowing several times to relieve the sudden dryness in her throat, she wondered how was she going to tell him that it was her first time, that she had never shared her body with a man.

"You're going to have to help me with this." Her fingers were splayed over his chest. "You're going to have to show me how to please you."

He pressed a kiss to her forehead, smiling. "You don't have to do anything. You please me because I'm here with you. You please me just by existing."

That was not what she meant, but he did not give her the opportunity to explain herself when he took possession of her mouth in a slow, drugging kiss that elicited a rush of moisture between her thighs. She squeezed them together to stop the pulsing, but to no avail. His mouth moved lower, to her breasts, and she was lost, lost in a maelstrom of desire which set her aflame with a surge of desire that shattered her dammed-up sexuality.

Regina had tried many times to imagine a man actually making love to her, and failed miserably. When she had executed her love scenes in *Silent Witness,* Oscar had outlined explicitly what he wanted from her and her costar. She had enacted the scenes like the professional she had been trained to be, but she had felt none of the responses Aaron now wrung from her.

The heat from his mouth swept from her own mouth to her core. Waves of passion shook her until she could not stop her legs from shaking. He suckled her breasts, worshiping them, and the moans she sought to suppress escaped her parted lips.

His tongue circled her nipples, leaving them hard, erect, and throbbing. His teeth tightened on the turgid tips, and she felt a violent spasm grip her womb.

Her fingers were entwined in the cotton sheets, tightening and ripping them from their fastenings at the same time she arched up off the mattress.

"Aaron!" His name exploded from her mouth as he inched down her body, holding her hips to still their thrashing. Shame replaced her passion when she realized where he had buried his face. "Stop! Please!"

But he did not stop. His hot breath seared the tangled curls between her thighs and she went limp, unable to protest or think of anything except the pleasure her lover offered her. She registered a series of breathless sighs, not realizing they were her own moans of physical satisfaction. Eyes closed, head thrown back, lips parted, back arched, she reveled in the sensations that took her beyond herself.

Then it began, rippling little tremors increasing and shaking her uncontrollably and becoming more volatile when it sought a route of escape.

Aaron heard her breath come in long, surrendering moans, and he moved quickly up her trembling limbs and eased his sex into her body. He was met with a resistance he hadn't expected. Gritting his teeth, he feared spilling his passion onto the sheets. He drew back, and with a strong, sure thrust of his hips buried his hardness in the hot, moist, tight flesh pulsing around his own.

Regina caught and held her breath, feeling if she had been impaled on a red-hot piece of steel when Aaron penetrated her virginal flesh, but the burning subsided the moment he began moving in a slow, measured rhythm, quickly renewing her passion.

Her arms curved around his waist as rivulets of moisture bathed his back and dotted her hands. She could not think of anything or anyone except the hard body atop hers as their bodies found and set a rhythm where they were in perfect harmony with each other.

Reaching down, Aaron cupped her hips in his hands, lifting her higher and permitting deeper penetration; he quickened his movements. Regina assisted him, increasing her own pleasure as she wound her legs around his waist.

Aaron's heat, hardness, and carnal sensuality had awakened the dormant sexuality of her body, and she responded to the seduction of his passion as hers rose higher and higher until it exploded in an awesome, vibrating liquid fire that scorched her mind and left her convulsing in ecstasy.

She hadn't quite returned from her own free-fall flight when she heard Aaron's groan of satisfaction against her ear as he quickened his movements and then collapsed heavily on her sated form. There was only the sound of their labored breathing in the stillness of the bedroom as they lay motionless, savoring the aftermath of a shared, sweet fulfillment.

He reversed their positions, bringing her with him until she lay sprawled over his body, her legs resting between his. "Did I hurt you, *Princesa?*"

"No," she drawled, placing tiny kisses on his throat and over his shoulder. There had been pain, but it was offset by the pleasure he had offered her.

"I hadn't expected you to be so small," he murmured in the cloud of curly hair flowing over his face. "I—"

She stopped his words when she placed her fingertips over his lips. "I'm all right, Aaron."

His right hand moved over her bare hip, caressing the silken flesh. She had no idea how sensuous her voice sounded in the dark. He drew in a deep breath, luxuriating in the intoxicating fragrance of her perfume mingling with the lingering scent of their lovemaking.

He could not believe the passion she had aroused in him; if possible, he had wanted to make love to her all through the night. Inhaling her scent, tasting her flesh, caressing her silken body, had tested the limits of his control. He smiled, knowing there was the possibility that he would make love to her many more times before they left Mexico. He did not want to think about her leaving, even though she had promised to come to Bahia.

If she did not come to him, then he would come for her. Now that Regina Cole-Spencer had become a part of his existence, he had no intention of letting her walk out of his life.

Chapter 13

Regina turned over, encountering an immovable bulk, and woke up. Realization dawned as she stared up at Aaron staring down at her. A gentle smile softened her lush mouth.

"¡Buenos dias!" she whispered shyly.

Slanting eyes crinkling attractively, he returned her smile. *"Bom dia,"* he replied in Portuguese. Shifting to his side, he placed an arm over her flat middle, pulling her closer. "How do you feel?" he continued in English.

She shrugged a slender shoulder. "Okay."

He arched a sweeping eyebrow. "Just okay?"

"Yes. Why?"

His expression sobered as he glared at her. "Why didn't you tell me you were a virgin?"

When he awoke earlier that morning he had noticed the dark-red stains on the sheet. He had felt as if someone had punched him in his gut once he realized the woman sharing his bed had given him the most precious gift any woman could offer a man.

His eyes clung to hers, analyzing her reaction to his accusation. He should not have been surprised when she did not flinch or glance away.

"I tried to tell you," she argued softly.

He frowned. "You didn't try hard enough."

"But I did. I asked for your help."

"Asking for help is not the same as saying that you'd never slept with a man." She lowered her gaze and stared at his smooth, bare chest. "You were married for eight years, *Princesa*."

"Oscar and I never shared a bed. Our marriage was in name only."

Anchoring his hand under her chin, he raised her face to his. "Why couldn't you have told me that?"

A slight frown furrowed her smooth forehead. "I told you everything I wanted you to know. What did or did not occur between Oscar and me in the bedroom was of too personal a nature to discuss with anyone. Even you."

"You're right—as usual," he conceded.

Curving her arms around his neck, she pressed her breasts against the solid wall of his broad chest, smiling when he gasped audibly.

"I'm going back to my bedroom to shower," she said quietly. "I'll see you later."

Aaron wanted to beg her to stay, stay with him until thirst, hunger, or the need to relieve himself drove him from her scented arms, but didn't. He knew it would be several days before they would make love again. He would wait for her tender flesh to heal before losing himself once again in the passion she evoked just by them sharing the same space.

Three weeks sped by as quickly as in a blink of the eye for Regina.

She and Aaron waited two nights after their initial passionate joining before sharing a bed again, while at the same time dreading the moment when they would be forced to part.

The courier her father had promised to send arrived in Mexico and escorted the fourteen paintings back to the States for safekeeping within days of their telephone conversation; the documents setting up the accounts for the Oscar and Arlene Spencer Foundation for Medical Research and *El Cielo*'s employees were finalized; all of her valuables and personal heirloom pieces were packed and shipped to her parents' home to await her arrival.

She spent her last night in Mexico in her garden, sitting on the stone bench facing Oscar's grave. Closing her eyes, she fought back tears. She was leaving her husband, not knowing when or if she would ever return.

"I'm leaving tomorrow morning, Oscar," she whispered. "I'm finally going home." Biting down on her lower lip, she forced a trembling smile. *I love you,* she added silently. She loved him, and she also had fallen in love with his son, and she was mature enough to realize her love for Aaron had nothing to do with their sexual encounters.

The days and nights when they did not make love offered her a modicum of objectivity. She craved his passion, that she would not deny, but she also treasured his companionship. But even more than passion or companionship, it was his protection she desired. She was able to sleep alongside him in an unlit room without waking up drenched in sweat or with tortured screams exploding from the back of her throat. The few times she whimpered in her sleep, he woke her with a gentle caress and whispered soothing, gentle words to reassure her that she had nothing to fear.

She would leave Mexico in the morning, reunite with her family, remain in Florida through the end of the year, and then perhaps take Aaron up on his offer to visit with him in Brazil.

* * *

Aaron stood on the second-story veranda outside his bedroom, staring down at the slender figure sitting by his father's grave. It was a sight he had grown accustomed to since he had come to *El Cielo,* and it was a sight that wrang a gamut of emotions from him. It saddened him to know he would never see, touch, or speak to Oscar again. The sight also rankled him, because for the second time in his life a woman he had fallen in love with also loved his father.

He lost track of time as he rested his arms on the wrought-iron railing, reliving the events of the past month. The past five weeks had changed him. Since he had become involved with the *São Tomé Instituto de Médico Pesquisa* he had never been away from his research for more than three weeks. Since becoming the director he had found himself traveling throughout the world at least twice each year to attend medical symposiums to share the institute's theories with others in his field of study. Medical research had been his passion for more than twelve years—until now.

Now his passion was Regina Spencer.

Regina said her final goodbye to Oscar and returned to the house to prepare for her last night on Mexican soil. The household was quiet, and all of the permanent household staff conspicuously absent. They had said their final farewells after the evening meal. The driver was scheduled to drive her and Aaron to the airport in Mexico City. He would board an early morning flight for Salvador, Brazil, while she awaited the arrival of the ColeDiz Gulfstream jet from the West Palm Beach airport.

Her footsteps were slow and sure as she climbed the staircase. She felt a heaviness in her chest which would not permit her to breathe normally. Swallowing back a wave of anxiety, she drew herself up straighter and visually examined everything around her, committing it to memory.

She would miss *El Cielo,* her garden, and the employees who had become her extended family. She refused to think of missing Aaron, because she had become too dependent on him. They had agreed not to spend their last night together.

Pushing open the door to her bedroom, she walked in and stopped abruptly as Aaron rose from the chair beside her bed. Her eyes widened when she saw an emotion in his dark gaze that was indefinable.

"What are you doing here?" Her voice was a low, breathless whisper. "We agreed not to see each other until—"

"*You* agreed," he interrupted, visibly annoyed that he had gone along with her plea. "Do you think it would make it any easier to say goodbye at the airport?"

"Yes, Aaron, it would." She threw up her hands in a gesture signaling hopelessness. "Why do you think I suggested it?"

His gaze narrowed as he moved toward her with the slow, stalking walk she had come to love. There were so many things about Aaron that she loved that she had lost count.

Reaching for her, he held her upper arms and pulled her to his chest. "I think you suggested it because you want to avoid what is going to happen right now."

She tilted her chin, giving him a direct stare. "And that is?"

"Not wanting to hear the truth."

"And what is the truth, Aaron?"

He studied her thoughtfully, his eyes betraying his innermost feelings and telling her what she knew before he uttered the words. "I love you."

Closing her eyes, she swayed slightly at the same time he tightened his grip. "Don't."

"Don't what? Don't love you? I'm sorry, *Princesa,* but I can't turn my feelings on and off the way you're able to."

She opened her eyes and glared at him. "Go away! Please," she continued in a softer tone.

He shook his head slowly. "No, Regina. Any other time I would oblige you, but not tonight."

Pulling out of his loose grip, she turned and walked out of the bedroom. She hadn't gone more than ten feet when he caught up with her.

"Why are you running away?"

She turned to face him. "I'm not running away. I just need to be alone."

The flash of anger in his dark eyes vanished, replaced by a tenderness that twisted her insides into knots. He loved her, while she was too much of a coward to let him know that she loved him.

She laid her hand alongside his jaw, feeling the throbbing muscles under her fingertips. "I'll come to you later."

Grasping her hand, he brought it to his lips and kissed each finger, his gaze never leaving hers. Bending over, he brushed his lips over hers. "I'll be waiting."

He released her hand, turning and walking down the hallway in the direction of his bedroom.

Aaron lay on the bed, arms folded under his head. He hadn't turned on the lamp because the eerie, silvered light of a full moon lit up the bedroom. He had told Regina he would wait for her, and now he had lost track of time, and still she had not come.

Closing his eyes, he felt a lump form in his throat. He had told her he loved her, and she recoiled as if he had struck her. *Fool!* He had been a fool to let her know how he felt. What was the matter with him when it came to affairs of the heart? Why was it he couldn't select a woman who would love him as much as he loved her? The whys attacked him relentlessly until he relaxed enough to fall asleep.

Within seconds something shook him into awareness. He detected the familiar, rain-washed fragrance, then the silken touch of her body as she moved beside him on the bed. Regina had come to him, as promised. She would spend the night with him.

"Please love me, Aaron." Her husky plea broke the pregnant silence.

And he would love her. He would make their last night together special. Moving over her naked form and supporting his greater weight on his arms, he cradled her face between his hands.

"This is not goodbye," he crooned seconds before he covered her mouth in a hungry, soul-searching kiss that indicated they would not be satisfied with a prolonged session of foreplay.

Aaron was relentless when he branded her throat, breasts, and her inner thighs with a passion which would linger in her memory during their separation. His rapacious mouth charted a path from her lips to her feet. Just when she recovered from one shock, she was assailed with another.

Her soft moans of pleasure escalated into long, surrendering groans, with a rising heat rippling under her skin. Her whole being was flooded with a desire that sucked her into an abyss of abandoned ecstasy.

She reached for him, hoping to capture the source which would end her erotic torment. She wanted his hardness in her; she needed him to relieve the burning ache which threatened to shatter her into pieces so that she would never be whole again.

Aaron felt her fingers close around his engorged sex, and groaned aloud. Pulling away from her, he picked up the packet on the bedside table. Making certain to protect her, he eased himself into her wet, hot body.

It became a battle of wills, neither willing to succumb to the explosive passion sweeping them beyond themselves. Tightening his grip on her waist, he reversed their positions, hoping to prolong his ecstasy. But it was not to be. The caress of her distended nipples on his chest, and the vision of her perfectly formed breasts in the full moonlight weakened his resolve, and he surrendered to the explosive passions sweeping him to a place where he had never been.

The triumphant growl of fulfillment floating up from Aaron's throat sent a shiver of chills down Regina's spine, and within seconds she, too, gave in to the hot tide of passion buffeting her up, down, and around until she collapsed on his body, weeping uncontrollably.

He reversed their positions again, withdrawing from her trembling body. Gathering her to his chest, he held her until her sobs subsided, then buried his face in her hair. A pain he had never known assailed him when he realized he had deluded himself. He could not leave her; he would not leave her.

Aaron woke up two hours before dawn reaching for Regina, but encountered an empty space where she had been. Sitting up, he reached for the lamp. Light flooded the room, revealing an envelope on the pillow where her head had lain only hours before. His hand was steady when he picked up the envelope and withdrew its contents. A check for his research institute was nestled between the folds of a single sheet of pale-blue parchment stationery.

He ignored the check as his gaze raced quickly over the neatly slanting script on the page embossed with her monogram. *Do not try to contact me. Please be patient. I will come to you. Regina.*

Closing his eyes, he slumped back against the pillows cradling his broad shoulders. She had ended it with three sentences, and her name. He opened his eyes, and the lethal calmness flowing from their depths matched the hardness of his unreadable expression.

He would not contact her. Not now. Not ever.

Chapter 14

Regina walked onto the tarmac of the private airstrip at the Mexico City airport, smiling broadly when she saw her father alight from the sleek corporate jet. He had come to take her back.

Racing into his outstretched arms, she flung herself against his solid body, reveling in his protective embrace. "Daddy, Daddy," she murmured over and over as she placed tiny kisses on his chin and jaw.

Martin Cole tightened his grip on his daughter's narrow waist, swinging her up into his arms and carrying her up the steps into the jet. He struggled to control his own emotions when he realized he finally was going to get his firstborn back after a ten-year absence. She was only twenty-seven, but it seemed as if they had been separated more than they had been together.

She had called him crying uncontrollably at 2:00 a.m. Eastern Time, begging him to come and get her. He couldn't understand her need to leave Mexico at that time, when the ColeDiz pilot was scheduled to meet her later that afternoon. He called the pilot, apologizing profusely for waking the man, then called the airstrip to have the jet fueled and ready for their departure within the hour.

They were now seated and belted inside the luxury aircraft. The pilot's voice came through the speakers. "Mr. Cole, I've been cleared for takeoff."

Regina held her father's hand, sharing a dimpled smile with him. A casually dressed Martin Cole was breathtakingly handsome at fifty-seven. His close-cropped curly hair was a luminous silver, complementing his sun-browned, olive skin. Perusing his features reminded her that she was truly her father's child, because she had inherited his coloring, dimpled smile, curly hair, large dark eyes, sweeping black eyebrows, high cheekbones, thin delicate nose, and full sensual mouth. Her father was in the full throes of middle age, claiming a network of attractive lines at the corners of his expressive eyes whenever he smiled.

Shifting an eyebrow, he stared at her. "Why the nine-one-one phone call in the middle of the night, Cupcake?"

Pressing her head back against the plush seat, she closed her eyes. "The closer I came to leaving the more I panicked."

What she did not say was that if she had not left when she did, she would not have returned to Florida as promised. Her dependence on Aaron had grown so that she feared not being able to leave him.

"Are you saying you did not want to leave Mexico?"

She hesitated, holding her breath as the plane taxied down the runway before increasing its speed for a liftoff. "Is it ever easy to leave home?"

Martin frowned. "Florida is your home."

She opened her eyes and shook her head. "Florida *was* my home, Daddy. Why do you find it so difficult to accept that I'm an adult now? I was a wife for eight years, and ran my own household in a country I had come to regard as home."

Martin bit back the sharp retort poised on his tongue, leaning over and kissing her forehead. His daughter had experienced what most women twice her age hadn't had to undergo—caring for a sick, elderly husband. She was back, and he did not want to do or say anything that would force her to leave—at least, not for a while. He wanted to hold on to her, knowing instinctively that even though Regina had decided to return to Florida her stay would not be a permanent one.

"Why don't you try to get some sleep? You're going to need it, because I doubt whether you'll get much once everyone realizes you're back."

She closed her eyes, but did not sleep. She did not know why it had taken her ten years to realize home was not a country or a structure, but the people you loved. She loved her family, Oscar, and she had also fallen in love with Aaron.

Aaron was everything his father had been—gentle, considerate, protective, and more. The more was the passion he offered her—a passion that transported her beyond herself, where she felt free to exist without her childhood fears tormenting her.

A wry smile touched her mouth. She would wait until the new year, then travel to Bahia in time for Carnival.

Regina felt a swell of emotion fill her chest at the same time her father maneuvered his favored Jaguar sports coupe into the circular driveway of the sprawling Fort Lauderdale structure that claimed the Atlantic Ocean as its backyard.

She was out of the car before he turned off the ignition, rushing to the entrance to meet her younger sister. Arianna had grown at least another inch since she last saw her. Her parents, brother, and sister had come to visit her in Mexico for her twenty-seventh birthday in July, and while it hadn't been three months, the change in Arianna was startling. It was as if she had grown up overnight.

"Ari! Baby sister," Regina whispered, hugging her tightly and kissing her cheek.

Arianna sobbed softly, clinging to Regina as if she were her lifeline. "If you go away and leave me again, I'll kill myself."

Pulling back, Regina examined her sister's pained expression. Fourteen-year-old Arianna had inherited her parents' best features: towering height, slimness, rich, deep, golden-brown coloring, her mother's green-flecked brown eyes and her mouth, and her father's curly black hair, which she wore in a flattering short style. At five-eight, she hinted of a sensuality which was certain to short-circuit any teenage boy's nervous system.

"I don't want to hear you talk about killing yourself," she admonished softly. "I just buried my husband, Ari. I came back here to reconnect with my family, not bury my only sister."

Arianna nodded quickly, forcing a tearful s mile. "I'm sorry."

"Where're Mommy and Tyler?"

"Tyler went out for a little while, and Mommy's in the house."

Martin Cole walked up to his daughters, his dark eyes shining with pride and happiness. He extended his arms at his sides. "May I escort my lovely princesses into the castle?"

Regina went completely still, staring at her father. *Princesa.* That was what Aaron had called her. She was thousands of miles from him, and still he haunted her.

"Is there something wrong?" Martin questioned.

Shaking her head quickly, she flashed a smile. "No. Not at all." Looping her arm through her father's, she walked into the home filled with both good and bad memories.

Parris Simmons-Cole lay on a chaise beside Regina, holding her hand tightly as they stared at the foam-flecked incoming tide. It had been a long time since she had all of her children together at the same time.

"You've aged me, Angel."

Regina stared at her mother, her mouth gaping. "You look beautiful. No one would take you for fifty."

And they wouldn't. Her mother's hair had grayed considerably, but her hair stylist had lightened some of the remaining dark brown strands, so the overall effect was that of a frosted look. Her flawless skin was smooth and completely wrinkle-free, and five years ago she had begun an intense exercise regimen that kept her slender body well-toned.

Parris closed her eyes behind her oversize sunglasses. "I'm not talking about how I look. It's how I feel. I've never hidden anything from you, so you know what I had to go through just to bring you into the world. Then I lost you for six days, and when I got you back I swore to myself that I would never let you go. But I had to let you go, or I would've spent the rest of my life hating myself if you did not fulfill your dream. It's not easy for a mother to let her firstborn go—especially since you were so young."

Squeezing her mother's fingers, Regina smiled at her. "But everything worked out, didn't it?"

Opening her eyes, Parris smiled and nodded. "Yes, it did. You made me very proud of you."

A shadow blocked out the strong rays of the early fall sun, and Regina glanced up to find her brother standing over her. She sat up quickly, offering him her hand. He pulled her up in one strong, swift motion.

"Tyler!"

Curving his arms around her waist, he picked her up, holding her aloft effortlessly, then released her. "Welcome home, Sis." He kissed her soundly on her mouth.

Staring at her brother, Regina's eyes were filled with pride as she visually examined Tyler Cole. At seventeen, he was as tall as his father, but claimed a lankiness that made him appear more delicate than he actually was. He flashed a rare smile, his dark eyes too serious for someone so young. He, too, had changed since she last saw him. She ran a hand over his head, feeling the stubble against her palm.

"What did you do, shave your head?"

He nodded. "I joined the swim team at school."

Regina wagged her head in amazement. "I don't believe it. The Coles have two swimmers in the family."

Tyler ducked his head, staring at his shoes. "Arianna swims to compete. I've starting swimming to build up muscle. I feel uncomfortable working out in a gym, so I felt swimming was the next best thing."

His head came up, and he stared down at his older sister. Taking her arm, he led her down to the beach and out of range of their mother's hearing.

"How long are you going to hang around this time?"

"Tyler!" she whispered.

"Answer my question, Regina."

"I can't, because I don't know."

"You can't imagine what Arianna and I have had to go through the past ten years."

Her body stiffened in shock. "What are you talking about?"

"Mom and Dad have us on lockdown. They've tightened the reins so much that we feel like we're under house arrest. They lost you and—"

"They didn't lose me," she countered angrily. "I graduated and I moved away. You still have another year before you complete high school, and Ari has four."

"But you were only sixteen," he argued.

"They could've stopped me if they'd wanted to."

"But they didn't."

"So, what's your beef?"

"My *beef* is that I'm not allowed to apply to colleges out of the state. I want to be a doctor, Regina, and for that I want to go to a college where I can get the best medical training available.

And in case you aren't aware of it, Meharry, Harvard, Stanford, and Yale don't have campuses in Florida."

Resting her hands on her hips, she shifted her eyebrows. "So, you really want a career in medicine?" Tyler nodded. "Have you taken your SATs?"

"I took the PSATs last semester."

"What were your scores?"

"I managed a combined score of over fifteen hundred."

She smiled. "My brother, the genius."

"Uncle Josh is the genius in the family. I just study my butt off, that's all."

She sobered quickly. "I had no idea what you and Ari were going through. When you came to Mexico to visit me, why didn't you say something?"

He shrugged his shoulders. "I don't know."

"I'll talk to Daddy about this. I won't let him know that I spoke to you. I'll bring it up casually, and feel him out."

Tyler gave her a wide smile for the first time. "Will you?"

"Of course. And what does Ari want?"

"She wants to be an Olympic swimmer. She's fast," he added quickly. "Very, very fast. Her coach had her try out for a possible spot on the team, and she beat everyone in the one- and two-hundred-meter freestyle competition. You should see her in the four-hundred-meter relay. She's awesome!"

Curving an arm around her brother's waist, she rested her head against his shoulder. "Narrow down the college of your choice, then give me a couple of weeks to see what I can do."

Regina had been in Florida exactly two weeks when she was finally reunited with the entire Cole clan, who had increased appreciably in her absence. Four generations gathered at the family estate in West Palm Beach early one Saturday afternoon.

Her uncle Joshua Kirkland and his wife Vanessa had flown in from Santa Fe, New Mexico, with their son and daughter. Emily had turned twelve, and Michael was now eight. Both children had inherited their father's electric green eyes.

Music producer David Cole and his nurse-wife Serena had doubled their family with a set of twins. Ana and Jason, who had celebrated their first birthday on September twenty-third, joined their older brother and sister, eight-year-old Gabriel and six-year-old Alexandra, adding to the never-ending activity going on at their Boca Raton beachfront home.

Her aunts, Nancy Cole-Thomas and Josephine Cole-Wilson, were grandparents, claiming a half-dozen grandchildren between them. Her grandmother, Marguerite Josephine Diaz-Cole, the family matriarch, had managed to maintain her regal beauty at seventy-eight, while M.J.'s husband of nearly sixty years exhibited signs of aging poorly with his declining health. Samuel Claridge Cole was now eighty-five, and most times now was confined to his bed. A debilitating stroke had left him with limited use of his right arm and leg.

Cradling the twins on either hip, Regina walked across the expansive lawn where everyone lounged under a large tent to escape the harmful rays of the intense Florida sunshine.

Emily Kirkland approached her, holding out her arms. "I'll take one."

Regina handed her Jason, then cradled Ana to her chest, but the child squirmed uncomfortably in her arms. She smiled at the tiny girl, and much to her surprise Ana returned her smile. She was the image of her father, with the exception of her eyes. Ana, along with all of Serena and David's children, claimed their mother's clear brown eyes and their father's dimpled smile.

"I'll take her if she's too heavy for you."

Turning around, Regina smiled at Serena. "I don't mind holding her. It's time this little princess and I became better acquainted with each other."

"Why don't you come back to Boca with us tonight, and hang

out for a couple of days? David and I would love to have you," she added when Regina hesitated.

"You, Uncle David, or Alex?"

Petite Serena Morris-Cole ran a hand through the profusion of short reddish-brown curls sticking to her moist forehead, flashing a knowing smile. She had recently celebrated her thirty-ninth birthday and had given birth to four children, yet could easily pass for someone in her late twenties.

"It's Alexandra. Ever since she realized her cousin was, as she says, 'a moo-vee star' she's been bugging me to ask you if you would come and tell her about your acting career."

"Doesn't the child know I only have two films to my credit?"

"Tell that to a six-year-old."

"I can't go back with you tonight. Arianna and I have plans to do some shopping in the morning. What I'll do is come up to Boca during the week and stay for a few days."

Regina handed Ana to her mother, then spent the next four hours relaxing, eating, laughing, and interacting with her many cousins. Everyone waited for their food to settle before they retreated to the pool house to change into swimwear.

Arianna and Tyler stood at the edge of the Olympic-size pool, their arms hanging limply at their sides as an eerie hush settled over the assembly. Regina glanced at her parents, who stood together, arms around each other. She smiled behind the lenses of her sunglasses, but at the same time an emotion she identified as jealousy welled up in her chest.

Her parents were still in love, and the man she had fallen in love with was thousands of miles away. She had seen Martin and Parris's furtive glances when they did not think she noticed, and on more than one occasion she saw her father caress her mother's body in a way that made her feel she was spying on them. Parris Simmons had been twenty-two when she met Martin Cole for the first time, but had to wait ten years before she could claim him as her husband and a father for her daughter.

Closing her eyes briefly, she tried imagining it was Aaron she had been married to, and not his father. Instead of becoming Oscar Spencer's widow she would be Aaron Spencer's wife, and probably the mother of his child or children. She opened her eyes, frowning. She did not want to think about Aaron, any more than she wanted to love him.

All thoughts of him vanished as she watched her brother and sister dive into the pool. Moving closer, she was transfixed by the form and speed of Arianna as she sliced through the water like a silent torpedo. There was complete silence, everyone watching her swim to the opposite end of the pool, turn, then push off to return. Arianna was halfway across the pool before her brother made his turn.

David Cole extended a hand to his niece, helping her from the water, and handing her a towel. He shook his head in amazement. "Martin, are you certain your daughter doesn't have webbed feet?" he teased with an attractive, lopsided smile.

Arianna blotted water from her short hair, grinning broadly. "Anyone want to race?" Despite the exertion, she was breathing normally. She pointed to her uncle with the silver-blond hair. "How about it, Uncle Josh?"

Joshua Kirkland waved a delicate hand. "Too full."

She snapped the towel in his direction. "Too full, or too frightened?"

Joshua gave her a warm smile. "Too old," he confirmed. "Why don't you challenge some of the younger guys?"

Arianna stalked her young male cousins. "Come on, guys. Don't tell me you're scared of a *girl?*" She encountered silence.

Nancy Cole-Thomas leaned over and whispered in her youngest son's ear and he stepped forward, pulling his T-shirt over his head.

The setting sun glinted off his brown back. "Let's go, Ari," he challenged. He didn't fare any better than Tyler. She beat him by an even larger margin.

Regina saw the exhibition of Arianna's prowess as the perfect opportunity to approach her parents. Moving next to her father, she wound her arm through his free one.

"Ari has the makings of a world-class champion," she said softly.

Martin arched his eyebrows, his impassive expression never changing. "You think so?"

"I *know* so, Daddy."

"What are you suggesting, Cupcake?"

"You should let her compete."

"She does compete."

"She competes locally. That's not enough."

Turning his head, he stared down her, meeting her direct stare. "Say what's on your mind."

"She needs to follow her dream, Daddy. And that dream is to make the next Olympic team."

"You think she could make it?"

"I *know* she could. Think of the publicity she would get, too, being an African-American swimmer instead of a runner, gymnast, or a basketball player in the upcoming summer games."

"That would mean that she would travel with the swim team and—"

"She would be away for a while, but she would always come back home," Regina interrupted. "I did," she added quietly.

Curving his arm around his daughter's waist, Martin pulled her closer and kissed the top of her head. "You're right, Cupcake. You did come back home."

Closing her eyes, Regina prayed for strength. She knew her stay in Florida was to become a short one—she doubted whether she would stay until the end of the year. She had tried filling her days and nights with activity when she redesigned her mother's flower garden and spent hours in her grandparents' formal gardens, but when she least expected it remnants of what she had shared with Aaron filled her thoughts. She felt his invisible pull, binding them together across thousands of miles.

Martin nodded, smiling. "I'll let her compete. Now, before you dance a jig, tell me what Tyler wants."

She stared at her father, complete shock freezing her features. "You knew?"

"Of course we knew," Parris replied, peering around her husband. Her deep, sultry voice was filled with repressed laughter. "We know our children a lot better than they think we do."

Regina hugged her parents, then kissed their cheeks. "You guys are so cool."

Parris affected a frown. "Your father and I aren't that *cool*. What we've come to realize is that Tyler and Arianna are growing up, and we have to do whatever it takes to help them fulfill their destinies. I'd love to have my children with me forever, but that's not realistic. You'll be faced with the same dilemma once you have your own children," she predicted sagely.

I hope I won't, she prayed silently. If or when she ever became a mother, she hoped she would remain objective enough to know when to let go.

Chapter 15

Bahia, Brazil

Aaron Spencer lounged on a chair in his study, staring at the images on the television screen. He could not remember how often he had viewed *Silent Witness* since he had ordered a copy of the movie two weeks ago, but after the first half-dozen times he activated the mute button on the remote and only watched the flickering images. There was no need for him to hear the dialogue, because he had memorized every line.

When the camera first captured the image of a seventeen-year-old Regina Cole walking through the AeroMexico terminal, he'd caught and held his breath until a lack of oxygen forced him to release it. It was as if her face and body made love to the camera. He'd been transfixed by the sultry sound of her voice, the way she moved, and her unabashed innocence. He did not know why, but he felt betrayed whenever he watched her love scenes with her costar, and had begun fast-forwarding those segments.

He had returned to Bahia and fully immersed himself in his work at the hospital, the research institute, and his coffee plantation. His foreman had predicted an excellent yield for an April or May harvest. What he could not do was erase the memory of Regina Spencer from his mind. She haunted his days, as well as his nights, and there were times when he sat up all night, only to fall asleep with the sunrise.

This night was to become one of those.

Fort Lauderdale, Florida

Regina left her bed for the first time in twenty-four hours, showered, shampooed her hair, and changed into a pair of sweatpants with an oversize T-shirt. She was sitting at the kitchen table drinking a cup of tea sweetened with honey and flavored with a slice of lemon when her mother walked in.

Parris gave her a warm smile. "Are you feeling better this morning?"

She nodded, grimacing as a wave of dizziness swept over her, bringing with it chills while leaving a layer of moisture on her brow. "A little."

Parris sat down at the table, peering closely at her daughter and noticing the hollows under her high cheekbones. She had lost weight. Placing the back of her hand against her forehead, she frowned.

"You feel a little warm. I'm going to call the doctor for an appointment."

Regina felt too weak to protest. Whenever her stomach churned and rejected its contents, she was left feeling lethargic and listless during the aftermath of several violent retchings.

"I'm going back to bed," she murmured, pushing to her feet. She met her father as he walked into the kitchen, tightening a silk tie under the collar of a pristine white shirt.

He stopped and kissed her damp hair. "Still under the weather, Cupcake?"

"Yeah," she moaned, moving slowly in the direction of her bedroom.

She flopped down across the bed, willing the tea to stay down. Her stomach settled itself, and she let out her breath slowly. She had been back for six weeks, and during that time she hadn't had a menstrual flow. She hadn't told her mother, but she did not need a doctor or anyone else to tell her that she was carrying Aaron Spencer's child. And she also knew exactly when it had occurred—the night she had offered him her virginity.

Regina waited until she was seated in the car with her mother, then disclosed the doctor's findings. "Congratulations. You're going to be a grandmother."

Parris's hand froze as she attempted to put the key in the car's ignition. "How? Who? Where?" The three words came out in a staccato cadence. Unbuckling her seatbelt, she turned toward her daughter.

"Which question do you want me to answer first?" Regina replied flippantly, then sobered when she saw a warning cloud settle on her mother's usually pleasant features.

"I'm sorry," she continued in a softer tone. "The who is Aaron Spencer. And the where was in Mexico." Parris's astonishment was apparent when her delicate jaw dropped slightly. "We hadn't planned for it to happen, but circumstances being what they were we became emotionally as well as physically involved with each other."

"Do you love him?"

Closing her eyes, she nodded slowly. "Yes."

"How long have you known him?"

"Not long at all," Regina admitted. "We spent a total of five weeks together."

Letting out her breath in an audible sigh, Parris managed a

knowing smile. She had been more than familiar with young love. "You're good. It took me about two weeks to fall in love with your father."

Regina smiled for the first time since hearing the doctor confirm her suspicions. "That's because he saved your life. Daddy was your hero."

Her father had saved her mother's life when her ex-husband tried to drown her after she had rejected his advances for a reconciliation. What she hadn't verbalized was that Aaron had become *her* hero, protecting her from all seen and unseen. With him she was safe.

"And he still is," Parris admitted. "Does Aaron know that you love him?"

"No."

"Why not?"

"I couldn't tell him."

"Do you know if he loves you?"

"He said he did, but I don't know about now. I left him without saying goodbye."

Parris touched her daughter's cheek. "What's going to happen now? I hope you're going to tell him about the baby."

Biting down hard on her lower lip, Regina turned to stare out the side window. "I've decided to tell him in person."

Parris closed her eyes briefly, willing the tears welling up behind her eyelids not to fall. "When are you leaving?"

"In a couple of weeks," she replied noncommittally, twisting the circle of diamonds around her finger.

"What about marriage?"

A slight frown furrowed her forehead as she turned to meet her mother's gaze. A shaft of sunlight highlighted the green in Parris's clear brown eyes, reminding Regina of a pairing of brilliant emeralds and warm golden topaz.

"I'm not going to marry a man just because I'm carrying his child."

Parris opened her mouth, then closed it just as quickly. Whatever impasse Regina would have with Aaron Spencer would have to be solved by them. She hoped the man her daughter had chosen to father her child would be puissant enough to withstand Regina's formidable personality.

Regina's planned departure from Fort Lauderdale was vastly different than the one of a decade ago. The early morning breakfast she shared with her parents, brother, and sister was filled with laughter and a few ribald jokes about scantily clad women from a normally serious Tyler when he promised to visit her in Bahia during Carnival.

Martin Cole glanced at his watch and stood up. He pushed back his chair. "Let's go, Cupcake. It's time we left." He would drive her to the airport, then return to the offices of ColeDiz International, Ltd. for a monthly board meeting. He looked forward to the meetings because they offered him the opportunity to spend a few days with his half brother. Even though Joshua Kirkland still maintained an apartment in Palm Beach, he preferred living with his family in the Southwest. He had relocated to Santa Fe after he retired from a career as the former decorated Associate Coordinating Chief of the Army's Defense Intelligence Agency.

Parris also rose to her feet. "And I have to go into the shop this morning." She had set up an interior design business in nearby Hollywood, Florida, after Arianna entered high school, but had limited her clients to no more than a half-dozen at any given time.

Regina stood up, holding out her arms to her brother and sister. The three hugged tightly while sharing a secret smile, then she walked over to her mother. "I'll call you as soon as I arrive," she promised.

"I pray you find a lasting happiness this time."

"So do I," Regina whispered.

Parris stared at her, tears filling her eyes, then turned and walked out of the kitchen to grieve in private. Tyler and Arianna stared at their mother's departing back and followed her.

Picking up her handbag from the countertop, making certain it contained her passport, traveler's checks, and an ample amount of Brazilian currency, Regina walked out of the house and to the garage, where her father waited beside his car.

Smiling up at him, she said teasingly, "I must have been a Gypsy or a bedouin in another life."

He dropped an arm around her shoulders. "You're a lot like I was at your age. It was as if I was living two lives simultaneously, traveling from country to country on business."

"When did it stop?"

He gave her a smile that reminded her of her own. "After I married your mother."

She shifted an arching eyebrow. "But I *was* married."

Martin's smile faded. "You married the wrong man the first time, Regina."

"Like my mother?"

He nodded. "I know you'll get it right the next time." Opening the passenger-side door, he helped her into the car, then took his position behind the wheel.

Both were silent during the drive to the airport, each lost in their private musings—Martin wishing the best for his willful daughter, Regina trying to imagine Aaron's reaction when he saw her again. He would notice the most obvious change first, leaving her to tell him of the changes going on within her body. What she did not try to predict was his reaction to the news that he was to become a father.

They arrived at the Fort Lauderdale Airport, she hugging and kissing her father once they neared the security sector. "I love you, Daddy."

He closed his eyes, smiling. "And I love you, too, Cupcake."

He opened his eyes, his expression sobering. "I want you to take care of yourself and my grandchild."

"I will," she promised.

"If you need me—for anything—I want you to pick up the phone and call."

"I will," she repeated.

Those were the last words they shared before she turned and made her way to the area where she would be cleared to board her flight. Half an hour later she was seated in the private jet, en route to Brazil.

Regina stared out the small window, her eyes widening in amazement as the jet lost altitude in preparation for a landing. She had not been able to fathom the size of Brazil with its magnificent Amazon River and awesome rain forest. Observing *Salvador da Bahia* for the first time from an aerial view was something that would stay with her forever. Built on a bluff, Salvador, Brazil's first capital, overlooked *Bahia de Todos os Santos*.

She recalled Aaron Spencer's deep voice when he had spoken of the beauty and majesty of the country he had decided to make his home. He had related that eighty percent of Salvador's two million people were black—as evidenced by the region's music, art, dance, cuisine, and festivals—but she did not understand why he was still an American. Even though he had lived in the South American country most of his life, he had elected not to relinquish his coveted U.S. citizenship status.

Regina felt the intense heat and humidity the moment she walked out of the *Aeroporto Dois de Julho* following the baggage handler, who led her to an awaiting car. It was the middle of November, and in another two weeks the Brazilian summer season would officially begin.

She ignored the admiring glances men threw her way as she passed them, her attention focused on the driver standing beside the car. He nodded, opened the rear door for her, then closed it.

Settling back against the leather seat, she closed her eyes and inhaled the cool air coming from the automobile's vents.

Her father's longtime personal secretary had seen to her travel arrangements, from securing a ninety-day visa to reserving a car and driver for the trip from the airport to Aaron's home. Philip Trent, ColeDiz's senior attorney, had made certain funds from her personal account were wired to a Salvador branch of *Banco do Brasil* for her use.

She was prepared to spend three months in Salvador, the capital of the northeast state of Bahia, then return home. The tentative plans she had made to secure her own home and set up a business were delayed because of her impending motherhood.

Thinking of becoming a mother wrung a satisfied smile from her as the driver drove quickly and expertly over cobblestone streets lined with ornate churches from the early sixteenth century.

There were times during her marriage to Oscar when she wished it had been a real one, in which she could actually feel like a wife. She had wanted to share her husband's bed and also his body, and there were times during the eight years that she thought about having a child. She had then dismissed the notion as quickly as it had come to mind. There would have been no way she could have cared for a child and a terminally ill husband at the same time. And it would not have been fair to Oscar, knowing he would never live to see his child reach adulthood.

A part of Oscar would now live on in his grandchild. Closing her eyes, she placed a slender hand over her flat middle, praying silently for a son, a son who would inherit the gentleness of both his father and grandfather. The rolling motion of the car lulled her into a state of total relaxation, and within minutes she succumbed to the drowsiness that seemed to envelop her now when she least expected it. When the driver turned off the local road and onto the one leading to the da Costa property, she missed the many acres of coffee trees putting forth their abundant yield for a May harvest. It wasn't until the car came to a complete stop that she opened her eyes and peered through the glass at the structure Aaron Laurence Spencer called home.

The driver opened the rear door, extended his hand, and pulled her gently to her feet. *"Obrigado,"* she said softly, pleased she had remembered the Portuguese word for thank you. She knew very few words of Portuguese, but her knowledge of Spanish would serve her better than if she didn't understand any of the language.

Standing beside the car, she waited for the driver to make his way across an open courtyard to the entrance of a two-story, stucco farmhouse with a red-tiled roof. There were several smaller buildings constructed in the same Spanish-Moorish architecture as the main house several hundred feet away, and Regina wondered who or what had occupied these buildings over the years.

The driver returned and retrieved her luggage from the trunk of his car, then motioned with his head for her to follow him. *"Por favor, Senhora."*

She followed the man, grateful that he spoke Portuguese and Spanish. Each step she took brought her closer to her destiny, and she knew even if she did not marry Aaron Spencer their lives would always be linked to each other because of the tiny child growing beneath her breasts.

The solid wooden door opened and a petite, dark-skinned woman with crinkling, graying hair pulled back in a tight chignon glared up at her. Observing her, Regina saw every race of Brazil etched on her face: African, European, and Native Indian. It wasn't possible to tell her age, because in spite of the graying hair her skin was flawless and wrinkle-free.

Her dark eyes saw everything, missing nothing—especially the diamond wedding band Regina wore on the third finger of her left hand. She drew in a quick breath, then let it out slowly, turning her attention to the driver. "Tell Senhora Spencer that Senhor Spencer is not here, but she may come in."

The driver translated in Spanish, and Regina smiled at the woman for the first time, nodding. She stepped into the entry and followed the woman through an inner courtyard open to the sky, then into a living room with a vaulted brick ceiling. She was not given time to survey her surroundings, since the woman gestured to her.

They made their way up a curving staircase with a wrought-iron railing, the driver following with her luggage, to the second floor. Thick, bare, white plaster walls and a brick flooring kept the interiors cool, offsetting the intense heat of a country set south of the equator.

The older woman opened the door to a room, and stood aside. Regina walked in, then the driver, who placed her luggage in a corner. A majestic octagonal ceiling rose twenty feet above bare, stark-white walls and a polished wood floor, making it a place of beauty. She knew instinctively it was Aaron's bedroom.

Opening her purse, she withdrew several *reis* notes and handed them to her driver. He thanked her profusely in Spanish before turning to the housekeeper and addressing her in rapid Portuguese. Whatever he said seemed to affect the woman, who nodded apologetically.

He turned his attention back to Regina. "Senhora Pires will bring you some refreshment before you take your *siesta*. I hope you'll enjoy your stay in our wonderful country."

"I'm certain I will," she replied, successfully stifling a yawn. What she wanted to tell the driver was that she did not want anything to eat or drink as much as she wanted to sleep, because she had eaten lunch during the flight. There was only a two-hour time difference between the eastern United States and eastern Brazil, so jet lag was not a factor.

Waiting until she was left alone, she removed her shoes, slacks, blouse and bra, but left on her panties. Then she pulled back a colorful handmade quilt and slipped under a cool cotton sheet. The scent of Aaron's cologne swept over her as she closed her eyes. Ten minutes later, the smell of coffee and fresh bread wafted in her nostrils, but she did not open her eyes.

If she had, she would have seen the cold fury in the depths of Magda Pires's malevolent gaze.

Chapter 16

Regina woke hours later, totally disoriented. Lengthening shadows crisscrossed the room, giving no indication of the hour. Rolling over onto her back, she stared up at the ceiling. Then she remembered. She was in Bahia, and in Aaron's bedroom.

"*Boa tarde,* Senhora Spencer."

Recognizing the deep male voice, she gasped, noticing Aaron's presence for the first time. He sat in a corner, his face hidden in the shadows.

Sitting up, she pulled the sheet over her naked breasts. "Good afternoon," she replied, her voice lower than usual with the lingering effects of sleep.

Aaron closed his eyes, and at the same time his grip on the arms of the chair tightened. He forced himself not to move, not to go to her. His housekeeper had called him at the institute, asking if he would be home for the evening meal because his *wife* had arrived, and he had known she was referring to Regina Cole-Spencer. If she had introduced herself as Senhora Spencer, then Magda would assume that she was his wife instead of his stepmother.

Opening his eyes, he visually examined the woman on his bed. She had changed. Missing was the waist-length curly hair, and in its place was a sleek style with the remaining glossy, black curls swept off her face and long neck. If possible, she was even more beautiful than he had remembered. She appeared older, more sophisticated.

Looping one knee over the other, he crossed his arms over his chest. "Why did you come?"

Her gaze widened. "Why? Because I told you I would, that's why."

"You did not *tell* me, Regina. You left me a note!"

"I left you a note because I couldn't face you."

"Why? Because you were too much of a coward to say whatever you needed to say to my face?"

Regina felt a rush of heat suffuse her face. "It had nothing to do with cowardice. I had to leave when I did or I never would've returned to Florida. I'd been away for eight years—eight long years."

Aaron uncrossed his leg, placing both feet firmly on the floor. "What are you talking about?" he questioned softly, rising to his feet and closing the distance between them.

Regina stared up at him in a stunned silence when she saw his face. If she had changed, he had, too. He still wore his hair close to his scalp, but he had added a moustache to his lean, clean-shaven face—a moustache that was an exact replica of Oscar's. Her gaze followed him as he sat down on the bed beside her. She flinched slightly when he laid his right hand along her jaw.

"If I had left Mexico with you I don't think I would've returned to the States," she confessed.

"Why?" He leaned in closer, inhaling the clean, feminine scent that was exclusively Regina Spencer's.

Her gaze fused with his. "Because I had fallen in love with

you, Aaron. It was easier for me to leave you at *El Cielo* than have you walk away from me at the airport."

Aaron flashed an easy, open smile for the first time since he had returned to Bahia from Mexico. He arched a sweeping eyebrow. "You love me?" He seemed amazed by her admission.

Regina lowered her gaze in a demure gesture. *"Sí."*

"And I, you," he whispered, pressing her gently back against the pillows cradling her shoulders. His mouth closed over hers, telling her silently how much he had missed her. What began as a tender joining, a series of slow, shivery kisses, became a hot, hungry possession as he devoured her mouth.

Succumbing to the forceful dominance of his mouth, Regina pressed her parted lips to his, capturing his thrusting tongue. The heat in his large, powerful body was transferred to hers, and her hands were as busy as his when she unbuttoned his shirt and pushed it off his wide shoulders.

Their mouths still joined, Aaron quickly divested himself of his slacks and briefs. There was only the sound of their labored breathing and the whisper of fabric against bare skin, followed by the satisfied moans of their bodies joining in a familiar act of possession.

He suddenly went still. His passion for the woman he held to his heart was spiraling out of control, and he wanted to prolong their fulfillment until the last possible moment. It was not to be.

Lowering his head, his mouth closed over an erect nipple, causing Regina to writhe sensuously beneath him. He suckled her breasts relentlessly, the motion sweeping down her body to the secret place between her thighs, her soft whimpers firing his blood. Everything that was Regina—her feminine scent, silken limbs, husky voice, and tight, hot, moist body—pulled Aaron in so that he forgot who he was.

"I've missed you, *Princesa*. I've missed you so much."

She nodded, unable to verbalize how much she missed him

as her hands moved over his back and down his hips. Her fingers tightened on the firm muscles of his hips when he began moving inside her.

Nothing mattered, only his comforting weight and the hardness between his muscled thighs sliding in and out of her throbbing flesh and increasing her fever-pitch desire for him.

Her lust for him overrode everything else, and she surrendered to the fiery passion, soaring to an awesome, shuddering climax as the screams in the back of her throat erupted and then faded away in a lingering sigh of sated delight.

Aaron's own pleasure peaked and exploded with a frenzied thrusting of his powerful hips and a deep, rumbling moan of gratification. His heart pounded painfully in his chest as he tried forcing air into his labored lungs. Not only were they man and woman, but she had become heart of his heart, and flesh of his flesh. He loved her; he loved her so much he feared losing himself if she ever left him again. Burying his face between her scented shoulder and neck, he rained kisses across the silken flesh.

Curving her arms around Aaron's strong neck, Regina pressed her mouth to his ear. "I have something to tell you," she whispered quietly.

Pulling back slightly, he stared down at her mysterious expression. "What?"

"Estou grávida," she confessed in Portuguese.

He withdrew from her warm flesh, reaching for her shoulders at the same time and pulling her to sit across his lap. He stared at her, complete surprise on his face.

"What did you say?"

"I'm pregnant," she repeated in English.

Aaron gave her a narrow, glinting look, and she silently berated herself for telling him about the baby. She had made a mistake. She never should have come to Brazil.

Pulling away from him, she attempted to scramble off the bed, but was thwarted when he curved an arm around her waist, not allowing her to escape him. He released her body, then captured her head between his large hands. There was no mistaking the smile of extreme joy lighting up his dark eyes.

"Oh, *Princesa*. You've just made me the happiest man in the world."

Regina collapsed against his chest in relief. "You want this baby?"

Running his fingers through her shortened curls, he wagged his head. "You beautiful, silly goose. What made you think I wouldn't?"

She shrugged a bare, slender shoulder. "I don't know." Her voice was muffled in his chest. "You just seemed so stunned."

He laughed softly. "Of course I was stunned. I'm still stunned."

Her soft laugh joined his. "You hit the jackpot the first time we made love."

"I hit the jackpot the day I met you," he countered.

She curved into the comforting warmth of his body and closed her eyes. "What do you want, Aaron? Boy or a girl?"

"It doesn't matter as long as it's healthy. Speaking of healthy, I assume you've seen an obstetrician."

"Yes."

"When are you due?"

"June twelfth."

"Perfect timing. We'll be harvesting this year's coffee crop in late April and early May."

"I won't be here for the harvesting."

He froze. "Why not?"

"I'm only staying three months."

Easing back, he stared at her as if he had never seen her before. "You can't!"

"I'm here on a ninety-day visa."

"You can always renew the damn visa. We'll travel to Argentina, then reenter the country with another ninety-day visa."

"No."

"You can't go back."

"I have to, Aaron. I want my child born on U.S. soil."

"It won't matter where the baby is born. Both of us are United States citizens."

"I can't stay," she argued.

"If it's a question of citizenship or the renewal of visas, we can always get around that by getting married."

She felt a fist of disappointment squeeze her heart when he mentioned marriage. He claimed he loved her, but had only mentioned marriage when she spoke of leaving him. He had equated marriage to a form of proprietorship. He wanted to hold on to her the way he held onto his coffee plantation—with a license or a deed.

Her gaze did not waver as she caught and held his. "I will stay six months, Aaron. Don't ask me to promise more than that. Then I'm going back to Florida to have my baby. I will schedule my return for the first week in May."

Aaron struggled to control his temper. "Oh, now it's *your* baby," he drawled sarcastically.

"Don't fight me," she warned softly.

"Fight? I'll make you sorry you ever drew a breath if you try keeping my child from me, Senhora Spencer."

Her eyes narrowed as she went to her knees. "Don't ever threaten me—"

"Or what?" he said, cutting her off. "You'll tell your rich and powerful father that I threatened his little girl?"

The very air around them was electrified with a tension thick enough to swallow them whole, neither willing to concede as they stared at each other.

Regina couldn't believe how their red, hot passion had turned to red, hot fury. Tilting her chin in a haughty gesture, she slid gracefully off the bed. Unmindful of her nakedness, she folded her hands on her hips.

"Please show me to a bathroom where I can wash before I get dressed."

Moving off the bed, Aaron towered over her, his arms folded across his bare chest. "This will be your bedroom. The bathroom is the door on the right, and your dressing room is on the left."

He reached for his slacks on the foot of the bed and slipped into them, his gaze never leaving her face. "We usually eat the evening meal at eight, but in deference to your condition we'll dine earlier. I'll tell Magda to expect us in an hour."

He turned and walked across the room, opened the door to the dressing room, and disappeared, leaving her staring at the space where he had been. She glanced at a clock on a table with several framed black and white photographs, noting the time. It was only five-thirty. She had spent the afternoon sleeping, making love, and arguing with Aaron. It was not what she had anticipated for her first day in Bahia. She would take a bath and change for dinner, but first she would call her family and confirm her safe arrival.

Picking up the telephone on one of the bedside tables, she dialed the international code for the United States, then the area code and telephone number for her parents' home. Arianna answered the call. She exchanged greetings with her brother, mother, and father. It was another fifteen minutes before she hung up to prepare herself to face Aaron again. Her delicate jaw tightened when she realized her relationship with him had changed, and it was the new life growing inside her that was responsible for that change.

She had promised him she would remain in Bahia for six months, and she prayed she would be able to fulfill that promise.

* * *

Regina took a leisurely bath in a bathroom from a bygone era. Ivy climbed up one wall through the wrought-iron grillwork of the windows, bringing the outdoors inside. The collection of blue glass vials, containers, and vases cradling grooming supplies and plant cuttings were a vivid contrast against the sand-colored stucco walls. The brick floor was nearly worn smooth from thousands of feet wearing down its surface over hundreds of years.

She stepped out of the tepid, scented water and reached for a thick, thirsty towel in a cobalt blue. Blotting her moist face, she walked over to a shelf and peered at a collection of elegant razors with handles inlaid with pearl, onyx, jade, and several semi-precious stones.

Bending down, she attempted to dry her legs and feet and slumped to the floor as the objects in the room began spinning. Gasping, she tried swallowing back a wave of nausea. Crawling on her hands and knees, she made it over to the commode.

At the same time, Aaron walked into the bathroom. He held her gently while she purged the contents of her stomach, then placed a cool cloth over her face and helped her brush her teeth and rinse her mouth before he carried her back to the bedroom.

He placed her on the bed where they had made love less than an hour before and held her until she rewarded him with a dimpled smile. "*Muito obrigado,* Aaron."

"You're very welcome," he replied, returning her smile. "How much Portuguese have you learned?"

"Just enough to be polite."

"You knew how to say I'm pregnant." She nodded, closing her eyes against his intense stare. "How often do you throw up?"

She opened her eyes. "At least twice a day."

"You're losing weight." It was more of a statement than a

question. "When I go to the hospital tomorrow I'm taking you with me. I want Dr. Nicolas Benedetti to look at you."

"I'm okay now," she said, pulling out of his loose embrace. "I'd like to get dressed." Aaron left the bed and returned to the chair where he had sat watching her sleep. Regina stared across the room at him, unable to believe he was going to sit and watch her dress. "Aaron, please give me a little privacy."

"No." He draped one leg over the other. "I'm not moving. You can get dressed with me right here. There's nothing you have I haven't seen before. Try to think of me as your personal physician."

"But, you're not."

He flashed a wide grin. "Oh, but I am, *Princesa*. Very few Bahian doctors make house calls."

She knew he was not going to leave, so she walked over to the loveseat where she had placed the dress and underwear she had selected to wear to dinner.

It was impossible to ignore his dark, burning gaze as she slipped into a pair of dark brown, lace bikini panties with a matching demi-bra. She thought she heard Aaron's intake of breath when she leaned over to pick up a loose-fitting dress made of an airy voile fabric in a soft, eggshell-white. She had just slipped her arms into the sleeveless garment that ended mid-calf when he rose to his feet and crossed the room.

Standing in front of her, he gently brushed her hands away and fastened the tiny pearl buttons lining the front. The heat of his freshly showered body caused her to sway gently, and he caught her shoulders to steady her. He was as casually dressed as she was. He had elected to wear a taupe-colored, short-sleeved cotton shirt with a pair of black linen slacks and loafers.

He smiled, exhibiting his straight, white teeth under his neatly barbered moustache when he glanced down at her narrow feet. "Are you going to take the phrase barefoot and pregnant literally?"

She wiggled her professionally groomed toes. "My shoes are in the smaller bag." She pointed to her luggage in the corner.

"I'll have Magda unpack your clothes and put them away." Walking over to her luggage, he recognized the superior quality of the kidskin leather. "Which pair do you want?"

"Any sandal."

He withdrew a pair of black, patent leather mules with a two-inch heel. Easing her down to the loveseat, he bent down and slipped them on her feet. Staring up at her, he smiled. "Do you need help with your hair?"

Regina wrinkled her delicate nose. "I think I can manage, thank you." Returning to the bathroom, she brushed her hair off her face, then outlined her mouth with a soft orange color. Turning, she saw Aaron standing several feet away, watching her every move. "I'm ready," she replied breathlessly.

He held out his hand, and she caught his fingers. Pulling her to his side, he examined her features intently. "If anyone asks about our relationship I'll tell them that you are my wife." He ignored her sharp intake of breath. "It will save a lot of explaining once your pregnancy becomes apparent." He did not say that if they lived the lie long enough perhaps it would become a reality.

She nodded, acquiescing. It wasn't as if she wasn't a Mrs. Spencer. She just wasn't Mrs. Aaron Spencer.

Regina and Aaron dined alfresco on a terrace garden under an allée of areca palms, which gave the appearance of an encroaching jungle in a civilized oasis. A cooling ocean breeze made eating under the sky possible once the sun traveled overhead in a westward direction.

The outdoor wooden furniture had acquired a natural patina, with a quartet of chairs covered with rush seats. A nearby bench was flanked by large clay urns overflowing with ferns indigenous to the region.

Aaron watched with amusement when Regina's gaze lingered

on overgrown sections of the untamed land. He cleared his throat, recapturing her attention.

"What do you think?"

Arching a sweeping eyebrow, she angled her head. "About what?"

"The garden."

"It has a lot of potential. How long has it been neglected?"

"Too long," he replied. "This garden was my aunt's pride and joy."

Regina took a long sip of chilled bottled water, meeting his gaze over the rim of her glass. "Would you mind if I suggested a few renovations?"

"I was hoping you'd ask. Every acre of this land is yours, *Princesa*. Make any change you want."

Placing her glass on the table, she laughed, her low, husky voice floating and lingering sensuously in the warm air. "I don't believe you would actually trust me with your precious coffee plantation."

I would trust you with my life, he said silently. "And why wouldn't I?" he queried aloud. "It's a known fact that Cole-Diz International owns and manages several coffee plantations throughout the Caribbean, and I'm willing to bet you know as much about the plant as I do."

"The only thing I'll concede at this time is that I've given up drinking it for the next year."

Aaron was right. She was very knowledgeable about the planting, cultivating, and harvesting of coffee.

His gaze went from her face to her chest. "Do you plan to breast-feed?"

"I would like to."

His eyes crinkled in a smile. "Good."

She picked up her fork and concentrated on finishing her meal, which consisted of a salad, *arroz, feijãao,* and *carne*—white rice, black beans, and steak—grilled with peppers and spices.

"How many acres do you use for your coffee fields?" she asked after a comfortable silence.

"Eight thousand out of a possible twelve."

"It didn't realize it was that large."

"It's the largest in Bahia. Leonardo da Costa's family was one of the largest landowners in Bahia for several centuries. They controlled the country's sugar industry from the time Salvador was the capital of colonial Brazil until the eighteenth century. After the decline in international sugar prices they lost most of their wealth. My aunt married the last surviving da Costa, and when she failed to produce an heir the bloodline ended with Leonardo."

Regina touched her lips with a cloth napkin. "May I have a brief tour of the garden before it gets too dark to see anything?"

Aaron rose to his feet and came around the table to pull back her chair. "I'll show you the coffee fields at another time. But if you're willing to get up at five, you can come with me when I drive down to meet with the foreman."

"I don't think so, Aaron."

He shrugged a shoulder in the elegant gesture she hadn't seen in a long time. "Just asking."

Holding her hand firmly, he guided her over a slate path to a world of overgrown trees, shrubs, and wildflowers. Ivy and ferns were growing in riotous disarray, spilling over stone walls and benches.

Regina stopped, pointing to a marble figure obscured by a tangle of climbing vines. "There's a fountain."

Releasing her hand, Aaron reached through the vines, trying to pull them away from the figure, which held a pitcher from which water had poured into a small pool many years ago.

He shook his head, sighing heavily. "They are going to have to be cut away. The vines are probably choking an underground pool. Look," he said, pointing to a damp area on the flagstone path. "The pool was over here."

Regina felt her pulses racing. Instead of designing a garden, she would undertake restoring this one to its former magnificence. Working on the garden would give her something to do while Aaron was away from the house during the day.

"Tomorrow I'll begin identifying flowers, vines, trees, and ferns," she said excitedly.

"You're going to have to postpone your project for a day. Remember, you're coming to the hospital with me tomorrow for a checkup with Nicolas Benedetti."

She nodded. "Can you hire an assistant for me?"

His hands slipped up her bare arms, bringing her closer and molding her soft curves to the contours of his body. "What else do you want, *Princesa?*"

Tilting her chin, she gave him a dazzling smile. "That's all for now."

He lowered his head until their lips were only inches apart. "Are you sure?"

She inhaled his moist breath, closing her eyes. "Yes."

"The assistant is yours," he whispered seconds before he claimed the sweetness of her lush mouth. He tightened his hold on her body, moaning slightly when she looped her arms around his neck and returned his kiss. Both were breathing heavily when the kiss ended.

Aaron smiled down at the dreamy expression on her face. "One of these days I'm going to make love to you in your garden paradise, because I want to experience what Adam felt when he made love to Eve."

"But theirs was the Garden of Eden," she argued softly.

"And ours will be the *Jardim da Costa.*"

"I have to see if I can find some fig leaves."

Shaking his head, he laughed deep in his throat. "Forget the fig leaves, Darling. The only concession I'm willing to make is a blanket to protect your delicate little behind."

"You're a wicked man, Senhor Spencer."

"Not as wicked as I'd like to be, Senhora Spencer."

"You have to remember I'm carrying a child."

"That is something I'll never forget."

Regina felt the invisible thread drawing them closer, closer than she wanted to be. What she would not think about was the time when she would be forced to leave Aaron, taking the fruit of their love and passion with her.

Chapter 17

Aaron led Regina out of the garden, experiencing a gentle peace he had not felt in years. For the first time in his life everything he had ever wanted was his: a medical profession, his direct involvement in medical research, the promise of harvesting the da Costa plantation's best coffee crop in more than a decade, and the realization that the woman he had fallen in love with was carrying his unborn child.

"Who lives in those buildings?"

Regina's query shattered his pleasant musings. "The larger one belongs to the foreman and his family, and Magda lives in the smaller one."

She glanced up at his distinctive profile, studying the set of his firm jaw. "Why doesn't she live in the main house?"

"After my aunt died I decided I didn't want to share the house with any of the employees. I value my privacy too much to have them lurking about."

"Have you caught them lurking about?"

He shook his head. "No. But I don't want to give them the opportunity, either. Magda comes at seven in the morning and is usually gone before ten at night." He tightened his grip on her fingers. "Come, I'll show you the rest of the house."

Regina followed Aaron in and out of rooms which were added to the original building erected by the first European da Costas, who had sailed across the Atlantic to the New World more than three-hundred-fifty years ago. Terra-cotta, stone, wood, and plaster were the basic ingredients of the traditional sixteenth and seventeenth-country structures. Even with the addition of indoor plumbing and electricity, the magnificent house had lost none of its exquisite beauty, as it claimed terra-cotta-tiled roofs and chimneys, rustic stone walls, vaulted ceilings, and stained glass windows.

Staring out a window on the upper level, she was enchanted by the panorama unfolding before her eyes. Countless numbers of shrubs bearing the fruit which would blossom with cherries containing coffee beans swayed gently in the cooling ocean breeze. She noticed that acre upon acre of trees were planted nearby to shade the coffee trees and developing fruit from the hottest sun.

She felt the heat from Aaron's body as he moved behind her. He curved an arm around her waist and pulled her back to lean against his chest.

"What blend do you grow?" she asked.

"Coffee arabica."

Smiling, she nodded. "My family has perfected a variety of an arabica that is known as San Ramon."

"If they're cultivating a dwarf strain, then they must harvest the Jamaican Blue Mountain."

"They do."

Turning her around in his embrace, he cradled her face between his hands, giving her a questioning look. "All you know about coffee is drinking it?"

She flashed a saucy grin. "I suppose you can say I know a little about the plant." Her grin faded when his expressive face changed, becoming almost somber, and an inexplicable look of withdrawal hardened his gaze. Her hands moved up and curved around his strong wrists.

"Aaron?"

He blinked, seemingly coming out of a trance. "Yes?"

"I'm going back to my room to lie down."

"Are you feeling all right?"

"I'm just a little tired," she admitted truthfully.

His hands dropped. "Do you want anything before you retire for bed?"

"Just water, please."

Leaning down, he pressed a kiss to her parted lips. "I'll bring you the water."

She turned and walked down the hallway to the bedroom Aaron had assigned her, leaving him to stare at her back. She retreated to the bathroom to wash her face and brush her teeth. By the time Aaron walked into the bedroom she had slipped into a nightgown and was in bed with a pile of pillows cradling her back. Light from an exquisite Tiffany table lamp lit up the space with a soft, golden glow.

He placed a carafe of water on the table beside the lamp. Removing the top, he filled it with water. Sitting down on the edge of the bed, he smiled at her.

"I've told Magda to prepare meals for you using only bottled water. Brazil's water can be unkind to those who aren't used to it."

She gave him a dazzling, dimpled smile. "Thank you, Aaron."

"Are you going to be all right sleeping here alone?"

Her lids lowered as her smile slipped away. "I think so."

"If you need me I'll be in the bedroom on the other side of

the dressing room. I'm going to leave the doors open, just in case…"

She placed her fingertips over his lips, stopping his words and savoring the feel of hair covering his upper lip. "Stop worrying about me," she chided softly. "I'll be okay."

His fingers curled around her wrist and he pressed a kiss against the silken flesh of her inner arm. "Good night, *Princesa*."

"*Boa noite,*" she whispered softly.

Her gaze followed him as he opened the door to the dressing room. "Remember, I'll be less than fifty feet away if you need me."

She nodded, then sank down to the pillows and stared up at the unusual ceiling, not seeing Aaron as he lingered in the doorway. Closing her eyes, she placed a hand over her belly. Her breathing deepened and within minutes she fell into a deep, dreamless sleep.

Sleep wasn't as kind to Aaron as he lay in bed hours later, staring at the half-moon suspended in the nighttime sky. The day had been one of surprises—Regina's arrival, and the news that she was carrying his child.

When she fled Mexico he had thought he would never see her again, despite her written promise that she would come to him. Now she had come, but not alone.

A wide smile split his face. He was going to be a father. It was after he had made love to Regina the first time that he realized it was the only time that he had slept with a woman and had not protected her. It had taken only that one time to get Regina pregnant.

When he offered to marry her she had spurned him. She was willing to share the next six months of her life with him, but would not commit to sharing her future or his child with him.

His fingers curled into tight fists. What was there about her

that made him so vulnerable? Why had he permitted her to challenge him over and over? What power did she hold over him so
that he thought of her first and himself second?

What he felt for her went beyond love. She had become his
obsession.

Regina woke two hours before dawn with a gnawing hunger
gripping her stomach. The glowing red numbers on the clock
were clearly displayed in the darkness. Her pulse quickened.
The room was dark, but she had not remembered turning off
the lamp.

Closing her eyes, she counted backward slowly, hoping to
quell the rising panic in her chest. She had nothing to fear; she
was safe. Aaron was not far away. His words came rushing back,
stemming her trepidation. *If you need me I'll be in the bedroom
on the other side of the dressing room.*

She did not want to need him, even though she did. Somehow
she forced herself to sit up and reach for the lamp. Her fingers
grazed the base, moving slowly upward until she pulled the delicate chain. Within seconds the room was flooded with warm,
comforting, protective, golden light.

The door to the dressing room stood open, and she smiled.
All she had to do was leave her bed, walk across the room, and
walk through the dressing room to find Aaron.

Instead of going to Aaron, she made her way to the bathroom
to splash water on her face and brush her teeth. The pangs of
hunger grew stronger, and she knew she had to put something
into her stomach.

Opening her bedroom door, she glanced out into the hallway. A lighted wall sconce at the head of the staircase provided
enough illumination for her to navigate the stairs safely. Her bare
feet were silent as she went in search of her pre-dawn snack.

She hadn't stepped off the last stair when she noticed the
silhouette of someone closing the front door, and she wondered

if Aaron had left the house to meet with his foreman. It was only a little after four o'clock, and he said he usually met the foreman at five.

Shrugging a bare shoulder under her revealing silk nightgown, she made her way into the dimly lit kitchen, flicking a wall switch for the overhead lights. Three minutes later she sat at a large oaken table, drinking a glass of chilled milk and eating a banana.

A low whistle punctuated the silence, and she turned and stared at Aaron as he leaned against the arched entrance to the kitchen, his arms crossed over his T-shirt-covered chest. He was casually dressed in a pair of jeans and work boots.

She flashed a shy smile. "Good morning."

He shifted an eyebrow, his lips parting in a mysterious smile. "Good morning back to you. I take it you're hungry?"

"Starved," she confirmed, wrinkling her delicate nose.

He pushed away from the wall and closed the distance between them. Leaning over her, he curved his fingers around her neck and dropped a kiss on the top of her head. "I'll fix you something to eat."

She inhaled the warmth of his clean, masculine body. "Are you going to join me?"

He stared down at her, and she stared up at him with an expectant look in her dark eyes. He usually ate breakfast after he returned from the fields, but that practice would change, along with everything else in his life, now that Regina lived under his roof.

He ran a finger down the length of her nose. "Yes." His mouth replaced his finger.

"Do you need help?"

Hunkering down in front of her, he held her hands loosely in his warm, strong grip. "I want you to sit and relax. I'll take care of you while offering you everything you'll ever need."

Regina studied the lean, dark face with the high cheekbones, slanting eyes, and the strong masculine mouth beneath the neat, clipped moustache. Placing her fingertips over his lips, she leaned over and pressed a kiss at the corner of his mouth, unable to believe she loved him as much as she did.

There was a time she had thought she was captivated by Aaron because he had come into her life when she had been most vulnerable, that he had filled a void no man, including his father, had been able to fill. Closing her eyes, she realized she wanted him to take care of her. In Mexico he had promised to protect her, and she came to a realization that for the next six months she would permit him to do that.

Opening her eyes, she met his penetrating gaze. "I think I could get used to that."

He smiled, but the warmth of the expression did not quite reach his eyes. "Whether you get used to it doesn't matter much, because you don't have a choice."

She inhaled sharply, frowning. "I can't believe your arrogance."

"It has nothing to do with arrogance or what you believe, Regina."

"Then what do you call it?"

Releasing her hands, he stood up and stared at her upturned face. "I *will* do whatever I have to do to take care of you. And whenever you doubt that, I'll be the first to remind you of it."

A sudden anger lit her eyes at the same time she bit back the acerbic words poised on the tip of her tongue. What was it about Aaron Spencer that set her on edge the way a scrape of a fingernail across a chalkboard sent chills down her spine? Within a span of seconds he could ignite her desire until she vibrated with passion, then without warning douse the flames until she found herself spewing virulent words like a shrew.

It would not happen this morning. He had goaded her for the last time. She schooled her expression to one of complacency. "I'll make certain you don't have to remind me, *Dr. Spencer.*"

His forehead furrowed in an angry scowl. "You just have to have the last word, don't you?"

"What are you talking about?"

"I've warned you about using my professional title."

"Are you or aren't you a doctor?"

"At the hospital, or at the institute. But never in my home."

She lowered her gaze in a demure gesture. "I'm sorry, Aaron."

Reaching down, he pulled her gently to her feet. "Are you really sorry?" His angry gaze softened, moving from her eyes to her shoulders and still lower, to the soft swell of breasts rising above the lace of her nightgown.

Rising on tiptoe, she moved closer, pressing her breasts to his chest. "No," she whispered inches from his mouth.

"I thought not," he murmured softly. His right hand moved slowly down her back until his fingers were splayed over a hip. "Why don't you go upstairs and put on something less enticing while I prepare something to eat, because if you continue to tempt me in that nightgown I'm afraid I'm going to be the only one eating this morning."

"You wouldn't take advantage of me like that." There was no mistaking the thread of disbelief in her incredulous tone.

He released her, his hands going to the waistband of his jeans. His fingers were poised on the zipper when Regina turned and rushed out of the kitchen, his unrestrained, ribald laughter following her departing figure.

She was right. He would never take advantage of her. Yet the lingering image of her slender, swaying hips stayed with him as he opened the refrigerator. The image was not of an erotic nature. Seeing Regina completely nude the day before had sent a warning signal to his brain when she revealed that she was pregnant. Her hips were narrow—much too narrow to allow for an easy delivery if she carried a large baby to term.

Aaron went completely still, his hand reaching for a bottle of milk and halting in midair. He was thinking as a doctor, not as a man who loved Regina and hoped to marry her, but she wasn' his patient. She would be Nicolas Benedetti's patient for the du ration of her stay in Bahia. He had to inform his colleague of hi concerns for the mother of his unborn child.

Half an hour later he looked up to find Regina striding into the kitchen with a *"Don't mess with me"* mien radiating from her face and carriage. His admiring gaze swept from her damp curly hair to a straight, slender, cotton skirt and matching blouse in a flattering melon-orange down to her well-groomed feet in a pair of leather sandals in the same melon shade.

"You look beautiful." The adoration in his eyes mirrored his statement.

She folded her hands on her hips, flashing a saucy grin. "Beau tiful enough to *eat?*"

Pulling out a chair from the table, he bowed from the waist. "Sit down, *Princesa,* and oblige me," he said teasingly.

"Perhaps another time, Sweetheart. Right now your baby and its mother need nourishment."

He seated her, lingering over her head for several seconds. Even though Regina had informed him that he had gotten her pregnant, she had been referring to their unborn child as *my baby*.

"Say it again," he whispered.

She went still. "Say what, Aaron?"

"Tell me it's my baby."

Turning slightly, she looked up at him, her expression softening. "It's not yours or mine, but ours."

Bending, his lips slowly descended to meet hers. "Yes, *Princesa,* it is ours."

Regina caught his hand, holding it tightly, and when their lips parted she pressed a soft kiss to his palm, rewarding him with a sensual smile.

Aaron straightened, reluctantly withdrawing his fingers and moving away to place the plates that he had kept warming on the table. The dreamy intimacy evoked by their kiss lingered far beyond breakfast.

Regina sat in the Range Rover beside Aaron, staring out the window as he drove slowly past acre after acre of coffee fields. He chanced a quick glance at her profile behind the lenses of his sunglasses.

"I divided this year's crop into four varieties, each one encompassing several thousand acres."

She turned to look at him. "Which ones have you decided to plant?"

"Conilon, Typica, Bourbon, and Caturra."

Smiling, she turned her attention back to the passing landscape. That explained why some of the plants were large bushes or shrubs while others were small trees.

"Do you usually get enough rainfall to sustain a good harvest?"

"Most times we do. But I installed a sophisticated irrigation system two years ago just in case the rainfall is lower than usual. Several years back nearly every coffee grower in Brazil suffered enormous losses when a frost swept the country."

Maneuvering off the single-lane unpaved road, he shifted into four-wheel drive and drove up a rutted road until he stopped at the top of a hill. A tall, thin man came out of a small cabin at the same time Aaron stopped and turned off the sport utility vehicle's engine.

A bright smile curved the man's mouth when he spied Aaron getting out of the late-model four-wheel drive vehicle. "*Bom dia,* Senhor Spencer. You are later than usual this morning."

"*Bom dia,* Sebastião," Aaron replied, a mysterious smile parting his lips. He rounded the Range Rover and opened the passenger side door for Regina. Extending his arms, his hands circled her waist as he lifted her effortlessly before setting her on her feet. His foreman's surprise was apparent when he snatched a worn straw hat from his head and crushed it to his chest.

"Sebastião, this is Regina Spencer." His arm tightened around her waist. "Regina, Sebastião Rivas, my foreman and the person most responsible for the excellent quality of da Costa's superior coffee crop year after year."

Sebastião bobbed his head up and down as he clutched his hat tighter to his chest. "*Muito prazer,* Senhora Spencer."

"He says he's pleased to meet you," Aaron translated the Portuguese into Spanish.

Regina inclined her head. "*Muito prazer,* Senhor Rivas," she replied, trying out her limited Portuguese again.

Sebastião's gaze was directed to her left hand, where the rising sun fired the diamonds that made up her wedding band. Aaron saw the direction of his gaze. Regina had not removed the ring his father had given her to symbolize their union, and he was grateful she hadn't, because it eliminated his need to deceive others who assumed they were husband and wife. He wanted to protect Regina from unnecessary gossip concerning what would be obvious with her impending motherhood.

Regina listened intently as Aaron and his foreman lapsed into a serious discussion of the number of laborers needed to harvest the current crop, she understanding less than half of what was said in rapid Portuguese. Her six months in Brazil would be put to good use: renovating the da Costa garden and learning Portuguese.

Aaron, with Sebastião's assistance, had modernized the da Costa coffee plantation. Higher labor costs were offset by using modern techniques, including the use of fertilizers, herbicides, pesticides, mechanization, and irrigation.

He ended his daily encounter with the foreman, shaking his hand. Turning, he directed his attention to Regina, who had walked to the summit of the rise and stared down at countless acres of coffee plants stretching down to the ocean.

Walking up behind her, he curved both arms around her waist, pulling her back to lean against him. "What are you thinking?"

She laid her hands over his and closed her eyes. "It's so beautiful here. So peaceful."

"That's why I live here." His voice deepened until it resembled a sensual growl against her ear.

And as beautiful as it is, I'll have to leave it, she said silently.

Aaron tightened his grip, inhaling the clean, rain-washed scent of her soft body. "Marry me, Regina. That way you won't have to go back to the States. You can stay here forever."

She stiffened in his embrace. "No," she whispered.

Turning her in his embrace, he cradled her face between his hands. Vertical lines appeared between his eyes. "Why not?"

"Why not? I'm surprised you have to ask me that."

"Am I missing something?" he questioned.

"You are, Aaron. I will not marry you just because I'm carrying your child. That is not reason enough for me to accept your offer of marriage."

"But I love you."

"And I, you. But if our love is strong enough, then we can wait until after the baby's born." Rising on tiptoe, she kissed his scowling mouth. "I'm still Mrs. Spencer."

"You were Mrs. Oscar Spencer," he spat out angrily.

"And I'll become your wife if the time presents itself."

He cursed under his breath, coarse, vulgar, obscene curses which surprised even him when they sprang to mind.

His expression changed, becoming impassive. "Let's go. You have an eight o'clock appointment to see Nicolas."

Chapter 18

Aaron arrived at Salvador's largest municipal hospital, parking in his assigned space in the staff parking lot. He attached an ID badge to the waistband of his jeans and escorted Regina through the staff entrance and into the elevator and up to the floor for gynecology and obstetrics. Dr. Nicolas Benedetti worked the 3:00 to 11:00 a.m. shift, and had offered to see Regina before he completed his morning rounds.

Knocking on the door bearing the name of his colleague, Aaron pushed it open to find Nicolas rising to his feet behind his desk.

"*Bom dia,* Nicolas. Thank you again for agreeing to see Regina."

Coming from behind the desk, Nicolas extended a large hand covered with a profusion of coarse, black hair. "*Bom dia,* Aaron. Anything for you."

Aaron moved closer to Regina, pulling her gently to his side.

"Regina, this is Dr. Nicolas Benedetti. He's the best obstetrician in the country. Nicolas, Regina Spencer."

She shrank from the large, hulking man, who claimed swatches of thick, black eyebrows that grew in wild disarray over his squinting black eyes. Forcing a smile, she extended her hand. *"Muito prazer,* Dr. Benedetti."

Nicolas, momentarily stunned by her dimpled smile, took her slender hand and held it gently. *"Muito prazer,"* he said repeatedly as if in a trance. "Please come with me," he continued in rapid Portuguese.

Aaron released her waist. "You'll have to speak either Spanish or English, Nicolas. Her Portuguese is very limited."

Nicolas shifted an eyebrow that looked very much like a hairy caterpillar inching its way up his forehead. "I hardly speak Spanish since living in Brazil," he said to Regina, speaking rapidly in that language. "I don't get a chance to speak English except with my American wife. You can correct me when I make a glaring blunder with my words."

"Then English it is," she confirmed, her smile growing wider.

Nicolas stared at Aaron. "Would you like to stay for the examination?"

Regina felt a wave of heat suffuse her face. It was one thing to share her body with Aaron, but having him present when another doctor conducted an internal examination made her uncomfortable.

He shook his head, relieving her of her increasing apprehension. "I'll be in my office. Call me when you're finished." Leaning over, he pressed his lips to Regina's forehead. "I'll see you later."

Aaron waited until Regina disappeared into the examining room with Nicolas, then made his way down the highly waxed corridor to the elevator. His steps slowed when he saw Dr. Elena Carvalho coming toward him.

She walked over to him, lips drawn back over her teeth. "You cowardly bastard!" she spat out, her voice low and controlled. "Why did I have to hear it from your servant that you are married?"

Reaching for her elbow, he steered her gently away from the elevator and over to the door leading to a stairwell. "We'll discuss this in my office."

Elena pulled back. "We have nothing to discuss, *Dr. Spencer.*" Her hazel eyes filled with unshed tears. "If you couldn't tell me to my face, then you should've called to let me know that you were married. I go out with you one night, and less than twenty-four hours later your servant tells me you can't come to the telephone because you are eating dinner with your *wife.*"

Aaron struggled to control his rising temper. "Magda is not my servant, but an employee, and the only person I'll ever owe an explanation to for *anything* in my life will be my wife. Is there anything about what I've just said that you don't understand, Dr. Carvalho?"

Elena recoiled as if he had struck her. "I understand everything, Dr. Spencer." Tilting her chin, she gave him a smile which successfully concealed her newfound hatred of him. "Have a nice life."

Aaron stood, watching the woman he had seen socially no more than a half-dozen times over the past year walk down the corridor to her office. Elena had achieved everything she had ever wanted in life, with one exception: a husband and children. And for reasons he could not fathom, she wanted to become Mrs. Aaron Spencer.

They usually attended hospital social events as a couple, and there were times when they shared dinner, a movie, or concert, but never at any time had Aaron ever misled her. He could count the number of times on one hand when he'd kissed her, and the kisses were always chaste ones.

He wanted to tell Elena that he had agreed to have dinner with her two nights ago because she had come to his office earlier that morning, threatening to cause a scene if he did not see her. Elena had wanted answers he was unwilling to answer, and she wanted to know the status of their relationship. He had told her firmly that there was no relationship. There never was, and never would be.

Shrugging a shoulder, he took the staircase up the two flights to the floor set aside for pediatrics. He was scheduled to see patients in the clinic at eleven o'clock, which gave him time to review patient records and then drive Regina back to the house before he began his shift.

He recalled Elena's parting words—*Have a nice life.* He shook off the chill that swept over his body. The four words stayed with him until he opened a chart and read the lab results on a child who had been hospitalized with a high fever which had not responded to the powerful antibiotic he had prescribed to combat the infection invading his tiny, six-year-old body.

He stared at the diagnosis and let out his breath slowly. The tests revealed the child had acute promyelocytic leukemia—APL, a particularly deadly form of the disease. Closing his eyes, he mumbled a silent prayer. The child would be spared, because a brand-new medicine developed by pharmaceutical company researchers had predicted an eighty percent survival rate with the new miracle drug.

He glanced at his watch, then picked up the telephone and dialed the number of the man who headed a U.S. pharmaceutical company, knowing the child's parents would never be able to afford the cost of the medication, but he could.

Waiting for the connection, he listened to the automated recorded message on an answering machine, then left his message. "Good morning. This is Dr. Aaron Spencer, and I'm calling from the *São Tomé Instituto de Médico Pesquisa* in Bahia, Brazil. I'd like to leave a message for Dr. Charles Sands. Chuck, please call me after noon Brazilian time—"

"Good morning, Aaron," said a male voice with a distinctive New Orleans drawl, interrupting the recording. "How's the research?"

"Slow, but very productive, Chuck," he replied truthfully. "I need a favor."

"Spit it out."

"I have a patient who was just diagnosed with APL, and I need some—"

"Say no more, Aaron," his former classmate interrupted. "I was just walking out the door to go to the office for a breakfast meeting. As soon as I get there I'll FedEx the drug. I'll have it delivered to your institute."

His telephone call lasted less than five minutes, and when Aaron hung up his smile was one of relief. Regina was right. He had executed a marriage of pediatrics and medical research with wonderful results. If only his personal life were as perfectly aligned.

The telephone rang softly, and he picked it up after the first ring before the secretary for the pediatric department could answer it. She waved to him as she walked into the large outer officer and took her position behind her desk.

"Dr. Spencer," he said softly. "Please hold on." He placed the receiver on the desk, stood up, then walked over to close the door. He did not want the secretary to overhear his conversation with Nicolas.

He returned to the desk, picking up the receiver. "Nicolas?"

"She's in excellent health, Aaron, for a woman who is ten weeks into her term. I don't foresee any complications, which means you can expect to become a father anytime between June twelfth and July eleventh."

"Where is Regina now?"

"She's sitting out in the waiting room. Why?"

"I have one concern."

"And that is?"

"The narrowness of her hips."

"You have a right to be concerned, Aaron. But I'll monitor her closely. Bring her back next month and I'll give her an ultrasound. I want you to watch her to make certain she doesn't gain too much weight during the last trimester, but if the baby is a large one which makes a normal delivery impossible, then we can't rule out her having a C-section."

"Thanks, Nicolas. I'll be there in ten minutes." He hung up, burying his face in his hands.

How could he tell Nicolas that Regina planned to leave Brazil six weeks before she was due to deliver their child? He had openly lied, telling Nicolas that Regina was his wife, and he wondered how many more lies he would be forced to tell before he would actually claim her as wife.

He lowered his hands and stared at a shaft of sunlight pouring into the room. He did not want to think about Regina leaving him and taking their unborn child with her.

Compressing his lips tightly, he shook his head. She had left him once, but it would not happen again—not as long as there was breath in his body....

Aaron drove Regina back to the house, giving Magda specific instructions about seeing to Senhora Spencer's meals, then changed his clothes before returning to the hospital. Regina walked with him to the garage, holding his hand and telling him of the plans she had made for her afternoon. He wasn't disappointed when she kissed him passionately, then turned and made her way back to the house. He stood watching her until she disappeared from view.

Regina's plan to identify and label plants, flowers, and shrubs was thwarted by a torrential downpour. She'd been sitting in an enclosed patio flipping through magazines and watching the falling rain when Magda brought her a midmorning snack of sliced fruit, cheese, bread, and chilled milk. After she ate, a weighted fatigue descended upon her, and she retreated to her bedroom for a nap.

She awoke once to relieve herself and then returned to the bed, where she slept through the afternoon and into the early evening. The second time she woke up it was to the now familiar feeling of gnawing hunger and the solidness of Aaron's body as he lay beside her on the large bed.

Light from the table lamp illuminated his smiling face. *"Boa tarde."*

She tried sitting up, but he eased her down to the pillows. "What time is it?"

He took a quick glance at the clock on the bedside table. "Five forty-seven."

"Aaron, I've slept the day away," she moaned, burying her face against his warm throat. "All I do is eat and sleep."

He laughed deep in his chest. "That's what you're supposed to do." Releasing her, he leaned over and offered her a glass of milk. She drained the glass. At the same time, he picked up a bowl filled with stew. "It's called *cozidos*," he explained, spooning small portions into her mouth. "It's made with a variety of boiled vegetables with different cuts of beef and pork."

"It's good," she said between bitefuls of savory vegetables and tender cuts of meat. "Where's yours?" she questioned after Aaron handed her a cloth napkin.

"I'll eat later."

Placing the bowl beside the glass, he turned back to her, smiling. "How was your day?"

Lying down beside him, she visually examined his face. There were lines of fatigue she hadn't noticed before. They were etched around his nose and mouth, and closer inspection revealed newer, deeper lines around his slanting eyes.

"Very uneventful. I watched the rain, read an old magazine, and slept. How was yours?"

"Hectic. I vaccinated at least a dozen infants against the most common childhood diseases, admitted an eight-year-old for pneumonia, diagnosed one child with PKU, and treated a little boy for impetigo." He did not tell her that a little girl died in his arms of dehydration because her parents had neglected to bring the child to the hospital after three days of vomiting and diarrhea from an intestinal infection.

"What are impetigo and PKU?"

"Phenylketonuria, PKU, is a rare, inherited disease that affects the body's ability to break down the amino acid phenylalanine. If it is allowed to accumulate in the body, phenylalanine damages the nervous system and results in mental retardation."

Regina's hand went to her belly. "What about our child?"

Aaron covered her hand with his. "Don't worry, Darling. PKU will be inherited *only* if both parents carry the PKU gene."

Her eyes widened. "Do you carry it?"

Lowering his head, he kissed the tip of her nose. "No."

She let out an audible sigh of relief. "What about the impetigo?"

"Impetigo is a bacterial skin infection most often seen around the lips, nose, and ear, even though it can occur anywhere on the body."

"What causes it?"

"Common skin organisms like streptococcus and staphylococcus, which are carried in the nose and on the skin."

"What does the infection look like?"

"The rash starts as small blisters, which break and crust over to become yellow-brown scabs that look a lot like particles of brown sugar."

She shuddered, moving closer to him. "Yuck."

He forced a smile, telling himself this would be the first and last time he would discuss his patients with Regina. He did not need or want her agonizing over unfounded fears for her unborn child when her only concern should be carrying a healthy baby to term.

Pulling away from Aaron, Regina rolled over and sat up. "I need to take a bath and change my clothes." She hadn't bothered to remove her skirt and blouse, which she had put on earlier that morning when she lay down to take a nap which had stretched into more than six hours of a deep, refreshing slumber.

"I'm going to shower and change, too."

Leaning forward, she pressed her lips to his, lingering and enjoying the taste and feel of his moustached mouth. "I'll see you later."

Aaron left the bed and picked up the tray with the empty bowl and glass. He winked at her as he made his way across the bedroom. Regina sat staring at the space where he had been, a comforting feeling of calm and confidence filling her entire being.

She loved him, loved him so much that she wanted to cry from the joy and passion he aroused in her. She thrilled to the touch of his hands whenever they grazed her body, and to the taste and feel of his lips on her own. When she least expected it she craved his possession, wanting to take him into her body so that they ceased to exist as separate entities. Joined, they became one in the same manner that the child growing beneath her breasts symbolized the blending of their ancestors.

She slipped off the bed and walked into the bathroom. Instead of turning on the electric lights, she lit several scented candles and positioned them on the tables under the windows. The fragrance of lavender blended with the powerful scents of damp earth and blooming flowers coming in through the windows.

She emptied a capful of scented bath oil under the flow of warm running water, filling the tub with her favorite fragrance as she brushed her teeth. The tub was half-filled when she stripped off her clothes and eased her naked body into the relaxing waters.

"Very nice. Very nice indeed."

Her head came up quickly, and she stared at Aaron standing

in the doorway smiling at her. He was naked, with the exception of a towel covering his loins.

A rush of heat swept over her face and settled in her chest. "What are you doing?"

He arched an eyebrow. "Getting an eyeful."

Sinking down lower in the water, she tried escaping his penetrating stare. "Aaron!"

His smile widened as he walked into the space, his gaze never leaving her face. "I've come to share your bath."

"Men don't share women's baths," she protested, her voice lowering to a seductive octave.

"How would you know?"

Aaron's hands went to his waist, and the towel fell to the brick floor. "I want your first bath experience to be a memorable one."

Regina wanted to pull her gaze away from his naked form, but couldn't. The rich darkness of his coloring was shadowed in the flickering candlelight. However, the definition and planes of his powerful upper body stood out in bold relief in the golden light.

She hadn't realized she was holding her breath until he stepped into the oversize tub behind her and pulled her back until her spine was pressed against his chest. The oil-slicked water lapped over her thighs and up to her belly.

Closing her eyes, she smiled. "You're going to smell like me," she crooned, enjoying the warmth and hardness of Aaron's body molded to her back.

"That's okay," he replied. There was a hint of laughter in his deep voice. His arms tightened around her waist and his hands moved up and cradled her moist breasts. "The smell of you lingered in my nostrils for weeks," he continued quietly. "Even after I'd returned to Bahia it seemed as if I could still smell you. And there were times when I imagined I could taste you in my mouth. So many weeks had gone by, but everything about you stayed with me. There was never a moment during the day or night that I didn't think of you."

Tears welled up behind her closed eyelids and slipped down her cheeks at his erotic confession. "I didn't want to leave you, Aaron."

His fingers tightened on her breasts, the thumbs moving up and down in a soft, sweeping motion over the erect nipples. "I know, *Princesa*. You did what you had to do." She gasped aloud, and his fingers stilled. "Do they hurt, Baby?"

Breathing heavily through her parted lips, she nodded. "They're very sensitive."

Aaron's hands went to her waist and he lifted her so that she faced him. Sitting up straighter, he settled her thighs until she straddled his. Long and short shadows flickered over her face, highlighting the sensuous smile curving her lush mouth.

Leaning closer, Regina pressed her breasts to his broad, hard chest and touched her lips to his. "I love you, Aaron Spencer," she whispered reverently.

Aaron cradled her face between his palms, increasing the pressure of her mouth on his at the same time his ardor escalated. He lifted her with one arm, while his other hand eased his sex into her body.

Regina did not have time to stifle a gasp when she felt Aaron's hardness filling every inch of her body without any pretense of foreplay. She stared up at him and detected an expression she couldn't quite identify lurking beneath the surface of his rising desire.

There was something feral, almost savage, in his gaze that aroused and frightened her at the same time. Something foreign, unknown, indicated that this coming together would be different than any other they had shared.

She did not know whether it was the atmosphere created by the candles in the darkened space, the intimacy of their sharing a bath, his passionate confession, or the physical changes in her body because of her pregnancy, but she knew she would recall the scene over and over for the rest of her life.

Curving her arms around his neck for support, Regina began moving over his aroused flesh. It began with a slow up and down motion, then increased to a frenzied rocking, and Aaron's upward thrusting splashed water over the sides of the tub and onto the brick floor.

Without warning, he reversed their positions, supporting her body, and his lower body pumped with the velocity of a piston as he wordlessly communicated his masculine dominance.

"Marry me," he gasped, his breath hot and heavy against her ear.

Sharking her head, she swallowed to relieve the dryness in her throat. "No, Aaron. I can't."

"Marry me," he repeated.

"No!"

"Marry me, *Princesa,*" he intoned, the supplication becoming a litany which rang in her ear like a chant.

Passion, desire, and rage surged through Aaron, one emotion fusing with the other until he did not know who he was. Claiming Regina Spencer's body wasn't enough; her carrying his child still wasn't enough. What he wanted was to claim her as his own, and that would not become possible until he made her his wife.

Without warning, he withdrew from her, rose to his feet, and stepped out of the bathtub. He reached for her, knowing he had startled her when she emitted a cry of surprise as he lifted her effortlessly and carried her across the bathroom and into the bedroom.

It had taken less than sixty seconds before he placed her on the bed where she had spent the afternoon, fastening his rapacious mouth to her sensitive breasts. Her keening cry fired his blood as his mouth journeyed down her body, tasting every inch of her silken flesh.

The primitiveness of the act awakened a primal hunger in

Regina as she writhed under the sensual assault, her husky voice begging him not to stop.

"I can't stop, Baby," he countered, moving up her wet, trembling limbs and joining their bodies.

Her fire spread to his, dissolving both in an inferno from which there was no escape. His tongue slipped into her mouth, keeping perfect rhythm with his hips as he drove into her over and over.

One hand moved over the curve of a breast and slid down her taut stomach and still lower. Arching his lower body, his finger found the tight nodule hidden in the downy hair at the apex of her thighs. The pad of his thumb massaged the engorged flesh, and she cried out shamelessly with the spasm of pleasure shaking her from head to toe.

Increasing the circular motion, Aaron bit back his own moans of pleasure, which threatened to drown him a maelstrom of ecstasy from which he did not want to escape.

Regina felt herself sinking further and further into the morass of immeasurable ecstasy as their bodies met in exquisite harmony with one another.

Her moans of erotic pleasure became unrestrained screams of ecstasy when she stiffened with the explosive rush of orgasmic fulfillment sweeping through her. The screams subsided to long, surrendering moans of physical satiation as she closed her eyes and registered the rush of Aaron's release bathing her throbbing flesh.

Tears leaked from under her lids. Aaron Spencer possessed the power to assuage her physical need for him, but unknowingly he also had the power to tear her soul apart. She prayed he would not ask her to marry him again, because at that very moment she would have consented.

They lay together on the bed until their breathing resumed its normal rate. Then Aaron picked her up again and returned to the bathroom. They were silent as they shared a shower, watching each other warily and knowing that the single passionate physical act had changed them—forever.

Chapter 19

Regina blotted the back of her neck with a linen handkerchief she had taken from an ample supply nestled in a drawer in one of the two massive armoires occupying the dressing room she shared with Aaron. The intense Brazilian summer forced her to work more slowly than planned. She had spent less than two hours in the late Alice Spencer da Costa's garden, and had uncovered an herb garden containing petunias, moonflowers, daturas, brugmansias, four o'clocks, and nicotianas.

A large field of pungently perfumed, colorful lavender grew in wild abundance, reminding her of the scent of the candles she had lit in the bathroom the night she shared the unforgettable bath with Aaron. He had shared her bath and her bed that night, establishing a ritual which would determine their relationship for the duration of her stay in Bahia.

Slipping the handkerchief into the pocket of her loose-fitting cotton dress, she squinted up at the sun through the lenses of her sunglasses. It was directly overhead, indicating the noon hour.

She would take her *siesta,* then return to the garden once the sun passed over in a westerly direction.

She hadn't taken more than a dozen steps when she saw Aaron striding toward her, holding a package in one hand. Vertical lines appeared between her eyes, and she went completely still. What was he doing home in the middle of the day? He was committed to working three days at the hospital in Salvador, and usually put in another three at the research institute.

Her pulse quickened as he quickly closed the distance between them. "What's the matter, Aaron?"

His quick smile allayed her fear. "Nothing, Darling. I just came home to bring you a package that was delivered at the institute this morning. The return address on the label bears the ColeDiz logo."

He handed her the package, and she stared at the familiar handwriting on the label. It was from Parris Cole. "I wonder what my mother sent me." She had celebrated her twenty-seventh birthday in July, and even though it was late November it was still too early for a Christmas gift.

Curving an arm around her expanding waist, Aaron pulled her to his side. "Let's go into the house. It's not good for you to be out in the heat."

He was right. She was at the end of her first trimester, and her body was beginning to show signs of her pregnancy. Her breasts were noticeably fuller, and she had discovered that many of her fitted garments were too tight in the waist. Aaron had driven her to Salvador, where she spent an afternoon shopping for clothes which artfully camouflaged her physical condition. Shopping for a new wardrobe served a twofold purpose. She and Aaron had received their first social invitation as a couple. They were invited to attend a surprise birthday party for Nicolas Benedetti's American-born wife Saturday evening.

Aaron led Regina into his study, seating her on the comfortable chaise they shared whenever they watched television. She

did not know why, but this room was her favorite in the large
house. Books filled the built-in shelves from floor-to-ceiling.
Aaron's desk was covered with papers stacked in neat piles, and
a profusion of live plants was nestled in every corner and any
available surface large enough to hold a clay pot.

It was into this room that Aaron usually retreated after dinner,
entering notes in his computer or communicating electronically
with researchers from all over the world. It was also into this
room that he came to watch videos or movies with her, translat-
ing the dialogue whenever some of the Portuguese totally eluded
her comprehension.

She had been in Bahia for three weeks and, despite Aaron's
urging she had not redecorated the house—not when she planned
to leave in five months.

Her fingers were steady as she peeled the paper off the package to reveal an exquisite, black-lacquered box. As she turned
a key in the lock, the top opened to reveal a collection of silver-
framed photographs nestled between bubble wrap.

Her eyes brightened in amusement. "She sent me photographs
from our last family reunion." Picking up the one on top, she
studied it closely, then handed it to Aaron. "This one shows my
grandparents and their children. My dad is behind Grandpa,
and my grandmother is standing between my uncles Joshua and
David. The two women are my aunts."

Aaron stared at the professionally shot photograph. "Everyone
resembles your grandmother, except one of your uncles."

She nodded. "That's because he's my grandfather's son from
an illicit affair with a young woman who was in his employ."

He gave her a questioning look. "I suppose the Coles have
their family secrets like everyone else."

"They *are* like everyone else. Having money does not exempt
them from having skeletons in their closets." She kept her features deceptively composed as she removed the next photograph.
"Here's me with my mother, father, sister, and brother."

Aaron took the photograph, staring intently at the two people who were responsible for creating the woman he had fallen hopelessly in love with. "I see where you get your beauty. Your mother is gorgeous."

"She is," Regina agreed. "But my sister Arianna looks more like her than I do." She removed the next two photographs. "These are my aunts, their husbands, children, and grandchildren."

Whistling softly, Aaron shook his head as he counted the number of people in the two photographs. "Your aunts are the prolific ones in the family."

Regina removed the next photograph. "My uncle David is gaining quickly. He and his wife have four children, and I don't think they're finished. He complains he was cheated when his wife delivered twins."

"You have twins in your family, too?"

She touched her slightly rounded belly. "Don't even go there, Aaron Spencer. You know I'm carrying one child." A recent ultrasound had verified a single birth, even though it was too early to detect the sex of the tiny baby.

"I was thinking about the next time," he explained.

"There may not be a next time," she murmured softly as she removed the last remaining photograph. "Here's Uncle Josh, his wife Vanessa, and my cousins Emily and Michael."

Aaron had felt a fist of fear squeeze his heart with her statement. *There may not be a next time.* Was she warning him in advance that they would never have another child—that when she left him she would never return?

His lean jaw tightened. "Have you thought of any names?"

"No," she admitted.

He forced a smile he did not quite feel. "Do you think it's too soon to start thinking about names?"

Regina shrugged a shoulder. "Not really. We can list a few for boys and a few for girls. Then we can wait and see what he or she looks like, then make a decision."

"I don't know about that," he stated, shaking his head. "I don't believe a child can actually resemble a name."

"Sure they can. Look at my brother and sister." She pointed to the photograph of her immediate family. "Tyler and Arianna fit their names perfectly."

He nodded. "I like those names. Look, *Princesa,* why don't we compromise? You select the name if it's a boy, and I'll select one for a girl."

Arching a sweeping eyebrow, she gave him a skeptical look. "You won't mind if I name our son?"

He shrugged his shoulder under a crisply laundered pale-blue shirt. "I trust you to come up with something befitting, where he won't spend half his life punching people out because his mother decided to name him Percival."

"Percival isn't that bad," she teased.

"Tell him that each time he's suspended from school for fighting."

Regina peered into the box and withdrew a sheet of paper. She smiled when she read what her mother had written: *A little something to remind you that we love and miss you. Mom.*

Moving closer to Aaron, she angled for a more comfortable position. "Whose decision was it to name you Aaron?"

There was a swollen silence before he answered. "It had been my mother's choice." He flashed a quick smile. "And you?"

"My mother."

"Your father agreed with her decision?"

Closing her eyes, Regina drew in a deep breath. She had to tell Aaron. She had to tell him of the family secret so jealously guarded by the Coles, because the child she carried beneath her breasts claimed the blood of the Coles and the Spencers.

"My father wasn't aware that he had fathered a child until I was nine years old."

He went completely still, his gaze narrowing. "Why?"

"Because my mother was forced to leave him before she could

tell him that she was pregnant. She was threatened with death if she did not leave Florida, and my father."

"But why?"

She opened her eyes and stared at the puzzlement on Aaron's face. "Because a very powerful, very wealthy man did not want his son to marry my mother. He paid someone to blackmail her, while threatening her with death if she ever returned."

A shadow of alarm touched Aaron's features when he analyzed what she had revealed. "Was that man your grandfather?"

"Yes, it was. He had had an extramarital affair when he was a young man, which resulted in the birth of Joshua Kirkland. My grandmother forgave him for his indiscretion, but apparently my grandfather couldn't forgive himself for turning his back on his own flesh and blood. So when my father began seeing my mother, Grandpa confused her with the kind of woman whom he had loved more than his own wife."

"How were your parents reunited?"

"Daddy got his half brother to look for us."

"Your grandfather finally accepted his illegitimate son?"

"That wasn't until years later. Uncle Josh was a career officer in military intelligence, so he knew where to look for us. My parents were finally married, then Daddy went into politics. The people Grandpa hired to get rid of my mother tried a few more times to kill her, and failed. One of the men needed money to pay off loan sharks who were looking for him, which led to me being kidnapped. You know the rest of the story."

She stared at Aaron staring back at her in stunned silence. "Now you know all of the Coles' dirty little family secrets. And after many years of bitterness they've declared a truce. My grandfather has had a lot of time to repent for his sins because he's been a semi-invalid for the past fourteen years. I still find it difficult to believe that he was once one of the most feared African-American businessmen in the world whenever I see him sitting in a wheelchair just staring into space."

Aaron shook his head in disbelief. "Have you forgiven him?"

"Yes, I have. You have to forgive in order to be forgiven."

He knew she was right. It had taken him twelve years to forgive Oscar for claiming the first woman he had fallen in love with. And Oscar had redeemed himself, because he had given him Regina in return.

His expression grew serious as he studied her intently. "You're luckier than I am, because I was never given the opportunity to tell my father I was sorry for turning my back on him," he said quietly.

"Tell him now," Regina urged softly. "He's listening, Aaron."

He lifted an eyebrow. "You think so?"

"I know so. There are times when I feel his presence, or I imagine I hear his voice. I had a dream about him several weeks ago in which he told me that he was overjoyed that I was carrying his grandchild."

Aaron wanted to laugh at her childish beliefs but did not, because he realized Regina had exhibited a maturity far beyond her years.

"My father forgave me before I forgave him."

Her brow furrowed in a frown. "When?"

"When Oscar told you to contact me. When he left his money to the institute so I could continue my research. And when he brought us together."

She shook her head. "Oscar had no way of knowing that we would end up together."

"But he did, *Princesa*. My father and I were more alike than dissimilar. The woman who was Oscar's second wife was engaged to me first." He ignored Regina's gasp. "She slept with me, then slept with my father. She told him she was pregnant to get him to marry her."

Regina's lids fluttered wildly. "But—she could've been carrying your child."

"That was highly improbable. I never slept with Sharon or any other woman without using a contraceptive. You were the first woman who did not fall into that category."

She blushed, nodding. "Was she actually pregnant?"

"No, and it did not take Dad long to realize that she had used him to further her acting career. But the damage had been done. I told myself that I didn't have a father, and after a while I came to believe it. Now you know the Spencers' dirty little family secret."

And now I know why you want to marry me, Regina countered silently. It had nothing to do with possession or ownership, but revenge. Oscar Spencer had married the woman Aaron loved above all others, and now he wanted to marry the woman Oscar had claimed as wife.

Her delicate jaw hardened with determination. "What we've shared today will stay between us. I don't want our child's life influenced by the heinous behavior of its decadent ancestors. It's time we begin anew."

"You're right," he agreed, leaning closer. His mouth covered hers, sealing their oath with a passionate kiss.

Regina surveyed her face in the mirror for the last time, her fingers smoothing back a gel-covered curl from her forehead. She walked out of the bathroom at the same time Aaron made his way through the connecting dressing room into their bedroom. He stopped short, his eyes widening appreciably when she stood in front of him.

Successfully concealing a smile, she watched him as he walked slowly around her while staring at her over his shoulder. His body language called to mind a matador challenging a motionless bull.

Tilting her chin, she smiled down the length of her nose at him. "Do I pass inspection, Senhor Spencer?"

Aaron found breathing difficult as he surveyed her tall,

ripening body in a sheer, gunmetal-gray sheath dress lined in black silk, with shimmering, floral beaded designs from neckline to hem. His gaze was fixed on an expanse of one pale-gray-covered leg from a thigh-grazing slit. The garment fit loosely at the waist, artfully disguising the slight swell of her belly. Her narrow feet were encased in a pair of gun-metal-gray, silk-covered, sling-strap heels with narrow ties encircling her slender ankles. The high heels put her within three inches of his own towering height.

He moved closer and stood behind her. She shivered slightly as his warm breath swept over the back of her neck. "You are perfect," he murmured.

Closing her eyes, Regina leaned back against his solid chest, savoring the warmth and the haunting scent of his aftershave. Even with her eyes closed she still could see the smoothness of his shaven jaw, the shimmer of hairdressing clinging to the short-ened strands of his close-cropped graying hair, and the contrast of the whiteness of the wing collar of his dress shirt against the rich darkness of his strong throat.

"I suppose that means you approve?" she whispered.

"I more than approve," he confirmed, his hands moving up and covering the fullness of her breasts over the sheer fabric. A jolt of white-hot heat swept through his groin when he appraised the weight and size of the flesh filling his large hands.

His fingers tightened slightly, squeezing gently. "You are the most enchanting woman I've ever seen in my life." Lowering his head, he pressed his mouth to the side of her neck. "And you're going to become even more stunning in the coming months."

Breathing heavily through parted lips, Regina felt the heat of his body course down the entire length of hers. One of Aar-on's hands moved over her belly, and a moan of ecstasy slipped through her lips. "I'm going to be fat in the coming months," she slurred.

"You're going to become the most beautiful mother-to-be in

existence." His hand inched lower, lingering over the warm area between her thighs.

"No, Sweetheart. Please," she pleaded. "We have to go out."

The passion clouding Aaron's mind lifted, and his hands went to her bare shoulders, turning her around to face him. For what seemed like the hundredth time he found it hard to believe he had fallen in love with a woman so exquisitely beautiful and passionate. It was as if fate had rewarded him for his patience.

"You're right," he replied reluctantly.

He released her, and Regina moved over to the bed. She picked up a small, sequined bag and the jacket matching her dress, while Aaron retreated to the dressing room to retrieve his white dinner jacket.

He returned, grasped her left hand firmly, and removed the diamond ring his father had slipped onto her finger eight years ago, replacing it with a wider band designed with alternating white and yellow round diamonds set in platinum.

Her temper flared, fingers curling into fists, but Aaron was ready for her quick temper. "My mother would've been honored for *her daughter* to wear her ring," he explained in a deep, soothing tone.

Lowering her gaze, she nodded in acquiescence. The virulent words poised on the tip of her tongue died quickly. She knew Aaron resented the fact that she hadn't taken off his father's ring. She would humor him and wear his mother's ring. But only for the one night.

Holding out her hand, she stared up at him, and wasn't disappointed when he dropped the circle of diamonds into her outstretched palm. She dropped it in the bottom of the small evening purse.

Aaron hadn't asked that she marry him since the night of their passionate bathtub encounter, and she hoped he would not broach the subject again until after she delivered. She did not doubt that he loved her, but she could not ignore the notion that his wanting to marry her was motivated more by revenge than that love.

Aaron offered Regina his arm, and she placed her hand over the pristine sleeve of his white jacket. He led her out of the bedroom, down the staircase, and out to the courtyard, where he had parked a low-slung, silver-gray sports car. Opening the passenger side door, he helped her in and waited until she was comfortably seated on the black leather before closing it. Removing his jacket, he placed it in the space behind the front seats, then slipped into the car beside Regina.

A liberal sprinkling of stars littered the navy-blue Bahian summer nighttime sky as he drove quickly and expertly along the unlit roads. He felt the heat of Regina's gaze on his right hand each time he shifted gears.

A glint of determination filled his eyes as he concentrated on navigating the dark road. A feeling of satisfaction filled his chest after he had gotten Regina to accept his mother's ring. It wasn't the ring he had purchased for their wedding, but that no longer mattered because she wasn't wearing the one his father had given her.

"I am thinking about buying you a car so that you can get around without waiting for me to take you into the city," he said after a while, breaking the comfortable silence.

Turning her head, she stared at his strong profile. "Save your money, Aaron. I don't need a car."

He gave her a quick glance. "My last name may not be Cole, but I'm a long way from being labeled a pauper, *Princesa*."

"It's not about money," she retorted. "I go into the city only twice a month. You take me in to see Nicolas, and I usually spend the rest of the day at the beauty spa. The only other time I go in is to have an occasional manicure and pedicure. Having a car is a waste for me."

Shrugging a shoulder, Aaron smiled at her. "I thought you

were bored hanging around the house and wanted a change of scene."

She laughed softly. "I spend more time in the garden than in the house. I've completely identified every plant in your aunt's garden from fern to herb, flower to lichen. Next week I'm going to create a blueprint design to lay out what I want to move."

"How is your assistant?" He had recruited a young man who usually worked in the coffee fields to help Regina in her garden.

"Christôvão is wonderful. He's teaching me Portuguese."

"He's supposed to be helping you with your work."

"He *is.*"

"He can't be, if he spends the day flirting with you."

Her mouth dropped open as she stared at Aaron, her eyes widening in surprise. "Don't tell me you're jealous of a boy, Aaron."

"He's not a boy. In case you haven't noticed, he's very much a man."

"He's only twenty-two."

"He's a *man,* Regina."

"And he believes I'm the wife of the man who pays him his salary. I don't think he would do anything that would jeopardize his employment."

"He'd better not," Aaron countered in a dangerously soft voice. "Losing his job will be nothing compared to what I'd do to him if—"

"Stop it, Aaron!" she admonished, cutting him off. "What's with your unfounded jealousy? And why would any man be interested in carrying on with a pregnant woman? In case you haven't noticed, I've lost my waistline."

"What I've noticed is that you're more beautiful now than when I first met you."

Glancing away, she stared out the window. "That's because it's your child I'm carrying."

"I'm not quite that vain, Senhora Spencer."

"But you do admit to being vain," she teased.

He shrugged his shoulder in the elegant gesture she loved to see. "A little."

"Mentiroso," she said accusingly.

"I'm not a liar."

"Yes, you are, Aaron Laurence Spencer. Aren't we living a lie?"

His fingers tightened on the leather steering wheel before he shifted into a higher gear. The racy car picked up speed as it seemed to fly over the uneven surface of the unpaved back road.

"Only temporarily," he ground out between clenched teeth.

Those were the last two words they exchanged until Aaron maneuvered into the courtyard of the sprawling Spanish Colonial-style home belonging to Dr. Nicolas and Jeannette Benedetti.

Chapter 20

Regina noticed raised eyebrows and startled expressions, and she registered questioning whispers as to her identity, when she and Aaron were ushered into the expansive Benedetti living room by a young man hired by the party planner to greet the invited guests. Another, acting as a parking valet, had parked more than a dozen cars on a remote section of the property and out of sight of anyone approaching the house.

Aaron nodded, smiling at the people waiting silently in the room, then settled Regina on a straight-back chair. Her loose-fitting dress artfully designed her ripening body. He stood behind her, his right hand resting possessively on her bare, scented shoulder. She smiled over her shoulder at him, then crossed her legs gracefully, giving him and everyone in attendance a glimpse of her long, smooth, shapely legs encased in shimmering pale gray. There was an eerie silence as the gazes of all the invited guests were fixed on the tall couple trading mysterious smiles.

The front door opened and then closed behind an attractive

couple who laughed softly, as if sharing a private joke. The woman's dark red hair was swept up off her neck in an elaborate twist. The color was the perfect foil for her clear, hazel eyes and honey-gold complexion.

Regina's eyes narrowed in concentration as she tried placing where she had seen the man before. Running various categories through her mind, she enumerated: actor, singer, athlete. Athlete! He was Fragancio Solis. As Brazil's most popular *futebol* player, he had attained superstar status similar to Pele, who had retired more than twenty years ago yet was still revered by all Brazilians as a national hero.

Fragancio Solis glanced around the room, acknowledging his renown as if it were his due while his red-haired date glared at Aaron, her golden eyes hardening like cold jewels.

Regina held her breath when she felt Aaron's fingers tightening on her bare shoulder. Reaching up, she covered his hand with her left one, and he eased his punishing grip on her tender flesh. She did not want to look up at him, but knew instinctively that things did not bode well with the man whose child she carried and the provocatively attired woman with the auburn hair.

Her obsidian gaze met and fused with one of gold, neither willing to concede, and Regina knew that during her tenure in Bahia she would never call the woman *friend*.

The parking attendant opened the door, slipped quietly into the room, then closed it quickly. "They're coming," he whispered excitedly.

Within minutes the front door opened again and a formally dressed Nicolas Benedetti walked into the living room. His dark gaze swept over the people sitting or standing quietly in his home, his solemn expression brightening.

"Come help me look for my wallet, Jeannette," he called out in heavily accented English. "It will go quickly if we both look."

Jeannette Jackson-Benedetti mumbled angrily under her breath as she stepped into the living room. Her scowl vanished, replaced by an expression of shock when she saw her husband's friends and colleagues smiling at her. Turning, she walked out of the house, Nicolas a half-dozen steps behind her.

"Come back, *Querida!*"

"No. You *didn't!*" Jeannette whispered harshly. "How could you, Nicky?"

Nicolas pulled his protesting wife back into the living room amid applause and hooting. "Are you surprised?"

Resting a hand over her heaving bosom, Jeannette smiled up at Nicolas. "Very."

She permitted him to lead her to a chair festooned with streamers of pink, white, and red ribbon. Sitting down, she lowered her head, forcing a smile. Her dark eyes were shimmering with bright tears when she finally glanced up.

"I don't know what to say," she began slowly, searching for the equivalent words in Portuguese, "except thank you all for coming to help me celebrate my thirtieth birthday." She shot her husband a lethal glare. "I'll take care of *you* later," she threatened in English.

Crossing his arms over his chest, Nicolas displayed a Cheshire cat grin. "How?"

"You'll find out soon enough." Jeannette stood up. "It looks as if everyone came to party," she continued in Portuguese. "So, let's have some fun!"

Two silent, efficient waiters escorted the dozen couples filing out of the living room and into a formal dining room to their assigned seats while another filled crystal goblets and glasses with wine and water.

Aaron helped Regina to her feet, guiding her toward the guest of honor. Jeannette's expression softened as she offered Regina an infectious, friendly smile. Jeannette was average height and favored a fashionable, close-cropped natural hairstyle. Her flawless cinnamon-brown skin, perfectly round face, slanting eyes, and high cheekbones made her an exotically beautiful woman.

Jeannette extended her right hand, the overhead light from a chandelier catching the blue-white brilliance of the enormous square-cut diamond on her finger. "I suppose you know I'm the birthday girl," she said in a laughing voice.

Regina took the proffered hand, flashing a dimpled smile. "Happy birthday, Jeannette. I'm Regina Spencer."

Jeannette's gaze widened, and she hugged Regina. "I don't believe it. A sister girl!"

Regina returned the hug. "Florida."

"I'm from North Carolina." Her grin widened. "We have to get together and talk."

Holding on to the sleeve of Aaron's jacket, Jeannette smiled up at him. "While you and Nicky are busy healing mankind, your wife and I are going to hang out together."

He returned her smile. "That sounds like a wonderful idea." He'd hoped Regina and Jeannette would bond quickly. He didn't like leaving her alone so much.

Nicolas curved an arm around his wife's thickening waist. "Come sit down, *Querida*. You must eat or you'll be sick."

When Jeannette placed a hand over her slightly rounded belly, Regina realized she was pregnant. The exquisitely designed gunmetal-gray-and-back dress had artfully concealed her own condition from anyone who hadn't been aware that she had just begun her second trimester.

Aaron saw the direction of Regina's gaze. "You two have a lot more in common than just being sister girlfriends from the States."

Satisfaction pursed her lush mouth as she looped her hand over the bend of his elbow. "Something tells me we're going to have a lot of fun."

Lifting his broad shoulders in an elegant shrug, Aaron nodded. "That's what I was hoping." Lowering his head, he pressed his mouth to her hair. "It's time we go in and sit down."

Regina sat on Aaron's right and opposite the soccer player and his date, successfully avoiding her malevolent glare as she listened to the conversations in Portuguese floating around her.

Nicolas, sitting at the head of the table, rose to his feet and raised a glass of burgundy-red wine. His thick, black, wiry hair had been tamed with the efforts of a styling gel, and he managed to look very elegant in formal wear despite his bulk. Most people who met him for the first time thought he looked more like a professional wrestler than a doctor.

"I'd like to propose a toast to my lovely wife in celebration of her birthday. I want to thank you for the happiness you've given me these past two years. Happy birthday, *Querida*."

Rising to her feet, Jeannette raised her goblet of water. "I'd like to thank Nicolas and everyone for helping me celebrate what will become a very special year for me. I extend my sincerest appreciation to all of my old friends, and the new ones to come." She glanced at Regina, giving her a bright smile. "God bless you all." A spattering of applause was followed by Nicky nodding to the caterer to begin serving.

Regina lost count of the number of dishes she had sampled as Aaron leaned toward her, quietly describing the contents and ingredients of each course. She found herself leaning against his solid shoulder or touching his hand when she least expected it, but the gestures were not lost on the other diners.

Nicolas waited for the end of the fourth course, then stood up again. "Most of us know one another, but there are a couple of people here for the first time. Aaron, would you like to make your introduction?"

Placing his damask napkin beside his plate, Aaron rose to his feet. His gaze was fixed on the short, black glossy hair Regina had brushed off her forehead. The sophisticated style displayed the perfection of her delicate features.

"The beautiful lady sitting beside me is Regina Spencer—my wife, soon to be the mother of my child."

Flashing a shy smile, Regina accepted the congratulations and good wishes of everyone in the room as Aaron took his seat.

Nicolas took a sip of wine. "Jeannette and I thank the Spencers for gracing our table." He turned his attention to Elena Carvalho. "Elena, will you please introduce your guest?"

Fragancio Solis pulled back Elena's chair, assisting her as she stood up, and towered above her by at least six inches. She inhaled, causing a swell of golden breasts to rise precariously from her dress's revealing décolletage, then let out her breath in a soft whisper.

"I'm certain this man needs no introduction," she began slowly enough for those who weren't fully conversant in Portuguese, "but for those who are not familiar with the celebrities in *our* country..." Her words trailed off as she glared across the table at Regina. "I'd like to introduce my very good friend, Senhor Fragancio Solis."

Fragancio inclined his head in acknowledgment, his gaze meeting and fusing with Regina's. A slight smile played at the corner of his sensual mouth, and as he sat back down he winked at her.

She felt waves of anger radiating from Aaron, even though she hadn't glanced at him. Placing her hand over his clenched fist, she leaned closer. "I have to use the lavatory," she whispered in Spanish.

Pushing back his chair, Aaron stood up, excusing himself. His hand cupped Regina's elbow as he eased her to her feet and led her out of the dining room.

Regina waited until they were concealed behind the closed door of an ultramodern bathroom, then asked angrily, "What is going on back there?"

He went completely still. "You tell me."

Her gaze narrowed. "No, Aaron, you tell me. Your redhaired girlfriend has been throwing daggers at me from the moment she laid eyes on me, and I don't like it. I suggest you handle your business," she warned softly.

"There's nothing to handle, because there's nothing going on between Elena and me."

"Then what was her snide remark about those not being familiar with *our* country all about? She doesn't know me or anything about me, yet that doesn't stop her from being downright bitchy. Muzzle her, Aaron, or I won't be responsible for what I just might say. After all, these people are your esteemed colleagues, not mine."

She brushed past him, opening the door and leaving him to follow her. She hadn't taken more than a half-dozen steps when he caught up with her, his fingers curving around her upper arm.

"Calm down," he ordered, holding her fast. His grip tightened as he pulled her against his chest in a comforting embrace. "Relax, *Princesa*." She went limp against his body. "Are you all right now?"

Closing her eyes, she smiled. "Yes."

His nose nuzzled her ear. "Do you know something?"

"What?"

"You're magnificent when you're angry."

Easing back, she couldn't help herself when she burst out laughing, and much to her surprise his low, rumbling laugh joined hers.

Winding her arm through his, she brushed her mouth over his. "Let's go back before they send out a search party for us."

They returned to the dining room, holding hands while sharing a secret smile. The rest of the evening sped by quickly as Aaron and Regina withdrew to their private world where no one or nothing could penetrate the invisible thread binding them even tighter than before.

They were silent on the return trip home. Aaron smiled to himself, concentrating on the uneven surfaces of the road illuminated by the car's headlights. After their confrontation in the Benedetti bathroom and he and Regina had declared a temporary truce, Elena had transferred her undivided attention to her flirtatious jock for the remainder of the evening.

Jeannette and Regina made plans to visit each other, and he was pleased Regina had found a friend. She needed more than her garden to keep her occupied.

They arrived home after midnight, and Regina hesitated going inside as she stood in the veiled blackness, inhaling the scent of Brazil.

"I can't believe the vastness of this country," she whispered softly to Aaron.

"It is mind-boggling, isn't it?"

Leaning back against his body, she stared up at the star-littered sky, placing a delicate hand over the mound of her belly. "I have a name for our son."

"What is it, Darling?"

"Clayborne Diaz Spencer."

Turning her around to face him, Aaron tried making out her features in the dark. "He would carry his grandfathers' middle names."

She nodded and moved closer. "Something tells me he's going to be very much like his grandfathers."

Bending slightly, Aaron curved an arm under her knees and the other under her shoulders. "If that's the case, then he'll become a man who should make us very proud."

Holding on to his neck, she buried her face against his throat, inhaling his sensual male scent as it mingled with his cologne. "I'm sorry about going off on you in the bathroom," she whispered as he pushed open the door beyond the inner courtyard and headed for the staircase. "I just couldn't sit there and watch Elena—"

His mouth swooped down on hers, stopping her words. "Shh,

Princesa. Don't ever mention her name in this house again," he warned softly between light, nibbling kisses.

"I won't," she whispered back.

As he lifted her higher, she gasped as the tiny purse she held in one hand fell to the floor. "Stop, Aaron. I dropped my bag."

He continued up the staircase. "Don't worry about it. You can get it in the morning."

And she did forget about it, and everything else, once she lay in bed with Aaron, welcoming him into her arms and into her body. Their lovemaking was a prolonged, tender joining, and when they finally released their dammed up passions both were filled with an amazing sense of completeness they had never experienced before.

Regina left the bed at sunrise and managed to complete her morning toilette without waking Aaron. It was Sunday morning, and she wanted to prepare breakfast for him for the first time.

Her step was light and carefree as she practically skipped down the staircase, stopping only to pick up the small sequined bag she had dropped the night before.

She walked into the kitchen and stopped abruptly. Magda was there, filling a coffeepot with water. It wasn't seven o'clock, and she hadn't expected to see the housekeeper before that time. The petite woman turned and stared at her, her gaze widening in surprise.

Regina gave her a warm smile. *"Bom dia,* Magda."

"Bom dia, Senhora Spencer."

Walking across the kitchen, Regina placed her evening bag on a countertop. "You don't have to make breakfast for Senhor Spencer this morning. I'm going to do it."

Magda stared at her, unmoving. "I always make Senhor Spencer's breakfast."

"Not this morning. I'd like to surprise *my husband—*" The instant the two words were out of her mouth she knew she thought of Aaron Spencer not only as the father of her unborn child, but as the man she would exchange vows with.

Magda shook her head as if she did not understand. "I'm sorry, Senhora, but I will make the breakfast."

Regina knew the housekeeper understood what she was saying. She had learned enough basic Portuguese from the young man who helped her in the garden to communicate with most Brazilians.

"I *will* cook," she said firmly. "You may go back home."

Magda put down the coffeepot, at the same time mumbling angrily under her breath. Regina stared, her mouth gaping when she recognized a curse she had heard two men exchange during a heated argument when she'd walked down a street in Salvador.

"What did you say?"

Magda spun around, her dark eyes narrowing with resentment. "*Nada,* Senhora Spencer." There was no mistaking the facetiousness in the title.

"Senhora Pires, I would like to see you—alone!"

Both women jumped at the low, angry sound of Aaron's voice. Neither had heard him when he walked into the kitchen.

"*Agora.*" Even though he hadn't raised his voice, Magda flinched. He wanted to see her *now!*

Regina took a step toward Aaron, hoping to explain to him that Magda probably hadn't understood her, but he shot her a warning glance which shouted *Don't interfere,* and she wouldn't.

Her gaze softened as it met Magda's when she followed Aaron out of the kitchen.

Aaron waited for the housekeeper to walk into his study before he closed the door. He gestured to the chair beside his desk. "Please sit," Magda nodded, taking the chair.

Waiting until she was seated, Aaron sat down behind the desk and laced his fingers together as he stared from under lowered lids at the woman who had come to work for the da Costas the year he turned twenty. He had always found her cooperative and efficient, and there was never a time since his stepmother-aunt had passed away that he'd ever found fault with her household duties.

Except now.

"Did you not understand Senhora Spencer when she said she would prepare breakfast for me?"

Magda kept her gaze fixed on her folded hands on her lap. "I understood, Senhor Spencer."

His forehead furrowed in a frown. "Then why did you not do as she asked?"

"But I always prepare your breakfast for you."

His frown deepened. "That was in the past, Magda. If Senhora Spencer elects to prepare breakfast, then I don't want you to challenge her. She is mistress of this house, and her word is final. Do you understand?"

She nodded, raising her head and giving him a direct stare. "Yes."

He offered her a gentle smile, his eyes crinkling attractively. "I've been thinking about giving you more time off." Her eyes widened with this disclosure. "From now on you will work from Monday through Thursday."

"You do not need me on Fridays?"

He shook his head. "No." He had decided to cut back his own work schedule. He was committed to the three days at the hospital, but now he limited his involvement with the research institute to one day. Medical research was an ongoing laborious task, and his need to care for Regina was much more immediate.

What he did not want to acknowledge was his fear—a fear that she, like his mother, would not survive childbirth. The fear surfaced when he least expected it, leaving him shaking and feeling powerless despite his medical training.

Magda forced a smile. "Thank you, Senhor Spencer."

"You're welcome, Magda."

He waited for the tiny woman to leave, then sat for several

minutes staring at the closed door. A foreign emotion had not permitted him to fire Magda though he registered the slur she made about Regina. It was as if something had swept away the red-hot fury, temporarily paralyzing his tongue.

He suspected Magda resented Regina's presence. For more than three years no other woman had occupied the house, and she had probably come to think of herself as mistress of the da Costa estate.

Aaron closed his eyes, shaking his head slowly. If Regina Spencer did not become mistress of his house, no other woman would ever claim that status.

Chapter 21

Regina sat at the dressing table in the expansive dressing room, outlining her lips with a brown liner before filling them in with a flattering, orange-brown color. A gleam of anticipation glimmered in her dark eyes as she looked forward to spending the afternoon with Jeannette Benedetti. They had agreed Jeannette would come to the da Costa estate for brunch for their first social engagement.

Surveying her face, Regina was pleased with the results. She had had her hair trimmed the day before, when she went to Salvador with Aaron for her monthly checkup with Dr. Nicolas Benedetti. Her trip to the hair salon was followed up with an afternoon of shopping for Christmas gifts for family members, and instead of waiting for Aaron to drive her back home she had secured the services of a taxi for the return trip. She offered the overly polite, friendly driver a generous tip, prompting him to propose his services as an on-call driver. She accepted his pager number, promising to call him whenever the need arose. Having a

private driver at her disposal would eliminate the need for Aaron
to purchase a car for her personal use.

The light from a lamp on the dressing table glinted off the
stones on the ring on her left hand, and she stared down at Arlene
Spencer's ring. She had promised herself she would only wear it
the night of Jeannette's surprise party, but two days had passed
since that event. Twisting the wide band around her finger, she
pulled it off and left it on the table.

Rising to her feet, she made her way over to the armoire
where her clothes were stored, opening one of many small draw-
ers. The sequined purse she had carried to the dinner party lay
beside another covered with a profusion of black bugle beads.
She picked up the purse, retreated to her bedroom, and poured
its contents out on the antique quilt covering the large bed. A
jeweled compact, tube of lipstick, and a small sable brush lay
on the bed covering. Vertical lines appeared between her eyes
as she shook the purse vigorously. The ring was missing!

Closing her eyes, she tried remembering the events wherein
Aaron had removed Oscar's ring from her finger. He had given
it back to her, and she had dropped it into the purse, she was
certain. But then she remembered dropping the purse on the staircase when he carried her up the stairs to their bedroom later that
night.

She opened her eyes. However, she had found the purse the
following morning in the exact place where she had dropped
it, and she was sure it hadn't opened to spill its contents on the
staircase.

A lump rose in her throat. The ring was her last inanimate link
with Oscar Spencer, and she wasn't ready to let him go—not
yet. There were times when she wondered why she had not accepted Aaron's marriage proposal, rationalizing there was no
rush to marry him because she was carrying his child. On the
other hand, there were occasions when she believed the enmity
between Aaron and Oscar continued despite the latter's death.

After all, Oscar had married the first woman Aaron had ever loved. And the memory of a first love usually did not fade—not even with time.

Her jaw hardened as she returned to the dressing room and retrieved Arlene's ring. It was safer on her finger than lying around. She intended as soon as Aaron returned from the hospital to ask him if he had removed the ring from her purse.

She made her way down to the kitchen to solicit Magda's assistance to set the table on the pergola. After their Sunday morning confrontation Magda had come to her and apologized profusely. She accepted the apology, with a promise it would never occur again.

Taking several steps back from the table in the pergola, Regina surveyed her handiwork. The round wooden table was set with a sunny, yellow linen tablecloth with matching napkins. Blooming yellow tea roses entwined with ivy, climbed over the trellis, filling the warm air with their delicate floral scent.

A closet off the kitchen contained century-old sets of china, silver, crystal, and linens, and she had selected a place setting of bone china with sprigs of yellow flowers circling the edges and sterling silverware with heavy handles designed with an elaborate baroque design.

She had spent the morning preparing a menu which was certain to surprise her guest, hoping to bring a touch of the American South to Bahia, Brazil. The sound of voices filtered in the warm summer air, and Regina turned to find Magda escorting Jeannette into the pergola.

"What's up, Girlfriend?" Jeannette asked, grinning broadly.

Regina hugged her new friend, returning the smile. "We're having soul food for lunch," she whispered close to her ear.

Jeannette pulled back, her mouth gaping in surprise. "Oh, no you didn't!" she exclaimed once she found her voice. "What did you make?"

"Oven-fried chicken, cornbread, sweet potatoes, and steamed

kale. I couldn't find any collard or mustard greens, so the kale was the next best substitute."

Jeannette's head bobbed up and down in slow motion as she wrinkled her nose. "Did you slip any smoked meat in the kale?"

"I put just a sliver in, for seasoning purposes only," she confirmed, feeling like a conspirator. "You know your husband's warnings about sodium intake."

Waving a hand, Jeannette glanced at the table set with the heirloom china, crystal, and covered silver serving dishes. "Nicolas can be a pain in the behind when he wants to. My blood pressure is normal, and my feet and legs haven't swelled, so I don't know why he monitors my diet so closely." She glanced down at the ballet slippers on Regina's narrow feet. "And judging from the spikes you were wearing Saturday night I know you haven't been retaining fluid."

Regina nodded. "I'm giving myself until Christmas for the heels, then I'm going to put them away for a while." Taking Jeannette's hand, she led her to the table. "Let's sit and eat before everything gets cold."

Jeannette Benedetti sat down, visually admiring her hostess. This Regina Spencer looked vastly differently from the one she had met at her dinner party. She looked younger, almost too young for Aaron Spencer. A pair of slim, black Capri pants she had paired with a tailored, white linen smock concealed her physical condition. Pregnancy agreed with her. Her skin was clear, her eyes bright, and her coiffed hair full and lustrous. Jeannette had been as surprised as her husband when Nicolas revealed that Aaron had married and his bride was expecting a child.

Jeannette took a forkful of each portion, shaking her head in reverence. "Girl, you can cook for me anytime. Where did you learn to cook like this?"

Regina raised her goblet filled with chilled lemonade and took a sip. "My father. He won't admit it, but he's always been a frustrated chef. I don't know how he does it, but he manages to make grilled franks taste wonderful."

Smiling, Jeannette stared at Regina over the rim of her own goblet of lemonade. "Does Aaron cook?"

"Yes. And very well."

"It seems as if you married a man like your father."

Regina's expression sobered when she analyzed Jeannette's statement. Aaron was more like her father than she realized. Both were tall and powerfully built. And whenever Aaron sat and draped one leg over his knee the motion was the same graceful movement she had seen Martin Cole execute over and over.

Even their personalities were more similar than dissimilar. Aaron saw to her every need in the manner that her father had taken, and continued to take, care of her mother. The most important factor was that they were honorable men, and she knew if she married Aaron it would be for a lifetime.

"You're right about that," she confirmed with a bright smile.

"I don't like spreading gossip, but you have to know that Aaron was quite the bachelor before he married you." Jeannette had lowered her voice. "I don't mean that he ran around with a lot of women, because he didn't. Some women were just downright shameless whenever they tried coming on to him."

"What did they do?" Regina did not know why she'd asked the question, but a part of her always wanted to know more about the man she now shared a house with before he had come into her life.

"It wasn't so much a *they* as it was one person in particular."

"Elena?"

Sitting up straighter, Jeannette stared directly at her. "You know about Elena?"

"What I do know is that we will never become friends."

Wiping a corner of her mouth with the napkin, Jeannette

frowned. "I'm surprised Dr. Elena Carvalho hasn't come at you with a scalpel."

Regina felt a flicker of apprehension race up her spine. "She's a doctor?"

"Aaron didn't tell you?"

"Aaron and I do not discuss the *lady*."

Jeannette registered the sarcasm immediately. "Nicolas and I have had long, heated conversations about her. She's one of the best surgeons on the continent, but she's also obsessed with Dr. Aaron Spencer. She had a prestigious position at a major hospital in Rio, but transferred to Salvador about eighteen months ago after she met Aaron at a medical conference. He was dating someone else, but that ended a week after Elena joined the staff."

"Was the other woman also a doctor?"

Jeannette shook her head. "No. She was a television news commentator."

"What did Elena do to her?"

"No one knows. The word was she handed in her resignation and left the country. I really can't say that Aaron and Elena were ever a couple, because the few times I saw them together I realized there were no sparks, no passion. I watched him with you Saturday night. Seeing the way he touched you and looked at you said more than a spoken admission of love. We had no idea that when he took a personal leave of absence for more than a month it was to get married."

"Aaron is a very private person," she said truthfully—so private he would not permit his full-time household staff to reside under his roof.

It was apparent Aaron had not told his friends and colleagues that he had left Bahia to bury his father—subsequently seducing his father's widow.

"How did you find your way to Bahia via North Carolina?" she queried Jeannette, smoothly changing the topic.

Jeannette's expression brightened. "I came here for Carnival three years ago and met Nicky. I was a partner with three of my college soros in a travel agency, and each year one of us visited a different place to update our travel packages.

"We offered trips to Rio for Carnival, then decided to add Bahia. I was chosen to cover the festivities, and after several hours of dancing and mingling with local Bahians and visitors I was literally cooling my heels in a small restaurant. I had taken my sandals off and put my aching feet up on a chair when Nicolas Benedetti walked in with two of his friends. They were seated at a table next to mine. He kept staring and smiling at me while I tried ignoring this hulk of a man who looked like the *after* for a Rogaine ad. I much preferred his taller, darker friend, whom I later discovered was Dr. Aaron Spencer."

Regina shifted a naturally arching eyebrow at this disclosure. She remembered Aaron saying that he stayed away from Carnival because it had become too boisterous for him.

"How did you finally meet Nicolas?"

"He walked over to my table, sat down, and began massaging my bare, dusty, aching feet. I was too shocked to do anything but stare at this gentle giant while he whispered softly in Portuguese about how much he liked my face. He said it reminded him of a beautiful sculpture he had on a wall in his house."

"You understood Portuguese?"

Jeannette nodded. "I was a language major in college. At that time I spoke fluent Spanish, French, and Italian. My Portuguese was limited, but my knowledge of Spanish helped a lot. I've lived here for two years, and there are times I still have to grope for the words because I find myself thinking in Spanish. Nicky was talking about me coming to his house to see his sculpture when most guys I knew would talk about taking a girl home to see the etchings on their ceilings."

Leaning forward, her eyes shining with anticipation, Regina said, "What happened after that?"

"I turned him down, but hadn't noticed that his two friends left the restaurant without him. When I told him why I was in Bahia, he offered to act as my tour guide. We spent the next six hours together, talking and laughing. He took me back to my hotel, and as we stood outside the door to my room his beeper went off. I let him in to use the telephone to return the page, and when he hung up I saw a very different Nicolas Benedetti. Gone was the smiling, joking man, and in his place a very serious Dr. Benedetti. He told me he had to get to the hospital to deliver a baby."

"He hadn't told you he was a doctor?"

Shaking her head, Jeannette said, "No."

"What happened after that?"

"He came back to the hotel around four o'clock the next morning, exhausted. His patient had been unable to deliver vaginally, and he'd had to perform a C-section. He laid across my bed and slept for six hours without waking up. When he woke up I ordered breakfast for us and we spent the day together until he left to go back to the hospital.

"I saw him every day until it was time for me to return to the States, and in all of the time we spent together he never tried to touch or kiss me. At first I thought that he hadn't found me attractive, but a month later he called me and he said he was sorry he let me go without kissing me. I told him that I would give him the opportunity when I came back to Bahia for the next Carnival."

"Did you?"

"No. I came back sooner. Nicky called me every Sunday night for four months, and we'd talk for hours. Then one day without warning I decided to fly down and surprise him. I told myself I was crazy, but I didn't care. I walked into the hospital, went to his office, and asked to see him. His bushy eyebrows shot up so far on his forehead that I thought they would never come down. I stared at him, realizing he looked nothing like the men I had ever dated in the States, but at that moment I didn't care because I had fallen in love with him.

"I spent the week with him at his house, and before I left Bahia to fly back to Winston-Salem, North Carolina, I had accepted his proposal to become Mrs. Nicolas Benedetti. My girlfriends thought I had lost my mind until Nicky came to the States to see me that Christmas. I invited them over to my apartment for a Kwanzaa party, and showed them my engagement ring. Needless to say, my three very beautiful, unattached girlfriends left later that night just a tad jealous."

"Where were you married?"

"We decided to marry in Bahia. My sister was my matron of honor, and Aaron was Nicky's best man. Aaron paid for the reception dinner at *Tempero da Dadá,* one of the more popular restaurants in Salvador. It was a very small gathering with my parents and Nicky's, who had flown up from Buenos Aires."

Regina sighed softly. "It sounds like a fairy tale romance."

"And it has been," Jeannette confirmed. "Earlier this year we decided to start a family, and I finally conceived in August."

"Which means we should deliver a month apart."

"Which means our children will grow up together. Our husbands are good friends, and I'm hoping you and I will also become good friends," Jeannette said, flashing a bright smile.

Reaching across the table, Regina squeezed her hand. "I'm certain we will."

She wanted to tell Jeannette that she had never had a girlfriend. Her female cousins did not count as girlfriends, and while in school she had never cultivated a friendship with any girl she felt comfortable enough to confide in. After her kidnapping she had found it hard to develop a closeness with anyone outside her family, and when most girls were flirting and hanging out in the malls with adolescent boys she had immersed herself in her studies, excelling, accelerating, and graduating a year ahead of her contemporaries.

She'd moved in with Oscar at seventeen, married him at ni◼
teen, and spent the next eight years caring for her elderly, si◼
husband. She planned to spend six months in Bahia, and duri◼
that time she was certain she would call Jeannette Benede◼
friend.

Aaron reread the newspaper article, the smile playing arou◼
his mouth widening as his gaze moved swiftly over the word◼

"Good news?" questioned Dr. Dennis Liu.

"It has to be, or why would we be sitting here with chill◼
champagne?" asked the doctor who headed the research tear◼

Nodding, Aaron glanced up at the brilliant young microbio◼
gist. "Very good news."

"Then share it with us, Aaron," a female research assista◼
pleaded softly.

Smiling at the eight people sitting around the conference tab◼
Aaron lowered his gaze and began reading.

"Doctors at the *São Tomé Instituto de Médico Pes-quisa* in Bahia, Brazil, have developed a new way to test fetuses for a potentially fatal blood problem known as RH incompatibility.

"The procedure, which is not yet in general use, is safer and faster than existing tests. Instead of inserting a needle through the mother's abdomen and into her uterus, the doctors draw blood, with test results available within a day rather than a week or more.

"RH incompatibility can cause anemia, swelling, and brain damage. The current tests for RH-factor incompatibility use a needle to extract amniotic fluid or tissue from the placenta. These tests are accurate, but there's a small risk—one percent to two percent—of their causing a miscarriage.

"The testing determines whether what is called the RH-factor in the baby's blood is compatible with the mother's. If not, the mother's immune system may create antibodies that attack the baby's blood.

"In a study to be published today in the *New England Journal of Medicine,* Dr. Aaron Spencer, the institute's director, said he found that the mother's blood carries enough of the fetus's DNA to determine the baby's RH-factor as early as fourteen weeks into pregnancy."

Folding the newspaper, he offered each person sitting at the table a warm smile. "Congratulations."

The man who headed the research team stood up and applauded as the others in the room followed suit, applauding one another.

The young doctor from China, who had joined the research staff a year ago, reached for the open bottle of champagne chilling in a container on the conference table, and one by one each person held out a flute to be filled.

Dr. Dennis Liu filled a glass, extending it to Aaron. "To you, Aaron. For believing in us, and for signing our paychecks."

"Hear! Hear!" the assembled chorused.

Aaron took the proffered glass and raised it. "To the finest research team in the world. This recognition could not have come at a better time, because this Christmas will become one that I will remember for a long time. And before we end this research year for our holiday recess I'd like to invite everyone to my home for a little celebratory soirée next Saturday evening. You may bring your wives, husbands, partners, or significant others." There was a stunned silence during which the eight exchanged questioning glances. "The festivities will begin at seven," he continued smoothly. Draining his glass, he savored the bubbles on his tongue before swallowing the premium champagne. "Excuse me, ladies, gentlemen. I'm taking the rest of the afternoon off."

Dennis Liu glanced at his watch. It was only two-thirty. He might have been the newest member of the research team at the *São Tomé Instituto de Médico Pesquisa,* but he was more than aware of the in-house rumors of Dr. Aaron Spencer regularly spending as many as three nights a week at the institute until he took a leave of absence several months ago.

He had returned to Bahia a changed man, and since his wife arrived he had exhibited another facet of his personality no one had ever seen before. He seemed more relaxed, smiled more often, and there were times when he seemed more human, not an automaton who existed for medical research. Yes, Dennis mused, getting married had had an amazing effect on the man who headed the *São Tomé Instituto de Médico Pesquisa.*

Aaron parked the Range Rover in the garage, then made his way toward the garden, where he was certain to find Regina. He slowed his pace, noting the obvious changes. All of the overgrown portions of the flower and herb gardens were cleared away, turning the garden into a civilized oasis. Water poured from the fountain into a pool, which flowed into a long runlet.

Walking along a wide avenue of stone, he noticed that the many flowers were living works of art. He touched the dewy petals of a dainty iris, and inhaled the distinctive fragrance of orchids growing in extravagant abandonment.

He had played hide-and-seek in his aunt's garden during his youth, usually ignoring its haunting beauty. Regina had painstakingly begun its restoration, and like a phoenix it now rose anew.

Making his way up a flight of stone steps, he smiled at a statuary swathed in palm fronds. He ran his fingers over the cool marble, tracing its smooth curves.

Movement caught his attention and he went completely still, listening.

He heard Regina's low, sultry voice then that of Christôvão's. Aaron did not know why, but he felt like a cuckold husband spying on his unfaithful wife. He waited until they emerged from the overgrowth of trees, startling both when they saw him.

"Boa tarde," he announced quietly, inclining his head.

Christôvão offered him a half-smile. *"Boa tarde,* Senhor Spencer." He gave Regina a shy smile. "I'll see you tomorrow."

Regina gestured to him. "No, Christôvão, don't leave."

"Let him go," Aaron commanded when the younger man quickened his pace and walked away.

Rounding on him, Regina glared at Aaron. "What are you doing? Spying on me?"

Folding his arms over his chest, he tilted his head at an angle. "Is there a reason why I should?"

Heat flooded her cheeks. "Of course not." She gave him a long, penetrating stare. "What are you doing home so early?"

His upper lip curled under the neatly barbered moustache. "I came home to share *siesta* with my wife."

"You delude yourself, because I'm not your wife," she shot back angrily.

His temper rose to match hers. "And what keeps you from becoming my wife, Senhora Spencer?"

Her gaze widened. "There are a number of reasons."

"Enumerate."

"I don't want to become a possession, Aaron. I don't want to feel as if you own me the way you own this land. And I don't want you to think I'm beholden to you because I'm carrying your child. Years from now I don't want you to throw it in my face that you married me because you didn't want your child to be illegitimate. I also don't want you to use me to pay your father back for marrying your fiancée. And, last but not least, I don't need your money to provide support for this baby, nor do I need your name, because I'm already a Spencer."

"Are you finished?" he questioned in a dangerously soft voice.

Raising her chin in a haughty gesture, she turned her back. "Yes, I am."

"Good." Taking two steps, Aaron swept her up in his arms and carried her into the allée of palms closing in around them. She struggled in his embrace, and he tightened his grip. "The only time you aren't verbally abusing me with that whip you call a tongue is when I make love to you, *Senhora* Spencer."

Her gaze widened as she froze. "You're not going to make love to me in—"

He stopped her words when his mouth descended on hers, robbing her of her breath. Pulling back, he drew in a lungful of air, then recaptured her soft, throbbing mouth.

Day merged into night the farther he retreated deep into the garden, the towering trees blocking out the brilliant Brazilian afternoon summer sun.

Regina, caught up in the dizzying spell of rising passion, remembered Aaron lowering her to the cool, damp earth, but nothing beyond that. It was later, much later that she found herself nude, lying on Aaron's shirt as he lay beside her breathing heavily. When his respiration returned to normal, he had plucked a flowering shell ginger and tucked it behind her left ear.

The cool earth absorbed the heat from her moist body as she closed her eyes, reveling in the aftermath of their passions having spiraled out of control.

"What are you doing to me, Aaron?"

Turning on his side, he smiled at her thoroughly kissed mouth. "I'm loving you, *Princesa*."

"No, you're not," she slurred.

"Oh, yes I am," he insisted.

"You're taking advantage of me. You're bigger, stronger, and—"

"And I love your life," he confessed, pressing his mouth to hers.

There was a low rumble as the earth vibrated under their bodies and both went completely still. It was thunder. They were lying naked in the garden while the threat of imminent rain threatened to cool their wanton coupling. There was another roll of thunder, followed by fat, warm drops dotting their fevered flesh.

They sprang to their feet, pulling on articles of clothing to cover their nakedness as they raced out of the garden toward the house. Aaron managed to slip on his slacks and Regina her slacks and top, both leaving underwear and shoes behind.

She clutched Aaron's hand, while holding her unbuttoned blouse together with her other. "Slow down!" she screamed to be heard above the intermittent rumbling.

He slowed enough to swing her up into his arms and raced the remaining feet to the house. Staring down at her flushed face, he smiled, his gaze moving down to her exposed breasts. The lush darkness of her distended nipples renewed his passion all over again as he pushed open the door to the inner courtyard.

Magda walked across the living room, staring at the rain-soaked couple, her knowing gaze taking in their state of half-dress. "Is Senhora Spencer all right?"

Regina pressed her face to Aaron's bare chest when she heard the housekeeper's voice. She wanted to tell Magda that she was wonderful. Aaron had just made love to her in the garden, and all she wanted to do was spend the rest of her life in his arms.

"She's fine, Magda," Aaron said, taking the stairs two at a time. He moved down the hallway, smiling at Regina. "Now, are you ready to take *siesta* with me?"

"Umm," she moaned, angling for a more comfortable position.

He placed her on the bed, removed her damp clothing, then removed his slacks and lay down beside her. "I love you, Regina Spencer," he whispered as he closed his eyes and joined her in a sleep for sated lovers.

Chapter 22

Regina awoke to a blue-veiled sky and an orange-colored full moon as the backdrop for a profusion of twinkling stars. She moaned softly as she turned away from the window.

"Did I hurt you?" questioned a deep voice in the velvet darkness.

"No. I'm just a little stiff from pulling up weeds."

Aaron sat up, reached over, and flicked on the table lamp. Turning back to Regina, he frowned at her. "What are you doing weeding? Isn't that why I hired Christôvão?"

She let out her breath in an audible sigh. "I was helping him."

Moving closer, he place a hand over her hip, massaging the tender muscles in her lower back. "Next time let the man do *his* job."

"I will," she promised. She moaned again. "That feels wonderful, Aaron."

Going up on his knees, he leaned over her prone body and

massaged her back and legs, his strong fingers working their healing magic.

"I want to host a Christmas party for the staff at the institute," he stated firmly.

There was a noticeable pause before Regina responded. "Where?" Her low, sultry voice floated up and lingered in the quietness of the room.

"Here."

"When?"

"Next Saturday."

A slight smile softened her full lips. "You're not giving me much notice, Aaron. I have to prepare a menu and decorate the house."

He ran his forefinger down the length of her spine. "We'll have a caterer provide the food. Meanwhile, Magda and I will help you with whatever else you'll need in the house."

Shifting, she sat up and pressed her back against the massive, carved headboard. "How can you help when you're working?"

Aaron moved over and sat beside her. His admiring gaze lingered on her delicate profile. "Tomorrow will be my last day at the institute for two months. And—"

"Two months?" she queried, interrupting him. It was apparent she was shocked at this disclosure.

"We always recess for two months. It gives everyone a chance to return to their native countries, or go on holiday. You'll get to see a lot of me until mid-February."

"Speaking of February, would you mind if I invited my brother and sister to come for Carnival?"

Curving an arm around her shoulders, he pulled her head to his chest. "Of course I don't mind. Invite whomever you want."

She smiled up at him. "You wouldn't be so generous if I decided to invite the entire Cole clan."

"Oh, yes I would," he said teasingly. "I don't know where

everyone would sleep, but I'm certain we could figure out something."

Regina stared at her left hand splayed over his muscled chest, her gaze lingering on the white and rare yellow diamonds in the wide band on her finger. Pulling back, she gave him a direct stare. "Did you take my ring from my evening purse?"

He frowned. "What ring?"

"The ring Oscar gave me."

"No, I didn't. Why?"

"I can't find it."

"When was the last time you saw it?"

"The night we went to Jeannette's party. You took it off my finger, but I put it in my bag."

"Do you think it could've fallen out?"

She shrugged both shoulders. "I don't know. I dropped the purse on the staircase, but when I picked it up the next morning it was still closed."

Moving off the bed, Aaron stood up. "After I shower I'll ask Magda if she found it."

Regina went to her knees and held on to his wrist. "Don't. I'll ask her. I don't want her to think you're accusing her of stealing it."

His eyebrows met in a frown. "I'd never accuse her of being a thief."

"Let me handle it?"

"Okay," he conceded. "I won't say anything." He extended a hand. "Come share a shower with me."

She grasped the proffered fingers. "Only if you promise to behave, Aaron Spencer."

Pulling her gently from the bed, he swung her up in his arms. "I can promise you anything but that."

"*Aaron,*" she wailed.

"Okay. But just this time." Walking across the bedroom, he

shifted her ripening body, smiling. She was gaining weight. "I've come up with a name for our daughter," he said mysteriously.

Her eyes brightened with amusement. "What is it?"

"Eden."

Lowering her gaze, lashes brushing her sun-tanned cheeks, Regina flashed a shy smile. "It would be very appropriate for a girl, but—" Her gaze moved up and locked with his.

"But what?" His voice was barely a whisper.

"But it's going to be a boy."

"How do you know that, Senhora Spencer?"

"I just know."

"We'll see."

"Promise me you won't ask Nicolas to see the ultrasound pictures."

"Have you seen them?" he countered.

"No. And I don't want to. Promise me, Aaron." His mouth tightened beneath his moustache. "Please, Darling," she pleaded, offering him one of her irresistible dimpled smiles.

"All right. I promise," he said between clenched teeth.

"I will finish bringing out the dishes and show the caterers where you want them to set up when they arrive, Senhora Spencer."

Regina smiled at Magda, nodding. "Thank you for your help. Everything looks beautiful." She and Magda had prepared all of the appetizers for the cocktail hour.

Cold fish dishes, along with other platters filled with assorted cheeses, a Mediterranean salad, a five-tomato salsa, stuffed tomatoes and mushrooms, chicken salads, oven-roasted artichoke slivers with thyme and marjoram, and prosciutto-stuffed figs all lined the tables set up in the courtyard, which was brightly illuminated with more than three dozen lanterns positioned around the perimeter. Strings of tiny electric lights cast an ethereal glow on the garden and beyond.

Regina had planned for an outdoor buffet dinner for twenty, followed by dancing under a navy-blue, star-littered sky. The oppressive daytime temperatures were alleviated by the setting sun, and a nighttime temperature of seventy-five with a warm summer breeze had helped create the perfect setting for a holiday gathering.

Magda offered Senhora Spencer a sincere smile for the first time since she had come to the da Costa estate. Her smile was still in place as she watched Regina retreat to the house to dress before the arrival of her guests.

Even though she resented the younger woman's presence, she had to admit she had treated her kindly. When Regina had questioned her about her missing wedding ring, she had readily accepted her response that she hadn't seen it.

She'd lied smoothly; it was she who had taken it from the small purse lying on the staircase. Discovering the ring had been divine providence. She had waited two days, then taken a rare trip to Salvador and sold it for a fraction of its worth. She could have haggled and gotten more money, but what she received was enough—more than enough to pay someone to make certain Senhora Regina Spencer and the child she carried in her womb would not survive the next harvest.

Aaron squeezed Regina's fingers, then smiled down at her as the first of the invitees walked into the courtyard. The invitation had indicated casual dress. The men arrived *sans* jackets and ties, and the women favored colorful sandals they had paired with dresses that revealed the maximum amount of bare flesh without being vulgar.

Regina felt almost overdressed in her silk ensemble of slacks and softly flowing top with a scooped neckline. She wore red, and Aaron had elected black: linen slacks, shirt, and imported Italian loafers.

She felt the excitement the moment she had descended the

staircase. Every room in the house was filled with flowers bringing the ethereal enchantment of her resplendent garden indoors.

The caterers and the musicians had arrived, and had set up quickly and expertly before their guests crossed the boundary line marking the da Costa property.

"Everything looks beautiful," Aaron whispered. "You look beautiful."

Returning his smile, she nodded. "Thank you, Darling."

Lowering his head, he pressed his mouth to her ear. "No, *Princesa,* thank *you*."

"I'm truly wounded, Aaron. You throw a party and forget to invite me."

Aaron's head came up quickly when he heard a familiar male voice. A bright smile crossed his face as he released Regina's hand and pulled Marcos Jarre into a quick, rough embrace.

"If you wanted an invitation, you should've let me know you were back."

Marcos Jarre's black eyes narrowed in concentration as he ignored the man who was more like a brother to him than his own brother, his gaze softening when he stared at the tall, slender woman standing beside Aaron Spencer.

Aaron did not miss Marcos's interest in Regina. Curving an arm around her waist, he smiled. "Regina, this gypsy is Marcos Jarre, our closest neighbor. Marcos, Regina Spencer."

Regina extended a slender hand, offering Aaron's friend a warm, dimpled smile. "My pleasure, Marcos."

He took her hand and pressed a kiss to her knuckles. His steady gaze did not waver behind the lenses of his round, wire-rimmed glasses when he catalogued every inch of her face and body. "No, Regina. The pleasure is mine. I can't believe my friend has been holding out on me."

"I wouldn't have to hold out on you if you called me more than once a year," Aaron teased. "Marcos has spent the last ten years of his life studying and teaching in Europe and Africa. And I must admit that he is a brilliant teacher and scholar," he explained to Regina.

Marcos shook his head, smiling. "You've changed, friend. Old age and marriage have humbled you."

"Old age!" Aaron retorted. "I'm only a day older than you are."

Regina examined the man who would be her neighbor during her stay in Bahia. She eclipsed his height by several inches, but his slender body made him appear taller than his five feet, eight inches. He affected a close-cropped haircut, while a neat goatee added character to his narrow face. His coloring reminded her of a polished pecan with rich, gold-brown undertones. His English was flawless, and she wondered whether he was a native Brazilian or had learned the language during his travels.

"In case you're not aware of it, your husband is also an excellent teacher," Marcos stated with a wide grin. "He taught me English—"

"And you taught me to speak Spanish," Aaron countered.

"And I taught you how to ride a horse, *amigo,* and you became a better horseman, even though I had grown up around them all of my life."

Aaron nodded. "That's because books were your passion, not horses. How long do you plan to stay in Bahia this time?"

"I've taken a sabbatical. I'll be here for a year."

As he placed a large hand on Marcos's shoulder, Aaron's expression softened. "Good. Welcome home, friend."

"Thank you."

"I hope you're going to join us," Regina offered in a quiet tone.

"I thought you'd never ask," Marcos teased, winking at her.

"He's seems very nice," she said to Aaron after Marcos made his way across the courtyard to where a portable bar had been set up.

"He's the brother I never had," Aaron admitted. "He's tru
brilliant, *Princesa*. He has become an expert on African histor
He has lived in most African countries, and has lectured at eve
prestigious university in the States and Europe. He just spent th
past two years at Oxford."

Curiosity and anticipation lit up her eyes. "I'd love to invi
him for dinner."

"Knowing Marcos, he won't wait for an invitation. Chanc
are you'll get to see a lot of him now that he's going to remai
in Bahia for more than a few months."

She inhaled, then let out her breath slowly. "I think it's tim
you introduced me to your guests."

"*Our* guests," he reminded her, spying Nicolas and Jeannet
as they made their way into the courtyard.

Regina spent the cocktail hour meeting and socializing wit
the people who worked at the research institute. She thoug
them too formal, stilted, until each had sampled a cup of pote
rum punch. After their second drinks inhibitions were shed, an
everyone exhibited a liveliness that was infectious.

The frivolity continued well into the night with drinking
dancing, and a nonstop consumption of food. Regina shared he
first dance with Aaron, then with every man present. A few o
the doctors from the institute flirted shamelessly with her, b
she laughed and ignored some of the more ribald comment
attributing the loose tongues to the intoxicating effects of th
punch.

Near the midnight hour she found herself in the arms o
Marcos Jarre, once the pulsing musical numbers had slowed
a classic, Brazilian love ballad. He had pulled her into a clos
embrace, then gone completely still once he registered the sligl
swell of her belly artfully disguised under the red silk.

"You're expecting a child?" His voice was a hoarse whis
per.

She shifted an eyebrow, smiling. "Yes."

He whistled softly. "My friend has really changed."

Her smile faded, replaced by a questioning frown. "Why would you say that?"

Marcos shook his head. "There was a time when Aaron took solemn oath that he would never marry or have children."

She forced a smile she did not feel. "I suppose anyone can change."

"That's true, Regina. But I just remember Aaron being so adamant about not wanting to get married." He swung her around in an intricate step, she following easily. "However, I can see why he did change his mind. You're stunning," he murmured in velvet tone.

Easing back, she stared at him. "Are you flirting with me, Marcos?"

"Of course," he replied flippantly.

She was forced to laugh even though she did not feel like it. Marcos and Jeannette had remarked how much Aaron had changed, and she wondered who was the real man she had reluctantly pledged her future to.

Had he proposed marriage because he truly did love her, or was revenge his intent? The question nagged at her until Marcos's voice shattered her musings.

"How much of Bahia have you seen?"

"Not too much. I visit Salvador several times a month. I'm currently spending a lot of time at home because I'm restoring the garden."

Marcos tilted his head at an attractive angle, flashing a knowing smile. "I know Aaron is probably up to his eyeballs with his work at the institute and at the hospital, so I'm going to appoint myself as your personal guide. And if you're willing to give up a few days working in your garden I'll show you a place unlike any other on the continent. A thorough tour of Salvador will take about five days, while I can also plan a few day trips to Caldas do Jorro or Lençóis. One thing you must see is a *candombl* ceremony."

"What is *candomblé?*"

"It is a religious ceremony that is wholly African in origin The participants worship various divinities called *orixás.*"

Regina gave him a skeptical look. "Brazil is a Catholic coun try, yet you're saying the people practice *candomblé?*"

Marcos nodded. "It's fascinating. I'll take you to a *candombl* ceremony, and let you judge for yourself. All I'll say is that Sal vador is known as the most deeply religious of Brazilian cities and has about one hundred-sixty churches and approximatel four thousand *candomblé terreiros,* or temples."

"I can't wait."

"Wait for what?" questioned a deep, velvety voice.

Regina turned to find Aaron standing less than three fee away, watching her dance with his friend. "Marcos has promise to take me to a *candomblé* ceremony."

His expression became a mask of stone. "I'd prefer that yo stayed away from those places."

Stepping away from Marcos, she moved over and wound he arm through Aaron's. "Why, Darling?"

"We'll talk about it later." He had addressed Regina, but hi angry gaze was trained on his friend and neighbor.

Recognizing the warning look in Aaron's eyes, Marcos nodde to Regina. "Thank you for the dance."

"You're welcome," she called out as he walked away.

Aaron turned to look at her, his hands cradling her face "What do you say we send our guests on their way, then go t bed?"

Her fingers curled around his strong wrists. "Before you d that I'd like to know something."

He gave her a sensual smile. "What is it?"

"This pretense of masquerading as husband and wife." He nodded. "Who are you trying to protect? Me, or yourself?"

His smile faded quickly. "What do you mean?"

She leaned closer, her gaze widening in the shadowed light from the minute bulbs hanging from the branches of a nearby tree. "I think it's your reputation you want to protect, not mine. It was you, Bahia's eminent Dr. Aaron Spencer, who swore he would never marry or father a child. But all of that has changed since—"

"Stop it, Regina!" He hadn't raised his voice, but the three words cut through the night like the crack of a whip.

"Stop what, Aaron? Stop wanting to live a lie? What's the matter with you that you can't accept the truth?"

"And what do you think is the truth?"

"That I've become a willing victim in your scheme to punish your father for marrying your fiancée."

He dropped his hands and turned away from her. "You're back to that again."

"I can't let it go, Aaron."

He turned slowly to face her, his impassive expression masking the rage threatening to explode. "And why not?" he questioned softly.

"You lost Sharon to Oscar, and you had to accept that. But why has it taken you twelve years to commit to marrying? Why me and not Elena, or some other woman? More importantly, why your father's widow?"

"You're asking questions I'm not able to answer, because there are no answers."

"You expect me to believe that?"

"Yes."

"Well, I can't, Aaron."

"Then you have a problem, Senhora Spencer. A very serious, personal problem."

"You're right about that," she confirmed. "Marcos told me about your oath that you would never marry or—"

"Marcos talks too much," he interrupted.

"But did you say it?"

Aaron silently cursed his friend for his loose tongue. He had never lied to Regina, even though they continued to live a lie. What Marcos revealed was true. After his aborted engagement he had returned to Bahia and confided in Marcos, leaving nothing out. And it was then he took a solemn oath that he would never marry or father children. He hadn't kept the oath because now he wanted to marry, and he looked forward to holding his child within the next six months.

"Yes, I did say it."

Closing her eyes, she nodded slowly. "Thank you for the truth."

It was Aaron's turn to close his eyes briefly, and when he opened them Regina had disappeared. He waited several minutes, trying to sort out what had just occurred between them. Marcos's return should've signaled a joyous reunion, but it hadn't. His friend had revealed a part of his past he had buried when he symbolically buried Oscar Spencer.

He had to get Regina to understand that his wanting to marry her had nothing to do with revenge. It was because he loved her, and wanted to share his life with her.

Exhaling, he let out his breath slowly. He would give her time and the space she needed to come to terms with their future. Then he would try to make amends for Marcos's careless comments.

Chapter 23

Regina felt the warmth of a hard body molded to her back; she opened her eyes, encountering darkness. Her eyelids fluttered before lowering as exhaustion descended on her like a warm, heavy blanket, but something about the darkness jolted her into a startling awareness as she sat up, blinking. Her gaze, fixed on the window closest to the bed, narrowed in concentration. A wavering orange glow dissected the night, growing brighter the longer she stared at it.

Her heart pounded uncontrollably in her chest, making it difficult for her to draw a normal breath. "Aaron!"

He came awake immediately, reaching out for her in the obscure shadows. "What's the matter?"

Her breath was coming faster as a momentary panic rendered her speechless. "The fields are on fire," she gasped, her voice sounding abnormally loud in the heavy silence.

Aaron was out of bed and turning on the table lamp in one motion. Reaching for the telephone, he pressed a button. Seconds later he shouted, "Turn on the sprinklers!"

Regina was still on her knees, staring out the window, when she heard Aaron pull on a pair of slacks and race barefoot out of the bedroom. Then she was galvanized into action, reaching for the bathrobe thrown over the arm of the chair in the sitting area.

Not waiting to search for her own shoes, she made her way down the staircase, out of the house, and across the courtyard to the garages. She shouted to Aaron as he shot past her in the Range Rover, but he did not see her or chose to ignore her as he drove in the direction of the coffee fields.

The orange glow glimmered brightly against the blackness of the night, along with the distinctive smell of smoke. All she thought of was the fire spreading quickly, incinerating everything in its wake.

And Aaron had gone out into the night to meet the inferno. Fear snaked its way up her body, tightening around her throat so that she couldn't make a sound. How could he fight a fire without equipment?

"Fool!" she screamed when she finally found her voice. "Let the damn fields burn!"

It did not matter if he lost this year's crop. She would offset his losses from the assets she had not drawn from since receiving her trust fund at her majority. She wanted to go after Aaron and tell him, but she couldn't. Even though he always parked his cars in the garage with the keys in the ignition, she did not know the landscape well enough to maneuver in the dark. She had only accompanied Aaron once to the coffee fields, preferring instead to remain close to the house or in the garden.

The child she carried in her womb was heir to the house, land and coffee plantation, yet she had not bothered to connect with any of it because she hadn't planned to remain in Bahia. She lived under Aaron's roof, shared his bed, but had yet to commit to share her future or that of his child with him.

The acrid smell of smoke increased as the orange glow

dimmed until a wall of blackness shrouded the nighttime sky once again. She murmured a silent prayer that Aaron and Sebastião had managed to extinguish the fire. Moving slowly to a chair, she sat down and waited for Aaron's return.

Something startled Regina, and her head jerked up. Pink and yellow streaks of light crisscrossed the sky, heralding the beginning of a new day. She stared at Aaron as if she had never seen him before when he hunkered down beside her, smiling.

"Bom dia," she whispered, stretching her arms upward and returning his smile.

"Good morning to you." He arched an eyebrow at her. "There are at least a half-dozen beds in the house, yet you prefer sleeping on a chair in the courtyard where anyone can see you in a state of undress."

Glancing down, she realized the bodice of her robe hung open, revealing a generous amount of breast spilling over the lace of a matching nightgown.

She pulled her robe closer to her body, her eyes widening when she remembered why she was in the courtyard. "Did you put out the fire? Was there much damage?"

Rising to his feet, Aaron swept her up from the chair, and headed toward the house. The smell of smoke clung to his clothes and flesh. "It's out. And thanks to you, we managed to contain it to less than ten acres. Sebastião activated the underground irrigation system, keeping the ground wet enough so that the flames did not spread."

She tightened her arms around his strong neck. "What do you think caused the fire?"

"I don't know."

Her gaze met his. "Have you ever had fires before?"

"A few times," he replied softly. "We had a fire three years ago that destroyed the entire crop. That year we never had a rainy season, and everything was as dry as paper. A flash of lightning

hit a tree, setting it afire. By the time we put it out we had nothin
left to harvest. After that disaster I decided to put in the irrigatio
system."

His bare feet were silent as he mounted the staircase slowl
He walked into the bedroom and placed Regina on the bec
Leaning over, he kissed her forehead. "I have to shower. Don
run away," he teased, forcing a tired smile.

"I won't," she whispered, pulling his head down and pressin
her parted lips to his. "Thank you for coming back safe."

Aaron gave her a questioning look before he removed he
arms from his neck and walked toward the bathroom. She lay o
the bed, staring up at the vaulted ceiling, knowing that when th
time came it would not be easy to leave Aaron Spencer—he ha
become so much a part of her existence that she did not know
when he hadn't been in her life—but she could not afford to le
romantic notions control her just because she loved him.

And she did love him, but more than love was the realizatio
that she had come to depend on him. It was as if the life sh
shared with Oscar had been reversed. Oscar had needed her, an
she needed Aaron.

No, a silent voice whispered to her. She had to curb her nee
and dependence. And for the first time since she had steppe
foot on Bahian soil she wanted May to come quickly, so that sh
could return to the United States.

Thinking of the States prompted her to pick up the telephon
and dial her parents' number.

"Good morning," she said softly after hearing her mother'
voice.

"Regina? Are you all right?"

"I'm fine."

"Then why are you calling me this early?"

She heard the repressed panic in her mother's low, sultry
voice. "It's only early in Bahia, not Fort Lauderdale." Her gaz
noted the numbers on the clock on the table alongside two smal

black and white photographs of Aaron's mother and stepmother-aunt. His features were an exact replica of the identical twin sisters. "I just wanted to talk to you."

"Don't fool with me, Regina," she warned. "We just *talked* two days ago. What's going on between you and Aaron?"

Staring at her bare feet, she noted a film of dust on her toes. When Aaron finished in the bathroom she would take her own shower. Her mother wanted to know what was going on between her and Aaron, and if she answered truthfully she would say nothing, because the problem wasn't Aaron but herself.

"It's me," she whispered.

There was a noticeable pause before Parris Cole responded. "What's wrong, Angel?"

"I don't know, Mommy. I don't know what's wrong with me."

"There's nothing wrong with you," Parris replied in a comforting tone. "You're pregnant and—"

"It has nothing to do with my physical condition," she interrupted. "It's more emotional." She hesitated, trying to form the phrases to explain how she felt about her relationship with Aaron. "I love him, Mommy. I love him more than I ever thought I would love a man."

"Loving him bothers you?"

"No. It's—it's a feeling of not trusting him that bothers me."

"Has he been unfaithful to you?"

"No. At least, I don't believe he has."

There was no way she could tell her mother that her libido was stronger than it had been before she slept with Aaron, matching and at times surpassing his fervid passion, which meant she gave him no reason to seek out another woman or women.

"I feel as if he's using me," she finally confessed.

"How?"

Taking a deep breath, Regina told her mother about Aaron's

and Oscar's estrangement, then related what Jeannette and Marcos had revealed about the man whom she had fallen in love with.

"He's very possessive," she concluded.

"And probably just as controlling," Parris added.

"He will not control me. I will never permit any man to do that." She smiled when she heard her mother's husky laughter come through the receiver.

"He's possessive because he's fears losing you. Remember, he lost one woman he loved, and I'm certain he doesn't want history to repeat itself."

"What I want him to be able to do is trust me. Trust me enough to return to Florida to have my baby before I come back to Bahia."

"You're asking a lot from him. It was different when you left him in Mexico, because he did not know you were carrying his child."

"Why are you taking his side, Mommy?" She felt the rush of hot tears well up behind her eyelids.

"I'm not taking sides, Angel. I've been down the road you're now traveling. For more than nine years your father did not know he'd fathered a child. And once he found you it was always his fear that he would not have you for long. And he was right, Regina. He had you for a very short time. I remember him voicing his fear one day when we were sitting by the pool and he was watching you swim. *'She's growing up so quickly, it's frightening. Every time I see her she's changed. I'll have her for such a short time. In eight years she'll be eighteen, and by then I won't be the only man in her life.'* I knew he was praying for at least eight years, but his prayers weren't answered. I withheld the first nine years of your life from him, and then you left home before your seventeenth birthday.

"I've learned a lot about Martin Diaz Cole in the almost thirty years since my first meeting him, and his love is strong and deep—his love for his family and his children. And something tells me that Aaron Spencer is a lot like your father. You did not call me this morning just to talk, but for advice. And I'm going to be a meddling mother, grandmother, and mother-in-law-to-be and tell you to give Aaron a chance to love you and his child."

"Are you saying I shouldn't come home in May?"

"I'm saying that your home is in Bahia with Aaron."

"But I thought you did not want me to leave."

"I want you to be happy, Angel."

"I am happy," she argued.

"No, you're not. If you were we would not be having this conversation. Stay in Bahia and have your baby. Give Aaron the chance to prove himself. And whenever you're ready to come to Florida for a visit, I'll have your father send the jet for you."

Regina's delicate jaw tightened in annoyance. "I suppose you want me to marry him, too."

"That must be your decision, not mine. I also lived with your father for several months before he proposed marriage. I turned him down, while committing to living with him. Living with a man is very different from being married to him. I don't have to tell you which is more fulfilling."

Letting out her breath slowly, Regina closed her eyes. "I'll think about what you've said. Thank you, Mother."

"Mother!" Parris repeated, laughing. "What ever happened to Mommy?"

Opening her eyes, Regina smiled through her tears. "I'm going to be Mommy, and you're going to be Grandmother, or whatever you want this baby to call you."

"Grandma will do just fine, thank you."

"I love you, Mommy."

"And I love you, daughter."

"Bye."

"Until the next time," Parris said, repeating her usual parting statement.

Regina replaced the receiver in its cradle. Turning around, she saw Aaron standing less than six feet away from the bed. He had reentered the room so silently that she had not been aware of his presence—but she had no doubt that he had overheard a portion—maybe even all—of her conversation.

He stood over her, resplendent in his male nakedness, long fingers splayed over slim hips. His face was a glowering mask of rage. "I am committed to you, Regina. I am committed as any man could be without being married to you. I don't know what you want from me, but whatever it is I can't give it to you at this time."

His gaze narrowed as he took a step closer. "You don't trust me. Well, right now I don't trust myself to be with you."

Her initial shock wore off as she rose to her knees. Tilting her chin, she glared up at him. "I hope you're not threatening me, Aaron Spencer."

He shook his head. "There's no need for threats, because I'm going to make this easy for you. No more lies, Regina. Our only connection will be that you're carrying my child. Your life is your own to control, and for the duration of your stay in Bahia we don't have to share a bed. However, I'll make certain you'll always know where to contact me if you ever *need* me."

She watched, paralyzed, as he picked up his watch from the bedside table, then walked out of the bedroom, closing the door. He hadn't bothered to use the connecting dressing room. The separation was not only profound, but complete.

The tears which had welled up in her eyes during her telephone conversation with her mother now fell, staining her cheeks and the silk fabric of her nightgown. Aaron's shower had not lasted long enough. If he hadn't overheard her telephone call she would have told him what he had been waiting to hear the first day she arrived in Bahia.

She would have consented to become Mrs. Aaron Laurence Spencer.

* * *

Regina woke up late Christmas Eve morning, not wanting to get out of bed, but the pressure on her bladder and the need to eat surpassed her lethargy. Pushing aside the sheet, she left the bed and walked to the bathroom. It had taken a week for the realization to set in that Aaron intended to keep his word about allowing her to control her own life. If she saw him, it was only at a distance.

He rose early, conferred with Sebastião, then—on Mondays, Wednesdays, and Fridays—he saw patients in the pediatric clinic at the municipal hospital in Salvador. His Tuesdays, Thursdays, and Saturdays were spent at the research institute, despite the fact that all of the staff were on holiday for two months. On Sundays she caught a glimpse of him whenever he entered or exited his study. Most times, he looked through her as if she were a stranger, but whenever they chanced a face-to-face encounter he usually acknowledged her with a smile.

Each morning he left a schedule of his whereabouts, along with telephone numbers, on a bulletin board beside the wall phone in the kitchen, but knowing where he was did little to assuage her feelings of loss and alienation.

Her stubborn pride would not permit her to go to him and tell him that she wanted to share his bed, his name, his life, and his future. She had promised him that she would stay one hundred-eighty days, and she would. Then, she would leave him and Bahia to await the birth of her baby.

Half an hour later, dressed in a daffodil-yellow sundress with a loose-fitting waist and matching leather mules, Regina descended the staircase. She stopped before she stepped off the last stair, staring at Aaron as he was making his way up the staircase. Moving aside, she noticed the difference in his appearance immediately. His face was leaner, and his eyes appeared sunken in their sockets. As he neared her she felt the warmth of his large body. Her gaze widened when she saw the layer of moisture dotting his forehead.

Without thinking she reached out and touched his forearm. The heat of his dry flesh burned her fingertips. "You're sick!"

He jerked his arm away. "Stay away from me."

Regina flinched at his angry tone, but recovered quickly. "You need a doctor."

His upper lip curled in a sardonic sneer. "I *am* a doctor."

"But not a very smart one," she snapped. "You should be in bed."

Closing his eyes, Aaron supported his sagging body against the banister. "That's where I was going."

She stood aside, watching him literally drag himself up the stairs. "Have you taken any medication?"

Aaron shook his head, chiding himself for attempting the motion. Every bone in his body ached, along with a pounding headache that would not permit him to think clearly. He knew what he had contracted. It was the flu.

Regina continued her descent, raced into the kitchen, and picked up the telephone. She called the Benedetti residence, apologizing profusely to Nicolas for disturbing him at home. He promised to come to the da Costa estate within the hour.

She hung up, then busied herself brewing a pot of green tea, at the same time nibbling on fresh pineapple, mango, and guava slices. Temporarily assuaging her own hunger, she prepared a tray with a cup of tea, freshly squeezed orange juice, and a small portion of applesauce.

Aaron was in bed, asleep, when she walked into his bedroom. This bedroom was an exact replica of the one she slept in, except that it was smaller and claimed an adjoining half-bath instead of a full one.

Placing the tray on a bedside table, she walked into the bathroom and soaked a small cloth with cold water. Returning to the bedroom, she placed the cloth over Aaron's head, and he came awake immediately. She noticed he hadn't shaved, and a coarse stubble of hair covered his lean cheeks.

He pushed her hand and the cloth away. "Go away, Regina. I don't want you to get sick."

She slapped at his hand. "I'm not going to get sick."

Closing his eyes, he let out his breath in a shuddering sigh. "Think about the baby," he slurred.

"It's not the baby that's sick," she retorted. "It's his father."

"*Her* father," he moaned, throwing a muscled arm over his forehead.

"*His* father," she insisted. "Move your arm, Aaron."

"No."

Leaning over his prone body, she pulled his arm down and replaced it with the cloth. "Don't fight with me. You can't possibly win."

A slight smile softened his jaw. "You're taking advantage of me because I don't feel well."

"When you're feeling better I'll offer you a rematch."

Opening his eyes, he stared up at her. "I don't want a rematch."

"What do you want?" Her husky voice had lowered to a velvet whisper.

"You know what I want."

"Say it," she challenged.

He closed his eyes again, a frown creasing his forehead. "No. I will not ask you again."

She wanted to tell him that she would marry him, but swallowed back the words poised on the tip of her tongue. She had time. They had time. They had five months to learn to trust each other before she boarded the flight which would take her back to the United States.

She managed to get him to take in half a cup of tea, several ounces of orange juice, and three tablespoons of applesauce before he drifted off to sleep. Then she lay down beside him, holding him close to her ripening body until Nicolas arrived.

Regina sat on an armchair in the corner of the bedroom while Nicolas checked his patient's vital signs, glancing away when he swabbed an area on Aaron's hip before injecting him with an antibiotic which was certain to bring down his high fever.

"How is he?" she asked after Nicolas motioned for her to step out of the room with him.

"He'll feel more like himself in a couple of days. I gave him something that will make him more comfortable, even though it will not speed his recovery. Only bed rest will do that."

"What's wrong with him?"

"He probably has a virus. Several of my patients have come down with the same malady." He handed her a vial filled with capsules. "Make certain he takes one of these twice a day. Give him the first one around nine o'clock tonight. If he's not feeling any better tomorrow morning, call me."

"I'm sorry I had to call you at home—"

"If you hadn't called, I would have been very annoyed with you," Nicolas said, stopping her apology.

She offered him an attractive, dimpled smile. "Thank you, Nicolas."

Leaning over, he kissed her cheek. "I want you to take care of yourself. You're much more vulnerable to the flu than Aaron."

She saw Nicolas to the door, then returned to the upper level and Aaron. She sat at his bedside, reading and watching him sleep, leaving only to eat. At nine o'clock, she forced a capsule between his lips and got him to drink a cup of water. When she lay down beside him, she noticed his skin was cooler than it had been earlier that morning.

Closing her eyes, she slept, one arm thrown over his flat belly.

Chapter 24

Regina and Aaron celebrated Christmas a week late. He left his bed before sunrise, but had not gone to the coffee fields.

They sat together at a table in the pergola, sharing breakfast for the first time in two weeks. He'd lost weight, the evidence reflected by the gauntness of his face. He had removed the week's growth of whiskers from his lean jaw, but had not trimmed his moustache to its former clipped precision. It was thicker, fuller, concealing most of his upper lip.

"Marcos stopped by yesterday with an invitation to a New Year's Eve party," she stated, breaking a comfortable silence. "His parents decided at the last possible moment to throw a little something to welcome him home."

"What did you tell him?"

"I declined the invitation."

Aaron shifted an eyebrow. "Why?"

"You're still recovering from the flu."

"That shouldn't stop you from attending."

Regina stared at him for a long moment. "I know I don't need your permission to accept an invitation. I declined the invitation for you because I didn't want you to relapse. I declined for myself because I did not want to attend without you."

Aaron was not successful when he tried concealing a satisfied grin. "Should I accept your not wanting to attend without me as a compliment?"

She felt a warm glow flow through her. "Yes."

He inclined his head. "Thank you."

Removing a slender, foil-wrapped box from the large patch pocket of a flowing smock, she pushed it across the table. "It's a little late, but Merry Christmas."

He grew still, staring at her over the rim of his coffee cup. "I wasn't expecting anything."

Lowering her head, she flashed a shy smile. "I bought it before you..." Her words trailed off.

Aaron placed his cup on the saucer. "Before I started acting like a horse's ass." Her head came up, her eyes crinkling in laughter. "Don't say anything, *Princesa,*" he warned softly. "I've called myself every name imaginable for being Bahia's biggest fool."

"Open it, Aaron."

"Don't you want to talk about it?"

"No, I don't. It's the past, Aaron. Let it remain in the past."

But he wanted to talk about it. He wanted to allay her fears, gain her trust, and offer her his name and protection for the rest of her life.

"Let me get your gift, and we'll open them together," he said instead.

Regina waited for Aaron to go into the house to retrieve the gift he had selected for her. She inhaled, then let out her breath slowly. They hadn't resolved their differences, but at least they were talking to each other.

Aaron returned to the pergola and handed her a gaily wrapped gift. Leaning down, he pressed his mouth to the side of her neck. "Merry Christmas."

She shivered noticeably, savoring the brush of silken hair on her sensitive flesh. "Thank you."

Her fingers were shaking slightly as she peeled away the paper covering a large, square velvet box. Even without lifting the top, she knew it contained a piece of jewelry.

Shafts of sunlight filtering through overhead trees caught the fiery brilliance of a necklace of graduated diamonds the instant she raised the cover. Tilting her head, her startled gaze met Aaron's amused one.

"Oh, Aaron. It's beautiful."

"I hope you like it."

"I love it. Thank you." Removing the necklace from the box, she handed it to him. "Help me put it on."

He draped the length of diamond around her neck, securing the clasp. Pulling her gently from her chair, he smiled down at her. "They are almost as beautiful as you are."

Her fingers caressed the flawless, blue-white stones. "I'll treasure it—always."

Cocking his head at an angle, Aaron studied her animated expression. He knew she was upset when she lost her wedding ring, and had felt the need to replace it with another dramatic piece of jewelry. He had considered giving her a bracelet until the jeweler showed him the necklace. Seeing the brilliant stones resting below the delicate bones of her clavicle verified he had made the right decision.

Moving closer, Regina curved her arms around his neck, burying her face against his shoulder. His arms came up, circling her waist and pulling her to his middle. Oh, how he'd missed her. He missed her more than he could have ever imagined.

The few times he had woken he'd found her asleep at the foot of his bed, but had been too ill to reach for her. Even in his weakened condition he had wanted to hold her, kiss her, love her.

And his love for her frightened him, because he feared he loved Regina more than he loved himself.

"Open your gift, Aaron," she urged softly, her warm breath caressing his throat.

He released her, feeling her loss the moment she pulled out of his embrace. He sat down and unwrapped his gift, closing his eyes briefly after he'd glimpsed the exquisite, solid gold razor with his name engraved on its gracefully curved handle, resting on a bed of navy-blue velvet.

He opened his eyes, smiling at her. "How did you know? Where did you get it?"

"Oh, Aaron, how could I not know?" She laughed. "You only have a half-dozen of them on the shelf in the bathroom adjoining the master bedroom. I called my mother and asked her to pick it up for me."

He sobered quickly. "I collect antique razors, but none of them are solid gold. You should not have spent so much—"

"Did I give you a limit on how much you could spend on my gift?" she countered, cutting him off.

He managed to look sheepish. "No, ma'am."

"I thought not," she crooned, giving him a smug smile.

The exchange of gifts signaled a change, a change which offered them a glimpse of what they had shared before mistrust and doubt had come between them.

They spent the evening in the garden, enjoying the ethereal setting when they sat on a stone bench near the gurgling fountain. The instant the clock tolled the twelve o'clock hour, heralding the advent of a new year, Aaron dropped an arm around Regina's shoulder; they watched the sky light up with fireworks set off by the revelers at the Jarres.

He stood up, smiling and extending his hand. "Will you share a dance with me to celebrate the new year?" She placed her hand in his, and he pulled her gently to her feet. "Thank you, Senhora Spencer."

"You're quite welcome, Senhor Spencer," Regina whispered, enjoying his closeness and masculine strength.

He cradled her waist, one hand splayed over her rounded belly, waltzing her around and around the fountain until she pleaded fatigue. Bending slightly, he picked her up and carried her across the courtyard and into the house. There was only the sound of their breathing when he climbed the staircase to the second level.

Holding her breath, Regina met and held his direct stare as he lowered her to her bed. She exhaled, closing her eyes when he pressed his mouth to her forehead.

"Happy new year, *Princesa*. I hope this is the year all of your dreams come true."

She managed a tremulous smile. "So do I, Aaron." *So do I, my darling,* she repeated silently.

Aaron hesitated, his penetrating gaze sweeping over her composed features. They had declared a truce; a very fragile truce for the beginning of a new year.

Regina did not move, not even her eyes, when her gaze fused with his. She knew he was waiting, waiting for her to invite him into her bed. She wanted him, she had missed him, but there was no way she could fall into his arms and offer him her body until they resolved their differences. And that would not happen with just a passionate session of lovemaking, because after a physical release the doubts would still remain.

They had time; she had time; she had months to commit to spending the rest of her life with Aaron Spencer, or walk away from him—forever.

Regina's new year began with a whirlwind frenzy of social activity. She spent time with Jeannette Benedetti. They shared lunch or shopping excursions. And she toured Bahia with Marcos Jarre. She suspected Aaron wasn't too pleased with the amount of time she spent with Marcos, but he had yet to voice his annoyance.

That all changed when she strolled into the house half an hour before midnight in late January.

He walked out of his study at the same time she headed for the staircase. "Where have you been?"

She stopped suddenly, staring at him, her forehead creasing in bewilderment. "If I was not here, Aaron, then wouldn't I have to have been *out*?"

He ignored her curt retort. "Out with Marcos?"

Her frown faded. "Yes. Why?"

Aaron struggled to control not only his temper but a surge of red-hot jealousy. "Is it not enough that he monopolizes your days? Must that also include your nights?"

"Lençóis is not around the corner. It was a six-hour drive, each way, from Salvador."

"I'm aware of the geography of Bahia, Senhora Spencer."

"Then what exactly is the problem, Aaron?"

"I want you to spend less time with Marcos."

Regina closed her eyes, sighing heavily. She was tired, bone tired, and she needed to take a bath to soak her tired and aching feet and legs before she fell into bed.

Opening her eyes, she stared up at Aaron glaring down at her. He still had not gained back the weight he'd lost when he had come down with the flu. The bones in his face were more pronounced than when she had first met him; she now thought of him as lean and dangerous-looking with the thick moustache.

"I wouldn't spend so much time with Marcos touring Bahia if you had offered to take me around. You close the research institute for two months, yet you still go in as if it were open."

"Why didn't you tell me you wanted to see Bahia?"

"I shouldn't have to ask you, Aaron," she countered angrily.

"I don't read minds," he argued, his voice rising slightly. "I offered to buy you a car so that you can get around independently, but you refused it. You said you wanted time in the garden. If ou're afraid of driving by yourself, then you should've said omething."

"I'm not afraid to drive."

"Then what is it?"

"Nothing," she replied wearily. "Look, Aaron, I'm exhausted, nd I have to go to bed." What she did not tell him was that he did not want any tokens of permanence, because when she eft Bahia she would leave with only her clothes and personal ems.

He inclined his head. "We'll continue this in the morning."

She gave him a tired smile. "Thank you. *Boa noite.*"

"Boa noite, Princesa."

She climbed the staircase slowly, one hand resting over her elly. She stopped, her eyes widening in shock. A dreamy smile oftened the lines of fatigue ringing her generous mouth.

Aaron saw her stop and was beside her in seconds. "What's he matter?"

Her head came up slowly as she rewarded him with a tearful mile. "I felt the baby move, Aaron." Reaching for his hand, she laced it over the area where she had felt the slight fluttering.

"It's called quickening." He could not disguise the hoarseness f his own voice.

"He just moved again," she whispered, leaning into him.

Aaron curved an arm around her shoulders and led her up he staircase to her bedroom. "You're practically falling asleep n your feet. I'll fix your bath and wash you—"

"No," she cut in, shaking her head.

"Yes," he stated firmly. "Don't fight with me, Regina. Even hough you've put on a little weight over the past few months, 'm still bigger than you are."

"You're a bully."

"Wrong," he countered, sitting her gently on the bed and re- moving her shoes. "I'm the man who loves your life."

He took off her slacks, smock top, and underwear, leaving

her briefly to fill the bathtub. A quarter of an hour later, she la
on the bed, her scented body tingling from the light pressure o
his magical fingers as he massaged the tight muscles in her leg
and feet.

"Aaron?"

"What is it, *Princesa?*"

"I'd like to make a request."

Covering her nude body with a sheet, he sat down beside he
"What is it?"

"Stay with me tonight."

Leaning closer, his mouth grazed an earlobe. "Are you askin
me to share your bed?"

"Yes." She slurred the single word, and within seconds sh
was asleep.

Aaron watched her features relax as she succumbed to th
exhaustion she had valiantly fought and lost. He combed hi
fingers through the raven curls falling over the top of her ea
his former anger fading.

Her outings with his childhood friend had begun inno
cently enough when Marcos offered to take her to the historica
churches, forts, and buildings of colonial Salvador. After tw
weeks their excursions escalated to day-long outings to Cachoe
ira, Ilhéus, and Caldas do Jorro. He was pleased that Regin
enjoyed Marcos's company and his vast knowledge of African
history, but he did not like Marcos's obvious obsession with th
woman who was carrying his child.

He had planned to confront Marcos, warning him to stay awa
from Regina before she revealed that she saw Marcos because h
had not been there for her. And she was right. Even though th
institute was closed, he still went into his office like clockwork
Regina had always been so fiercely independent and solitary tha
he had not thought of spending more time with her. Now tha
would change. Moving off the bed, he headed to the bathroom
to shower, then returned to lie down beside her.

She felt the power of his large body as it settled against her back. Stirring slightly, she moved toward the source of heat.

"Go back to sleep," a deep voice crooned close to her ear.

"Te amo," she whispered in Spanish.

"And I love you," Aaron confessed, pulling her closer.

Regina stopped pacing long enough to give Aaron a tortured look. "Where could they be, Aaron? The jet landed more than an hour ago."

He stood up, took her hand, and eased her back down to the seat beside his. "Sit down and relax. They're probably being held up in customs. It's Carnival time, and the whole world comes to Brazil to party."

"But my father always has us pre-cleared before we arrive." Aaron gave her a look that said he did not believe her. "I never wait with other passengers when I fly on the corporate jet."

Money and rank have their privileges, Aaron mused silently. "Don't worry, *Princesa,* they'll be here." Nodding, she rested her head against his shoulder.

Aaron was not as relaxed as he appeared. Two days ago Sebastião woke him up with the report of another fire. This time more than a hundred acres were destroyed before the fast-moving blaze was extinguished.

When the people who worked in the fields reported to work that morning, he gathered them all together and lectured them sternly about smoking. No one—and he reiterated, *no one*—was allowed to smoke anywhere on the da Costa property. A single infraction was cause for immediate dismissal.

"There they are!"

Aaron stood up, staring at a tall, attractive couple as they followed a baggage handler. Their resemblance to Regina was startling—especially her brother.

Arianna Cole spotted her sister and raced ahead of Tyler, her arms outstretched, while he slowed his pace and stared over his broad shoulder at a beautiful, dark-skinned Brazilian girl who flirted shamelessly with him as they passed each other.

Regina hugged her sister, then kissed her cheek. "I've been pacing the floor waiting for you guys. Welcome to Bahia."

Arianna pulled back, her clear, green-flecked brown eyes surveying her older sister. "You look beautiful."

Regina wrinkled her nose. "I look fat."

"Pregnant women are supposed to gain weight." She examined Regina's rounded face, softly curling short hair, fuller breasts, and the hint of a rounded belly under an exquisitely tailored bright orange linen smock over a pair of slim black slacks. "You look better pregnant than not."

Arianna's gaze shifted to the tall man standing several feet behind her sister, arms crossed over his chest. Her eyes widened when she noticed that there was something about the man that reminded her of her own father. "Is that Aaron?" she whispered *sotto voce*. Regina nodded, smiling. "Good grief! He's hot!"

Shaking her head in amusement, Regina directed her sister over to Aaron. "This is Arianna. My very talented sister just earned a spot in our next Olympic swim team."

Aaron smiled at the teenage girl, his teeth showing whitely under his moustache. Leaning over, he placed a kiss on her cheek. "It's a pleasure to meet you. Congratulations on making the team."

Arianna flashed a bright smile. "Thanks."

Tyler walked over to Aaron and extended his right hand. "Thanks for having us, Dr. Spencer. Tyler Cole."

Aaron shook the proffered hand, then pulled Tyler to him in a rough embrace. "None of that Dr. Spencer business, Tyler. It's Aaron."

Tyler nodded, offering him a smile so reminiscent of his older sister's. "Okay, Aaron."

Dropping his arms around the shoulders of the Cole siblings, he smiled at them. "Welcome to Bahia. Regina and I will give you time to settle in, rest up, and get used to the heat. Then after that it's party time."

"When does Carnival begin?" Tyler asked.

"It starts up around Friday, but by Saturday it's in full swing. And for four full days all business stops for what becomes a street party."

"Is it only at night?" Arianna questioned.

"It's all day and all night," Aaron replied.

"Hot damn!" Tyler whispered under his breath.

Aaron gave him a sidelong look. "Did you come to party, or did you come for the girls?"

"Both," he said, flashing his attractive shy grin.

Regina laughed. Her very serious brother had finally discovered the opposite sex. She had begun to give up on him, because in the past he'd much preferred reading a book to interacting with girls his own age. Tyler was his father's son. He had inherited his height, astounding masculine beauty, and the famous male Cole charm.

Her brother and sister had planned to stay a week, and a week was enough for Regina, because having them with her would counter her occasional spells of homesickness.

Chapter 25

Aaron helped Regina and Arianna into the Range Rover before directing the baggage handler to store the Coles' luggage in the cargo area. He tipped the man, then slipped behind the wheel beside Tyler.

Slipping on a pair of sunglasses against the rays of the fiery Brazilian sun, he waited patiently until he could maneuver out of the traffic jam at the Salvador airport. The area's population had almost doubled with the influx of tourists for Carnival. While the festivities surrounding Rio's Carnival had waned over the years, the reverse had not been true for Bahia. It had become one of the most spontaneous street festivals on the face of the earth. It was not only spontaneous, but uninhibited, and unadulterated fun. He had stayed away for the past three years because seeing everyone celebrating with such fervid abandonment had reminded him of how empty his life had become. He had existed for his medical research, and nothing more. But now he awaited the birth of his child; a child who would give him a purpose for existing beyond his career.

He took a quick glance at Tyler Cole's perfect profile. "Your sister says you're thinking of a career in medicine."

Tyler smiled. "I am."

"What schools have you considered?"

"I'm thinking of applying to the big ones—Harvard, Yale, Stanford. Where did you go?"

Aaron smiled. "Johns Hopkins. If you think about attending, let me know and I'll write you a letter of recommendation."

"Would you do that?" There was no mistaking the excitement in the younger man's voice.

"Of course. It's the least I could do for the uncle of my son or daughter."

"Do you know what sex the baby is?" Arianna asked from the backseat.

"No." Regina and Aaron had spoken in unison.

"Why not?" she asked.

"Regina doesn't want to know," Aaron replied, glancing up at the rearview mirror.

Arianna sucked her teeth. "I think I'd want to know."

"So would I," Aaron concurred.

"It's going to be a boy," Tyler predicted.

Reaching forward, Regina patted her brother's shoulder. "I think you're right."

"If it is a boy, then Daddy is going to lose his mind," Arianna stated with a big smile. "He's already set up a stock portfolio for the baby. All he's waiting for is the name."

Aaron wanted to tell Arianna that he could afford to provide for his child, but swallowed back the words. He had to remember that his son or daughter was also a Cole, and the Coles had established their own traditions. On the other hand, he intended to establish a few Spencer traditions which would be handed down from one generation to another. The land he owned was still known as the da Costa estate, even though the last of the da Costa line ended with Leonardo. After the birth of his son or daughter he would officially change the deed to read Spencer.

Regina showed Arianna to her bedroom. "This is it," she said, gesturing with a slender hand.

Arianna walked slowly into a room where a massive, four-poster iron bed dominated the space. Panels of antique ivory lace floated around the bed, offering furtive glimpses of lace-trimmed pillows, shams, and bolsters. A pedestal table cradled a vase filled with a profusion of fragrant white and pale pink flowers. A Chippendale-style chest-on-chest and a burgundy brocade armchair and matching footstool were nestled in a corner near a door which opened to a full bath.

"This house and everything in it is magnificent, Regina. I hate to say it, but you're a better decorator than Mommy."

"Bite your tongue, Ari," Regina teased. "I can't take credit for anything you see here. Aaron's aunt was mistress to these treasures long before I arrived."

Closing the door softly, Arianna leaned against it. "When are you going to become the mistress?"

"Say what?"

"When are you going to marry Aaron?"

Regina felt a rush of heat suffuse her face. "Who told you to ask me that? Mommy? Daddy?"

"I'm not going to answer that. You can tell me to mind my own damn business—"

"Arianna Cole!"

Pushing off the door, Arianna threw up both hands. "Don't act so shocked. I've said worse. Back to my question. When are you going to marry Aaron? Even though I'm not sexually active, I know when a man loves a woman. I've seen Mommy and Daddy together enough to know. And your Dr. Spencer has it real bad."

Tilting her chin, Regina stared down the length of her nose

at her younger sister. "If you know so much, then you'd see that
love him."

"Love him enough to marry him?"

"Yes."

"What's stopping you?"

"He hasn't asked me—lately."

Arianna's mouth dropped open. "Lately?"

"We've had a few squabbles, and even though we live under
the same roof we've been somewhat estranged."

"Which means?"

"He sleeps in his bedroom, and I sleep in my bedroom."

Rolling her eyes upward, Arianna shook her head. "You're
both too old to play games."

"And you're not old enough to understand the dynamics. I suggest you take *siesta,* because we're going to Salvador later tonight
to eat. Then tomorrow night we're throwing a pre-Carnival party.
Our neighbor has cousins visiting from the Dominican Republic
who are around your age. They will probably want to hang out
with you and Tyler."

"Cool!"

Regina wrinkled her nose. "Yeah, cool. Did you bring something to party in?"

"I have a few outfits."

"How would you like to go to a beauty spa with me tomorrow morning? You can have your hair trimmed, get a manicure,
pedicure, facial, and massage. And if we have time we can always
visit a few boutiques to pick up a few more party outfits. Remember, Carnival is four days of nonstop fun."

Arianna executed a dance step, spinning around on her toes.
"Yes!"

Aaron sat across from Tyler Cole, silently admiring the
younger man's enthusiasm. Tyler had elected to forego *siesta*
when he urged him to talk about his research projects.

"What are you working on now?"

"We have two projects going at the same time," Aaron replied. "Several of the doctors have developed an oral antiviral agent which has been used experimentally in children and adults with meningitis to shorten the course of the disease."

Leaning forward on the sofa, Tyler rested his elbows on his knees. "But viral meningitis, unlike the bacterial version, is not life-threatening."

"You're right about that. But the picornaviruses are small viruses that, once inside the body, can travel to many different tissues, causing disease, inflammation of the heart muscle, otitis media or inflammation of the middle ear, meningitis, and the common cold. And viral meningitis also causes incapacitating headaches that can last two weeks or more."

"What's the drug's reaction time?"

"Most patients feel better on the first day, and many had their painful headaches disappear within a week. Most patients in the study recovered within nine days instead of taking the usual fourteen for the infection to run its course."

"That sounds exciting."

"It is for infectious-disease doctors," Aaron confirmed. "I'm personally involved in a project where we have successfully developed a bandage that can stop severe bleeding in seconds, potentially saving thousands of lives on battlefields and highways. I received a grant two years ago from the U.S. Army after I'd sent a proposal to the Pentagon for funding to develop the experimental bandage and a related foam and spray that contain freeze-dried clotting agents in concentrations fifty to one hundred times greater than human blood."

Tyler wagged his head in amazement. "Have they begun using it?"

"Clinical trials are to begin in a couple of months at an army hospital in Texas, where the bandage will be applied to the gushing wounds from prostate removal surgery."

"What will the foam and spray be used for?"

"The foam is intended for bullet wounds and other punctures that bleed from deep inside the body, while the clotting spray is for seeping wounds like severe burns and torn muscle."

Tyler continued with his questioning. "What did you use for the clotting process?"

"A protein called fibrinogen and the enzyme thrombin."

"Isn't thrombin derived from plasma?"

Aaron nodded, smiling. There was no doubt Tyler Cole was a brilliant student and would probably gain admission to any college he selected. "When the fibrinogen and thrombin come in contact with blood, they instantly begin forming a sticky lattice called fibrin that adheres to live tissue and eventually becomes a scab."

"Oh, man, that's incredible."

"We are pretty excited about it. By the way, what branch of medicine are you interested in?"

Tyler shifted his sweeping black eyebrows. "I don't know yet. I've thought about obstetrics, but I keep vacillating between that and epidemiology."

"Have you considered pediatrics?"

Tyler registered Aaron's smug expression. "You're a pediatrician, aren't you?"

Smiling broadly, he nodded, then glanced at his watch. "We have some time before we have to be ready to go out for dinner tonight. How would you like a tour of the hospital and research institute? Maybe seeing everything up close and personal will help you make up your mind."

Tyler sprang to his feet, then seemed embarrassed by his eagerness. "I'd love that, Dr….Aaron," he said, correcting himself quickly.

"Wait here for me. I have to let your sister know where we're going."

Aaron took the stairs two at a time, then made his way down the hallway to Regina's room. Knocking lightly on the door, he pushed it opened. A tender smile curved his mouth when he saw her lying on her side, facing the open window.

"Have you come to share *siesta* with me?" Her sultry voice sent a warming shiver down his spine.

He walked around the bed and sat down beside her. "You should've asked me before I promised Tyler that I'd take him on a tour of the hospital."

She placed a hand over his. "I'll take a rain check."

"Will that rain check be valid for other than *siesta?*"

She lifted an eyebrow. "What are you asking?"

Leaning over, he pressed his mouth to hers. "How about tonight?"

"I'll let you know," she whispered against his parted lips.

"When?"

"Tonight."

Increasing the pressure on her mouth, he cradled her head between his palms and drank deeply, temporarily assuaging a gnawing thirst he had been forced to endure for weeks.

"Tonight," he repeated, reluctantly pulling away. Running a finger down the length of her delicate nose, he winked at her. "I'll see you later, *Princesa.*"

Regina stared at him, holding his gaze as he stood up and backed away from the bed. She waited until he closed the door behind his departing figure, then closed her eyes. She lay motionless, enjoying the feel of the tiny life moving in her womb. A feeling of peace invaded her as she imagined holding a nursing child to her full breasts. Then she fell asleep, a gentle smile mirroring the peace she had discovered since Aaron Spencer had walked into her life.

"Aaron, please help me put my necklace on."

He took the length of glittering diamonds from her fingers

and looped it around her neck, securing the clasp. "We wouldn't be late for our guests if you hadn't wanted to stay in bed," he whispered close to her ear.

"Oh, now it's my fault *you* wanted to spend the afternoon in bed."

Curving an arm under her breasts, Aaron eased Regina back to lean against his chest. "It's your fault that I've had to undergo a long and agonizing period of abstinence. So don't blame me if I got carried away. Do you want to have another go at it?"

"Behave, Aaron," she chided softly.

"I am."

Turning in his loose embrace, she raised her face for his kiss, and she wasn't disappointed when he left her mouth burning with a passion that rekindled her desire all over again.

Pushing gently against his chest, she moaned softly. "Go and greet our guests. I'll be down as soon as I repair my makeup." She had to run a comb through her hair and reapply her lipstick.

Aaron had waited twenty-four hours to redeem his *rain check*. They had shared *siesta,* and each other's bodies, for the first time in more than a month. She had been humiliatingly conscious of his scrutiny when he stared at her naked body before placing a large hand over a pendulous breast. She looked very pregnant, with and without her clothes. There were times when she did not feel very attractive, and she feared Aaron would not find her attractive or desirable. Her fears were unfounded, though, when he closed his eyes and traced every curve of her body with his fingertips as if he were a sculptor idolizing his creation.

Their lovemaking was tender, passions tempered, until it finally exploded in a soaring ecstasy that had been building for more weeks than she could remember. The rush of sexual fulfillment had rendered her unable to move as her breath had come in long, surrendering moans of amazing completeness. Then she slept for hours, long past the time when she had allotted to prepare herself for the pre-Carnival party she and Aaron planned to host for her brother, sister, their friends, and neighbors.

She retouched her mouth with a shimmering copper lip color, then ran a comb through her professionally coiffed hair. The image staring back at her reflected a woman in love. She literally glowed: her eyes and flawless skin competed with the length of flawless diamonds draped around her neck.

She had elected to wear midnight-blue silk—sleeveless top with a scoop neck banded in satin, and matching silk slacks. Her shoes were low-heeled, navy-blue patent leather pumps with satin bows. Her jewelry was Aaron's mother's wedding ring, his Christmas gift necklace, and a pair of diamond stud earrings she received from her parents to celebrate her sixteenth birthday.

Checking her reflection for the last time, she went downstairs to join her guests.

Taped music blared from a sound system set up around the courtyard and pergola. Regina and Aaron had catered a sit-down dinner for twelve following a buffet where platters of fish and meat appetizers and potent drinks to wash down the spicy fare were served by silent, efficient waiters.

Dinner included grilled meats and chicken and *feijoada,* a dish consisting of black beans, sausage, beef, and pork served with rice, finely shredded kale, orange slices, and *farofa.* Regina had quickly developed a taste for *farofa,* which was manioc flour that was fried with onions and egg. She avoided most dishes prepared with coconut milk, dende oil, and the fiery malagueta pepper. Certain foods she had been able to consume before becoming pregnant were now shifted to a DO NOT EAT list.

Throughout dinner she watched Tyler interact with Marcos Jarre's female cousin and her sister flirt with his two male cousins. Arianna had elected to wear a black tank dress that showed off more flesh than Regina had ever displayed, creating a stir among the younger males, who were stunned by the perfection of her strong, lean athletic body. Dinner was a leisurely affair, lasting nearly three hours before everyone retreated to the courtyard to dance or walk off the ample portions of food that were followed by a number of rich, sweet desserts.

Marcos approached Aaron and patted him on his back. "Excellent party, friend. Good food, good music, and perfect weather for a gathering of old and new friends." He gestured with a hand holding a glass filled with a well-made *caipirinha*. The concoction of *cacahaça*—a high-proof, sugarcane alcohol—lime, sugar, and crushed ice, was Brazil's national drink. "Your niece and nephew seem to have hit it off well with my cousins."

Aaron took a sip of his own *caipirinha* as he watched Tyler lean closer to whisper in the ear of the sixteen-year-old girl from Santo Domingo. Tyler and Arianna, like Regina, were also fluent in Spanish.

"What can I say, Marcos? They are teenagers."

Marcos nodded, withdrawing a slim cigar from the pocket of his jacket. He snapped open a lighter, and within seconds the flame caught and lit the fragrant tobacco.

His hand tightening around his glass, Aaron stared numbly at Marcos. "When did you start smoking?"

Taking several more puffs to ensure the cigar was lit, Marcos blew out a stream of smoke, watching it curl in the air. "About a year ago. I took a side trip to Turkey and decided to sample one of their renowned blends. After a couple of puffs, I was hooked." He held the cigar between his thumb and forefinger. "It's not Turkish, but it's the best Brazil has to offer."

"Be careful where you put it out. I've had two fires in my fields this season."

"I thought I smelled smoke the other night."

"You did. I've lost a little more than a hundred acres. I've banned all smoking on the property."

"I'll be careful." Even though Marcos had spoken to Aaron his gaze was fixed on Regina as she laughed at something his Dominican-born mother had said.

Aaron saw the direction of his gaze, and a shadow of annoyance settled onto his features. Since he had spoken to Regina about spending so much time with Marcos she had curtailed her outings with him, but apparently that had not stopped his boyhood friend from seeking her out.

Marcos had called one morning asking to speak to her, but was disappointed when Magda informed him that Senhora Spencer had gone to Salvador with her husband.

"I've been meaning to speak to you about Regina," Aaron began in a dangerously soft tone.

Marcos lifted his head alertly, but did not look at Aaron. "What about her?"

"I want you to stop seeing her so often."

Turning, Marcos glared at him from behind the lenses of his glasses. "Are you telling me to stay away from her?"

"That's not what I said."

"What you are asking is impossible."

"And why the hell not!"

"Because I love her, Aaron."

"Don't even go there, Marcos."

"And why not? We wouldn't be having this conversation if you paid more attention to her."

Aaron's left hand shot out, his fingers grasping the front of his neighbor's shirt. Tightening his grip, he jerked Marcos closer. "I'll forget you ever said that because I've always regarded you as a brother. But if you ever cross the line and try to come between me and Regina, I'll forget the oath I took when I became a doctor and take your life." His chest rose and fell heavily as he tried curbing the rage coursing throughout his body.

Marcos had seen Aaron angry once, and that one time was

enough. He would not test him further. He had told him the truth. He loved Regina—her beauty, intelligence, sensitivity, and her enthusiasm for learning—but he wasn't *in* love with her, at least not enough to test his lifelong friendship with Aaron or his volatile temper.

"I would never disrespect you or Regina," he offered in apology. "At least, not the way you think." He let out a sigh of relief when Aaron released him. "You're a lucky man, Aaron, because you have what most men spend all of their lives seeking. You have a beautiful, intelligent woman who loves you selflessly. You are the heir to lands whose history is documented in books written about this region, while the woman you love is carrying a child who will eventually inherit not only his property, but also a heritage which he or she will be able to trace back to the powerful and mighty kingdoms of ancient Africa."

Aaron took several steps, then stopped and stared up at the clear summer sky. He was losing it. He hadn't realized how close he had come to injuring Marcos until after he had grabbed him. If he hadn't been holding a glass in his right hand he was certain he would've hit him.

For several seconds it had become déjà vu. He had loved Sharon, and so had Oscar. Now, he loved Regina, and so did Marcos. He had lost Sharon, but he had no intention of letting Regina go. He would fight to keep her, and if necessary give up his own life in the struggle.

"I'm sorry." The two words came out in a hoarse whisper.

Marcos closed the distance between them, placing a hand on Aaron's shoulder. "No, friend, *I'm* sorry."

Glancing over his shoulder, Aaron smiled at him. Seconds later the two men were hugging and thumping each other's backs. Marcos extended his glass, touching it to Aaron's before they drained the contents.

Grimacing, Aaron shook his head. "I should test this stuff at the lab. I'm certain it's responsible for minimal brain damage."

Marcos nodded in agreement. "I think you're right. Let's get another glass to make certain."

The two men returned to the small crowd of people talking, dancing, and sitting on chairs under the clear, nighttime Brazilian sky as they anticipated the start of Carnival.

Chapter 26

Regina survived the first night of Carnival, but declined Tyler and Arianna's offer to accompany them the following evening. She could still hear the nonstop, ear-shattering music coming from live bands atop trucks packed with musicians, singers, and gyrating dancers.

After several hours of dancing, she had been swept along in a sea of people, losing Aaron and the others in their party in the crowd until she took refuge in a restaurant and waited for them to search each establishment until they found her. She was jostled without regard to her physical condition, and there had been a time when she feared for the life of her unborn child.

Marcos, Tyler, Arianna, and the Jarre cousins decided they hadn't partied enough, so she and Aaron returned home. The sky had brightened with the beginning of a new day when the Cole siblings stumbled in and fell across their beds fully dressed.

"What's the matter, Sis? Can't hang?" Tyler teased.

Cradling her belly with both hands, she squinted at him.

"You've got that right. Do me a favor. Try not to come in with the sun."

Arianna's head jerked up. "You sounded like Mommy."

"She's just practicing," Tyler teased.

"I'm serious." Her expression mirrored her statement.

"She's right," Aaron concurred, speaking for the first time. "Your parents entrusted us with your safety, and as long as you're under our roof you'll follow the rules."

Tyler sobered quickly. "What time do you want us to come home?"

Regina stared at Aaron and inclined her head. She would let him establish the curfew.

"Tell Marcos I want you in before one."

Arianna and Tyler shared a smile of relief. That would give them at least six hours to party.

"Thanks, Aaron. One it is," Tyler confirmed.

Waiting until the teenagers left the living room, Aaron moved over to sit beside Regina. "I'm not even a father and already I'm setting curfews."

Resting her head on his shoulder, she closed her eyes. "I don't even want to think about it. I just hope and pray I'll survive weaning, toilet training, and teething."

"You'll do okay, *Princesa*. You'll be a wonderful mother."

I hope you're right, she mused. The more she advanced in her term the more doubts she had. Would she be able to breastfeed? Would she have enough milk for the baby? Would the baby be colicky? Would she undergo a period of postpartum depression?

"*Princesa?*"

"Yes, Aaron."

"We are going to have to go to Argentina next week."

Her eyes opened and she stared up at him. "Why?"

"You have to renew your visa," he reminded her.

"I can't believe I've been here for almost ninety days. Time has passed so quickly."

Too quickly. Aaron did not look forward to the next time when her visa expired. This time he would have to prepare to put her on a plane for her return to the States. He hadn't proposed marriage again since the time he made love to her in her garden. Each time she rejected him he gave up a little piece of himself. One more rejection, and he would cease to exist. And he had to survive—not only for himself, but for Regina and the child kicking so vigorously in her womb.

Regina stood at the window in her bedroom, staring at the ripe coffee plants stretching for acres and beyond her range of vision. Within two weeks the workers would begin harvesting the crop, while she would prepare to leave Bahia.

She inhaled, holding her breath when the baby did what she imagined was a somersault inside her. She had just entered her eighth month, and her overall weight gain of fifteen pounds made her feel large and lumbering whenever she walked up the staircase. It was time she considered occupying one of the first-floor bedrooms.

She missed Aaron. He had been gone only three days, but it seemed more like three months. He had been invited to lecture at the Walter Reed Army Institute of Research on the process that was used to produce the bandage that miraculously minimized blood loss.

He had been reluctant to leave her, but she gently coerced him into going, saying she would be waiting for his return. She expected his return the following afternoon, and she had managed to keep busy in his absence.

She was nearing completion of restoring the garden. Her greatest satisfaction had been uncovering a kapok tree concealed by the overgrowth of other trees and shrubs. The tree, native to Asia, had probably been planted before Alice da Costa had passed away.

They were known to survive centuries and grow to heights of more than a hundred feet. Its massive twisted trunk and branches would provide a canopy of shade for generations to come.

The soft chiming of the telephone shattered the silence, and she moved over to the table to answer it.

"*Olá.*"

"Hello, yourself. How's it going?"

Her eyes crinkled in a smile. "I'm here, Marcos."

"How would you like to go to a *candomblé* ceremony tonight?"

"I don't know."

"Didn't you enjoy the last one?"

"Yes," she agreed reluctantly. She had enjoyed it, even if her baby hadn't. Hours after she left the temple and returned home the baby moved and gyrated as if he still heard the rhythmic passion of the drummers beating out the sounds of Africa.

"How about I pick you up and we go into Salvador for dinner. We'll hang around for a while, then head over to the *terreiro.* If we get there early we'll be able to get a good seat."

She did not want to share dinner with Marcos, even though she wanted to see another *candomblé* ceremony before she left Bahia. The ancient religion mimicked the Catholic worship of saints with their own native gods. At first she associated *candomblé* with the voodoo ceremonies of the Caribbean, but Marcos quickly reminded her that there was a major difference between the two. Unlike voodoo, *candomblé* was not aimed at producing bad luck for one's enemy. *Candomblé* was used only to produce positive results for the worshiper. There were no dolls with pins sticking in them in any of the ceremonies.

"I'll meet you there."

"Don't you want to eat out?" he insisted.

"No. I'm on a very bland diet nowadays." Recurring heartburn and indigestion made it impossible for her to ingest anything with the spices indigenous to the region.

"What time should I expect you?"

"I'll call my driver and tell him to pick me up around eight-thirty."

"Then I'll expect you at nine-fifteen."

"I'll see you later, Marcos."

Regina walked into the kitchen to get several bottles of water to take with her. Magda glanced up, halting stacking dishes in the dishwasher.

"Are you going out, Senhora?"

"Yes, Magda. I should be back around midnight."

"With Senhor Spencer gone, would you like me to stay in the house until you come back tonight?"

"That won't be necessary. But thank you, anyway."

She retrieved the bottles from a shelf in the pantry, slipped them into a large woven tote, then walked through a door at the back of the house and made her way around the courtyard to wait for her driver.

The driver pulled up within minutes of her arrival. He jumped out of the large, battered sedan and opened the rear door for her.

She stepped into the car and settled back against the aged leather seat, closing her eyes. The driver shifted into gear and the car rolled smoothly across the courtyard and down to the main road leading to Salvador.

They hadn't been on the road for more than five minutes when Regina sat up straight and opened her eyes. Sniffing, she turned and glanced out the rear window. An orange glow lit up the sky. Fire! Someone had set the coffee fields on fire again.

"Turn around!" she screamed at the driver. She shouted at him again, then realized she had spoken English.

"Stop and go back!" she demanded in Portuguese.

The driver hit the brake, the car skidding dangerously off the road, sliding precariously into an embankment. Panic spurted through her when she was slammed against the door of the car and fell to the floor. Pain ripped through her middle as she stifled a cry of agony.

The driver put the car in reverse and accelerated, and the vehicle eased back onto the solid road surface. Meanwhile Regina crawled onto the seat and lay down, fighting the waves of pain washing over her.

She lost track of time when she concentrated on the waves of pain slicing through her abdomen. The acrid smell of the smoke drifted through the open windows the closer they came to the coffee fields.

The car stopped in the courtyard, and when the driver helped Regina from the car she forgot her pain when she saw the orange glow that illuminated the night sky.

"The world is on fire," she whispered to herself.

"Senhora?" the driver asked, his voice trembling.

Reaching into her tote, she grabbed a handful of bills and threw it at him. "Get help," she ordered.

She did not wait to see what he would do as she made her way toward the house, both hands cradling her belly.

As she walked into the house, the telephone rang. Her hand was trembling uncontrollably when she picked up the receiver.

It was Sebastião. He was shouting into the phone, and she could not understand what he was saying. She thought she heard something about water, but any and everything around her faded with the next wave of pain, which brought her to her knees.

She knelt, staring at the widening circle of liquid pouring onto the floor. She had lost her amniotic fluid. "No," she moaned. The baby couldn't come now. It wasn't time. It was not full term.

Somehow she crawled across the floor and made it to one of the bedrooms on the first level. The contractions were coming faster when she pulled herself up to the bed. If she delivered on the bed, then maybe her baby had a better chance of surviving than on the floor.

Regina had no idea of how long she lay on the bed as waves of pain washed over her in measured intervals. One time she opened her eyes to find Magda standing over her.

Reaching out, she caught the housekeeper's hand. "Help me," she pleaded.

Magda's mouth curved into a sneer. "*Puta!* You need me to help you birth your brat, don't you?" She leaned closer, and Regina saw her own death in the woman's eyes. "You will die, and so will your baby. I will see to that."

Falling back to the pillow, she could not stop the tears that flowed down her cheeks. "Why?"

"Why, *puta?* Because you took the man who was supposed to marry my daughter. She should have been mistress of this house, not you."

"I don't know what you're talking—" She could not finish the sentence because another contraction seized her, this time stronger and longer than the others.

"Elena, *puta*. Elena Carvalho is my daughter. The beautiful child I had to give up because the woman in whose house I worked could not bear a child. So like Hagar, I lay with my Abraham and gave him a child his wife could not have. Elena had everything she could ever want—all except Dr. Aaron Spencer. And she did not believe me when I told her that I would get him for her."

Clenching her teeth against another contraction, Regina sat up and swung at Magda, her fist grazing her cheekbone.

Magda reacted quickly, pushing Regina away and slapping her across her mouth, cutting her lip and drawing blood. She slapped her again and again until the stinging in her face matched the pain in her belly.

Then it stopped abruptly. Someone pulled Magda away from the bed. There was a resounding thump, followed by a whimper of pain and the keening sound of someone sobbing.

Biting down on her cut lip, Regina stifled a moan when a

contraction threatened to tear her in two. "Aaron." His name came out in a trembling moan.

"I'm here, *Princesa.*"

She was dreaming. Aaron couldn't be in Bahia. He wasn't expected to return until the next day.

Between contractions, she opened her eyes to find him sitting beside her on the bed. "The fields are burning," she mumbled tearfully.

"It's all right, Darling."

"You'll lose everything."

"No," he countered in a soft tone. "Only if I lose you, I will have lost everything."

Aaron worked quickly, expertly, as he relieved Regina of her clothes. He had to examine her to find how her labor had progressed before he called Nicolas.

"My—my water broke."

"It's okay, Baby."

She drew in a sharp breath as another contraction gripped her. Aaron slipped two pillows under her hips, then pulled a table lamp closer to the bed. She was dilated, but he prayed the baby was facedown in the pelvic cavity.

Leaning over her, he touched the side of her battered face. "*Princesa,* listen to me. I'm going to leave you for a few minutes. I have to call Nicolas. Then I'm going to wash up. If Nicolas doesn't get here in time, then I'm going to have to bring our baby into the world. And for that I need your help."

"Okay," she slurred between contractions.

He kissed her forehead before he moved away from the bed, stepping over the prone figure of Magda Pires, who lay motionless on the floor.

Regina drifted in and out as she heard voices floating around her. She detected the familiar fragrance of Aaron's aftershave and savored the gentle caress of his hand on her distended belly.

She opened her eyes once and found him kneeling on the floor at the foot of the bed as he eased her gently toward him.

"Aaron?"

"When I tell you to push I want you to bear down and push. Push, Regina! Push harder."

She tried pushing, but gave up quickly. "I can't."

"Yes, you can. Pretend you have to go to the bathroom. That's it, Sweetheart. That's good."

Aaron waited until another contraction gripped her before he ordered her to push again. She did, and minutes later she heard the wavering cry of an infant.

Tears of joy and relief filled her eyes and flowed down her bruised cheeks. "It's a boy, isn't it?"

"Yes! Yes! Yes!" Aaron said, blinking through his own tears.

"Nice job, Aaron."

Still holding his son, Aaron glanced over his shoulder to find Nicolas Benedetti standing several feet away. Putting down his medical bag, Nicolas slipped on a pair of latex gloves.

"Put the baby on his mother's belly. I'll take over now."

Aaron complied, then removed his bloodstained gloves. He sat down on the bed beside Regina, holding her hand while Nicolas cut the umbilical cord and removed the mucous from the baby's nose and mouth. He wrapped the tiny, shivering boy in a blanket and handed him to Aaron.

"You can clean up your son now, Doctor."

Cradling the baby to his chest, Aaron took him to the kitchen, placed him on the counter next to the sink, and washed him gently with warm water.

The baby let out a frantic cry when the water touched his face. "Shh, Clayborne Diaz Spencer. This is as bad as it is going to get for a while. Right now I have to clean you up before you meet your mother," he crooned softly. "You must remember that you always have to look nice for the ladies."

He ran a finger along the infant's cheek and instinctively he turned his head in that direction. His son was small, but he was perfect—as perfect as the woman who had carried him.

The smell of burnt coffee beans wafted in through the windows, but Aaron could not think of anything but the woman who could have been lost to him if he hadn't returned when he did. Walking over to the window, he stared out into the night and whispered a prayer of thanks. A haze lingered, concealing the full moon. A gentle breeze blew in from the ocean, and the sky brightened as a silvery glow illuminated the earth. The moon appeared larger and brighter than at any other time of the year. It was then that he realized it was the night of a harvest moon, as well as his own birthday. His son had arrived in time to help his father celebrate his thirty-eighth birthday.

Lowering his head, he kissed Clayborne on his forehead, then returned to the bedroom, where he would introduce him to his mother.

Aaron returned to the bedroom to find Nicolas kneeling beside Magda, waving a bottle under her nose.

Regina sat up in bed, a gentle smile creasing her battered face as she reached for her son. Aaron sat down on the side of the bed and kissed her bruised mouth.

"Thank you for the birthday present."

Her eyes widened when she registered what he had said. "You came back early to celebrate your birthday?"

Nodding, he watched Regina guide the baby's mouth to her breast. After a few misses, he found the nipple and began sucking vigorously.

"Aaron, I can't imagine what would've happened if you hadn't come back when you did."

"If anything *had* happened to you, I probably would spend the rest of my life in jail, because I would've done more to Magda than just slap her."

"She tried to kill me because she thought having me out of the way would make it easier for Elena to marry you."

He frowned. "I never would've married Elena. Why would Magda think I would?"

Regina related what Magda had told her about being Elena's mother, watching disbelief freeze Aaron's features. "I wonder if Elena even knows Magda's her birth mother. I doubt that, because last week Elena announced her engagement to her *futebol* player."

"So now Magda will go to jail for nothing."

"No, *Princesa,* it will not be for nothing. She will be charged with attempted murder and arson. Those are pretty serious charges in Brazil."

The sucking motion stopped and Regina smiled down at her son. His last name might have been Spencer, but his features said he was a Cole.

Her head came up slowly as she gave Aaron a seductive look. "Do you think you can make an honest woman out of me, Aaron Laurence Spencer?"

He leaned closer. "I think I can."

"When?"

"As soon as you're better."

"Better how?" Her gaze was fixed on his sensual mouth.

"As soon as your doctor gives you the okay that you can travel."

"Where are we going, Darling?"

"Florida, *Princesa.* We'll have a double ceremony. We'll have a priest marry us, then baptize the baby."

She laid her head on his shoulder. "It sounds as if we're going to have quite a party."

"I'm ready," he crooned, sealing his pledge with a kiss that promised forever.

Epilogue

Parris Cole held her grandson, tears filling her green-flecked brown eyes when she watched her husband lead her firstborn down the aisle where Aaron Spencer waited to make her his wife. The tiny baby slept peacefully, unaware of the danger that had threatened his very existence.

Her gaze shifted from the tall man reaching for and grasping her daughter's hand to the baby who represented another generation of Coles. Clayborne was his mother's child, from his black curly hair to his delicate features and the twin dimples that were passed down from his Cuban-born great-grandmother.

Parris had to admit that Regina had chosen wisely. Aaron would be a good husband and father. The wedding ceremony ended with the exchange of vows, rings, and kisses. Then Regina, Aaron, and the priest, along with Tyler and Arianna, moved over to the baptismal font.

Rising to her feet, Parris handed Tyler his nephew. Clayborne wailed—his cry joining the voice of the priest intoning the prayer washing away original sin—then water was poured on his head. His crying continued until Tyler handed him to his mother. At six weeks of age, he had bonded quickly with her.

Martin moved closer to his wife, holding her hand gently. "We will have her for such a short time," he whispered close to her ear.

Parris saw the shimmer of tears in her husband's eyes. Regina and Aaron had planned to spend a month in Florida before they flew on to Mexico. They had promised to return to Florida to visit with the Coles at least twice each year: after Aaron harvested his coffee crop, and during the Christmas holidays. It wasn't much, but she would take it. She would take any time given her from her children.

Regina led Aaron through the formal gardens at her grandparents' estate, pointing out the differing plants and flowers. She had fed Clayborne, and he now slept in the nursery where many a Cole baby had slept over the years.

Aaron stopped and smiled down at the face of his bride. "Do you know what I was thinking, *Princesa?*"

She arched a naturally curving eyebrow, shaking her head. "No, Aaron. This is not our garden."

"No one will see us?" he whispered.

"I don't care."

"How about a kiss, Mrs. Aaron Spencer?"

"One kiss coming up," she crooned, putting her arms around his neck.

Six weeks had passed quickly. Magda and her accomplices were in jail, awaiting trial for attempted murder and arson. Sebastião had activated the irrigation system, saving more than half the crop.

She and Aaron would spend a month in Florida, then fly to Mexico to introduce Clayborne to his paternal grandfather. Then they would return to Bahia, to begin to live out their dreams without demons lurking in the background to thwart their happiness.

Pulling back, Regina glanced around her husband's broad shoulder. "I don't think we're the only ones making out in the garden," she whispered.

"She looks a little young—"

"Emily!" Regina scolded, startling her twelve-year-old cousin.

Emily Kirkland's dark green eyes widened in surprise. "Please don't tell my father," she pleaded as she approached the newly married couple.

"Who were you with?" Turning, Emily pointed to a tall, handsome young man who strolled casually from behind a wall of hedges.

Regina arched an eyebrow at Matt Sterling's stepson. "Chris?"

He cleared his throat several times before saying, "I would never touch her, Regina. Her father would kill me."

Regina gave him a knowing look. "I'm glad you realize that. I think the two of you should go back and join the others before your fathers come looking for you."

Christopher Delgado extended his hand to Emily Kirkland, who hesitated and then placed her hand in his. Regina and Aaron watched until they disappeared from view.

"Young love," he said softly.

"Dangerous love," Regina countered. "His sister is my cousin's best friend."

"Is her father your uncle with the silver hair and green eyes?"

"The same."

"That boy likes living on the edge, doesn't he?"

"You've got that right."

"Right now I feel like living on the edge, Mrs. Spencer," he crooned, pulling her deeper into the boxwood garden.

There was only the sound of their laughter before it ended abruptly with the exchange of a passionate kiss.

Hand in hand they returned to the house, smiling at everyone who had come to help them celebrate the harvest of their lives.

* * * * *

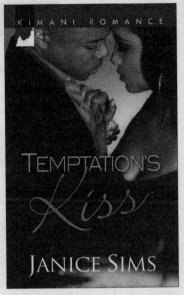

REQUEST YOUR FREE BOOKS!

2 FREE NOVELS
PLUS 2 FREE GIFTS!

KIMANI™ ROMANCE

Love's ultimate destination!

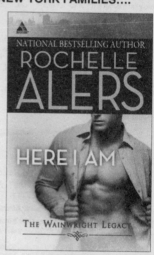